AMERICA'S M...
ROMANCE...

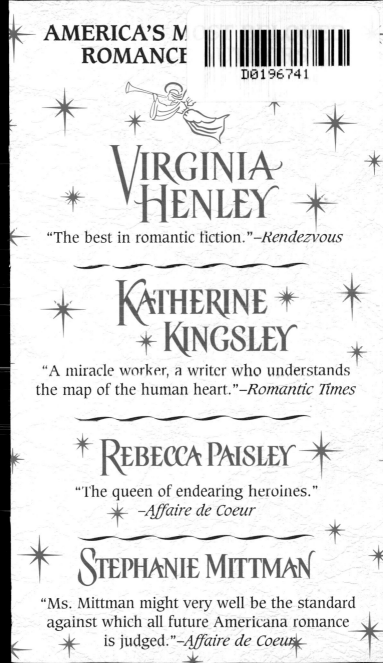

VIRGINIA HENLEY

"The best in romantic fiction."–*Rendezvous*

KATHERINE KINGSLEY

"A miracle worker, a writer who understands the map of the human heart."–*Romantic Times*

REBECCA PAISLEY

"The queen of endearing heroines."
–*Affaire de Coeur*

STEPHANIE MITTMAN

"Ms. Mittman might very well be the standard against which all future Americana romance is judged."–*Affaire de Coeur*

A Christmas Miracle

Virginia Henley

Katherine Kingsley

Rebecca Paisley

Stephanie Mittman

A Christmas Miracle

Island
BOOKS

ISLAND BOOKS
Published by
Dell Publishing
a division of
Bantam Doubleday Dell Publishing Group, Inc.
1540 Broadway
New York, New York 10036

If you purchased this book without a cover you should be aware
that this book is stolen property. It was reported as "unsold and
destroyed" to the publisher and neither the author nor the publisher
has received any payment for this "stripped book."

LOVE AND JOY copyright © 1996 by Virginia Henley
UPON A MIDNIGHT CLEAR copyright © 1996 by Katherine
  Kingsley
IN A TWINKLING copyright © 1996 by Rebecca Paisley
ANGELS IN THE SNOW copyright © 1996 by Stephanie Mittman

All rights reserved. No part of this book may be reproduced or transmit-
ted in any form or by any means, electronic or mechanical, including
photocopying, recording, or by any information storage and retrieval sys-
tem, without the written permission of the Publisher, except where permitted by law.

The trademark Dell® is registered in the U.S. Patent and Trademark
Office.

ISBN: 0-440-22290-7

Printed in the United States of America

Published simultaneously in Canada

December 1996

10 9 8 7 6 5 4 3 2 1

OPM

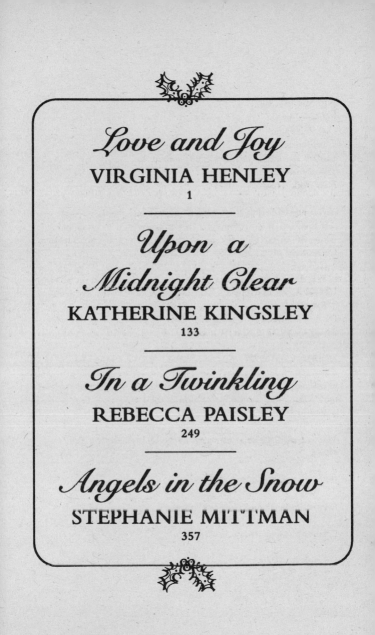

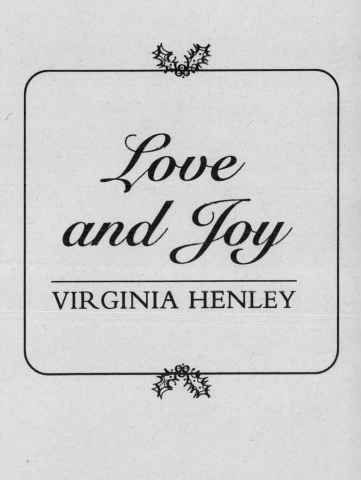

Love
and Joy

VIRGINIA HENLEY

Chapter 1

"Stop!" Joy Ashley cried, fleeing across the big kitchen.

"Don't you mean: Stop, *my lord*?" corrected the young man who'd had far too much to drink.

Astonished, she blurted, "You're not a noble of the realm!"

"'Ods balls, Richard, there's insolence for you," drawled his friend Carlton. "A scullery maid with the airs of a lady."

"I warrant a lady would be more forthcoming with her favors than this little baggage," Dick Humphries complained, cornering the maid once again.

"Leave me alone!" she bade both young men in her sternest voice, knowing from experience it would do little good. They had come home for the weekend from the University, and had had more than their share of drink this night.

"I only wish to share a little *Joy* with my friend," Richard said. "Where's the harm in that?"

Carlton St. Clare laughed at the witty word-play on the little wench's name and moved across the kitchen to aid his friend. "And I want the same, to share Joy with Dick," he added lewdly.

"You're drunk and disgusting!" Joy cried, spying her opportunity to push her employer's lecherous and spoiled son up against the hot kitchen oven.

As she shoved him, he staggered back, more from drink than force, and though his knee breeches and heavily embroidered waistcoat protected him from the cast-iron oven, he did burn his hand slightly when he saved himself from falling. "Little bitch!" he hissed. "It's time you learned to respect your betters."

"I may not be able to read or write, but that doesn't make you my better! A Cambridge education obviously hasn't turned you into a gentleman."

Carlton roared with laughter. "She's right, old man, you can't make a whistle of a pig's tail."

Richard made another grab for her and as she tore away from his grasp, the cloth of her much-washed cotton dress ripped apart, revealing a pair of deliciously tempting breasts. A foul epithet dropped from his lips. He glared at his companion, demanding, "Can't you help me?"

"I'd rather help myself," Carlton drawled, suddenly realizing the little wench had a rare beauty.

A plump figure immediately filled the kitchen doorway. "For very shame, Master Richard!" cried Bessie Bumble, the cook whose kitchen they were despoiling. "The little maid has bin on her feet for fourteen hours. The last thing she needs is to fight off a ravishing!"

"Shut your mouth and get back to bed, old woman, if you want to keep your job here." Dick Humphries' tone was so threatening, Bessie Bumble stepped back in alarm.

The two gallants managed to corner the maid between the pantry and the Welsh dresser that boasted a collection of pewter Joy had polished to look like silver only this morning. Her breasts rose and fell as she panted with apprehension. All she could think of was the knife drawer, but it was forty feet away on the other side of the kitchen.

When Dick Humphries' hands took hold of her breasts, as if they were peaches ripe for plucking, Joy dipped her head and fastened her teeth into his thumb.

"You shouldn't have done that, you little whore." With deliberation he tore what was left of her dress and petticoat from her trembling body.

With a sob, Joy snatched off her mobcap and held it in front of her to cover her nakedness. The moment she did so, a mass of red-gold curls tumbled down about her shoulders.

"Glory of God, she looks like Botticelli's Venus rising from the waves," Carlton St. Clare said with appreciation. "Since I'm your guest, Richard, 'tis only fitting I go first."

"Not bloody likely, but you can hold the little wildcat for me, then I'll return the favor," Dick said, fumbling with the front of his breeches.

Bessie Bumble panted up the backstairs holding a shawl over her night rail with one hand and a fluttering candle with the other. She rat-a-tatted on the master bedchamber door, then tried to catch her breath.

Presently, the mistress of the house, Hortense Humphries, opened the door and demanded, "Whatever is it?"

"Oh, ma'am, ye must come down to the kitchen and put a stop to the shameful goings-on."

"What *is* going on?" Hortense again demanded.

"It's Master Richard, ma'am, and that friend of his . . . they're foxed, ma'am, and making a shambles of my kitchen."

"How dare you? My son has never been intoxicated in his life!"

"No, ma'am," Bessie said, "but ye'd better come quick to put a stop to their fornication."

Hortense's long face froze. "Lewd language is forbidden at Humphrey House, Mrs. Bumble."

"It's lewd acts ye should be worried about," Bessie muttered under her breath.

Hortense was about to ring for her ladies' maid, then decided to put on her dressing gown without help. "You do realize it's after midnight?" Hortense said darkly as she followed Bessie down the backstairs.

The lamps still ablaze in the kitchen lit the room up to reveal to Mrs. Humphries exactly what was happening. One word from Hortense was enough to shrivel her son's rampant desire along with his cock. "Richard!"

As the two young wastrels stepped away from the girl, their long waistcoats covered their private parts, but revealed Joy Ashley's nakedness in all its youthful glory.

"I am appalled to learn what has been going on in my own kitchen!" Hortense Humphries' lips were stiff, her words stilted. "Ashley, you are dismissed. I will not tolerate a strumpet on my staff. Collect your things and begone!"

"Nay, ma'am," Bessie Bumble protested, "ye cannot put the lass out on a London street in the middle of the night!"

"It seems to me the street is where she should be plying her trade. Oh, very well, I suppose I'm a soft-hearted fool. The girl may stay until morning. But she had better be gone by the time you cook breakfast or you may find yourself accompanying her."

The male miscreants had slipped through the doorway unscathed, vanishing into the upper west wing before Hortense had even rendered her verdict. With one last disdainful glance at the servants, the mistress herself swept from the kitchen to return to her bedchamber.

Bessie pulled off her shawl and wrapped it about Joy's shoulders. "Are ye all right, love?"

"Thank you, Mrs. Bumble, they had me cornered."

"Don't thank me, I managed to get ye sacked."

Joy shuddered. "It's not the first time and I don't suppose it will be the last."

"Yer shivering; go to bed, child. Ye'll catch yer

death standing on this cold flagstone floor. We'll figure out something in the morning."

The cook's room was off the kitchen and Joy's cubbyhole adjacent to it. As she lay in the darkness, she thought, *Why am I always a victim?* The answer of course was as plain as the nose on her face. She was a servant, a member of the underclass. She had been trained as a ladies' maid, but once the lady of the house discovered the fatal attraction Joy Ashley had on the male members of the family, be they husband or sons, she was either dismissed or relegated to the rank of scullery maid where her pretty face and figure were never again seen above-stairs.

Joy had not been born into the servant class. Her father, Thomas Ashley, had been a captain in the king's army. They lived in a lovely manor house on two acres of land on the banks of the river Thames in the country outside London. Then Fate reared its ugly head in the form of Civil War.

Her father was a king's man, known as a Cavalier. He was garrisoned at Oxford, only fifty miles from home, and they saw him frequently. His tales of the Roundheads kept Joy wide-eyed, but never afraid, for her handsome father was the strongest, bravest man in the world who would protect both her and the king from all harm.

But on Joy's fifth birthday, January 30, 1649, the Parliamentary forces, bent on regicide, beheaded King Charles I. Her father along with the other Cavaliers rallied round the king's son, but were forced to flee the country as fugitives. Only a year later, Thomas Ashley was killed at the Battle of Dunbar in Scotland.

Joy's pretty, laughing mother was devastated, but that was only the start of their misfortunes. Without her husband's pay, Mary could not feed and clothe them and keep up with the expenses of lovely Ashley Manor. So she rented it out and found a live-in job in service where she was allowed to keep her child.

Joy didn't have many happy memories of that time. Her mother had taught her the alphabet, but now Mary worked such long hours, there was never time or energy to teach Joy her letters properly. Her pretty mother stopped laughing and Joy learned to be quiet as a mouse as she sat in a corner of the kitchen while her mother worked.

In bed at night, Mary told Joy of her plans and dreams. By the end of the year they would have enough money saved to move back to Ashley Manor. But once again Fate stepped in. England became a commonwealth and Oliver Cromwell, her Lord Protector.

"Lord Protector indeed! Old Noll is a disciple of the devil," her mother whispered.

Property owned by Royalists was now confiscated by the Puritans. The man who rented Ashley Manor declared himself a Parliamentarian and applied for the manor house. It almost killed her mother when she lost their lovely home. Mary began to live on dreams. Some day the king's son would regain the throne and reward those who had sacrificed all in the Stuart cause.

By this time, Joy was quite old enough to scrub

vegetables or weed the herb garden. Eventually she
learned to polish silver, iron linen, and sew a fine seam.
But the Puritan houses in which Mary was employed
were joyless places indeed. Londoners now lived bleak
lives where even innocent pleasures such as music and
laughter were considered sinful. The fashions for both
men and women were dull and drab, and the clothes of
the servants downright severe. All life had become sub-
dued by a somber and puritanical religion.

Once a month, on their day off, Joy and her mother
took a wherry ride on the river to see Ashley Manor
and dream about the day it would be returned to them.
Mary lived on her dreams, teaching Joy the pretty manners of a lady so that when the monarchy was restored,
they would be able to resume their life where they had
left off when their world turned upside-down.

Joy turned her face to the wall and squeezed her eyes
closed to prevent the tears from falling. "It's not fair!"
she whispered intensely. But her eighteen years had
taught her that life was not fair and that it was foolish,
even dangerous, to live on dreams. Shattered dreams
had killed her mother as surely as if she had had a knife
plunged into her heart.

Four years ago when Mary Ashley learned Old Noll
was dead, she told her daughter, "Oh, Joy, this is the
first step to getting our home back! You'll see, England
will demand that her rightful king, Charles II, will
wear the crown." And as her mother had predicted, in
a year's time a new Parliament was formed which everyone knew would call back the king.

A great lump came into Joy's throat as she remembered how her mother began to smile again, and even sing the merry little songs she had taught Joy in happier times. Then when Joy turned sixteen, they learned that Charles Stuart was returning to Whitehall. Mary was ecstatic! They joined the throng on the streets of London as they watched and cheered his triumphal return.

But her mother's happiness was short-lived. Among other things, Charles agreed not to disturb the owners of estates confiscated from Royalists in return for the throne of England! The news was such a blow that within hours Mary came down with a cold that rapidly developed into pneumonia. Within a week her mother was dead, along with her shattered dreams.

With tight fists, Joy dashed the tears from her eyes. "I will not feel sorry for myself," she vowed. She forced her mind away from the past. "I must think of the future!" But her future loomed before her like a dark cave, almost overwhelming her with fear of the unknown.

Joy tossed and turned on the narrow trundle bed as one question chased another through her mind. *Where will I go? What will I do?* The last two years had shown her how much her mother's presence had protected her against lechery. Joy had lost a succession of jobs because of it. Perhaps she was a fool to refuse her employers' advances. Other maids had scorned her, telling her it was inevitable that sooner or later a male of the privileged class would steal her virginity, which was a useless thing in the first place.

Joy sighed heavily. It was the inevitability of life that
she found the hardest to bear. She had never minded
hard work, never craved luxuries, but she bitterly re-
sented never having a choice about anything. "Five
o'clock comes early; get some sleep," she told herself,
and finally about an hour before dawn, she did drift off
into exhausted slumber.

A dream began where she found herself in a beautiful room. Before her were dozens of silver serving trays
displaying exquisite little iced cakes known as *petit fours*.
Each and every one was a different shape and color.
There were round, square, triangular, stars and crescent
moons all covered with icing in palest green, yellow,
pink, mauve, and white, all decorated with candied
violets, rosebuds, and silver balls.

Unbelievably, Joy was invited to select whichever
cake stole her fancy. It gave her untold pleasure to look
them all over at her leisure and choose. Seeing them,
touching them, smelling the violets and roses was only
half the pleasure. Soon she would actually taste the one
she had selected, and the anticipation was absolutely
delicious.

Next, Joy found herself in a large chamber decorated
with gold-leaf moldings and mirrors. The room was
filled with gowns, each more beautiful than anything
she had ever seen. Every style, color, and material was
displayed for her pleasure alone. Again, she was invited
to choose a gown for herself.

Deciding which she wanted from the myriad collection gave her as much pleasure as actually possessing
one. She was allowed to touch the material and hold

the gowns up against her before the mirrors to see which one best suited her red-gold hair.

It took a long time to pick one, for all of them were exquisite. The pastel satins made her look pretty, the taffeta rustled deliciously, and the stiff brocades were fit for a queen. But Joy finally chose a rich emerald velvet that set off her coloring to perfection.

Once again the dream changed. At the far end of the room, doors swung open to a ballroom that beckoned her inside. The chamber was lined with gentlemen. At first they reached out their hands to grab her, but she hurried past them without looking back, until finally, miraculously, the men stood respectfully and she was expected to make her own choice. There were fair men, dark men, tall and short. There were men with long hair, cropped heads, mustaches and beards. Kings, earls, lords, rich men, poor men, beggarmen and thieves; the choice was hers.

Suddenly, her eyes flew open and she realized it was dawn. A dark feeling of apprehension almost smothered her as she contemplated the day before her. She lay unmoving for long minutes, then she gathered her courage and flung back the covers. She laughed at the irony of her dreams, where she had been able to make her own choices. Such a thing was not possible, not in this world!

Chapter 2

Joy quickly lit the candles and poured water from the jug into the washbowl. Then she donned a clean petticoat and a brown cotton dress. Until last night's disastrous encounter she had owned two such dresses and petticoats, but now the only clothes she possessed were the ones on her back.

Bessie Bumble came into Joy's small room carrying a thick slice of freshly baked bread and a chunk of Lancashire cheese wrapped in a linen napkin. "Get this inside ye, child. Even if ye get nothing else today, it'll stave off the pangs of hunger."

"Thank you, Mrs. Bumble," said Joy, plaiting her lovely red-gold hair into tight braids. "The only thing I can do is go to every big house in the neighborhood and ask at the back door if they need any kitchen help."

"I've been searching my brain for houses that need servants and I remembered something the new cook next door told me. Lord Huntingdon is looking for a governess for his little girl."

"Lady Huntingdon would never hire me; she'd think me too young."

"There is no Lady Huntingdon. The child's a real handful, from what I hear. Half a dozen governesses have been dismissed in the last six months alone. Her father even sacked the cook because the little tyrant turned up her nose at the food she prepared. But if ye could get the job it would be much more suitable to someone with your fine manners than being a scullery maid."

"It's worth a try. No matter how bad she is, a spoiled daughter has to be easier to handle than a lecherous son. And if I don't get the position of governess, I might get a kitchen job. What's the address, Mrs. Bumble?"

"It's Huntingdon Hall just up the river."

"Huntingdon Hall?" Joy asked in surprise. "Well, I certainly know where that is. Ashley Manor, where my family lived, is almost adjacent to Huntingdon Hall. How the devil did Lord Bloody Huntingdon manage to get his property back, when others didn't have a rat's chance?" Joy bristled. "I suppose rank carries special privileges the rest of us can only dream about!"

"If wishes were horses, beggars would ride. That's what my old mother used to say. Now I won't take *no* for an answer; here's a shilling to help you out. She shouldn't be allowed to turn you out without wages; it's scandalous."

Joy was so touched by Mrs. Bumble's generosity, she was almost undone. "Thank you so much! I'll pay you back the minute I'm able to do so."

"I know that, child. Oh Lordy, Mrs. Humphries is ringing already. Must want a special breakfast laid on for Master Richard and his dissolute friend."

"I'd better go before horse-face Hortense finds me still on the premises. Too bad you haven't got some saltpeter to sprinkle on their kippers."

Bessie winked. "I warrant that's what Hortense uses to keep the old man from getting ideas!"

Joy and Bessie shared a last moment of laughter before the pretty young woman slipped out the back door of Humphrey House and made her way toward Charing Cross, where there were several secondhand clothing shops.

When Joy went inside one, she stood bemused for a moment. As in her dream she was in a room filled with dresses, but there the similarity ended. These old clothes were shabby, faded, and worn, but Joy knew she would have little trouble finding something suitable.

The fashions in London had changed so drastically since Charles had returned to the throne. These days ladies wanted rich fabrics covered with gold embroidery or beads, with low-cut necklines trimmed in lace or fur. Nobody would be caught dead in the prim Puritan fashions of yesterday, and as a result the secondhand shops were overflowing with the outdated garments.

Joy selected a gray poplin with white collar and cuffs and a white cotton petticoat to go under it, very suitable for the role of governess. She also bought some black cotton stockings and a black wool shawl. Though it was a lovely October day outside, Joy knew winter was just around the corner and the specter of pneumonia always lurked in the shadow of her thoughts.

She bartered with the shopkeeper for every item she bought. Finally they agreed on tenpence for everything because Joy made it clear she would go to another shop if the woman wanted more. That only left her tuppence for the wherry ride to Huntingdon Hall, which was a penny each way.

Joy left the shop in an optimistic mood carrying her purchases in a brown paper parcel tied with string. Her shame over what the two young men had done to her was beginning to recede. Though they had stripped her to the buff, they hadn't succeeded in their ultimate goal. It was true that she was presently unemployed, but the sunshine momentarily banished the darklings and some of her anxiety melted away along with her shame.

She began to hum a song from her childhood as she walked briskly down to the Whitehall water stairs, passing milkmaids and piemen hawking their wares to the many Londoners who were already abroad on this fine autumn morn.

"Westward ho," called the waterman as he poled the barge out into the Thames traffic.

Joy had made this trip downriver many times when she and her mother visited their lost home, Ashley Manor. She enjoyed the boat ride past Richmond and historic Hampton Court, where King Henry VIII had spent so much time. Her imagination took flight for a moment as she considered the plight of his six wives. How ironic that even a queen could be a victim in this world. Joy was thankful she would be disembarking at Chertsey, rather than the Tower of London where poor Anne Boleyn and Catharine Howard had been taken on their last ride on the river.

As the boatman pulled over to the Chertsey water stairs, Joy noticed two other women preparing to depart the wherry. Her heart sank. Where else could they be going but Huntingdon Hall? One was a tall, long-limbed woman with strong, hawklike features and a back as straight as a ramrod. The other was a heavyset woman with an imposing bosom and two chins. Both were garbed in expensive bombazine, both were more than a decade older than Joy, and both looked infinitely more suited to dealing with a child who was rumored to be unmanageable.

Joy slowed her steps so that she fell far behind the two women, who seemed to be in a footrace to see who could get through the wrought-iron gates of the estate first. Her confidence flagged; she didn't stand a chance. Both women wore hats and one of them even had on gloves.

If Joy had had any other prospects, she would have turned around and gone straight back to London. *You won't get a job if you don't even try,* she admonished herself, looking down in dismay at the shabby brown dress she was wearing. On an impulse, Joy slipped into a grove of rhododendron bushes and unwrapped her paper parcel. She shook out the prim gray dress with its white collar and cuffs, then quickly changed clothes. She smoothed down her hair, which was still neatly plaited, unaware that the dampness of the river had created tiny spirals of pale red-gold across her brow.

She added her brown dress to the parcel and hid it beneath the rhododendrons, then stepped back onto the long driveway that led up to the magnificent house. It would be so much easier to go to the back door and seek kitchen work, but Joy stiffened her resolve, marched up the stone steps, and rapped upon the heavy oaken door.

It was opened immediately by a majordomo who bade her to take a seat with the other applicants in the spacious entrance hall. Both women looked her up and down, dismissed her as posing no threat, and went back to eyeing each other. Soon, there was another knock on the front door and a small, dark woman joined their ranks. She wore a black cloak and clutched a black portfolio that Joy feared was filled with references. Her last ounce of confidence drained away.

Everyone sat up straight as an inside door opened, but it was only a child who came into the entrance hall. The little girl, who was perhaps nine or ten, had straight, jet-black hair, black eyes, and a rather sullen mouth. She was not a pretty child. She approached the first woman, stopped directly in front of her, and stared in an extremely rude manner. After two full minutes she moved in front of the next woman and subjected her to two minutes of silent scrutiny.

When it was Joy's turn, she took the opportunity to study the child. Her firm little jaw showed more than a hint of stubbornness, while her piercing black eyes revealed a shrewdness beyond her tender years. When her ritual was complete, she left through the same door she had entered.

By this time, two of the women were bristling with affront, while the third compressed her lips so tightly they disappeared altogether. Suddenly, voices were heard in argument. The deep timbre of the voice of a man who had lost all patience ordered, "Be silent, Amanda!"

"I shan't be silent," a child's voice defied. "I won't have a dragon, a toad, or a witch!"

The male voice rumbled again, in a lower tone, then the door was flung open and once more in marched the little girl. She went straight up to Joy, pointed her finger, and said, "This one! I'll try this one!"

A man followed the child into the entrance hall. The pair were obviously father and daughter; their black hair and eyes were identical.

"I humbly apologize, ladies." His voice was beautiful, his manners perfection, but despite his words, there was nothing humble about Lord Noel Huntingdon. "Mr. Burke!" His raised voice summoned his steward, who came in, took the young girl by the hand, and led her away. Lord Huntingdon then invited the first applicant into his library. After ten minutes, the first woman departed and the next was taken into the inner sanctum.

By the time it was Joy's turn, her palms were damp and she rubbed them surreptitiously down her skirt before the man offered her his hand.

"Good morning, I'm Noel Huntingdon."

"Good morning, my lord, I'm Joy Ashley."

"Pray be seated."

Joy swallowed hard and noticed his piercing black eyes were more shrewd than his daughter's, if that were possible. When she sat down, his six-foot physique looming above her was most intimidating. He wore his own hair long in Cavalier fashion and his dark face was in startling contrast to the snowy lace at his throat.

Joy wondered if he was as arrogant as he looked or if it was simply self-confidence. She was in no such doubt about his dominance. She was willing to wager his daughter was the only female he'd ever indulged. His black eyes swept over her from head to foot, without missing the smallest detail. He crossed booted ankles and leaned his great length against his massive desk.

"Amanda lost her mother at five and as a consequence she has been much indulged. Now I find myself with a willful little tyrant on my hands. What makes you think you could handle her?"

"I love children," Joy said with great enthusiasm.

Huntingdon made no effort to hide his mocking amusement. "Perhaps because you are scarce more than a child yourself."

A spark of resentment flared within her. Lord Bloody Huntingdon wasn't going to hire her without references anyway and she felt a need to bring him down off his high horse. His title and friendship with the king allowed him to live in splendor.

"I'm a woman full-grown, my lord. At eighteen did you not consider yourself a man?"

He quirked an eyebrow as black as a raven's wing at the impertinent question. "I did indeed, Mistress Ashley. I was fighting in the front lines at the Battle of Worcester."

That makes him almost thirty, Joy thought and immediately felt a blush warm her cheeks at the personal information.

"Being a woman full-grown leads you to believe you could take my daughter in hand?" he mocked.

"I can identify with her situation," Joy said softly. "I too lost a parent when I was five."

"Your mother?" he asked, unmoved.

"My father. He was killed at the Battle of Dunbar, my lord."

His face hardened as his eyes flicked over her prim, Puritan dress. "A Parliamentarian?"

"No, my lord, a Royalist," Joy said proudly.

Huntingdon's face changed immediately. His dark brows drew together in thought. "Ashley? Not Captain Thomas Ashley? 'Sblood, he was never your father?"

Joy nodded.

"He was my captain at Dunbar! Gave his life so his men could retreat. You don't live far from here—doesn't your land join mine?"

"Ashley Manor was confiscated from us after my father died. Unfortunately the king did not restore it to us," Joy said matter-of-factly.

The hard planes of his face softened. "I'm sorry, my dear. Charles' hands are tied. To regain his crown, he was forced to acknowledge Parliament's powers."

She wanted to ask how he was still in possession of Huntingdon Hall and its vast tract of land, but held her tongue. He had softened toward her and she did not want to lose the advantage.

A wave of guilt washed over Noel Huntingdon as he looked at Joy Ashley. Her father had made the ultimate sacrifice for the Stuart cause, yet his daughter, obviously a cultured young woman, was forced to hire herself out for wages. The corner of his mouth lifted wryly. "You are well aware Amanda preferred you over the others. She made that plain at the top of her lungs, I'm afraid."

Joy smiled for the first time. *Miracle of miracles, he isn't going to ask for references!*

His face sobered. "I must point out to you that the little minx probably prefers you because you are young, with a sweet face, and she no doubt thinks that in a contest of wills she would win, hands down."

"I wouldn't let it turn into a contest, my lord. Amanda and I would be on the same side."

Noel's brows raised slightly. Perhaps the young woman was wise beyond her years. It would certainly be more pleasant to sit at table with this lovely young creature than the last dragon-faced governess. "Can you start tomorrow, Mistress Ashley?"

She gave him a radiant smile. "Oh yes, my lord. Thank you very much! I shall do my utmost to look after Amanda, Lord Huntingdon."

He moved around his desk and picked up a book. "Her lessons have been sadly neglected of late. She's gotten to the point where she refuses to even open a book. I promised my wife I would give our child a fine education. I want you to try to instill a love of the classics in her."

Joy's mouth fell open. She quickly covered it with her hand and pretended to cough. *Don't tell him, you fool . . . don't tell him you cannot read or write. It could take a week before he learns of it and sends you packing. In the meantime you'll be fed and housed.*

He was discussing wages and she hadn't heard a word. "Yes, my lord," she murmured.

"Splendid. Then I can expect you tomorrow."

His dazzling smile made her heart turn over. Her blood was singing inside her eardrums with her own recklessness and the next thing she knew she was on the outside of the large oaken doors.

" 'Sdeath," she muttered, "where will I hide myself until morning?" On impulse Joy decided to take advantage of her "day off" and visit her old home. It was about three miles downriver and the walk would be delightful on such a cool, sunny day. Before she set out, she went into the rhododendron bushes to change back into her brown dress. Then, leaving her new clothes now hidden beneath the bushes, she made her way down to the riverbank and strolled quietly where she could enjoy nature at its loveliest.

Ducks and an occasional swan floated among the bulrushes and it seemed that squirrels were everywhere as they gathered nuts and acorns for the coming winter. Bee-covered goldenrod and purple Michaelmas daisies grew taller than Joy as she picked her way through the wildflowers, brushing off the burrs that clung to her stockings.

When Ashley Manor came into view, she stood perfectly still so that she could absorb its beauty. It seemed impossible that she had been born here and spent her first years dabbling in the fish pond and playing in the orchard. The manor house was small, but it had such graceful lines that pleased the eye, and it was in such a lovely setting, that it was no wonder others had coveted such a jewel. She wondered if they had kept up her mother's herb garden where she had spent so many happy hours.

Joy did not trespass near the house. Instead she walked in a wide circle until she reached the orchard at the back. She reached up to pick an apple and bit into it lustily, laughing as the juice ran down her chin. She sat down with her back against the bole of a tree and watched the butterflies flit about the milkweed. Soon her patience paid off as a field mouse approached to gather seed pods from the tall weeds. Joy sighed with contentment, wishing every day could be as pleasant as this one, but just as the squirrels and the tiny mouse knew that a day was coming that was much harsher, Joy realized that tomorrow might not be as kind to her.

Before she left the orchard, she picked a pear and another apple. She would eat one for her supper and tuck the other away for her breakfast. She idled the rest of the day away watching the traffic on the river and reliving happier times when the love of her parents wrapped her in its protective cocoon.

When the sun began to set, she returned to Huntingdon Hall, retrieved her parcel of clothes from beneath the rhododendrons, and slipped behind the stables where the hay for the horses was stacked. As darkness fell and the stars came out, one by one, she thought about Noel Huntingdon's daughter, Amanda. To Joy, the child seemed unhappy, though she had every material comfort.

In Joy's experience, it was the little things in life that brought happiness, like morning dew upon a rose or the heavenly smell of freshly baked bread. Wealth and privilege seldom touched the heart of a child.

Joy's thoughts strayed from Amanda to Noel Huntingdon himself. How handsome he was and sinfully attractive too, if she admitted the truth. Wickedly, she wondered just how adamantly she would fight off his advances if he were so inclined. She shivered at the disturbing thought and burrowed deeper into the sweet-smelling hay.

Chapter 3

Joy awoke at first cock's crow. She looked down in dismay at her wrinkled brown dress with bits of hay sticking to it. Her belly rumbled loudly, so she reached into her pocket for the pear, which she devoured in less than a minute. After a swift glance that told her no one was about, she slipped off the brown dress and exchanged it for the gray.

She tied up the string on her parcel of clothes, then unplaited her hair, combed it with her fingers, and braided it up again. As she walked toward the big house, she wondered how she would bear the humiliation of Huntingdon seeing her meager belongings.

Pretending a bravado she did not feel, she lifted her chin and tapped on the front door. It was opened by the steward, who miraculously did not look down his nose at her, but addressed her respectfully.

"Good morning, Mistress Ashley. Lord Huntingdon

isn't available yet. My name is Burke; I'll take it upon myself to show you to your room."

Joy attempted to conceal her parcel behind her, but Mr. Burke didn't even glance down. "Thank you, sir." She tried not to stare at the luxury of the furnishings as she followed Mr. Burke down a hallway and up a wide staircase hung with portraits of past Huntingdons.

"Your chamber is in the west wing, close by Miss Amanda's room. They are connected by a bath chamber."

Mr. Burke opened a door and allowed Joy to precede him into the room. Compared with what she had come to expect, the chamber was luxury itself. A poster bed with matching dressing table and chest of drawers stood upon a thick moss green carpet. A tall, leaded window, with green and gold brocade drapes stood opposite a small fireplace with black oak mantel. He walked to the connecting door and opened it to show her the water closet and bathtub.

"Here is the bell pull." He indicated the tasseled rope on the wall beside the bed. "You must have broken your fast at a very early hour, so if you would like something else to eat, just pull the bell and tell the maid what you would like. We have a new cook in the kitchens who isn't quite up to Lord Huntingdon's standards yet, but at least we're not starving," he said with gentle humor.

"Now, let's see," he continued, "the schoolroom is downstairs. We have a laundress who will wash your things for you and Miss Amanda has a mademoiselle who makes all her clothes and looks after her wardrobe.

Maude was Lady Huntingdon's maid when they lived
in France; she stayed on with the family after," he hesitated slightly, "the unfortunate business. Her chamber
also is in this wing, just down the hall."

"Thank you, Mr. Burke, it is very kind of you to
make me welcome."

"Not at all, Mistress Ashley. If there is anything I
can do for you, anything at all, simply ask."

Alone in her chamber she realized that Mr. Burke
was a gentleman. She had encountered few real gentlemen of employment in a manor home in the last two
years. Mr. Burke was a welcome relief. Joy untied the
string on her parcel and put the things she had purchased in the dresser; they took up only half of one
drawer. She decided to rinse out the brown cotton
dress herself because she was too embarrassed to give it
to the laundress, and she would wash her petticoat tonight when she took it off.

Joy had only two personal possessions which her
mother had passed on to her. One was a hairbrush with
tortoiseshell back, the other a silver brooch which had
been a gift from her father. She took both into the
bathroom and stopped dead in her tracks as she saw her
reflection in a large mirror. *Lord, how disgustingly young
I look!*

A cake of soap caught her eye and some spotless
linen towels. She picked up the soap and held it to her
nose. Joy closed her eyes as she breathed in the heady
fragrance of lavender. Such a luxury! She washed her
hands and face immediately, deriving a great deal of
pleasure from the simple act. She fastened the silver

brooch at her throat and brushed her hair back from her brow, then sighed with resignation as the red-gold tendrils sprang back into curls.

Joy filled the washbasin with water, rinsed out the brown dress, then hung it over the towel rack to dry. She heard her bedchamber door open, though no one had knocked. When she reentered her room, Amanda was standing there with her small hands on her hips. In a challenging voice she asked, "What's your first name?"

"It's Joy," she replied with a smile.

"That's a strange name. Do you mean like in the Christmas carol, 'Love and Joy'?"

"Yes, I suppose it means the same," she replied.

"Must I call you Mistress Ashley?" she demanded with a sulky mouth.

"Not when we're alone."

Because the new governess allowed the liberty, Amanda immediately took another. She climbed up on the bed and began to bounce up and down on her knees. When she wasn't reprimanded, she stood and jumped even higher. "I *hate* my name!" she declared.

"Amanda is a beautiful name."

Amanda shook her head. "It's ugly, like me."

"You're not ugly! Wherever did you get such a notion?"

"My mother. She rejected me because of it."

Such a thing could not be true, but Joy was alarmed that Amanda seemed to believe it. "You have lovely hair and beautiful black eyes."

Amanda stopped jumping. "Do you *really* think so?"

"I do."

"I'm too dark," Amanda insisted. "My mother was fair."

"You look like your father. He's an extremely handsome man."

"Do I hear my name being taken in vain?" Noel Huntingdon asked from the open doorway.

Joy flushed, knowing he had heard her personal remark.

"Daddy! Joy says my eyes are beautiful!"

"Amanda, you mustn't call her Joy; her name is Mistress Ashley."

"I don't mind," Joy assured him.

"That's very kind of you. I've decided Amanda should have a couple of days holiday this week instead of plunging into lessons. That way we can all get to know each other. Amanda, go down to breakfast and I'll join you in a moment."

The child's shrewd glance went from one to the other. Amanda was curious, but reluctantly went downstairs.

Noel Huntingdon spread his hands in a deprecating manner. "I don't want you and Amanda to get off on the wrong foot. She has my stubbornness, I'm afraid, and if she takes an instant dislike to you, she will make our lives hell until I dismiss you."

"Is that what happened before?"

"Half a dozen times," he admitted ruefully. "I have to go to Whitehall next week, so I'd like Amanda to enjoy the next two days. We've been at odds with each other lately; it's been one battle after another. Will you join us for breakfast?" he asked politely.

"Oh, I couldn't, my lord," Joy murmured, lowering her lashes over wide green eyes.

He cocked an eyebrow. "Force yourself."

Her thoughts flashed about like quicksilver. She'd have to be on her guard about her shameful secret for the next few days, but once he went to Whitehall she might be able to keep this job for weeks. She sketched him a curtsy. "Thank you."

As he walked along beside her, he realized it felt good to bend this beautiful, young creature to his will. She was so small, he had to look down at her and she made him feel excessively masculine and powerful. She was every bit as attractive as the ladies of the court without the artifice of makeup or the advantage of expensive gowns and jewels. He felt a sudden desire to see her with her red-gold hair tumbling about her shoulders.

When they arrived at the breakfast room, Amanda was already sitting at table. When Lord Huntingdon held a chair for Joy, she hid her surprise and sat down. Mr. Burke brought Amanda a small bowl of porridge which she immediately covered with a thick layer of brown sugar and then picked up the cream jug. "I love sugar!"

"So do I," Joy said wonderingly. She hadn't tasted castor sugar in years, but remembered well its delicious sweetness.

Amanda giggled. "You're not supposed to say that.

You are supposed to press your lips together disapprovingly, like this, and say, *It'll rot your teeth, you naughty child!"*

Joy looked at Lord Huntingdon. "Will it?" she asked.

Noel smiled lazily. "Too much of anything isn't good for you. But I've been known to overindulge myself upon occasion." Joy didn't think he was talking about sugar.

"That's the same dress you wore yesterday," Amanda said bluntly.

"It's rude to make personal remarks," her father said repressively.

"I know," Amanda replied. "Why are you wearing the same dress?"

"Because I washed my other dress and it isn't yet dry."

Amanda's dark brows drew together exactly as her father's did. "You've only *two* dresses?"

"Amanda!" her father roared.

"Oh for God's sake, we might as well lay our cards on the table. We can't address the problem unless we discuss it openly, Daddy."

"Her rudeness is inexcusable, Mistress Ashley."

"She's obviously imitating the things you say, my lord. To you it seems inappropriate, but she models her speech after you because she loves you."

Huntingdon realized immediately that *was* the way he spoke, bluntly, with no patience for subterfuge.

Mr. Burke hid a smile and inquired what they would like for breakfast. Her mouth watering for the taste of sugar, Joy asked for porridge and some bread with honey. Lord Huntingdon ordered a fillet of beefsteak with eggs. He had a healthy man's appetite and when his breakfast arrived he attacked it with gusto. But as he ate, his enthusiasm dwindled.

"The new cook leaves much to be desired," he told Mr. Burke.

"We had a wonderful cook where I was last employed," Joy said, mainly to add to the conversation rather than sitting mute.

"Could she be lured away from London?" he asked.

"Oh, I wouldn't want your new cook to lose her position. My conscience would play havoc."

Noel was amused. "A woman with a conscience; what a unique concept."

"His rudeness is inexcusable, Mistress Ashley," Amanda mimicked. In the midst of their laughter, Amanda's face lit up with a new thought. "We still haven't resolved Joy's wardrobe. I'll tell Maude to make her some new clothes."

"I believe Maude should be *asked,* not *told,* Amanda, and I also think it would be more appropriate if *I* did the asking."

"Good. That's settled," Amanda said, and both adults realized she had achieved her goal by blatant manipulation. "Since this is a holiday, why don't we go riding? You can show off Huntingdon's acres and I can show off my new palfrey."

At the child's suggestion, Joy's face fell.

Again, Lord Huntingdon's brows drew together. "What?" he demanded.

"I'm not an experienced rider," Joy admitted. "I had a pony when I was a child, but I've had little opportunity to ride since."

"It's unthinkable that Captain Thomas Ashley's daughter cannot ride. I'll give you some lessons."

Joy tried to protest, but he held up an all-powerful hand. "*My* conscience would play havoc!"

Amanda jumped up from the table and dragged on Joy's hand. "Come and help me change into my riding habit."

Lord Huntingdon rose to his feet. "I'll meet you at the stables." He plucked a straw she had missed with her brushing from Joy's thick plait. "You know where they are." The mocking amusement was back in his eyes.

Damn you to hell, you arrogant devil! Joy said silently, glad to escape his dominant presence.

Noel looked down at the straw in his fingers and pictured her naked, lying in hay. His groin stirred and started to pulse before he could banish the vision. What the hell was the matter with him, lusting after the young daughter of his old army captain? Then he grinned. It wasn't his conscience that was playing havoc with him!

"Oh, Amanda, this is lovely," Joy exclaimed as she took a sapphire blue riding habit from the child's wardrobe.

"Maude made it; she's very clever. She wears beautiful clothes too—makes them all herself."

Joy tried to picture the Frenchwoman with the

fancy clothes who had remained with Lord Huntingdon long after his wife's death. If she was so clever, why wasn't she Amanda's governess? *Because she's his mistress!* The thought came unbidden into Joy's mind and she wondered why it was so disturbing.

"There! Just look at yourself in the mirror," Joy urged.

"I don't look in mirrors; they are hateful things," Amanda declared.

Joy felt a catch in her throat. Who had destroyed this child's image of herself? "Please, Mandy?" Joy implored, holding out her hand.

Perhaps because she had used a diminutive of her name, Amanda reluctantly placed her hand in Joy's and allowed herself to be led before the looking glass.

"The blue velvet makes your dark coloring absolutely vivid!"

Amanda cocked her head to one side and gave herself a critical appraisal, devoid of admiration.

"When your father sees how pretty you are, I warrant his eyes will light up."

Amanda gave her a look halfway between disbelief and hope. "Let's hurry. He doesn't have much patience with females."

Then he certainly makes an exception in your case, little lady, Joy thought privately.

Joy and Amanda made a race of it, with Joy determined to reach Noel Huntingdon first. "Say she's pretty," Joy hissed beneath her breath.

Huntingdon gave her a startled look before his attention moved to his daughter. As comprehension dawned, he said, "Why, Amanda, how pretty you look."

Happy surprise transformed the child's face. "Joy said I'd make your eyes light up!"

The man and woman exchanged a fleeting glance of conspiracy.

A groom led out a cream-colored palfrey with a small saddle. "This is Jerome, he's been giving me lessons," she told Joy. Then she turned to her father. "You won't believe how much I've improved."

"That's because you spend every day at these lessons rather than your school lessons."

"Oh, but all that will change now that I have Mistress Ashley," she said sweetly, taking the reins in her hand.

"Butter wouldn't melt in your mouth . . . that's a load of codswallop."

"He means horse dung," Amanda explained to Joy.

The child was so droll, Joy couldn't help but like her. Jerome led out a sleek black animal and a roan gelding he had saddled. Huntingdon took the reins of the black and nodded toward the roan. "That fellow is for you. When you ride with Amanda you can have one of the mares, but my stallion would go mad trying to cover her if we mounted you on a mare today."

Joy was amazed that he spoke so matter-of-factly in front of the child. No wonder she was wise beyond her years.

"You're not watching me!" Amanda accused.

"Forgive me, Your Highness," he teased.

When she was certain she was the center of attention, Amanda placed her booted foot in the stirrup and swung up into the saddle in one graceful movement.

"Excellent!" her father approved.

"Oh, Amanda, you're so good, you put me to shame."

Amanda's face shone with pride. "Just do what I did," she instructed.

Joy was thankful it wasn't a ladies' saddle or she truly wouldn't have known how to mount. She put her black walking shoe in the stirrup, then swung her other leg over the gelding's back. Her gray skirt billowed up to show her plain white petticoat and black stockings, but her movements were not clumsy.

"You haven't forgotten at all," Huntingdon said. "You'd have a natural ability . . . if it wasn't for that wretched dress."

Joy flushed and bit her tongue. *We're not all born with a silver spoon in our mouths, Lord Bloody Huntingdon!*

The trio set off in a sedate manner, but that didn't last long. A brachet hound, loose from the kennels, came crashing through the trees toward them, in hopes of going on a hunt. The dog startled Amanda's small saddle horse, which half-reared in fright. The reins were jerked from Amanda's hands and she slid off, landing on her bottom. Her father dismounted in a flash and scooped her from the ground.

"May I have the dog?" she asked him.

"No!" he thundered.

"But it tried to make friends with me," she protested.

Suddenly Noel Huntingdon began to laugh with relief. "'Odsfeet, I thought you broke your neck and all you can think of is the blasted dog!"

A bubble of laughter escaped from Amanda and Joy's look of alarm turned into a smile. The brachet hound, which hunted by scent, was running in circles sniffing the ground. "Why can't I have the dog?" Amanda wheedled.

"You know we can't have dogs in the house; Maude is terrified of them."

Joy suddenly felt irritated at the woman she had never even met. Lord Huntingdon's stallion, left unattended, took a sudden dislike to the roan and bit it hard on the rump. Joy's horse screamed, then bolted with her on it!

Noel cursed and sprang into his saddle. He spurred Cavalier and in less than a minute his stallion overtook the roan. Huntingdon reached out powerful arms, plucked Joy from its back, and set her before him on his saddle.

She was gasping, but not from fear, from laughter. "I was in no danger, my lord, but it was a most gallant rescue and I thank you."

Noel threw back his head and let the laughter roll from his throat. A laughing Amanda caught up with them.

"Mandy, don't let go of your reins, you're laughing so hard you'll fall off again," Joy warned, in no danger herself with Noel's arm firmly about her waist.

"'Sdeath! Riding out with you two wenches is hazardous to a man's health."

As Joy turned to look up at him, her heart jumped

into her mouth. His flash of white teeth, his corded throat, his rugged maleness almost overwhelmed her. She suddenly became acutely aware of everything about him, his strength, his scent, his hard, muscled body snug against her backside, and she had to drag her eyes away from him.

"Oh, Daddy, this is fun. I wish you'd play with us every day."

Joy's lashes flew up and her glance collided with Noel's and held for a moment. When she saw the teasing light in his eyes, she was so afraid he was going to say something scandalous, she put her hand over his mouth. The gesture was so intimate, she gasped at what she had done and dropped her lashes, but not before she saw his mouth curve with sensuality.

Chapter 4

In her chamber, Joy went rapidly over the day's events with mixed emotions. She knew that she and Amanda were compatible and it gave her a measure of satisfaction that the child's sulks had been replaced by laughter, at least for today. Her feelings about Noel Huntingdon were not as clear-cut.

She had had an exhilarating day and thoroughly enjoyed the grand tour, riding about the acres of hops that provided the Huntingdons with every luxury. The only problem was that it galled her to think Ashley Manor was lost forever, while Huntingdon Hall re-

mained firmly in her employer's hands, solely because
of his friendship with the king. At the same time she
felt guilty over her uncharitable thoughts. She assured
herself that she didn't wish Lord Huntingdon to lose
his property; she simply wished to regain hers.

A knock on her door chased away her introspection.
When she opened it, Mr. Burke delivered a message.
"My lord wishes you to dine with them tonight. He
has persuaded Maude to join you for dinner."

"Thank you, Mr. Burke." As soon as she thanked
him, he withdrew. Since he did not await her reply,
she knew it was simply taken for granted she would be
there. It was not an invitation, but a summons. A spark
of anger ignited inside her. If his mistress wanted to
inspect her and put her through her paces like a filly at
a horse fair, Joy wanted no part of it! She knew how
cruel a woman could be to another female. On top of
everything else, Joy had nothing to change into for
dinner, while Maude was reputed to possess a fashionable wardrobe. Damnation!

Amanda came in, still wearing her riding habit and
trailing a white dress by its sash. "Joy, will you help
me?"

Joy looked at her in surprise. Amanda was capable of
ruling Huntingdon Hall, so she was perfectly capable of
changing her own clothes. But as Joy began to unbut-
ton the blue velvet habit, she realized that Amanda was
starved for attention.

"You have a very good eye for color, Mandy. This
white dress contrasts beautifully with your black hair."

Amanda digested the compliment for a moment. "I

think you are right. With your red-gold hair you should wear emerald green, and just think of all the different shades of purple you could wear."

Joy smiled wistfully. "I try not to yearn for things I cannot have."

"You can have pretty clothes. Daddy will tell Maude. I'll remind him."

"No, Mandy, you mustn't do that! Oh dear, is saying *no* to you like waving a red flag in front of a bull?"

Amanda giggled. "Usually it is. Come on, I'm hungry. 'Odsfeet, I hope the food has improved."

Joy sighed and followed her with resignation; as usual she did not have a choice.

When Joy entered the dining room, the first thing she saw was the back of a stunning wine velvet gown on the woman who was talking to Noel Huntingdon. Joy, filled with envy, went stiff with resentment.

Lord Huntingdon said, "Mistress Ashley, I want you to meet Maude."

As the Frenchwoman turned, her impact on Joy was like a heavy jolt of lightning. Maude's face was completely disfigured by pockmarks. Joy's envy turned to shame and her heart overflowed with compassion. "Maude, I'm delighted to meet you, I've heard so many lovely things about you."

"*Merci*, I 'ave little English," she apologized.

"You are most eloquent with your needle," Joy praised.

"Indeed she is," Lord Huntingdon agreed. "Amanda's new governess is in need of your services,

Maude. I think her most pressing need is a riding habit."

"She needs day dresses too," Amanda added. "I'm sick to death of that wretched gray thing."

"*Alors!* Manners!" Maude scolded.

"It's all right, Joy knows I have none."

"A situation which Mistress Ashley will be addressing, and soon I hope," asserted her father. When Mr. Burke brought in the first course, Noel said, "Set a place for yourself, man, I'm outnumbered tonight."

Shortly, Burke brought in a joint of meat, set it before Lord Huntingdon for carving, and sat down at the table with them.

As he served each of them, their host made a disclaimer. "The cook, I am sorry to say, is not as eloquent with her spoon as Maude is with her needle."

"England is notorious for its bad cuisine, but it has other compensations," remarked Mr. Burke.

"If that's a pointed reminder I'm better off here than at the Hague, I stand reprimanded," Lord Huntingdon drawled.

"I didn't like the Dutch," Amanda said bluntly.

With heavy sarcasm, her father said, "Strange, they adored *you*."

Mr. Burke almost choked on his brussels sprouts.

Amanda turned to Maude to reassure her. "I *did* like the French, though."

"Probably because they are more tolerant of oddities," teased her father.

"Oh, am I an oddity?" Amanda asked, quite taken with the idea.

Noel rolled his eyes at Joy and she answered him with an amused smile.

The dessert, although unremarkable, was at least palatable. Maude said to Joy, "Aftair, I will measure you, *non*?"

Amanda piped up, "I shall join you; I have a very good eye for color."

"I would value your suggestions," Joy said sincerely.

As Noel watched and listened to the new governess converse with his daughter, he thought, *She treats Amanda as an equal, she never belittles her because she is a child. Her predecessors all tried to put her in her place, and all failed miserably. Perhaps this new approach will work.* As he leaned back, sipping his wine, he tried to picture Joy in a fashionable gown. He didn't quite succeed. He had no trouble seeing her without the wretched gray dress, but that's as far as he got.

The two women and the little girl spent a pleasurable hour talking colors, material, and style. Since autumn was upon them, with winter rapidly approaching, Maude suggested wool for two new day dresses and velvet for the riding habit.

Joy agreed with gratitude; she had worn nothing costlier than cotton for many years. After much serious discussion, Amanda and Joy finally agreed on one dress in peacock, one in a shade of lavender, and black velvet for the habit.

When Joy told Amanda it was time for bed, the child's sulky mouth reappeared. Joy ignored it and went through the motions of helping her bathe and preparing her for bed. As Joy turned back the covers, Amanda hung back. "Will you read me a story?"

Joy bit her lip in frustration. "My eyes are tired, but I'll *tell* you a story if you like."

Amanda got into bed immediately and listened with rapt attention as Joy told her a fable of a princess who met an elf. When the story was finished Amanda was most reluctant to have her leave. "Can't you sleep in here?" she asked wistfully.

"No. What are you afraid of? The dark?"

"Not really," Amanda denied.

"Then what, I know you are afraid of something."

"Ghosties," Amanda admitted in a small voice.

"Oh, darling, there's an easy way to keep ghosts at bay," Joy told her solemnly.

"Honestly?"

"Absolutely! In a big loud voice you must shout that you're not afraid of them. That gives you power over them. If your voice reaches to every corner of the room, they can't come into your chamber. Go on, try it."

"I'm not afraid of no ghosties!" Amanda bellowed.

"I'll just turn this lamp down low," Joy told her, making a mental note to put it out once Amanda slept.

Noel Huntingdon waited until Joy went to her own chamber, then he went into his daughter's room and sat on the edge of the bed. Putting a finger to his lips and keeping his voice low, he asked, "Do you like her?"

Amanda nodded vigorously.

"Then we must conspire to keep her." Noel was at his wits' end with the war his daughter had declared on governesses. Joy Ashley had given him a glimmer of hope. He decided to try to get Amanda to cooperate for once. "I don't think Mistress Ashley has had a very easy time of it. When she was a little girl she lived at Ashley Manor, two or three miles downriver. Her father fought for the king, just as I did, but he was killed in battle. After that her home was confiscated and she had to go to work for a living."

"Blasted Roundheads!"

"Exactly. So if you're not difficult and obstinate, perhaps she'll stay."

"I'll pretend to be good," she whispered. "It'll be our secret, Daddy. May I have a drink of water?"

Joy closed the brocade drapes across her window and lit her oil lamps. What luxury to have a whole room to herself. She removed her sturdy shoes and dug her stockinged feet into the thick pile of the rug. She took off the gray dress with the white collar and cuffs and held it up before her. "I thought you were quite fetching, but my lord thinks you are *retching*!"

In her petticoat she went to the dressing table, picked up her tortoiseshell brush and unplaited her hair. When it was brushed out it swirled about her like a glorious cloak, all molten flames and fire. She couldn't resist looking at her reflection. She hadn't felt this happy in a long time. Huntingdon Hall was a magnificent place to live. It couldn't last, of course; once his lordship discovered she was illiterate, she'd be out on her ear, but in the meantime . . .

Joy took off her petticoat, and naked save for her stockings, carried it to the bathroom so she could wash it. She opened the connecting door and came face to face with Lord Huntingdon. Joy gasped in horror, the petticoat slipped from her nerveless fingers, and there she stood clad only in black stockings.

Noel Huntingdon stood transfixed, his mouth dry at the sight of the naked girl cloaked in a nimbus of red-gold hair. She immediately turned to flee, giving him a spectacular view of long black legs going all the way up to her delicious bum cheeks. Amanda's drink was totally wiped from his mind.

Much later, as Joy lay in bed, her mind re-created the indelicate scene over and over. She told herself it was accidental on both their parts and Lord Huntingdon had no prurient interest in her. But her imagination wouldn't leave it there. Once again, would the inevitable happen? Now that he had seen her unclothed, would he step over the bounds and expect intimacies because he was her employer? When he plucked her from the horse and their bodies were pressed together, she had stirred his desire. Or was it her desire that stirred?

Fleetingly, she thought of her dream and the room filled with men whom she could choose among. Joy dismissed the dream. *What nonsense; I'll never have free choice!*

Then slowly an idea came to her. Perhaps she *could*

have free choice. The idea was seductive and she examined it carefully. Joy presumed she would be deflowered sooner or later against her will. But what if she was bold enough to choose the man and give herself to him? What if she chose Noel Huntingdon? The idea seemed so outrageous, she dismissed it. But it refused to leave.

As she lay there, all Joy's senses heightened. She became aware of the linen sheet against her skin and recalled his male scent. It would be like taking control of a part of her life. Control was such a heady thought, she shivered with anticipation. Doubt assailed her. Perhaps she couldn't seduce him. Then her mouth curved in a secret smile. Perhaps she could!

The next thing Joy knew, it was morning, and Amanda was climbing onto her bed. "No ghosts!" she said triumphantly.

"I told you," Joy said happily.

Amanda stroked her hair as it lay across the pillow. "Oh, I wish I had golden hair."

"Your hair is beautiful, Mandy. And I warrant it will soon become all the rage to have black hair like the new queen."

"Daddy has promised to present me to Queen Catherine. Of course I've known the king all my life. We lived at his impoverished court in France and then Holland."

Joy smiled wryly. Though the Stuart court had gone hat-in-hand across Europe, impoverished was hardly the word to describe it. "Give me a few minutes to dress, then I'll come to your room and help you."

"I'm going to tell him we want to go on the river today."

"Mandy, ask him nicely, don't tell him. You catch more flies with honey than vinegar."

Joy's cotton stockings were dry, but her petticoat was still damp about the edges as she dragged it over her head. She donned the old brown dress and took the black woolen shawl from the drawer. If they were going on the water she would need it.

She found Amanda amid a pile of garments she had pulled from her wardrobe. To help her make up her mind, Joy suggested she wear something warm. The green dress Amanda picked had a matching green doublet and Joy complimented her choice. As Amanda looked in the mirror, Joy caught sight of her own reflection with dismay. Her outfit was the antithesis of seductive. She quickly dropped the hideous black shawl; she'd rather freeze than be seen in it.

"Are you trying to make yourself ugly?"

"I promise you I'm not," Joy replied.

"Then why did you do that to your lovely hair?"

"My position requires me to look neat and tidy."

"Then tie it back with a ribbon," Amanda suggested. "Here's a pale green one, the color of your eyes."

When Joy looked unconvinced, Amanda cajoled, "I'll wear one too."

Joy smiled her capitulation, realizing Mandy was taking on the role of adult, with her the child.

An hour later as Amanda clambered aboard the Huntingdon barge, Joy was thankful she had taken the child's advice, for as Noel Huntingdon saw her hair blowing loose in the breeze, she knew he was thinking of last night. Using her feminine wiles, she hesitated on the water stairs and felt a surge of elation as he strode toward her to lift her down to him.

The river breeze billowed her skirts, revealing ankles clad in black stockings and she saw with her own eyes that it physically aroused him. Her lashes lowered to her cheeks, her voice murmured a soft *thank you,* and her hands clung to his wide shoulders for a long, drawn-out moment before she deliberately moved away to join Amanda. She smiled inwardly as he followed.

"Take us downriver to Ashley Manor," Amanda directed.

Her father shot her a warning glance. "Perhaps that would be painful for Mistress Ashley."

"Oh no, it has such a special place in my heart, I would love to see it again."

As the elegant barge floated out to midstream, Amanda and Joy made themselves comfortable against plush red cushions. As they glided downriver on the tide, Noel Huntingdon's dark gaze returned again and again to the young woman with the glorious hair. His fingers itched to undress her. He allowed his imagination full rein, touching her, tasting her, inhaling her woman's scent. There was an innocence about her that drew him irresistibly, lured by his instinct to hunt and capture that which perhaps no other male had possessed. The thought of awakening the mysteries of her own sexuality was like an aphrodisiac to him.

As Ashley Manor came into view, Lord Huntingdon watched her rapt gaze. Her lips parted and a look of longing, of hunger, transformed her face. He would like her to look at him in just that way, so he could satisfy that hunger. His arousal became iron-hard as he envisioned sheathing himself in her, almost hearing her cries of passion.

Though Joy had eyes only for her old house and pointed out various things to Amanda, she was acutely aware of Noel Huntingdon. He hadn't taken his eyes from her since he lifted her aboard. Her female instinct told her he was tempted, but she imagined he was waging an inner battle with himself. Womanlike, she knew she must do something to tip the scales so that he lost the battle.

"Are you warm enough, Amanda?" she asked.

As the child nodded happily, Joy began to shiver. Noel saw immediately and closed the short distance between them. She jumped up as he came close. "You're cold," he murmured, instinctively wanting to put his arms about her.

Joy swayed slightly toward him, then pulled away. "Pray don't concern yourself, my lord."

"You should have brought your cloak."

Joy's eyes looked into his, giving him the full impact of her green gaze, then she lowered her lashes and blushed to show her embarrassment.

Lord Huntingdon understood immediately. *Damn, she has no cloak!* Unable to keep his hands from her, he touched her shoulder. "We'll remedy that," he assured her.

She gasped prettily. "You read my thoughts." The moment was an intimate one.

Noel Huntingdon reached for his own cloak and with sure hands draped it across her shoulders, then wrapped its folds about her. "Let me warm you," he murmured.

She looked at him with a refusal on her lips. Then suddenly she surrendered. "All right."

Huntingdon's vast experience with women told him this was her first small capitulation. Though she hadn't the least notion of it, he decided that soon, soon she would warm his bed.

Chapter 5

The day of recreation was a resounding success. They ate a picnic lunch aboard the barge, then sailed on to Hampton Court Palace and Windsor Castle, where they explored the medieval buildings and Elizabethan gardens. By the time they returned on the evening tide, a full-scale flirtation was underway.

Mr. Burke greeted Lord Huntingdon with a problem he could not fully resolve. "When I was in the kitchen this afternoon, I discovered the cook preparing lamb that had gone off. When I told her such a practice was unacceptable here, she argued that meat and game had to be hung many days before it was consumed. I told her that applied to venison and game, but that lamb was another thing entirely."

"To cut a long story short, you had words and she left in a huff," Noel said wryly.

"That's it in a nutshell, my lord. I took over the kitchen and prepared dinner the best I could."

"Thank you, Mr. Burke. I shall endeavor to find a replacement."

When Joy and Amanda went upstairs, Maude couldn't wait to show them the riding habit she had worked on all day. She was rewarded by Joy's reaction. "Oh, how very fashionable! It's the loveliest thing I've ever owned."

The black velvet had a nipped-in waist above a full skirt. But the thing that made it vivid was a tight black-and-white-striped satin vest beneath the jacket. Maude also had fashioned a hat in Cavalier style, with sweeping ostrich feathers, one black, one white.

Amanda clapped her hands. "I was right about black velvet; it will set your hair ablaze!"

Joy experienced a moment of panic. Amanda's lessons were to begin tomorrow. When her deception was uncovered, and she was dismissed, would that deprive her of this beautiful outfit? "I must try it on," she said, then added silently, *at least one time.*

When she helped Amanda bathe and get ready for bed, once more the child clung to her when it was time for her to sleep. "Will it work again tonight?"

Joy, clearly seeing her anxiety, sought to reassure her. "Of course it will work; tonight and every night. Is there a particular ghost you fear, Mandy?"

The dark head nodded solemnly. "I dream about her. She has long pale hair like spiderwebs and her face is covered with red, oozing lumps."

"It was just a nightmare, darling, there is no one like that."

"My mother," Amanda whispered. Then she lowered her voice even further. "She didn't want me, but I think she's changed her mind . . . she's coming for me."

"No, Amanda," Joy said firmly. "You are safe here with your father. I won't let anything come near you." She sat down in a chair beside the bed, determined to stay until the child fell asleep.

"I'm not afraid of no ghosties!"

Joy smiled at the way she pronounced the plural of ghost. She supposed, as her governess, it was her job to correct her pronunciation, but in Joy's wisdom it was the child's fear that needed correction.

Once Amanda drifted off, Joy enjoyed a long bath. *No wonder they say cleanliness is next to godliness; hot scented water makes me feel divine!* Again she washed out her petticoat and stockings, then slipped her brown cotton dress over her nakedness.

Back in her room she brushed out her hair, recalling how liberating it had felt to wear it loose today. When she answered a low knock on the door she was surprised to see the tall, dark figure of Lord Huntingdon. A swift intake of breath indicated how the sight of him affected her.

"May I come in, Joy?" He used her name in a familiar way, as if he were caressing it.

She held the door wide, inviting him to enter. Roses tinted her cheeks. He had wasted no time pursuing her. She held herself stiff as if poised for flight, then forced herself to relax a little and remember that she had chosen him, not the other way about.

"Amanda's asleep."

"Yes. I stayed awhile to calm her fears." Silence stretched between them. She felt compelled to fill the void. "Did her mother have smallpox?" The moment she mentioned his wife, she could have bitten off her tongue, for it was surely the most effective way of destroying intimacy between them.

"Yes, she died of smallpox in France. Maude nursed her selflessly and caught the dreaded contagion."

God above, that's why he has made a home for Maude. "I am so sorry, my lord."

"It was four years ago." He walked to the window and looked out into the darkness.

"Amanda remembers it," Joy said softly.

"She remembers so much. She was only five, I thought she'd forget."

"Five is old enough to remember everything."

He turned from the window and deliberately changed the subject. "So, you seem perfect for Amanda. I want to give you your salary before I forget. It was remiss of me to leave you without money." He took out five pounds and laid it on the mantel.

Joy had never had so much at one time. She was tongue-tied. *Thank you* seemed inadequate. Her skin tingled all over. Perhaps it was from the bath, but more likely it was his proximity which affected her so profoundly.

Lord Huntingdon cleared his throat and once more changed the subject. "You spoke of an exceptional cook at your last place of employment."

"Yes, Mrs. Bumble."

"If I take you to London tomorrow, do you think you could persuade her to come to Huntingdon Hall?"

"Why, I'm sure I could. She has no great affection for Hortense Humphries."

"You are an angel of mercy," he teased.

Joy swayed toward him and suddenly his lips came down on hers in a tentative kiss. When his hands discovered she wore nothing beneath the cotton dress, his mouth became demanding.

She reveled in the hard feel of him, becoming breathless at his possessive touch. She permitted him to kiss her, then allowed him to kiss her deeply.

"Joy . . . sweet . . ." he murmured against her throat, as one arm held her captive against his swollen phallus. One powerful hand cupped her breast, his thumb teasing her nipple to a hard ruby.

Suddenly, she remembered the money he had placed on the mantelpiece and knew that she could not give herself to him this night. She stiffened beneath his roving hands. "My lord," she protested.

He loosened his ironclad hold on her, but he did not apologize. He reached for her hands and drew them to his lips. "You intoxicate me." He knew she was not rejecting him completely, only begging time to accustom herself to the unfamiliar emotion of awakened passion. She was panting and it increased his desire for her a thousandfold. He wanted to sweep her up and carry her to his bed, but the thought of pleasure delayed for one more day stopped him. It would make his possession infinitely more intense.

He brushed his lips across hers. "Good night, Joy. I look forward to taking you to London."

After he left, she leaned against the closed door, a weakness stealing through her limbs. Her fingers touched her mouth in wonder. She could still feel his kiss. She licked her lips, imagining she could still taste him, and his scent, like suede leather, lingered.

Her heart raced as she thought of London. She had been reprieved from lessons tomorrow. How fortuitous that she had something fashionable to wear!

At breakfast, when she told Amanda that she and her father were going to London to get a new cook, Amanda's mouth turned sulky, but when Joy asked her to help Maude with the new dresses, she reluctantly agreed. "I hope I'm successful in getting Mrs. Bumble to be the cook here. Her food will melt in your mouth."

"Mrs. Bumble? What a comical name!"

"Bessie Bumble; it is rather droll," Joy conceded, glad to see the smile return to Amanda's face. When Mr. Burke told her Lord Huntingdon awaited her in the carriage, Joy swept up her hat and bent to kiss Amanda's cheek. The child stared after her, stunned as a bird flown into a wall.

"I'm sorry to keep you waiting, my lord, I thought we'd be going by barge," she said breathlessly.

His gaze swept her from head to foot and his eyes told her he liked what he saw. "We need transportation once we arrive in London and I didn't think you'd want to ride."

He handed her into the coach and took the seat opposite her so he could look his fill. "You need some riding boots to complete that stunning outfit. If you succeed in getting us a competent cook, I'll take you shopping, if you'll let me." His voice was deep and intimate.

She raised her green eyes to his. "I'll let you," she said slowly, softly.

Noel hardened instantly. "When we are done, I should stop at Whitehall."

"I understand King Charles is a personal friend."

"He is. Sometimes I have to pinch myself that I'm not just dreaming he regained the throne. Our Fate has been tied together since we were youths."

"Your Fate and your fortune," Joy said lightly.

A mocking look came into his eyes. "I don't usually explain myself to women," he drawled, "but in your case I'll make an exception. I don't owe thanks to Charles Stuart for Huntingdon Hall, actually I owe it to my father."

Joy felt her cheeks grow uncomfortably warm.

"My father changed his coat and backed the Parliamentarians. When they beheaded the late king, I was incensed at his beliefs and lack of loyalty. We quarreled, violently, I'm afraid, and I followed Charles into exile.

My father and I never spoke again. He died over two years ago, just before Charles was restored to the throne." He paused, then continued, "No one was more surprised than I that he never changed his will. He left me everything."

"I'm sorry, Lord Huntingdon. It's none of my business whatsoever." Joy truly felt contrite.

" 'Ods feet," he drawled, "do you have to call me Lord Huntingdon? Can't you call me Noel?"

"I . . . I can't," she protested prettily.

He bent his dark eyes upon her face. "You shall," he promised. He looked for all the world like a predator that had scented its prey. Joy smiled inwardly. He hadn't the faintest notion that he was the hunted, she the huntress!

Lord Huntingdon let Joy Ashley off at the corner of Bedford Street and the Strand, and told her he would wait for her. She walked along to Humphrey House, then went around the back and knocked on the kitchen door.

Bessie Bumble's mouth fell open. "Lord love a duck, look at you!"

"I got the job as governess at Huntingdon Hall, Bessie, thanks to you."

"Come in for a minute, lass, there's no one about."

"I've come to see if you want to work there too! Lord Huntingdon needs a cook and has brought me to London to see if you'll take the position."

"Are ye serious?"

"I am, Bessie. It's a wonderful place to live. Please say yes?"

"Well, I don't mind if I do. Just let me tell horse-face she can shove her job up her backstairs and we're off to Tipperary!"

"Will tomorrow be soon enough?"

"Perfect. It will give me time to give her nibs notice and pack me bag." She looked Joy up and down. "What are ye up to? No, don't tell me; I don't want to know," Bessie said with a wink.

"You won't regret it, Bessie, I promise you."

"I hope you'll have no regrets either," Bessie warned lightly.

"There'll be no regrets, Bessie. For the first time in my life, I'm calling the tune. No matter what happens, I'll be willing to pay the piper."

When Joy returned to the carriage, Lord Huntingdon was standing conversing with his coachman. "Drop us at the Royal Exchange," he instructed, "then you can take the carriage to Whitehall and stable the horses."

"Bessie Bumble is honored to become Huntingdon Hall's new cook. She's Irish and a very dear lady."

"If she can tell a bee from a bull's foot, I'll be thankful."

Joy gave him a saucy look from beneath her lashes. "I doubt that, my lord. I warrant your standards are exacting."

* * *

At the exchange, their first stop was a bootery where Joy had her foot measured and was then presented with a dozen pairs of riding boots. She took her time, reveling in the luxury of free choice. Finally, she tried a pair of soft black leather that reached all the way to her knees. She lifted her skirts so that her companion could admire them. "What do you think?"

"I'd be arrested if I told you," he grinned.

"Then I think these will do nicely, thank you."

He insisted on carrying them for her and offered her his arm as they strolled through the exchange. Half a dozen times he greeted acquaintances and whether they were men or women, all turned to stare at his female companion with speculative eyes.

Joy stopped at a stall displaying exquisite undergarments of lace and embroidered silk in a palette of pastel shades. All her pretended nonchalance dropped away as she stood mesmerized. Suddenly, remembering she was with Lord Huntingdon, she tried to hurry on so she wouldn't embarrass him.

Noel pulled her back. "They were designed to tempt the male every bit as much as the female. I don't mind in the least if you'd like something." Since he'd been both a husband and a widower, she realized women's undergarments were no mystery to him.

Her fingers could not resist a pale aqua silk embroidered with forget-me-nots. Wistfully, she tore her eyes away from it and selected a white cotton one which, despite its lace frills, was infinitely more practical than the delicate silk. Hoping he wouldn't think her greedy, she also chose a pair of white lace stockings.

As they were being wrapped, Noel pointed to the aqua silk. "We'll have that one, too."

"Oh, you shouldn't!" Joy protested.

"Didn't you ever do something you shouldn't?" he murmured wickedly.

She slanted him a sideways glance and said provocatively, "Once," then watched his imagination take flight.

When she refused to let him buy her anything more, he took her to lunch at Lockets in Charing Cross. Afterward, they strolled through Covent Garden, where Joy lingered to watch a puppet show. "Oh, how Amanda would enjoy this. Have you ever brought her to London?"

"Not in the past, I haven't."

"Perhaps when you bring her to meet Queen Catherine, she could see a bit of London."

"She told you that?"

Joy examined his amused expression carefully. "You did mean it? Amanda said you promised."

"Well, perhaps if you'll accompany her," he invited.

Damn men! They are so free and easy with their promises, then what they promise goes straight out of their heads. A child can live a year on a promise, perhaps even a lifetime.

"Do you enjoy the play?" he asked as they strolled down Drury Lane toward the Theatre Royal.

"I've never attended," she admitted.

"But the king reopened the playhouses two years back!"

Lord Huntingdon was in need of an education.

"When one is in service, one has neither time nor money for the play."

"Now that you are in my service, I shall change all that," he promised.

Joy listened avidly as a crier told all and sundry about the performance. *"The Maid's Tragedy,"* he bawled. "Learn what happens when a servant girl seeks diversion with a man above her station!"

"Would you care to see it?" Noel offered. "Oh, sorry, we're too late for the four o'clock performance. Another time, perhaps."

Joy was profoundly grateful. She didn't wish to learn the maid's tragedy just yet.

They finally walked back down the Strand to Whitehall. Joy, who had never dreamed of visiting the palace, plucked up enough courage to put on her hat. It took a great deal of confidence to wear a hat, especially a slouch Cavalier style adorned with ostrich feathers. Yet once it was on her head she felt transformed. In a heartbeat she acquired poise, pride, and panache, and it felt fabulous to be at the king's palace on the arm of Lord Noel Huntingdon.

Everyone greeted him, including the liveried footmen, which told Joy he spent a good deal of time at court. Noel handed her purchases to one, along with a word of instruction. Everything fascinated her from the magnificent furnishings to the fashions worn by the men and women Noel greeted. Though her outfit was the smartest she'd ever worn, Joy realized she was not suitably dressed up for an evening at court, but then neither was Lord Huntingdon, and he didn't seem to spare a thought for such trifles.

They walked up a gilt staircase and down a wide hall hung with brilliant chandeliers. A tall, dark figure hailed them. "Noel, the very man I need at this moment."

Lord Huntingdon swept off his hat. "Your Majesty, I am ever at your service. May I present Mistress Joy Ashley, my daughter's governess."

Charles made her a leg and took her hand to his mouth. "My very great pleasure, mistress."

As the king turned to Noel, Joy did her best to regain her composure.

"Catherine is having a drawing room this evening and so far very few of the ladies have attended. Barbara is boycotting it, perverse little jade that she is. Do me a favor, old man, and get her down here. You're one of the few men who can intimidate her. In the meanwhile I'll take Mistress Joy Ashley to meet Her Highness."

She looked at Noel with open mouth. He gave her a nod of encouragement. "A lady couldn't be in finer hands, my dear. I'll join you in Queen Catherine's drawing room shortly."

Joy didn't quite know how her feet carried her along at the king's side. But his manners were so easy, his words so charming, he almost put her at ease.

She curtsied low to the queen. Catherine was extremely dark with a sallow skin and was small-boned like Joy herself. Her clothes were quaintly old-fashioned. She had only been in England for a little over five months and had not yet adopted the flamboyant dress of the English courtiers. The little queen was touchingly eager to make Joy's acquaintance.

"This is Mistress Joy Ashley, who teaches Noel Huntingdon's daughter her lessons."

"I too needa the English lessons," Catherine said, using her fan to cover her smile. "Where is Noel?"

"He'll be here shortly, Catherine," Charles assured her, throwing a conspiratorial look at Joy.

Queen Catherine said, "I adore children; you too?"

"Well, I am certainly very fond of Amanda Huntingdon. She is longing to meet you, Your Royal Highness."

Catherine clapped her hands. "Good! You must bring her to me soon." The queen sat down at a small games table and bade Joy sit with her. "You know the cards?"

Joy smiled apologetically. "Not very well, Your Highness."

"Me too," Catherine said, "but I learn."

The Queen's drawing room began to fill with courtiers. Noel Huntingdon brought a woman forward on his arm to make her curtsy to the queen. Joy tried not to stare at the voluptuous female with hair the color of burgundy, for she had heard it whispered that the king's mistress was Barbara Palmer and Joy decided this must be she.

Barbara sketched the briefest of curtsies and moved off with her friends. Noel and Charles exchanged a meaningful glance. Catherine said, "Good evening,

Noel. Mistress Ashley has promised to bring your daughter to see me."

"Charles knows how difficult Amanda can be. Perhaps we should postpone that visit, Your Highness."

She tapped him with her fan. "No, no; I insist. I adore little girls."

Noel bowed. "You are very kind, Your Highness."

It was becoming quite crowded about the queen, so Joy stepped away to Noel's side. "Adore? She's more likely to abhor my little girl."

"If I had a fan, I'd slap you," Joy teased.

He bent his dark head toward her. "Do you think we could slip away from this throng?"

Joy knew this was the moment she had been waiting for. Once she made her choice and committed herself, there could be no turning back. She smiled up at him innocently. "Don't you have rooms here at Whitehall, my lord?"

Noel covered her hand possessively. "I do indeed, my beauty."

Chapter 6

When Joy entered Lord Huntingdon's apartment, which was down by the bowling green, the first thing she saw in the dimness were the packages he had given the footman. She felt suddenly shy. She pictured herself modeling the aqua silk he had bought her, and didn't believe she could be so bold.

She stood in the center of the room while Noel lit the lamps, then remained there as if her feet were rooted to the floor. He poured two glasses of golden wine, then closed the distance between them. When she still did not move, he took her hat from her fingers and replaced it with the wine. He lifted his own glass and murmured, "Here's to this moment, and the moment yet to come."

His dark eyes gazing at her mouth made her excitement build so quickly she wanted to scream; instead she took a sip of wine. She watched Noel remove his doublet and bend to light the fire which a palace servant had already laid, then he went into the bedchamber to light more lamps.

Joy did not follow him, but slipped off her walking shoes and sat down on a cushioned settle before the fire to sip her wine. Her feminine instincts told her she need do nothing further. She had snared her prey, all she need do now was allow him to assert his role as predator.

Joy was becoming quite warm from both the wine and the fire. With great daring she removed her black velvet jacket and sat in the striped satin vest, which exposed her bare arms and neck.

Noel sat down close beside her and slipped his arm about her waist. "Isn't this preferable to being crushed in a room of toad-eaters?"

"It is infinitely cozier," she admitted, breathlessly.

His fingers toyed with a curl. He held his glass up so that the firelight shone through it. "Your hair is just the color of this golden wine, and has the same intoxicating effect." He set his glass down and brought the tress of hair to his lips. It simply wasn't enough; his arms enfolded her and his hard mouth slanted down on hers. "You're so small," he marveled.

With trembling lips she whispered, "Good things come in small packages."

"I can wait no longer to unwrap you." He took her mouth again, kissing her deeper than before. Joy did not feel his fingers on the buttons of her vest, but she glanced down quickly when she felt her breasts being cupped in warm, strong hands. She felt as if the flames from the fire had spread into her belly, and threads of molten heat were spreading both up and down inside her, melting her very bones.

Joy clung to him, willingly, eagerly, wanting him to teach her everything. She felt his hand go boldly beneath her skirts and peel the stockings from her legs, so that he could caress her bare flesh. His fingers knowingly sought her woman's center between her thighs and Joy experienced her first fluttering arousal.

Noel picked her up and carried her to his bed. He undressed her, stripped off his own shirt, then laid her back against the pillows to look his fill. The lamp glow bathed her creamy flesh, showing her uptilting breasts and mons, arched incredibly high, covered with delicate red-gold curls.

Noel Huntingdon was only human; he tasted the feast laid out before him. When his lips dropped a kiss upon her high mons, he saw Joy's green eyes widen in amazement. Noel was thrilled with her reaction. "This is new to you," he murmured happily.

She had half-expected an assault; though she thought what he did excessively wicked, she also thought it exceedingly gentle. Joy watched his dark head poised above her golden triangle and found it unbelievably sensual. She watched his tongue dart out to delve into her scented cleft and could not help moaning at the deep pleasure he gave her. "I'm sorry, my lord," she gasped.

"It's all right to cry out. There's none to hear but me and I love it! Say my name, Joy."

Although it was a command, she did not think she could obey him. Then he plunged deeply, thrusting his tongue all the way into her and suddenly she could not stop crying his name. "Noel, Noel, Noel!" She arched herself high into his beautiful mouth, unable to control her mounting passion.

Her climax was so intense, she came up off the bed with a scream, then her body seemed to curl up. She felt Noel's firm hand cup her mons to gently massage her. Joy relaxed against the pillows and smiled up at him with eyes that had darkened to brilliant emerald.

Noel stripped off his remaining clothes, then lay down beside her and gathered her against his naked length. His cock pressed into her soft thigh like an iron poker, its heat scalding her flesh. Everything about him turned hard and male and demanding, as he unleashed the fierce desire that had been riding him for days.

Wildly, she wondered if that was herself she could taste on his lips. She watched him straddle her body, felt him open her with his fingers, then he buried himself in her silken sheath. Joy cried out at the sharp pain, and put up her hands as if to push him away. But her fingers came into contact with the smooth, rippling muscles of his chest and she discovered the power of his male strength.

In a heartbeat the revelation transformed her from a girl into a woman, a woman with sexual needs of her own. Her hands stroked his magnificent body, urging him on to take that which she so generously longed to give. She became splendidly uninhibited as she reveled in the hot, sliding friction of their joined bodies. What happened between them was primal and so cataclysmic that when he spent, she surrendered all.

Long minutes passed before either of them were aware of anything beyond their own pounding heartbeats. Then, finally, he withdrew and looked down at her. Tears like diamonds hung on her lashes, then Noel saw the drops of blood on the sheet. "I'm sorry, sweetheart."

She covered his mouth with her hand. "Please don't say that."

He pressed his lips into the palm of her hand. "Then I'm not sorry, so long as you are not."

Joy wrapped the sheet about her nakedness and Noel brushed back the glorious tangle of hair from her brow, then touched her cheek with the backs of his fingers. "Your first time, was it heaven or hell?" he asked softly.

"Both," she answered truthfully, "but the pleasure was far greater than the pain."

Noel felt elated that he was her first lover, even though there was a drawback. An experienced female would understand the nuances of dalliance, with no strings attached.

She looked at him from beneath her lashes and confessed, "I *chose* you for my first lover."

Noel threw back his head and his laughter rolled all about the bed. Joy had discovered many things about Noel Huntingdon, not the least of which was that he loved to laugh. She threw him a saucy look. "Of course, that was before I met the king," she teased.

"That may stop my head from swelling, but it has little effect on my other parts," he countered outrageously. He dipped his head to kiss her, but in the middle of the kiss they both broke into laughter.

She touched a fingertip to his laugh lines, then traced the dark shadow along his jaw.

"Would you like me to shave?"

"No . . . I liked the rough feel of your skin against mine."

Noel laughed again, this time at her ingenuous answer, which told him she'd had little practice at dissembling. It pleased him, for he hated deceit with a vengeance.

"Why don't you try on your new things?" he suggested.

Joy slipped from the bed, still wrapped in the sheet, and picked up the parcel that held the aqua silk.

"I meant the other one." Noel's dark eyes were alive with wicked amusement.

She picked up the parcel that held the long, black boots and when she took his meaning, blushed to the roots of her hair. She turned her back to hide her face from him, and heard his amused laughter. Joy's wicked juices began to bubble and she decided to be bold. She slipped on the boots and smoothed the black leather up to her knees. Then she turned to face him, tossed back her hair, and dropped the sheet.

Before dawn arrived, Joy realized she'd never be the same again. He had made her laugh, made her cry, and made her fall in love. She knew she must hide *that* at all costs!

Just as they were about to enter their coach in Whitehall's vast courtyard, King Charles with half a dozen spaniels at his heels was taking his early morning walk through the mews.

Lord Huntingdon made his bow. "Good morning, Your Majesty."

" 'Ods blood, Noel, were you so eager last night you couldn't stay for five minutes?" Charles held up his hand before Noel made his excuse. "I understand; beauty and brains are a rare combination." As the king turned to Joy, one eyelid slowly descended in a wink. "If I'd seen you first, this damned fellow wouldn't stand a chance."

Joy smiled radiantly. "I've already explained that to him, Your Majesty."

Charles whooped with laughter. "Don't forget, Catherine wants to meet Amanda."

Noel rolled his eyes. "It's on your head, Sire."

When the carriage stopped at Bedford and the Strand, Mrs. Bumble was waiting on the corner with her trunk at her feet. Noel handed her into the coach beside Joy, then sat down facing them.

"Lord Huntingdon, may I present your new cook, Mrs. Bessie Bumble."

The two slipped into a comfortable discussion of food, with Noel describing his favorites from childhood. Joy had no qualms about recommending Bessie Bumble; her friend was far more qualified for her position at Huntingdon Hall than Joy herself was.

When they arrived home, Amanda was awaiting their return at the gates of the estate. "Stop the carriage," Joy cried. She climbed out and the coach rumbled on to the house. She tried to hug Amanda, but it was obvious the child was furious. "Why didn't you come home last night? I waited and waited!"

Joy was suddenly covered with guilt. "I'm sorry, Mandy. Mrs. Bumble couldn't come until today." She felt wretched lying to the child and vowed not to make a habit of it.

In a small voice Amanda said, "I was afraid you wouldn't come back."

"Silly goose." Joy took her hand. "We'll spend the whole day together if you like. Come and meet Mrs. Bumble and for heaven's sake, do say hello to your father."

As Bessie opened and closed cupboard doors in her new kitchen, Amanda said, "May I call you Bumblebee? I shall call you that behind your back, so you might as well say yes."

Bessie considered for a moment. "Yes, if I can call you cockroach."

Amanda's brows lowered like a threatening storm. Then suddenly the skies cleared and she laughed. "You're funny, Mrs. Bumble."

"Come on, we'll clear out so the new cook can orient herself with her new domain."

"I know what that means, but where did a word like *orient* come from?"

"I haven't the faintest idea," Joy admitted.

"But you're my tutor, you're supposed to know."

Joy cleared her throat. "Amanda, why don't you show me your frog pond. We should be outside on such a lovely autumn day; there won't be many left."

"It isn't a frog pond, it's a fish pond," Amanda corrected.

"Take some bread," Bessie said, thrusting a stale-looking lump into Joy's hands.

They sat at the edge of the pond feeding crumbs to the carp. "I had a pond like this when I was little. I loved to watch the frogs."

"This one doesn't have any frogs."

"Well, I think it should. Shall we catch some?"

"That would be great fun, but where does one catch frogs?"

"At the river," Joy informed her.

"Really? Can we?"

"We'd better change out of our good clothes, then we'll get a bucket and go frogging!"

* * *

Mid-afternoon, as Noel Huntingdon stood at his bedchamber window gazing down into the gardens, a pair of disreputable-looking females, liberally spattered with mud, caught his attention. He wondered where they had been, and what the devil they were up to. As he watched, he saw Joy remove her shoes and stockings, tuck up her skirts, and wade into the fish pond. Then he watched Amanda follow suit.

They appeared to be shifting rocks among the water plants, then both reached into a bucket to pull out what could only be frogs. Not only were the pair absorbed in what they did, they were laughing like a couple of lunatics. His gaze centered on Joy. Even in the shabby brown frock, soiled with river mud, she was desirable. He transferred his attention to his child. It did his heart good to see Amanda having fun, but perhaps a gentle reminder about her lessons wouldn't be amiss.

When Joy and Amanda arrived in the dining room, they had been transformed into respectable ladies. Both wore new dresses of aqua wool, which Maude had created, with Amanda's insistent suggestions.

Noel looked from one to the other. "Ladies, you look lovely this evening."

"Yes, we know," Amanda agreed. Joy made a note to show Amanda how to accept a compliment with a little more grace.

When Mr. Burke carried in the first course, the look of anticipation on his face, combined with the appetizing aromas floating from the kitchen, filled the diners with hope. First came a hearty Cheddar and ham soup, followed by a braised brisket of beef, deviled cauliflower, buttered peas and pearl onions, with a watercress salad. By the time the pear and almond tart was served, the verdict was unanimous: Bessie Bumble was a treasure!

As Lord Huntingdon sipped his port, he bethought to remind Amanda about lessons. "Did you study today?"

Amanda licked glazed pear from her fork. "Yes, Daddy."

Noel blinked at the blatant lie. "What did you study?" he asked bluntly.

"Today we had a biology lesson."

Noel's eyes sought Joy's just in time to see her mouth curve in irrepressible amusement over Amanda's clever retort.

Noel Huntingdon let it pass. He was thankful that Huntingdon Hall was no longer in chaos. He had been excused from court while he put his house in order and was hopeful that he would now be free to return to duty. Huntingdon was one of the King's Gentlemen of the Bedchamber and he had recently been appointed to sit at the King's Council for Trade.

Noel decided this was an opportune moment to let them all know he would not be in residence for a while and to inform them of what he expected of them in his absence. He invited Mr. Burke to join them for wine and Stilton, then asked for everyone's attention.

"I believe you are all aware I must return to Whitehall. The King's Council for Trade sits in Mercers' Hall next week and I am appointed to it. His Majesty tells me I can use my talent to make money for the crown, as well as myself. In my absence, I leave Mr. Burke in full charge."

He fixed his daughter with a commanding stare. "Amanda, I want you to obey Mistress Ashley and to study your reading and writing. If I get a good report on you when I return, I shall consider that visit to meet Queen Catherine."

"I promise to be good, Daddy, in spite of your blackmail."

"Amanda, it is not blackmail, it is a simple bribe," he corrected.

"What's the difference?"

"One carries a threat, the other a reward; a visit to the queen versus a good thrashing."

"I see," Amanda said thoughtfully.

"I wondered if you would, since no one has ever laid a disciplinary hand on you. Of course things could change."

"*That* was a threat," she pointed out.

"How quickly you grasp things." Her father laughed and everyone joined in, relieved that the wonderful meal hadn't ended in a battle of wills.

After Joy put her charge to bed and told her another story, she sought the solitude of her own chamber to relive the exciting hours she had spent in London with Noel Huntingdon.

When she undressed, Joy stepped before the mirror to look at her body. She was surprised to see that it looked the same, yet it felt so different. Her skin seemed to have become sensitized to touch. Even the material of her petticoat heightened awareness of her body.

She slipped the aqua silk over her head and let it slither down her legs. Though Joy had never owned anything made of this material before, she knew immediately that she loved it. It made her feel special, extravagant, slightly sinful. She decided she would wear it to bed.

As she lay there, Joy knew it was a good thing that Lord Huntingdon was going to Whitehall. If he were here he would continue their liaison. Then when he tired of her, as he inevitably would, he would rid himself of her. The separation from Amanda would be painful, probably for both of them. Joy warned herself not to be too possessive. Yet inside, she feared it was too late. Amanda had already stolen her heart and she was mad in love with Noel Huntingdon. She sighed. Yes, all in all, it was a good thing he was going away.

Joy sat up in bed at the sound of her door opening. She assumed it was Amanda, until the husky whisper dispelled the assumption. Noel came to the bed and reached for her hand.

Her heart quickened to a staccato beat and she was suddenly breathless. "What do you want?" she whispered faintly.

"I want you to give me a biology lesson," he murmured wickedly, urging her from her bed and taking her with him to his own chamber. Noel closed the door, then gathered her into his arms. "Then I want to give *you* a biology lesson." The amusement in his voice set her off laughing. "There's so much I want to teach you," he said, running possessive fingers through her silken mass of hair.

Joy pushed away the dread of what he would do when he discovered her deceit. No one could take tonight away from her.

Chapter 7

J oy was back in her own chamber long before dawn lightened the sky. But her lover's touch stayed with her, a tangible thing almost as powerful as his presence. Although she doubted the wisdom of what had happened between them, she would not have changed it to save her soul. He was a magnificent lover who encouraged her to match his own passion.

She did not know if it was the world that had changed, or just her, but suddenly colors were more vivid, birdsongs more haunting, even the nip in the air was more invigorating!

After breakfast the first thing Amanda insisted upon was visiting the frog pond. "I hope they haven't hopped away in the night." But when they got there, she was overjoyed to see there were twice as many as they had put there yesterday. A large frog sitting on the edge of the pond croaked loudly.

"Good God, it spoke!" she exclaimed.

"The others heard him and that's why they came. I think it's a mating call."

"So you think they'll all stay?"

Joy nodded.

"What will they do when it snows?"

"I think they bury themselves in the mud and stay there all winter."

"I'm going to give them all names," Amanda decided. "I suppose we can't put off the lessons any longer. Daddy doesn't think much of biology lessons."

Joy blushed. *On the contrary, he has a passion for them!*

In the schoolroom, Joy looked at all the books in dismay. She sat down at the big desk and handed a leather-bound volume to Amanda. "Why don't you read me something?"

Amanda sat down at her own smaller desk and opened the book. "This passage was written by Abelard, describing Eleanor of Aquitaine's court."

The garments of the court ladies are fashioned from the finest tissues of wool or silk. A costly fur between two layers of rich stuffs forms the lining and border of their cloaks. Their arms are loaded with bracelets; from their ears hang pendants enshrining precious stones. For head dress they have a kerchief of fine linen which they drape about their neck and shoulders, allowing one corner to fall over the left arm. This is their wimple, ordinarily fastened to their brows by a chaplet, a fillet, or a circle of wrought gold. Gotten up in this way, they walk with mincing steps, their necks thrust forward; and furnished and adorned as only temples should be, they drag after them a tail of precious stuff that raises a cloud of dust . . .

*Some you see who are not so much adorned as loaded down
with gold, silver, and precious stones, and indeed with everything that pertains to queenly splendor.*

Joy sat entranced; listening to Amanda had conjured
a picture from medieval times. "Amanda, that was
wonderful! You read so well, I can see everything viv-
idly. I had no idea you were so clever. Oh, I could see
you were clever right away," Joy amended, "but you
are so well educated, it leaves me speechless!"

"My other governesses never praised me, but I always thought I read well, in spite of their carping.
However, I have a confession to make. My writing is
atrocious. It looks like a spider fell into the inkwell and
crawled across the page. How is your writing?"

"Nonexistent."

"Pardon?"

Joy knew she was taking a terrible risk. Amanda had
practiced being a wretched little beast for years. Giving
her this knowledge would give her power that could be
disastrous. Joy took a deep breath. "I too have a confession to make. I have a shameful secret I want to share
with you, if I can be sure you won't betray me."

"Daddy and I share a secret. I see no reason why I
can't share one with you, especially if it's a shameful
one," she said eagerly.

"I cannot read or write."

Amanda stared at her in utter disbelief. "Not at all?"

"I was taught my alphabet, then the lessons stopped.
Will you teach me to read, Amanda?"

The child was so flattered by the request, she agreed
eagerly. "If you work hard and apply yourself, I'll have

you reading in a fortnight!" Amanda had already taken on the role of teacher. "I get the big desk, you sit here." She handed Joy a slate and a piece of chalk, then began to scrawl on the wall blackboard.

Noel Huntingdon walked into the room. He did not notice Joy blanch. "I've come to say good-bye." He looked at Amanda with the wooden pointer in her hand, then at Joy sitting at the small desk. "What's going on?"

For one terrifying moment Joy thought Amanda would tell him, but she remained silent. "Amanda is taking a turn at being the teacher today. I thought it might rekindle her interest in her books." Joy's heartbeat thundered inside her eardrums. She knew her deception would be discovered any minute.

"What a brilliant idea."

Amanda, needing to be part of the deception, said, "We've been reading Abelard's description of the court of Aquitaine."

Lord Huntingdon gave Joy a look of approval. "That's rather ambitious. I'm very proud of you. I shall miss you." His eyes looked over the child's head at Joy. She knew his words were meant for her too.

"Good-bye, Amanda."

"Good-bye, Daddy." She gave him a swift hug.

"Godspeed, my lord."

When Joy was sure Lord Huntingdon had left, she heaved a sigh of relief. "Why don't we go to the kitchen to see what Mrs. Bumble is concocting?"

"Just a moment, young lady. When you have copied

down the twenty words I shall put on the board, you
can run off to the kitchen, and not before!"

In the afternoon, Amanda informed Maude of her
impending presentation at court.

"*Alors,* I would be terrified!"

Joy realized how difficult Maude found it to appear
in public and meet new faces, but she was unprepared
for Amanda's sensitivity.

"I too am afraid, Maude. I know I'm not pretty and
I live in fear of people looking at me with pity in their
eyes. Especially people who knew how beautiful my
mother was."

"Mandy, you may not be pretty in the conventional
way, but you have many attractive features," Joy
pointed out firmly. "Your hair shines like the blue-
black plumage on a raven's wing and your eyes are like
black velvet pansies."

"*Oui, oui,*" Maude agreed. "I weell make a peenk
gown for court."

Amanda wrinkled her nose. "Pink was *her* favorite
color."

Both women knew she referred to her mother.
"Not pink," Joy decided, "but peach. Peach is the
most complimentary color in the world for someone
with black hair."

"Peach velvet weeth the trimmings of swansdown,"
Maude suggested.

"Thank you, Maude, that sounds excellent."

Maude raised her eyebrows at Joy and put her hand
to her heart. "Manners, what a shock!"

Amanda giggled. "It's a conversion, like St. Paul on the road to Damascus."

Joy was amazed at the things Amanda came out with. Was there anything she didn't know?

"We're off to the kitchen to amuse ourselves," Amanda said.

"Won't you come and meet Mrs. Bumble?" Joy coaxed Maude, knowing she kept solitary because of her disfigured face. "She's the most comfortable woman in the world; do come."

In the kitchen, Bessie Bumble curtsied to Maude, then gave her a compliment. "The French are the finest cooks under the sun. I warrant ye could show me a thing or two."

"Non, non. I know ze clothes only. But pairhaps you teach me?"

"Me too!" Amanda insisted, refusing to be left out. "What are you making?"

"This is a potato and mushroom galette. I have sliced russet potatoes and I am about to blanch them." Mrs. Bumble handed Amanda a slotted spoon. "Ye can take the slices out of the boiling water and lay them to dry on this linen towel."

"I'll wash the mushrooms," Joy volunteered. "I didn't know there were so many different kinds."

"That's what enhances the delicate flavor. I use button mushrooms, wild mushrooms, and these here are oyster mushrooms," Bessie said, melting butter in a skillet so she could sauté them. "Amanda, I need yer skill with that slotted spoon again."

Maude chopped the chives, Bessie brushed the soufflé dish with olive oil, and then instructed Amanda to layer the dish with potatoes and mushrooms, and flatten them with the spoon as she went along.

"Is that it?" Amanda asked.

"Yes. All it needs before baking is salt, pepper, and grated cheese. When it's cooked, I just cut it into wedges."

"I can't wait for Christmas!" Amanda said. "May I help you make some of the fancy holiday dishes?"

"Since ye did such a good job today, ye certainly can help with Christmas. And though it's a short time off yet, it's not too early to start the Christmas cake, nor the Christmas puddings."

That night, after Amanda was asleep, Joy worked late at learning her letters. She felt extremely inadequate. Maude was an accomplished seamstress, Bessie was a gourmet cook, and Amanda was intelligent beyond belief. Joy wished there was something she was good at. It never occurred to her that making a child happy took a special talent which she possessed in abundance.

Joy rubbed her weary eyes, blew out the candle, and climbed into bed. Though she was pleasantly tired, sleep eluded her. Bed provoked thoughts of Noel. She could see his dark eyes fill with amusement, watch his mouth curve in a mocking smile, hear his deep laughter roll over her in the darkness.

She cupped her breasts with her palms to still their ache, wishing all the while it was his possessive hands that covered them. Joy closed her eyes and relived his lovemaking; slowly at first, making her skin feel like hot silk. Then she relived the moment when he lost all restraint. That was her favorite part, for it showed her how much power she had over him, if only for a fleeting hour. Already she missed him sorely, and in her heart she suspected it could only get worse. If days stretched into weeks, her body would be crying out for his touch.

Noel Huntingdon found himself in much worse shape than Joy, as he lay in bed in his apartment at Whitehall. He had unwittingly compared every courtesan he encountered at the palace with Joy Ashley, and each had come up wanting. After a twelve-hour day of business, he had spent the late evening hours gambling with Charles and his other friends at the Groom Porter's Lodge and could have had his pick of any of the courtesans offering their ample charms to the card-players.

This certainly put him in the mood for dalliance, but tonight the ladies looked overblown, underdressed, and slightly shopworn. Because of his jaded mood, he had retired alone. But as he lay abed, he wondered if he had made the wisest choice.

Noel's testes ached with a heaviness that made sleep impossible. But it wasn't only his body that hungered. His mind clung to Joy's image as tenaciously as a terrier with a bone, and refused to let it go. Try as he might, he could not dispel the thought of all the pleasure they gave each other in bed. The memory of her love

sounds made his blood run heavy and his body felt as if
it were starving.

With a foul oath he flung himself from the bed and
paced the chamber like a caged animal aroused to near-
violence. He poured himself wine, but its golden color
reminded him of Joy's hair. As he gazed at his hands, he
recalled how they looked cupping her breasts, tracing
her silken flesh, threading through the red-gold curls
atop her high mons. He set the wineglass aside and
tipped the decanter to his lips, determined to induce
sleep.

At the crack of dawn, Amanda awoke Joy with an
impatient shake. "Come on, sleepybones, you have
much to learn today."

Joy groaned with pretended reluctance. "You have
turned into a dragon. Must you be so strict?"

"You should have had some of my tutors. One
rapped me over the knuckles so hard, she broke her
wooden pointer, simply because I blotted my copy-
book."

No wonder she doesn't like writing, Joy thought. *I'll
have to find a way to change that.*

At mid-morning, after a two-hour reading lesson,
Joy took out a large sheet of parchment and began to
sketch. "Huntingdon Hall doesn't have a herb garden.
I thought we'd plan one on paper, so that it can be
planted in the spring."

"You draw beautifully, how did you learn?"

"Thank you, Amanda. I've always loved to draw,
though I've never had many drawing supplies."

"I have lots of charcoal and paints, but they are locked in that cupboard."

"Why is it locked?"

"I spilled paint on the carpet. It was rather a mess and the governess had to clean it up. She made certain I never touched my paints again."

"That's ridiculous! I'll get Mr. Burke to unlock it for us. I'll draw this plan for the garden, then you can write in the names of the herbs."

An hour into the project Amanda said, "I enjoy doing things together, Joy."

"I enjoy it too, Mandy. You know, we could plan a butterfly garden for around the fish pond. It will give us something pretty to think about on cold winter days."

"What is a butterfly garden?"

"Certain plants and flowers attract butterflies. The water already attracts dragonflies, so when the warm weather arrives it will be an enchanted place to sit quietly beside the pond."

"There's a book on butterflies here somewhere. Oh, here it is. Do you think we can attract bright ones like the painted lady?"

"Of course; they just love nettles."

"What about red admirals?"

"They like Michaelmas daisies, and these yellow butterflies with orange tips like lady's-smock."

"Joy, you are so clever!"

"Beside you, I'm a dunce."

Amanda giggled. "I shall make you a dunce cap and

if you are not reading in a fortnight, I shall make you
wear it!"

The days rapidly disappeared along with the fine
autumn weather. Only a week after Noel departed,
November winds rattled the shutters and whistled
down the chimneys of Huntingdon Hall. Whenever
Amanda was nervous about the night noises, Joy told
her it was the north wind blowing Christmas closer
every single night.

One evening not long after she'd gone to bed, Joy
heard her chamber door open softly and, thinking it
was Amanda, looking for comfort from the wind raging outside, sat up to light the lamp.

"No, don't disturb the darkness," a deep, familiar
voice murmured.

"Noel," she breathed, "I thought you were at
court."

"I was, and come morning I shall be there again, but
till then . . ."

His arms went around her and his hands slid up her
back, drawing her into his embrace. "God, how I
missed you!" He kissed her hair, her eyes, then his lips
found hers and his tongue explored her warm mouth.

"I must lock the door . . . Amanda . . ." she
whispered.

"No, Joy." He swept her high against his heart and
carried her softly to his own wing and his own bed.

If either of them could have held back the dawn,
they would have done so. After they had exhausted

themselves, he lay cuddling her, reluctant to abandon their warm cocoon.

"How can you leave without seeing Amanda? What will I say if she learns you were here?" Joy hoped it didn't sound as if she was clinging so he would not leave.

"No one will know, love. I came by river so I wouldn't have to stable my horse. In about a week, I'll come and take Amanda to court, I promise."

Joy hoped he wouldn't forget. To some men nothing weighed less than a promise.

Chapter 8

Before the week was over, snow began to fall. Amanda was overjoyed because here was concrete evidence that Christmas really was coming. The weather curtailed their riding lessons, but the extra time spent indoors helped Joy with her reading. Single words no longer presented a problem, but she still stumbled when reading sentences.

They broke out the paints and spent whole afternoons being colorfully creative. To encourage Amanda to practice her writing, Joy suggested illuminated letters. Both of them enjoyed writing out a word whose first letter they could turn into a painted picture of a fiery dragon or a medieval sword.

In the evenings, before a roaring fire, Joy and Amanda talked endlessly of Christmas and Amanda told Joy she planned to make gifts for all her favorite people. The staff of Huntingdon Hall was far too large for her to make gifts for everyone, but certainly she intended to make something for her father, Joy, Maude, Mr. Burke, and Mrs. Bumble.

All conversations about Christmas presents were conducted in whispers and Joy tried to find out what Amanda wanted so she could inform her father. Excitement began to build in Amanda, not only about Christmas but about her impending visit to London and Queen Catherine's court.

Noel Huntingdon finally returned, closer to the end of November than when he had actually promised, but the moment he arrived, his tardiness was forgiven. He lifted Amanda and swung her around. "Did you miss me?"

"Of course I missed you, Daddy, but only a little; I had Joy!"

Noel grinned. "Still scrupulously truthful, I see. Will you be as blunt with the poor queen, I wonder?"

"Of course. I only flatter people when I want something."

"A trait inherited from your mother, no doubt."

Amanda's mouth turned sulky and Joy rushed to her rescue. "Wait until you see Amanda's court dress, my lord. She chose the color and design herself."

"And what about you, Mistress Ashley? I trust Maude has outdone herself."

"Yes, my lord, I have a fine gown, but I don't have a cloak." Joy blushed. "May I have your permission to ask her to make me one?"

"Mistress Ashley . . . Joy, surely you don't think you need my permission for something as basic as a cloak? How on earth have you managed without one?"

"She's stayed inside with her nose in her books," Amanda said with admiration in her voice.

"And you still approve of the lady? Wonders never cease!"

Joy and Amanda exchanged a secret look of conspiracy.

"Get packed for London, we leave day after tomorrow."

Amanda clapped her hands. "Would you like to play with us, Daddy?"

Joy could feel his dark gaze sweep over her, but did not dare to encourage him, for fear his reply would be outrageous.

"Can we go out in the snow?" Amanda asked.

"Joy doesn't have a cloak."

"I have a shawl," Joy said eagerly.

He bowed formally with a wicked glint in his eyes. "Then I shall be delighted to play with you."

They made a snowman on the lawn, then Amanda insisted he needed a snow-woman, a snow-child, and a snow-dog. "I want them to be happy."

When Joy had a moment alone with him, she said quickly, "You must be more discreet, my lord . . . Noel. You shouldn't come to me in the night, Amanda is bound to discover us."

For a fleeting moment he thought how cozy it would be if Joy were his wife—that way Amanda could see them in bed every morning. He dismissed the thought immediately. He had been cured of marriage for a lifetime. "Then would you consider meeting me in the stables?"

"Of course not, that would be even more indiscreet!"

Noel threw back his head and laughed, then he launched himself at Joy and took her down in the snow. "Then it will have to be right here and now," he teased.

In a flash Amanda was on top of them both. The two females pushed him on his back and began to heap snow on him. "That should cool you down," Joy teased.

"Surrender! Surrender!" Amanda cried.

He threw up his arms. "That's it, I surrender; I'm licked!"

The following day, Noel decided to take them for a sleigh ride. The small cutter was taken from its storage shed and a harness with jingle bells was found for the horse. Joy, in her new hooded cape, climbed in next to Amanda and Noel covered them with a thick fur lap rug.

He took the reins and drove the sleigh all the way to Richmond. The snow-covered trees made the landscape picture-perfect in every direction. Amanda chattered away the whole time, telling her father that Joy was teaching her to paint, and then asking him endless questions about the court and Queen Catherine.

When they arrived back at Huntingdon Hall, Amanda whispered to her father, "Please take Joy for another ride. I want to work on her Christmas present and I want it to be a secret."

"Off you go," he urged, then turning to Joy said, "Stay where you are; I have orders to spirit you away for a while." He drove the sleigh around the back of the house so they could stop at the kitchen where Mrs. Bumble heated some spiced cider for them before they resumed their sleigh ride.

When they climbed back into the cutter, Noel tucked the fur about Joy, then slipped his arm around her to draw her close beside him. With the other hand on the reins he urged the horse downriver.

"I've found out what Amanda wants for Christmas, but she doesn't think you'll get it for her."

"Then she's probably right," he warned.

"She wants a dog."

"That's impossible. Maude is terrified of dogs."

"Actually, she isn't." She hesitated over the information she was about to impart, then plunged in. "Maude told me your wife, Elizabeth, hated dogs. She concocted the story that Maude was afraid of them so you would get rid of a greyhound you used to own."

Noel's mouth tightened. It sounded exactly like something Beth would do. She always drew the snake from the hole with another's hand. He immediately changed the subject. "Now I have you to myself, I don't intend to waste time talking of others. I almost came to you a hundred times last night. You are my torment, and my Joy."

He bent his head swiftly to steal a kiss. Their lips were icy cold when they touched, but before he withdrew his mouth from hers, they were both on fire. He withdrew his dark gaze from her so he could guide the horse, but his hand beneath the furs stole to her breast and cupped it possessively.

Noel Huntingdon's destination was Ashley Manor. When they arrived, he drew rein in front of the house so she could look her fill.

"Oh," she breathed, "how lovely it looks in the snow, but you shouldn't have brought me here."

He looked down at her quizzically. "Why not? I thought it would give you pleasure."

Joy sighed. "For years my mother and I lived on dreams, wishes, and flights of fancy. It was wrong."

"That's not altogether bad. Hope was all Charles and his loyal Cavaliers had to live on for years. When a wish eventually comes true, it is like a miracle."

Suddenly, more than anything in the world he wanted to make Joy's dream come true. He wanted her to have her miracle. He cupped her face with his hands and drew it close. "You have snowflakes on your lashes."

As the heat of his body seeped into hers, Joy had never felt so warm and wanted in her life. *If only every day could be like this one.*

The following day started off with a flurry of activity. The plan was to leave for London as early as possible so that everything could be accomplished in one day, then return to Huntingdon Hall without a stopover. Joy's and Amanda's court gowns were carefully packed so they wouldn't sit in them and crease them on the journey. Maude could not be persuaded to accompany them to London, but Joy reassured Lord Huntingdon that she could easily manage to dress herself and Amanda at his Whitehall apartment.

They arrived in the city with time aplenty on their hands, so before they went to the palace, Noel took his daughter to the Piazza in Covent Garden to see her first puppet play. All three ate an *al fresco* lunch from the carts of the street vendors, who did a brisk trade with their meat pasties, black peas, hot-cross buns, and roasted chestnuts.

Her father thought Amanda might be amused by the antics of an organ-grinder's monkey, but she was appalled that the man made money by exploiting the poor little devil and making it perform tricks that were unnatural to a creature who should live in the jungle, not the city of London!

" 'Tis a good thing we didn't eat where they have a turnspit-dog in a cage above the oven," he murmured to Joy.

Lord Huntingdon gave Amanda some money to spend on whatever she wished, so she bought China oranges, ribbons, a box of Christmas crackers, and a bouquet of hothouse flowers for the queen. All too soon their time melted away and the carriage delivered them to Whitehall Palace, where Noel left them in his rooms and told them he would be back in an hour to escort them to Her Royal Highness.

Joy helped Amanda bathe, then dressed her in her peach velvet trimmed with swansdown. She brushed the child's hair until it shone and, in Joy's eyes at least,

Amanda looked beautiful. Then she hurried into her own gown, which was a deep emerald green velvet; her only jewelry was the silver brooch from her mother. Finally, Joy brushed her hair into a heavy chignon and fastened it at the nape of her neck.

When Noel took Amanda and Joy to the queen's apartments, she was glad that her gown was dark, for Catherine and her attendants wore mostly black.

"They look like crows," Amanda whispered.

Joy squeezed her hand to warn her and whispered back, "And you look like a bird of paradise, darling."

When Amanda curtsied to the floor, then presented the flowers with a murmured, "Your Royal Highness," the queen was enchanted with her. Even the Portuguese attendants lost some of their stiffness at the sight of the dark child.

"Sucha beautiful hair—sucha big eyes," Catherine said wistfully, wishing she would soon be blessed by a daughter like this one.

Because she was given an inch, Amanda took a mile. She looked at the women who all carried the same book. "Is that the only book they allow you to read— the Bible?" she asked, wrinkling her nose.

"An *English* Bible," Queen Catherine informed her. "I must learna English. Can you read, Amanda?"

"Yes, Your Highness. Joy . . . Mistress Ashley and I read together. Actually, we do everything together, paint, ride, catch frogs. We are planning a butterfly garden for the spring."

"How fortunate you are to hava such a lady. Maybe I steal her from you," Catherine teased.

"Oh, I shall never part with her. I shall keep her for my own children when I am grown up."

Joy was taken off-guard by Amanda's sentiments, and was deeply touched.

When Noel and Charles entered the queen's apartments, Amanda immediately made her curtsy to the king. "Your Majesty," she murmured with perfect grace, then spoiled it by asking, "Are you wearing a wig, Sire?"

Charles lowered one eyelid. " 'Tis the fashion, what can I do?"

"But you set the fashion!" Amanda pointed out.

"Insanity is hereditary—parents get it from their children," Noel murmured to Charles.

"Don't fret over what she says; children have a disarming way of speaking the truth. I envy you; I wish she were mine."

"Are you referring to me or Mistress Ashley?" Amanda teased.

"Both," Charles whispered confidentially.

"May I go out on the balcony, Your Royal Highness?" she asked the queen. The balconies of the queen's apartments overlooked the river Thames.

"Charles tellsa me that by Christmas it may freeze anda the people will . . . how you say . . . skate!"

"Christmas is the best time of the year. You will love it!" Amanda told the queen.

"Yes, we will hava great festivities for twelve days. Please join us if you wish."

"You are too kind, Your Royal Highness," Noel interjected before Amanda could take over the court.

While Amanda and her father spoke with the queen, Charles engaged Joy in conversation. "You are doing an excellent job with Amanda; she used to be such a sad little girl. If Lord Huntingdon ever gives you the sack, come to court and tutor Catherine." The king's eyes glittered with the same amusement she often saw in Noel's. Joy blushed for she realized Charles knew that she and Noel were intimate. His invitation could be interpreted many ways.

Once King Charles' spaniels returned from their afternoon walk, Amanda was in her glory. She would have stayed forever playing with the dogs if her father had not put his foot down and made her say her good-byes.

Amanda talked their ears off as the carriage bowled along in the dusk. "I had no idea that London would stink so badly or that the streets by the river would be ankle-deep in mud. 'Tis an exciting place to visit, but I'm glad I don't have to live here." It wasn't until they were almost at Huntingdon Hall that she crawled into her father's lap and fell asleep with her head pillowed against his broad shoulder. He carried her straight to her bedroom, where Joy undressed the sleeping child and tucked her into bed.

Noel took hold of Joy's hand to take her with him and wouldn't accept no for an answer. "I'll be on my way back to London and you'll be safely in your own chamber long before Amanda stirs."

They had been denied each other for so long, the

mating was fierce and cataclysmic, assuaging their yearning, aching need in a primal and shocking way.

Afterward, they lay entwined as they talked of the day's events. Joy began to press him for a dog for Amanda. He refused outright at first, until she coaxed him to say *perhaps*. Still not satisfied, she traced her fingertips over his hirsute chest and cajoled, "A spaniel like the king's?"

As he had done the previous day in the snow, Noel threw up his arms. "That's it, I surrender; I'm licked!"

She smiled seductively and pushed him back upon the pillows. "Not yet you're not, my lord," and her wicked tongue came out to do the deed.

Chapter 9

"Promise you'll come home a week before Christmas?" Amanda demanded as her father prepared to leave for London.

"I'll get away as soon as I can. Christmas is a busy time here at Huntingdon; it's when we plan the crops for next year. Work hard at your lessons so you can have a Christmas holiday away from them."

"Don't forget the presents," Amanda reminded.

Noel exchanged a look with Joy that told her he would remember to bring the spaniel, and yet he knew Amanda wouldn't be half as surprised as Joy would be with the Christmas gift he had planned for her. Noel was excited about Christmas for the first time in years; he could hardly wait.

As the days of December sped past, they were filled with activities. Joy and Amanda, with Mr. Burke's help, cut holly, ivy, and mistletoe to decorate the hall. Maude was making Amanda a Christmas dress of red velvet, and Bessie Bumble filled the house with the tantalizing aromas of special treats she was preparing for the holiday festivities. In just one day the fragrance of rosemary could float from the kitchen, followed by cinnamon, and then the pungent spices of mince. Bessie showed Amanda how to shape tiny houses and animals from almond-flavored marzipan.

Joy was delighted that she could now read, even if it was only on a child's level. Amanda was a wonderful teacher and Joy was exceedingly grateful for her enthusiasm as well as her patience. The little girl had kept their secret sacred and Joy had begun to love her dearly. In bed at night, Joy burned her lamp until after midnight, reading page after page of some simple, mundane book, hoping that soon she would be able to graduate to Shakespeare's superb sonnets.

Amanda's fears and nightmares lessened considerably and Joy secretly wished some of the credit belonged to her. As she climbed into bed, Joy smiled to herself recalling Amanda's insistence that Maude make a matching red Christmas gown for her. Though immensely flattered that Amanda wanted to look exactly like her, Joy pointed out that she could not wear red with her clashing shade of hair.

Instead, she suggested Maude put a green taffeta sash on Amanda's red velvet, and make a red sash for Joy's green velvet gown, which she had worn to court. That way, they would look the same, but different!

Tonight, Joy had chosen the Bible to read in bed. As she opened it and began to leaf through the pages, she realized parts of it were difficult to read, while other chapters didn't hold her interest. That is until she came upon Solomon's Song of Songs.

Let him kiss me with the kisses of his mouth . . . your lips are like a thread of scarlet . . . honey and milk are under your tongue . . . your navel is like a round goblet . . . His cheeks are as a bed of spices . . . his belly as bright ivory overlaid with sapphires . . . his legs are as pillars of marble.

Joy closed the book before her longing for Noel became unbearable. She had had no notion the Bible was erotic!

In the schoolroom, Joy suggested that they each make a huge Christmas card. They would each choose a Christmas carol and write out the words using beautifully painted illuminated letters.

Amanda thought it a lovely idea, but made Joy promise not to look until she was finished. "I won't peek at yours either. That way it will be a surprise. On Christmas Day we can show off our cards and sing the carols."

Joy immediately chose "The First Noel" for her card and Amanda selected "The Wassail Song."

One week before Christmas a note arrived from

Lord Huntingdon, telling them he would arrive on the morrow as promised.

Joy and Amanda joined Bessie Bumble the next morning to learn what she was preparing for his return.

"Salmon *en papillote* with almonds and ginger," Bessie declared with a flourish.

Amanda giggled at the way she pronounced the letter T at the end of the French word, but nevertheless she was wildly curious about the dish.

"I grate lemon peel, then sprinkle it onto the salmon fillets along with sliced almonds and fresh ginger. Then I wrap the salmon in parchment paper an' bake 'um."

"It sounds divine," said Joy.

"May I help?" Amanda begged.

"Ye can toast the almonds. I've planned all the menus through Christmas. Tomorrow we are to have roast pheasant and the following day beef tenderloin spread with pâté then wrapped in pastry."

"What's Christmas dinner to be, Mrs. Bumble?"

"Roast goose with port wine gravy!" she boasted. "Apple, onion, and sage stuffing, Yorkshire pudding, leeks, carrots, and parsnips, pickled walnuts—"

"Stop! I shan't have room for mince pies, Christmas pudding, or trifle. You *are* making a trifle, Mrs. Bumblebee?"

"Yes, my little cockroach; just for you!"

Amanda flung her arms about Joy. "This is going to be the best Christmas, ever. Nothing can spoil it!"

* * *

After lunch, Joy and Amanda went for a ride. It was a beautiful crisp day with the sun turning the ice and snow that lay upon the fields to glittering crystal.

Amanda spotted the carriage first. "Daddy! Daddy! He's home!" she cried, galloping across the field toward Huntingdon's gates. The coach turned into the driveway and Amanda and Joy followed it to the stables.

Joy was even more excited than Amanda. Her gaze focused on the carriage door, eager to see his broad shoulders, his dark head, and his handsome, slightly cynical face emerge.

Noel alighted first, then a young man followed him. The smile of welcome froze on Joy's face.

"Uncle Carl!" Amanda exclaimed in surprise.

"Mistress Ashley, permit me to introduce my late wife's young brother, Carlton St. Clare. This lady is Amanda's tutor, Joy Ashley."

The man and woman who stood looking at each other did not reveal by look or word how well they were already acquainted. Joy watched his eyes sweep over her expensive black riding habit, then fill with knowing speculation. She saw his mouth curve with lust.

Carlton St. Clare made her a leg. "Mistress," he seemed to savor the word, "what an unlooked for pleasure."

Amanda's words reverberated in Joy's brain: *This is going to be the best Christmas, ever. Nothing can spoil it!* Joy's belly tightened into painful knots. The scene before her changed as if the sun went behind a cloud, but she knew it was Carlton St. Clare's shadow that cast its dark threat over her.

"Are you out of school for the holidays or have you been sent down?" Amanda questioned.

"Cheeky brat!" Carlton said. He smiled but his eyes were empty of amusement. "Actually, Cambridge closed early because of a rumor of smallpox." He watched with satisfaction as Amanda shuddered. The very sound of the word filled her with dread, as he knew it would.

Carlton's eyes returned to the tempting little maid. *Calling herself a tutor now, is she? Well, she may be able to pull the wool over Noel's eyes, but I know better. The cunning little bitch is living a complete lie!* Her audacity appealed to him. If he didn't take advantage of the situation, he would be a bloody fool. And Carlton St. Clare was nothing if not an opportunist. He'd been taking advantage of Noel Huntingdon since his sister's demise.

Carlton watched Noel lift his daughter from the saddle and heard her incessant chatter about Christmas and the hall's decorations. He took her palfrey's reins. "I'll stable your horse, brat. You'd better go up to the house before you catch cold."

Joy stiffened in the saddle. Clearly he was ridding them of Noel and Amanda so they would be alone in the stable. Her nightmare had begun. She walked her horse inside and dismounted quickly before he could offer his assistance. She watched him hand over Amanda's palfrey to a groom, then approach her.

"Such a small world," he drawled. "I am filled with Joy, though I prefer it the other way about."

"Leave me alone!"

"Those were the very words you threw at me last time we met, but nevertheless I still managed to have you naked within minutes."

Joy relived every humiliating moment. "If you play with fire, you're bound to get burned as your friend did."

"Is that a threat? Christ, you have the audacity of a bloody duchess! I hold all the cards, darling, and well you know it."

Joy knew she could not appeal to his better side, he had none. If she begged, it would be an added fillip to his lust. Her heart was heavy as a stone in her breast; she was caught like a rabbit in a snare. When the groom approached them to take her horse, Joy made her escape.

Noel awaited her at the front door. He took her hands into his and squeezed them. "Keep Amanda occupied while we spirit the spaniel to Mr. Burke's apartment."

Her mouth was so dry, she couldn't speak. She nodded her head in understanding. How could she have forgotten about the dog she had begged him to bring?

The next few hours were a blur of misery. Joy was so preoccupied with her thoughts she didn't hear anything Amanda or anyone else said to her. Dinner was a dreadful ordeal. Bessie Bumble's salmon *en papillote* tasted like ashes in her mouth, but the worst part was having to politely respond to Carlton's calculated conversation.

"You look amazingly familiar to me, Mistress Ashley, what was your last position?"

"It was in London, sir. I much prefer the country."

"I am studying the classics at Cambridge, perhaps we could read together."

"She's my tutor, not yours," Amanda pointed out.

"You must learn to share, Amanda. Surely you will share Mistress Ashley with me?"

"Surely, I won't!" Amanda responded.

Her father smiled apologetically. "She's grown very possessive of Mistress Ashley."

"Your manners are in tatters, Amanda. Your mother would not be pleased."

Joy wanted to stab him with her fork. Not only had he spoiled her dinner, he was doing his best to ruin Amanda's.

"I had a wonderful invitation to join my friend Richard Humphries for Christmas but this special time of year is for families."

When Mr. Burke poured the burgundy, Noel said, "That was the best meal served at Huntingdon in years. Let's have Bessie in to take a bow."

"No!" Joy almost shouted. She turned to Noel. "It would embarrass her terribly. I'll convey to her how very pleased you are, my lord."

As the men took their wine into the drawing room, Joy slipped into the kitchen. She took Bessie aside from the kitchen maids and gave her the bad news. "I don't know what I'm going to do. Whether I give in to him or I don't, I know he will make sure my job is finished here. Keep out of his way, Bessie, or you'll be out of a job too."

Amanda came looking for her. "I don't like Uncle Carl. Why did he have to come and spoil our Christmas? I wanted it to be just you and me and Daddy!"

"Oh, darling, nothing must spoil Christmas for you, promise?"

Amanda slipped her hand into Joy's. "Let's stay together until bedtime." Joy nodded reassuringly and squeezed her hand.

As Joy told Amanda a bedtime story about a snow queen, Lord Huntingdon came into his daughter's bedchamber to bid her good night. He listened in silence as Joy wove her magical tale of a queen who wore a crown of snowflakes and a necklace of icicles.

It was so obvious that the woman and child had formed a bond of affection, it made his heart sing. Joy had wrought a miracle. She had transformed a sad child into a happy one, and turned his home into a warm haven he had begun to miss when he went to London.

His home wasn't the only thing he missed. Whenever they were apart, Joy filled his thoughts and turned his long, empty nights into a torment of longing. He found himself in a constant state of arousal, which could be assuaged only when she spent the night in his bed. Noel suspected he was falling in love with his daughter's governess.

When Amanda's eyes finally closed and Joy tiptoed away, Noel followed her into her chamber. Before the door barely closed, he had her in his arms, his hot mouth seeking the rapidly beating pulse point in her throat that told him how wildly he affected her. "God's blood, I missed you," he said thickly.

Joy felt him rise against her belly, hot and hungry. She loved the feel of his fingers splaying through her hair to capture her for his mouth's ravishment. She felt the heat leap between them as he caressed her body with his. She knew she could not spend the night in his bed with a guest in the house, but also knew they would have to quickly slake their desire before they could bear to part with each other.

As Noel's possessive hands went beneath her skirts and his fingers found her throbbing woman's center, she opened to him with a cry of passion he took into his mouth. Joy clung to him, terrified that this might be their last time together. When she rejected Carlton's St. Clare's advances, she knew he would retaliate by exposing her shameful secrets to Noel.

Should she confess all to him here, now, while he was inflamed with his need for her? She knew she could not. Lord Huntingdon would never believe she had not invited Carlton St. Clare's advances. Yet that seemed a small matter compared with the deceit she had practiced in pretending to tutor his daughter. That, she knew he would never forgive.

"It's damned uncharitable of me, but I wish we didn't have company."

Joy caught at straws. "Could you not persuade him to visit his friend?"

"We are all the family he has, and it *is* Christmas," Noel said regretfully.

"I'm sorry, my lord."

"I'm sorry too. Sorry I can't carry you to my bed and keep you there till Christmas, or perhaps next year."

In the morning, Noel was out and about early. He and his land steward were meeting with all his tenant farmers, deciding which fields would be planted in hops, which in strawberries, and which would be planted in clover for grazing the animals.

St. Clare lost no time in seeking out Joy. "I suggest you keep the brat away from you, unless you want her to get a lesson about the facts of life, which I'm sure she'd be happy to tell her father about."

As if on cue, the child appeared. "Maude has finished my Christmas dress; come and see."

"Mandy, I'll see it later. I need some time alone to get ready for Christmas. There are only three days left until Christmas Eve. Why don't you get Jerome to give you a riding lesson?"

Amanda gave her a knowing look. "You are trying to get rid of me because you have a surprise present for me you want to wrap!"

Joy smiled at her. "You are too clever for me. Will you go?"

"Come and help me put on my habit and I promise to stay out all morning."

They went up to her chamber where Joy helped her into her riding dress, then added a quilted jacket for good measure. Amanda pulled on her gloves, picked up her crop, and dashed from the room.

No sooner did Amanda leave than St. Clare filled the doorway. She watched in fascinated horror as his mouth curved with satisfaction, knowing she was trapped. He closed the door and advanced toward her. "Undress for me; I know you don't want me to tear your pretty gown."

"No, I will not," she defied, caring little for the consequences.

Incensed at her defiance, he threw her down on Amanda's bed and began to tear at her clothes.

"Stop, or I'll scream," she vowed, suddenly filled with fear as she realized how much brute strength he possessed.

He laughed in her face. "I think not, you lying little whore. The last thing you want is the servants to see you copulating on your pupil's bed."

Joy felt his hard, obscene cock press into her soft thigh and at the same moment his mouth came savagely down on hers, effectively silencing her. She tore at his face with her nails, bit down into his lip, and began to scream until she felt her lungs might burst.

It was Mr. Burke who came running. Mr. Burke who witnessed her shame. St. Clare flung from the room, but not before he pierced her with a look that promised to destroy her.

Chapter 10

Joy ran through the connecting door to her own chamber and locked it for the first time since she had been at Huntingdon Hall. Then she locked the other door that opened onto the hallway. Her hands were trembling so violently, she had difficulty turning the key.

She sank down on the bed, head in hands, and began to sob. It was part relief at her escape, and part hopelessness. When her life was happier than ever before, why had this specter from her past materialized at Huntingdon to destroy her? Was this her punishment for living a lie? She pushed away the Puritan ideology and wiped at her tears ineffectively. She wasn't being punished, but she *had* brought it on herself. Through her sobs, she heard someone banging on the door.

"Joy, what's the matter? Why are you crying? Open the door, please," Amanda cried, her voice filled with anxiety.

Joy's heart broke all the more, knowing she was about to lose both the man and the child she had grown to love.

Carlton St. Clare awaited Noel Huntingdon at the stables. He would tell his story to his brother-in-law before he went up to the house. Carlton saw Amanda and her groom return from their ride, but the little brat wouldn't give him the time of day. He wondered again how a beautiful girl like his sister had produced such an ugly child. As his covetous gaze wandered about the imposing stables, it came to him that if anything happened to the brat, he would most likely be Lord Huntingdon's heir.

When Noel rode in on Cavalier, St. Clare lost no time taking the animal's reins and rubbing its glossy neck. "Noel, my conscience is playing hell with me; there's something I must tell you."

"In debt again, old man?" Noel asked, trying to make light of his problem.

"Nothing like that. It's Amanda's supposed governess. I know her—you could say I know the little trollop intimately."

"What the hell are you talking about?" Noel demanded coldly.

"She was a scullery maid at my friend Richard Humphries' house in London. The last time I saw the little doxy she entertained my friend and I nude in the kitchen. She's illiterate; how in the name of God did she fool you into thinking she could tutor Amanda? Unless of course you know all this, and she's simply warming your bed. In which case I'll say no more."

Lord Huntingdon's face turned dark and dangerous. When a groom came forward to take his horse, the lad stepped back in alarm. Every servant at Huntingdon knew enough to give him a wide berth when the master was in this mood.

Huntingdon strode up to the house and took the stairs two at a time.

"Daddy, Joy is crying!"

"Go to your room this instant."

Amanda obeyed immediately. His was the ultimate authority and he was wielding it.

He rattled the doorknob. "Open!"

Joy ignored the order. She had wiped away her tears, reminding herself that she had called the tune and must now pay the piper.

With one vicious kick, Lord Huntingdon opened the door.

She stood to face him, her heart hammering inside her chest. She had never seen his face like this before. It looked as if it were chiseled from cold marble.

"If there is one thing I abhor more than any other it is deception. I've had a bellyful in my dealings with women." He paused, then shot, "Do you know Carlton St. Clare?" His words flew at her like steel-tipped arrows and found their mark.

"Yes!" she flung. "He is a ravisher of young girls." Joy could only imagine the lecherous swine's accusations and she was unwilling to take the blame this time.

"Do you, or do you not, know how to read?" he demanded.

Joy closed her eyes in anguish. She had deceived Noel Huntingdon on that score. How could she deny it? She opened her eyes and squared her shoulders. "I do," she said, and then went on. "But only because Amanda has taught me. When I first came, I could not."

She saw his cold anger turn white-hot. "You made my daughter a part of your deception?"

"I gave her things she needed more than lessons. I

gave her attention, I soothed her fears . . . I gave her my love."

"Love?" he mocked with contempt. "You gave *me* a generous serving of your *love* while you were at it. You are not the first woman who has used sex to get what you want from me, but by Christ you'll be the last!" Noel Huntingdon laughed. The sound was not pleasant. "I thought you were different. How could I have been such a blind, stupid fool?"

Joy's cheeks were flaming. She wanted to smash his arrogant face, but knew he would retaliate and she would lose every last shred of dignity. "I'll pack and go immediately." She'd be damned if she'd leave without her new wardrobe; she'd earned it!

"Good. Just be sure you have no contact with my daughter before you leave."

Maude, with sad eyes, helped her to pack her clothes in a wicker carrier. When Joy descended the stairs, the house was strangely silent. She slipped into the kitchen to say good-bye to Bessie.

"Joy, let me go to Lord Huntingdon and tell him about Carlton St. Rotten-Clare."

"No, Bessie. St. Clare can do no wrong. He'd say we were in cahoots. You would lose your job immediately."

"But, my lamb, where will ye go?"

"I have an invitation to court for the Christmas festivities. Perhaps their majesties were not serious when they issued it, but I have nowhere else to go. It will give me time to try to find work. Don't worry about me, Bessie. Amanda is going to be very upset over all this. Be kind to her." Joy slipped out the back door before her tears undid her, and carrying everything she owned in the world, trekked from the estate down to the Chertsey water stairs.

For two solid hours Amanda did nothing but cry. Her father decided to let her cry it out, wishing he had some way to vent his own emotions. The noise got progressively louder until the sobbing permeated every corner of Huntingdon Hall. Finally, Noel had had enough and climbed the stairs.

"You will stop this caterwaul now, Amanda. Wash your face and come down to dinner."

She lifted a woebegone face and issued her ultimatum. "I shan't eat until Joy comes back!"

"Then you will starve to death, for she is never coming back," he said bluntly.

"What did you do to make her cry? What did you do to make her leave?" Amanda accused, hiccuping between dry sobs.

"Mistress Ashley was an unfit governess! When you found out she couldn't even read, why didn't you come and tell me?"

"It was our secret!" Amanda said passionately. "She was a brilliant pupil . . . I had her reading in no time and now you've spoiled everything. I hate you!"

"That's it! I've had all the insolence I will take. Downstairs immediately."

With every step she took, her distress turned to anger. Without realizing it, she followed her father's example, using anger to vent her emotions. When she entered the dining room, Carlton gave her such a smug look of satisfaction, Amanda was torn between screaming or smashing something; she did both. She picked up the soup tureen by its handles and flung it at her uncle.

St. Clare jumped back in alarm so that the missile missed him by inches, but the table and the carpet were saturated with bisque. Carlton roared at Noel Huntingdon, "If she were mine, I'd give her a damn good thrashing!"

Horrified, her father ordered, "Stop this tantrum!" and grabbed her by the shoulders. She was so hot to his touch, he stared at her in disbelief. Her face was dull red and her eyes had a glazed look. "My God, she's fevered."

"She has worked herself up into a fever," Carlton accused. "Stick her under a cold tap!"

Noel's anger drained away, replaced by concern for his child. He put his hand to her forehead and realized her skin was on fire.

Amanda swayed toward her father. "I don't feel very well; I want Joy."

He picked her up and carried her to a couch before the drawing room fire. Both Mr. Burke and Maude followed. "She's coming down with something," Noel said tightly. He did not voice his fear of what it was; he did not need to. Everyone in the room was thinking the same thing.

Amanda was having dry heaves. "I'm afraid . . . I want Joy."

At this moment, Noel Huntingdon, too, wanted Joy. "Hush, darling. I won't let anything happen to you. I'll get you a drink." Maude followed him to the kitchen. He said, "Just to be on the safe side, I think we'd better isolate her. You and I are the only ones who should have further contact with her until we rule out smallpox."

Maude crossed herself. "She likes strawberry juice."

Bessie Bumble filled a glass with Amanda's favorite drink and handed it to Lord Huntingdon. "I'll brew a tisane to help bring down her fever."

Her father carried Amanda up to her bed and asked Mr. Burke to keep all the household servants on the ground floor. Maude gave Amanda a sponge bath while Noel plied her with cool drinks, yet her fever seemed to climb.

Amanda lapsed into silence, uttering only one word every now and then: "Joy? Joy?"

Noel looked at Maude. "We'll know by morning." Both of them had been through this before. If the red pustules did not appear in the first twenty-four hours, danger of the dreaded contagion would be over.

Carlton St. Clare was torn between two thoughts. He hoped he hadn't carried the dire disease from Cambridge, yet if Amanda had been infected, she would almost surely succumb and her father would have a new heir!

He told himself the brat had made herself ill and likely didn't have smallpox at all. Nevertheless, he would not take the chance of going upstairs to his bedchamber, but instead went into the library where there was a liberal supply of brandy.

Amanda did not drift into a peaceful slumber as her father hoped, she vomited, then tossed and turned the entire night, growing more restless every hour, until finally she became delirious. Noel cradled her, hoping to soothe her, but by dawn he was at his wits' end. He shied away from the services of a physician; their practices could be barbaric.

Again, Maude brought tepid water and a sponge. When she raised Amanda's night rail, a gasp of horror escaped from her lips. Noel and Maude stared down in dismay at the red spots that were beginning to erupt on the child's body.

Christmas at Whitehall was spectacular. King Charles' courtiers had lived at the opulent French court for many years and now the decorations lavishly reflected this. Angels with gilded wings, some carrying golden harps, others blowing golden trumpets, were suspended on wires as if they were in heavenly flight. Gilt cherubs were perched on pedestals and newel posts, and a hundred musicians strolled the labyrinths of the palace, filling the very air with merriment. Thousands of candles, in chandeliers and candelabra, flickered day and night, turning the court into a glittering, extravagant tableau.

Joy's breath was taken away by the spectacle, and yet at the same time she knew the decorations of holly and ivy they had used at Huntingdon made it far more warm and welcoming. Not that she hadn't been welcomed at court. She had, especially by Queen Catherine. Her Royal Highness had had new gowns created for Christmas in cloth of gold and white satin encrusted with jewels, but she felt extremely self-conscious in the garments which were the antithesis of the farthingales she had brought from Portugal. She liked Joy's company because she was completely uncritical, unlike the English courtesans who laughed at her behind their fans.

Joy hoped and prayed Queen Catherine would employ her at court to help her improve her English, but inside she was heartbroken. She couldn't get the scene with Noel out of her mind. Joy had never seen anyone that angry before. He was incensed at her deception, almost to the point of violence. Huntingdon Hall had begun to feel like home and its inhabitants like her family. Now, in spite of the throngs of merrymakers, she felt utterly alone.

Joy missed Amanda with all her heart and knew with a sadness she could not dispel that Amanda would miss her too. Inside, she ached for Noel and the knowledge that she had brought it all on herself did not assuage the pain one iota. She should never have allowed Amanda to insinuate herself into her heart; she should never have allowed herself to fall hopelessly in love with Lord Huntingdon. How foolish she had been to let them inside the iron carapace she had built around her heart.

Joy had every opportunity to indulge in flirtation, as

every gentleman at court was looking to indulge in a liaison, but the loose morals at Whitehall secretly appalled her.

Noel patiently held the basin while Amanda vomited, then gently cleansed her mouth with the sponge. She looked at him with pitiful eyes. "Daddy, I want Joy," she whispered.

"So do I, darling," he said tenderly, knowing he would pay any price to have Joy Ashley back at Huntingdon. His heart felt like a heavy lump of lead in his chest as he saw that the spots on his child's body had turned to papules and her face was now covered with red dots.

With tender hands he held the cup to her mouth and encouraged her to swallow the tisane laced with poppy, then watched as she fell into a light doze. Noel Huntingdon stood and stretched; he had no option but to tell the others the dreaded news.

He found Carlton in the library. Noel was too preoccupied to realize he was sodden with drink. "It's as we feared, Carlton. Amanda has smallpox."

"It's my fault. I brought it from Cambridge, I should never have come!"

"Don't blame yourself, man. There are outbreaks all over London. It can strike anyone at anytime. We both know that."

"You have enough to do without worrying about me. I'll leave at once."

Noel saw his fear and understood it. Carlton had lost his only sister in France to the pestilence when he was a lad of fourteen. Noel found Mr. Burke in the kitchen with Bessie Bumble. "I'm certain it's smallpox," he said tightly. "The red spots have turned into papules and her fever has come down slightly because of it. Thank God Maude is immune, but you two should leave until the danger is passed."

"My place is at Huntingdon, my lord," Mr. Burke said quietly but firmly.

Bessie wiped away her tears. "My place is right here in this kitchen. Is there anything I can get for Amanda?"

"All she has asked for is Joy, but I am glad Mistress Ashley is gone and is out of harm's way."

"Beggin' yer pardon, my lord, Joy would be mad as fire if she knew her little Mandy was poorly. She'll never forgive ye, if ye don't tell her. Worse, she'll never forgive herself for deserting the child in her hour of need!"

"I don't even know where to look for her." Noel ran a distracted hand through his hair.

"She's gone to court—to the queen. She had nowhere else to go. She knew St. Clare would try to ravish her against her will. He tried it before at Humphries'!"

"It's true, my lord, I caught him in the act."

Noel cursed beneath his breath. He knew his late wife's brother was a lecherous young wastrel but turned a blind eye to it. He saw clearly now that if St. Clare couldn't ruin Joy one way, he would do it another. No one knew better than Noel that she was a virgin when she came to him. Why had he listened to St. Clare's

foul accusations? "Mr. Burke, please inform the staff
they are free to leave until the danger is past."

When Noel returned to Amanda's chamber, both
she and Maude were dozing fitfully. How could he
leave her when she was so ill? What if she died while
he was gone? On the other hand, how could he deny
Amanda the comfort Joy would bring her? He made
up his mind in a heartbeat. He would go to Whitehall
and beg Joy to return. If he hurried, he could be back
in less than three hours.

Chapter 11

Noel left the carriage at the mews where the vast
stables for Whitehall were located. Royalist
nobility from the surrounding counties swelled the
grounds and hallways of the palace. None wanted to be
left out of the first Christmas celebration held by King
Charles II and his queen, Catherine.

Noel searched through the crowded rooms hoping
for a glimpse of red–gold hair. He soon found Charles,
surrounded by a coterie of friends, both old and new.

"What's amiss?" asked Charles, taking one look at
his friend's haggard face.

Noel did not want to panic the king and court. "I'm
searching for Joy Ashley. Amanda has taken ill and is
crying for her."

"You'll likely find Mistress Ashley close by Catherine. I'll send one of my personal physicians down to

Huntingdon. Let's hope Amanda improves in time for Christmas."

"Thank you, Your Majesty. I beg you to excuse me."

When Noel spotted the queen, he could clearly see that Joy was not with her. His heart sank. He did not wish to waste time chattering with Catherine and her ladies. Her apartments were overheated and he felt as if he would suffocate. He slipped outside into the garden and was rewarded by a small hooded figure by the fish pond. Without hesitation he strode a direct path to her.

"Joy, I am so sorry about what happened. I know Carlton St. Clare is no damn good."

Joy searched his face and sensed something dreadful had happened. Had he and St. Clare fought? Had Noel killed him? "Whatever is amiss, my lord?"

"It's Amanda. She's ill and is asking for you."

Joy's hand flew to her throat. "Oh no. Let me thank Queen Catherine for her hospitality and I will come with you immediately."

"Hold a moment, Joy. I am afraid it is smallpox. Asking you to come to Huntingdon may be a death warrant. Consider your decision with care."

"There is no decision, my lord. I am coming."

Noel took her wicker carrying case and handed Joy into the carriage. Then he took the opposite seat so he could face her while he talked. "Joy, I behaved most shabbily toward you. When I found out you deceived me about your tutoring credentials, I was absolutely livid. I vowed never to let a woman deceive me again after my wife's faithlessness at the French court, and the things St. Clare told me made me believe it was all happening again."

"I'm sorry, Lord Huntingdon. I should have told you the truth."

"Christ, don't call me that! Can I not be Noel to you?"

"Let me finish before you ask that. I took the job looking after Amanda before I realized she needed a tutor. Then when you started talking about the classics I kept my mouth shut because I was resentful that you were in possession of Huntingdon Hall, while Ashley Manor had been confiscated. It was childish of me, as well as dishonorable."

"Joy, when Amanda became ill and I could see it was smallpox, I suddenly realized how unimportant it was whether or not you could read the classics. You gave Amanda so much more. The things you gave her were priceless. When she became fevered she wanted only one thing: she wanted you. And suddenly, I realized that I wanted you too!"

"Oh, Noel. Everything will be fine, you'll see."

"No, Joy, we mustn't fool ourselves. She's very ill. There's every chance that we may lose her."

Joy moved to his side and took his hand. "Noel, don't give up. Maude survived the terrible disease and so will Amanda." Joy wondered if she'd said the right thing when Maude was so tragically disfigured, but scars were infinitely preferable to death.

Noel shook his head and laughed bitterly. "I had such special plans for Christmas."

Joy squeezed his hand, trying to comfort him and bring him hope at the same time.

He raised his eyes to hers. "Thank you for this selfless gift. No matter what happens, I shall always be indebted to you."

"Noel, when I give, there are no strings attached."

When the carriage arrived at Huntingdon, Joy sprang out, lifted her skirts, and ran into the house.

"Thank God you are back, Mistress Ashley," said Mr. Burke as he held open the door.

She gave him a quick smile of thanks and, without pausing, carried on up the staircase. When Joy saw Amanda's face, she had to fight back her tears. She saw the child's eyes brighten in spite of how ill she felt. "Mandy, darling, I'm so sorry you are poorly."

"Joy, don't leave me."

"I won't, I promise I won't." Joy took Maude's hands. "Thank you! Get some rest, Maude, you are worn to the bone."

Joy dropped a kiss on Amanda's fevered brow. Up close she could see the red spots were vesiculas of water and there was little doubt she had contracted pox.

When Noel came in, Joy could see he was trying to hide the stark fear in his eyes. She gathered her courage, knowing she must do everything she could to keep the fear of both the man and the child at bay.

She gave Amanda a drink, then sat beside her and described the Christmas decorations of the royal court. Joy's calm voice and natural manner were at total odds with the panic she felt inside. She silently pleaded with

God, then bargained with Him, then threatened, and finally went back to begging.

Amanda closed her eyes. Now that Joy was back, she seemed able to rest more contentedly. Every half-hour or so, the child's eyes would fly open as if in panic until she saw Joy was still there, then they would close again.

Joy walked behind the chair Noel was sitting on and began to massage his neck and shoulders. He was drawn so tight, he looked as if he might snap. She felt his muscles relax slightly beneath her hands. He took her fingers in his and drew them to his mouth.

"Thank you, Joy."

She knew he was not just thanking her for touching him, but for coming back and touching his little girl.

Later in the day, Noel brought them food. Though Joy did not feel like eating, she forced herself to encourage Noel to eat something. Amanda turned her face away from every delicacy, but she did continue to drink whenever Joy coaxed her.

The day seemed to have a thousand long hours, yet darkness inevitably came. Joy gave Amanda a cool sponge bath. She was silently horrified when she broke a few of the water blisters on Amanda's body and before she gently pulled a fresh nightgown over her head, saw the broken vesiculas had begun to crust over.

"The king said he would send his personal physician, but I don't want him to bleed her. I want him to leave her in peace."

"Perhaps he won't come," Joy ventured.

"Daddy, I'm afraid."

"Darling, I won't let him touch you!"

"I'm afraid of her," Amanda whispered.

Joy moved to the bed and took her hand. "Hush, love."

Amanda clutched her hand. "She's coming for me."

"No, she is *not*. I shall hold your hand all night. Daddy and I will be here until daylight. We will not let her take you."

"Promise?"

"I promise, Amanda."

Noel's dark brows drew together in hopeless perplexity. "Who?" he silently mouthed to Joy.

She shook her head and murmured, "Later."

When Amanda fell asleep, Joy told Noel about his daughter's fear that her mother finally wanted her. He began to talk quietly, telling Joy of his unhappy marriage.

"If anyone had told me I would ever consider marrying again, I would have thought them a candidate for Bedlam. Yet here I sit, wishing you and I were wed and this was *our* child."

Joy's heart was filled to breaking. "She *is* our child, Noel. No two people could love a little girl more than we love her."

"That's true. If love alone can cure her, she will recover."

Still keeping hold of Amanda's fingers, Joy sank down and rested her weary head against Noel's knee, but fought the urge to close her eyes. She felt like a guardian angel.

* * *

Darkness began to fade and dawn broke across the sky. Joy felt Amanda's hand squeeze hers. She pulled herself up and looked down at the small figure in the big bed. *Thank God she's still with us.* "It's morning, Amanda."

"Is it Christmas morning?" she asked eagerly.

Noel came up out of his chair to stare down in disbelief.

Joy felt the child's forehead. "Her fever is gone!"

"Is it Christmas morning?" Amanda persisted.

Both Noel and Joy laughed. "My days are a bit mixed up—I think it's Christmas Eve."

There was a commotion at the chamber door as Mr. Burke knocked and entered. "The doctor is here, Lord Huntingdon."

Before Noel could say, "Show him in," the thickset gentleman entered and advanced upon them.

"Good morrow, Huntingdon, I am Dr. Marley. Is this the patient?"

Noel's manners were impeccable, even though he did not want the king's physician or any other attending his child. "Thank you for coming all the way from London, Dr. Marley, especially at Christmastide. My daughter, Amanda, seems much improved this morning. Her fever has gone and at last we dare to hope."

"Let me examine her."

Joy saw Noel hesitate, then graciously step aside. But she could see that Noel still stood guard, ready to eject him from the chamber if he did anything more than examine the patient.

"Mmm," Marley said, looking intently at Amanda's face. "Lift up your gown for me."

"Gentlemen don't look beneath nightgowns!" Amanda said with outrage.

"Doctors do," he insisted, lifting it himself. "Mmm, how do you feel?"

"Very well, thank you, sir," Amanda said primly.

Dr. Marley lifted her eyelids, looked inside her mouth, then chuckled. He stood, picked up his bag, and turned to Noel. "I'm happy to be able to tell you she does not have smallpox. She has contracted swinepox as most children do, sooner or later."

"Dr. Marley, thank you. You have no idea how relieved I am—we are," he amended, ushering the physician from the chamber, but not before his eyes met and held Joy's with triumph.

Maude, Mr. Burke, and Bessie Bumble came up to visit the patient, overjoyed at the news.

"I want to get up. I can't waste Christmas in bed."

"Christmas is tomorrow," Joy reminded her.

"No, I want it today; I can't wait."

"Neither can I," her father agreed from the doorway. "Bessie, cook that goose!"

Noel awaited them at the bottom of the stairs. As they descended, hand in hand, Joy in her green velvet, Amanda in her red, Noel knew he was about to seize this chance for happiness with both hands. He stepped to one side to reveal the King Charles' spaniel in Mr. Burke's arms.

Amanda flew down the remaining stairs. "Daddy! Daddy! Thank you!"

The minute Mr. Burke set it down on the carpet, the little dog peed. Joy and Amanda found that highly amusing. Noel rolled his eyes, knowing his patience was about to be tried yet again.

Amanda was allowed to rule the roost, unwrapping her gifts and giving out the ones she had made specially for the people she loved. Then she rushed to the schoolroom to get the huge Christmas cards she and Joy had painted. "We picked our favorite carols, so we could sing them. Joy picked 'Noel'! I knew she would! I was more subtle," she informed her father. "I chose 'The Wassail Song' because it says: Love and Joy come to you!"

In the afternoon Noel ordered the sleigh harnessed. "May I bring Lu-Lu?"

"No, young madam, you cannot go outdoors yet. Joy and I are going alone. I happen to love the lady as much as you do."

Noel tucked the furs about Joy, then took the reins and drove along the river road. When he stopped before Ashley Manor, he reached into his breast pocket and handed her a crackling parchment. "Happy Christmas, Joy." He watched her intently so he would not miss the rapture on her face when she realized Ashley Manor was hers.

Joy's eyes flooded with tears and she buried her face against his broad chest.

His arms enfolded her. "Don't cry, love, please don't cry."

She lifted her face to his. "These are tears of joy."

He kissed her eyelids. "I love you so much. Will you marry me?"

For answer, she reached up her lips to his and opened softly. Noel groaned and crushed her against him. "In that green gown with its red sash, you look just like a Christmas present waiting to be unwrapped." It was a long, long time before he turned the horses toward Huntingdon Hall.

When they came through the front door, Joy was glowing with love and happiness. Amanda looked at her father and saw the same rapt expression. Her dark eyes swept back to Joy. "Will you marry us?" Amanda pleaded.

"Yes, I will, yes," Joy said, laughing and crying at the same time.

"It's a Christmas miracle!" Amanda declared, and her face had never looked more beautiful.

Upon a Midnight Clear

KATHERINE KINGSLEY

Chapter 1

Arkengarthdale, North Yorkshire
November 1816

Emerald green, the fresh, fragrant stretch of grass gently caressed by breeze, a rich carpet that reached as far as the eye could see. Cobalt blue, the bright glimmer of the sky reflected in the broad lake, its surface still and peaceful. Red, orange, yellow, the vibrant hues of leaves in their last glorious stand before the onset of winter winds took them flurrying to the ground. All the colors of a rainbow lit the landscape, and Jenny threw her head back and laughed in sheer pleasure.

And then the image rippled and faded and the dark took over—the dark that shrouded the world and extinguished its brilliance, leaving Jenny without even the stars to light her way . . .

She shivered as the chill of morning seeped through her bones, bringing her fully awake. She buried her face in her pillow for a moment, holding on to her dream, and then released it with a sigh. Rolling over on her side she searched for the warm, comforting shape of her dog's solid head. She smiled as a cold wet nose burrowed into her palm and delivered one long, sloppy lick, a lazy canine morning greeting that indicated Maddie wasn't the least interested in rising. Jenny couldn't say she blamed her.

"It's another cold morning, isn't it, girl, but there's not a thing we can do about it," she murmured. "I'm afraid we've seen the last of warm weather for this year. Come on, up you get."

Jenny shrugged into her dressing gown and slid her feet into the slippers that always rested in precisely the same place on the floor. Cautiously she made her way over to the fireplace that still gave off a modicum of warmth. Maddie padded along beside her mistress, her tail beating against Jenny's thigh like a metronome, as if to say that although she might not like it, she really didn't resent being ordered from her warm, soft pallet.

Jenny crouched and embraced her beloved dog around the neck, stroking the soft fur with the palm of her hand. In some ways, Maddie was all she had in the world—which wasn't to say that Jenny disregarded her aunt and uncle, for she depended on them completely.

Still, they weren't the most reliable of people. Aunt Lucinda would probably faint if Jenny ever summoned the nerve to imply as much, since Aunt Lucinda considered herself a paragon of virtue in every way. On the other hand, Uncle Harry would probably be highly complimented, since in his opinion the highest of virtues was complete, utter eccentricity in which unreliability played a key role.

As far as Uncle Harry was concerned, all great artists were not only eccentric and unreliable but also admirably irresponsible, and he took great pleasure from filling Bigslow Hall with as many of the prototype as he could find as often as possible, in the belief that he was furthering genius. That's what came of being a patron of the arts, she supposed. Unfortunately, his greatest pleasure was the bane of Aunt Lucinda's existence.

Over time Aunt Lucinda's prized auburn hair, which she claimed had turned many a head in her youth when she'd been Darling of the Ton, had gone pure white as a result of the strain of entertaining the constant stream of artists. Or so Aunt Lucinda said. Jenny suspected the loss of color was a natural consequence of aging, but since Aunt Lucinda had long ago frozen her age at precisely thirty-eight years, Jenny declined to point out the logical effect of her aunt's advancing age on her looks. Logic wasn't Aunt Lucinda's strongest suit. She was much more suited to high drama, which she practiced on every possible occasion. In any case, contradicting Aunt Lucinda was a sure invitation for trouble.

Jenny turned her head, listening momentarily, and then with a slight smile on her lips, she called for her maid to enter before the knock came at the door. Ella could always be heard a mile away, her heavy wheezing

and even heavier footsteps a sure portent of her impending arrival.

"Oh, so you're up then, miss," Ella said between
breathless pants, the floorboards vibrating with each
plodding step she took. "It's a good thing too, for your
auntie's on a rampage today. Seems your uncle forgot
to mention he's expecting another of those artists of his
this very day, Lord Somebody-or-Other. And his lordship'll be staying through Christmas at the very least,
which didn't please Lady Bigslow one little bit."

Jenny rubbed one finger over her temple, feeling
one of her dreaded headaches starting up at the
thought of being subjected to another one of her aunt's
fits of temper, as famous as her once-famous hair. The
news that another impossible artist was taking up residence only increased the throbbing. "Oh, dear," she
said, frowning. "Is Auntie in a terrible state?"

"Indeed she is, Miss Jane, and I can't say it looks as if
she's going to calm down any time soon. She's summoned you downstairs for breakfast this morning, so
you might as well give up the idea of a nice peaceful
tray in your room and prepare yourself for a stormy
repast." She paused just long enough to draw breath.
"Sir Harry said to her that he couldn't be expected to
remember everything, and she should be grateful he
received a letter from this Lord Whomever to remind
them he was coming today, and *she* said she'd have his
lordship to stay over her dead body, not when the last
guest destroyed the Green Suite in a fit of pique when
his work wasn't going as well as expected, and that they
couldn't afford another disaster—"

"Never mind, Ella," Jenny said, quickly cutting the maid off, for she'd only hear it all again from her aunt later. "It sounds as if your asthma is giving you trouble again. Did you take your powders this morning?"

"Who has time to take powders when it's the devil to pay down below?" Ella said tartly, laying the fire with a great deal of clattering and banging. "I don't know why I stay in service here, miss, I really don't. It's a wonder I don't have heart palpitations on top of all my other troubles. Sir Harry's already thrown a teacup *and* a saucer and it's not yet gone nine. It's a miracle John the footman didn't lose his ear when they went flying by."

Jenny winced. If her uncle had resorted to throwing the bone china, the situation really was bad. "I'll dress and go directly down," she said, resigning herself to refereeing another battle of wills between her aunt and uncle. "Don't worry about bringing up hot water; I can make do with what's left in the pitcher. But I would appreciate your laying out my clothes and letting Maddie out. I have a bad feeling that Sir Harry's newest guest is going to bring nothing but disaster down on our heads."

"Right away, Miss Jane," Ella said with obvious relief. "If anyone can dampen the fire, it's you. It's a miracle those two haven't killed each other before this, and I say your uncle should be grateful to have you to defend him. Although I can't say I'm too pleased myself that we have another one of those so-called artists arriving on the doorstep." She sniffed indignantly. "Lechers, the lot of them, and it's not easy to run like the wind when your arches are fallen and your lungs grabbing for air all the time. Maybe it's a good thing most of them are drunken louts to boot and trip over their own feet faster than I can flee—although look at what happened to that poor chambermaid Mary." She clucked loudly. "A sad day that was, a sad day indeed, and not a bit of it her own fault from what I heard."

"What you need is a Maddie of your own for protection," Jenny replied, remembering well the day that Mary had been forced to pack her bags and return to her family. "She won't let any strangers near *me,* bless her loyal heart." And a good thing it was, she added silently to herself, for if she found herself ruined as Mary had been, her aunt would probably force her to leave too, and that really would put her in a predicament.

Ella bent down to give Maddie an affectionate pat, her beefy hand making a loud business out of it. "She's a good girl to look after you so well. Who could have known the runt of the litter would turn out so smart? But I reckon all that love and care you gave her in the beginning made her loyal as the day is long."

"She's certainly that," Jenny said, warming her hands in front of the fire that now crackled briskly. "I never knew a pup that small and frail could survive."

Maddie had been nothing more than a soft handful of fur when the kennel-keeper first brought her to the house, a puppy of only three weeks, rejected by her mother and hounded nearly to death by her littermates. Even though Jenny had been warned that the puppy would surely die and it was foolish to become attached, she fashioned a feeding bottle with a nipple made from an old cloth and coaxed her to drink from it. She slept by the fire with her tiny charge so that she could feed her hourly and left her only long enough to look after her own simple needs.

But amazingly enough, the puppy gradually gained strength and soon was cavorting alongside Jenny's heels. Jenny named her Madeleine Sophie Louisa on the theory that a puppy that small and brave deserved a long and dignified name.

It had been seven years since then and Maddie rarely left her side. She brought Jenny not only joy and companionship, but also the freedom to do what Jenny loved best. Daily, no matter how inclement the weather, they explored every available inch of the surrounding countryside. Neither her aunt nor uncle objected, for they knew Jenny was safe from danger in Maddie's company.

And that made Madeleine Sophie Louisa the greatest blessing in Jenny's life, for without her dog the world was a dark and inaccessible place. But with Maddie at her side, Jenny might not have sight, but at least she had eyes to guide her.

"Damnation!" Stuart Blakeney, Viscount of Middleton, bent down to rub the toe he'd banged on the doorjamb of his bedroom. Nothing was going right. But then nothing had gone right since the day two years before when Penelope had cried off one week before their wedding and run away with his second cousin Noddy, a bloody bounder if ever there was one.

Stuart still felt the sting of humiliation every time he
allowed himself to think about that miserable day,
which was not very often. The pair of them could rot
in hell for all he cared.

Worse, far worse, was that his artistic skill had dried
up from that day forth, withering like a plum drying in
the hot sun. A desiccated prune, that's what he'd become—not that he'd ever been overflowing with brilliance to begin with. But at least he'd been technically
proficient if nothing else. Promising, his teachers had
called him. Talented. Now he couldn't even claim to
be that. Stuart Blakeney. Even his signature on the bottom of his paintings had become a joke.

Stuart sat down and pulled his boot gingerly over
the offending digit that was already swelling and throbbing with a vengeance and swore under his breath.

"I might as well shoot myself now and be done with
it," he muttered, glowering at the two large trunks
waiting to be loaded into his carriage.

He wasn't even sure why he was going to Bigslow
Hall for an extended stay, but the invitation had come
the same morning that he'd had a letter from his
mother informing him that bloody Noddy and Penelope were coming for a family Christmas at Northrup
House, and she felt he ought to be forewarned. That
had been incentive enough to sit down and immediately pen an acceptance to Sir Harry's suggestion that
he spend two or three months on a painting retreat,
drawing inspiration from the spectacular landscapes and
the promise of uninterrupted peace.

The idea that he would find inspiration at Bigslow

was absurd, since nothing had inspired him in a good long while, but Sir Harry's invitation was a convenient excuse to escape an impossible situation at home and his mother had accepted his explanation without rancor. She still had belief in his so-called talent, the dear misguided woman.

So now he was stuck with the unattractive prospect of forcing himself to sit in front of an easel and slap paint on a canvas for ceaseless hours, weeks on end. Still, he was tired of being hounded to death. Returning with a few wretched landscapes might silence his mother, his friends, and his teachers once and for all. He already knew what to expect: every time he'd picked up a brush in the last two years, all he'd managed to produce was a mess that closely resembled his bleak inner landscape—certainly nothing anyone would gaze upon with pleasure, which was why he hadn't shown any of his recent work to a single soul, preferring everyone to think he simply wasn't applying himself. And in truth, for the last eight months he hadn't been, finding the whole process far too excruciating.

"Your lordship's carriage is waiting," his valet, Newton, announced from the door, standing back as two footmen heaved the first trunk onto their shoulders and carried it away. Stuart scowled, envisioning the blank canvases contained inside, the tubes of pigment, the brushes and turpentine, all mocking him to do something brilliant with them.

He sighed heavily, allowed Newton to help him

into his coat, and limped downstairs to embark upon the next phase of the farce his life had become.

"So there you are at last, Jane," Aunt Lucinda said, as usual refusing to use the pet name that Jenny's parents had given her when she was a baby. "And about time too, I say, for I cannot abide people who are late for breakfast," she added unfairly, or at least unfairly as far as Jenny was concerned, since she was rarely invited to join her aunt for the first meal of the day.

Aunt Lucinda's voice had a sharper edge than usual to it, and Jenny steeled herself as John led her to her chair and went to fill a plate from the sideboard for her. "I beg your pardon," she said as contritely as she could. "Good morning, Uncle," she offered hesitantly, not certain if he was still in the room.

"Your uncle has left the table, and all I can say is good riddance," her aunt replied in frigid tones. "He has informed me that we are expecting another of his horrible artists this very day, and what position does that put me in, may I ask? One would think I was merely a housekeeper in my own establishment, with no say over the riffraff who come and go at your uncle's invitation." Her knife fell loudly onto her plate, setting Jenny's sensitive ears to ringing.

"I'm sure Uncle Harry means to consult you," Jenny said in her uncle's defense. "He's just forgetful at times." She carefully felt for her cup and picked it up by the handle, which the footman had thoughtfully positioned at a quarter past three so that she wouldn't knock the cup over and slop coffee all over her front.

"Forgetful? Look at how you arrived on the doorstep fifteen years ago without Harry saying a word to me. It's a bit much to *forget* to tell me that his younger brother and his sister-in-law had been killed, leaving a child for me to raise."

"But you were away in France at the time of the accident, Aunt Lucinda," Jenny said reasonably as the footman set a plate in front of her. She smelled the heady fragrance of kidneys and eggs and kippers, but her appetite had deserted her.

"That is beside the point," Lucinda replied dismissively, as if that important fact had no bearing on the matter. "I do wish you'd attend, Jane—you're as absentminded as your uncle. The point is that Harry never tells me anything, nor does he listen to me. Now there's to be yet another hanger-on for months, even years for all I know, while Harry's looking for supposed genius, the silly fool!" she said, her voice rising with emotion. "What he doesn't seem to understand is that they're looking just as hard for free meals, a soft bed, and servants to wait on them hand and foot. All this poppycock about seeking hidden inspiration is just an excuse for having someone else support them. This ridiculous obsession of your uncle's is a terrible strain on our finances!"

Jenny knew that to be true, but she couldn't help feeling sorry for her uncle, who believed in every fiber of his being that one day he really would discover true genius and thus enrich the world. "Who is coming this time?" she asked, absently picking up her knife and fork, wishing her head didn't feel as if it had been caught in a vise.

"Someone utterly insignificant. He is supposed to be a viscount, but I've never heard of him," Aunt Lucinda said, her voice dripping with sarcasm. "He obviously isn't a very *important* viscount—most likely he comes from an impoverished and obscure family. But title or no, I'm sure he's as dreadful and unkempt as the rest of them, or why would he be coming to us? He's most likely been turned out by his own family for unsavory behavior, just like that nasty Jasper Ogilvy, and *he* was a baronet. It goes to show that a title is no guarantee of good manners."

Jenny's stomach twisted. She well remembered Jasper Ogilvy, who had not only eaten them out of house and home during his three-month stay but had also invited a steady stream of his rowdy friends to help him. Jasper Ogilvy vanished one day without a word, leaving the west wing in ruins, poor Mary the chambermaid in a compromised condition, and Aunt Lucinda in a state of shock.

Jenny could only be grateful it hadn't been she who had been left carrying his bastard child. One awful night Jasper had lain in wait and cornered her in the dark kitchen just after she'd put Maddie out before bedtime. He'd tried to maul her, his breath reeking of spirits, but one swift kick on the shins had disarmed him long enough for her to jerk the door open and let a ferociously barking Maddie in. Maddie had taken a sizable piece out of the back of his britches, and he hadn't troubled either of them again.

"I do hope you are attending me, Jane, for I have a deeply distressing announcement to make," Lucinda said, her tone of voice softening now and its timbre deepening, and Jenny knew from long experience that the next scene would include tears.

"What is it, dear Auntie?" Jenny said, trying to sound concerned. After fifteen years of life with Aunt Lucinda, she found it difficult to summon up enthusiasm for each new dramatic episode.

"You see, my dear, I'm afraid your uncle and I have come to an impasse." Here she added a little vibrato to heighten the tragic effect. "I told your uncle in no uncertain terms that I would not tolerate another invasion—this time he would have to choose between me or his newest derelict."

Jenny's head shot up in shock and she stared blankly in her aunt's direction. She now had a better idea of why Uncle Harry had let the china fly. Her aunt had never before gone so far as to give her husband an ultimatum, and a cold thrill of alarm ran through her veins. She sat up very straight. "What are you saying, Aunt Lucinda?"

"I am informing you, as I informed your uncle when he refused to change his tune, that I am removing myself to the Dower House." Her voice caught on a sob. "Oh, that he could be so cruel, so callous as to choose a—a *stranger,* yes—a complete, idle *stranger* over his own wife! It is unthinkable, Jane. Unthinkable!"

What Jenny thought was unthinkable was that Aunt Lucinda, despite her dramatic tendencies, would go so far just to prove her point. "But—but surely Uncle

Harry doesn't believe that you're going to actually leave him?" she stammered. "You are devoted to each other. He'll be lost without you . . ." She trailed off, at a loss as to how to correct the situation at this late date. Her aunt was as stubborn as she was temperamental and that was saying a great deal.

"Then let him be lost without me," Lucinda said on a strangled sob. "Let him realize what I have been to him—a devoted wife and helpmate, patient as the day is long, putting up with all of his eccentricities."

Jenny nearly choked on the sip of coffee she'd just taken. That Aunt Lucinda would describe herself as patient was laughable. "Oh, please, won't you reconsider?" Jenny pleaded, the concern in her voice genuine this time. "Uncle Harry won't have the first idea how to go on by himself."

"That is his problem now. I wash my hands of him. I wash my hands of Harry and Bigslow Hall and anything to do with either of them." She sniffed. "I'm not changing my mind, Jane, so there's no point in wasting your breath. Your uncle has made his own bed. Let him lie in it, and he'll be lucky if anyone remembers to instruct the maids to change his bed linens."

"But, Auntie—"

"No. I've made up my mind, and that's all there is to it. My bags are being packed as we speak. I have nothing else to say."

Jenny heard the scrape of Lucinda's chair as she stood, and then a torrent of weeping. She pushed her own chair back and felt her way to Lucinda's side, pulling her shaking body into an embrace. "I wish you wouldn't go," she said softly. "Christmas is coming, and it won't be the same without you. Oh, please, don't stand on your pride."

"My pride has nothing to do with it," Lucinda sobbed. "It's my sanity that is at risk—my sanity and my health. I cannot go on like this, never knowing what the next day is to bring, what calamity is around the next corner. Your uncle will never change, Jane; he has no desire to change, any more than he has any regard for my happiness or welfare." She pulled herself out of Jenny's arms. "He has made his position perfectly clear, and given that, I really have no choice but to leave. I must be off now to supervise the packing of my belongings, but I hope you will not suffer too severely, my dear. You have been like a daughter to me, but you must stay with your uncle, for it is he who is your blood relative."

It was the first time Lucinda had ever made mention of regarding Jenny as a daughter rather than an obligation, but Jenny supposed the sentiment struck the right note in the moment. Still, she couldn't help but wish that her aunt meant it in some small way. "May I come and visit you?"

"I don't think that would be appropriate," her aunt replied with another loud sniff. "I am cutting myself off from every connection with your uncle, and therefore with you."

And with that parting comment, Lucinda swept from the room in a rustle of skirts, leaving Jenny standing alone in the middle of the room, torn between wanting to strangle her aunt and wanting to cry like an abandoned child.

"I'm sorry, Miss Jane," the butler said when Jenny inquired as to her uncle's whereabouts, "but Sir Harry is no longer on the premises. He left in a terrible state, swearing that he wouldn't return until Lady Bigslow had vacated the hall. I heard all about the trouble from John, who witnessed the whole thing."

"Oh, Partridge, this is ridiculous," Jenny said, releasing an impatient breath. "The two of them have always fought like cats and dogs, but they never fail to resolve their disagreements. Do you think my aunt really will leave?"

"I saw her ladyship off only ten minutes ago, miss, the carriage piled high with her cases. She's taken Clarissa with her, and they both looked grim as could be, so I do not believe this time she is putting on one of her shows."

Jenny chewed on her bottom lip thoughtfully. "Maybe if you told the new guest when he arrives that the house has been quarantined for the pox, he'll go away again and Aunt Lucinda will return?"

Partridge chuckled. "There never was anything wrong with your imagination, miss, I'll give you that. But I don't think Sir Harry would approve of having his friend driven away with such a bald-faced lie. I'm afraid we're just going to have to wait until the dust settles and either your aunt or uncle backs down."

"I suppose you're right," Jenny said, but she didn't like the way matters were shaping up in the least. She decided a good long walk was the only way to blow the troubles out of her brain and Partridge obligingly fetched her cloak and helped her into it.

She took firm hold of Maddie's harness, a clever contraption that her uncle had fashioned long before from an old pair of reins, and set off across the front lawn, forcing herself to concentrate on nothing more than the feel of the brisk breeze blowing in her face and the smell of the crisp autumn leaves that crunched satisfyingly underfoot. Her head was now pounding in earnest, and she fervently hoped that the fresh air would help before the headache turned into a full-fledged migraine and she had to take to her bed with a cold cloth over her brow.

As she and Maddie walked farther across the lawn, she heard the distant sound of hoofbeats on the main road and the rattle of a carriage. She wondered for a moment if her aunt had changed her mind and turned her landau around, but her aunt would never be traveling at such a speed under any circumstances, and Jenny had no doubt that this carriage was going at a full clip, for it was at the top of the drive in a matter of moments.

Without warning, Maddie sprang forward with a volley of excited barks, abruptly pulling the harness out of Jenny's hand.

"Maddie!" she cried with real alarm. "Maddie, come back!"

But Maddie paid her no heed, her frenzied yapping coming from the direction of the drive down which the carriage was barreling at an unabated pace. Jenny's heart froze with dread, knowing that the one thing that caused Maddie to lose her normal good sense was a strange carriage invading her territory.

She could only hope that Maddie would be clever enough to stay well out of the way, but her worst fear was realized when Maddie's barks were abruptly silenced and a sharp howl of pain split the air, followed by a series of whimpers and the sound of the carriage coming to a sudden halt. Jenny cried out in panic and started to run as fast as she could, her hands outstretched in front of her. A man's voice shouted something, but she couldn't make out the words, only that it sounded like a volley of angry swearing. And then her foot caught on something and she went hurtling through space, flying for what seemed an age, then landed abruptly on the ground, her forehead hitting with a great crack that reverberated in her ears.

The last thing she remembered was the odd and unexpected sight of stars swimming in her eyes. And then there was nothing at all.

Chapter 2

"Oh, damnation!" Stuart cried as the girl who had been barreling toward him came a cropper on the hard ground. He heard the crack from where he was kneeling, inspecting the poor dog that had been stupid enough to get too close to the carriage and had been kicked by one of his horse's hooves. And now the horses were snorting and prancing about, threatening to trample the driver, who was desperately trying to calm them.

As if it wasn't bad enough that the dog's leg was obviously broken, he'd be lucky if the idiot girl hadn't broken her neck, for she hadn't budged from her prone position.

"Damn and damn again," he cursed, gently picking up the trembling retriever in his arms. "Here, take the animal," he commanded an alarmed Newton, who had alighted from the carriage, flapping about like an agitated hen. "Gently. Support her leg like this. I'm going to see what the girl's done to herself—not an auspicious beginning to our stay, but why should I be surprised?"

He passed the dog over, thinking that Newton looked as if he'd just been handed a sack of vermin. Handling dogs was not part of what Newton considered his esteemed duties as valet, and from the expression on his face, he was probably convinced that he'd catch fleas.

Stuart took off at a swift pace despite his sore toe, loping across the lawn to where the girl lay, still motionless, her face obscured by leaves, dirt, and a mass of fair hair that had shaken loose from a chignon. He knelt and carefully rolled her onto her back, feeling for broken bones. But there was no sign of any injury other than a nasty knot on her forehead that was red and angry-looking.

"Miss?" he inquired, lightly shaking one of her shoulders. "Is anyone home?" Nothing. Not a stirring, a single murmur. He felt for a pulse, which he was relieved to find was strong and steady, then sat back on his heels and looked at her more carefully.

She couldn't be above twenty, he concluded, a pretty thing. A very pretty thing indeed, with fine bones in a heart-shaped face. But that face was too pale for his liking, and he wasn't pleased at all that she showed no signs of coming around. He lifted an eyelid to discover one beautiful eye, an extraordinary shade of pale blue, not unlike the shell of a robin's egg. Sadly, it gazed not at him, but skyward.

With a resigned sigh he dropped her eyelid and scooped her up in his arms, finding that she weighed no more than a feather. She was small and slight, her slender shape easy to make out beneath the bulk of worn cloak.

He returned to the carriage at the same swift pace. Under other circumstances he might have lingered, relishing holding such a soft, sweet, unprotesting woman, but even he had his limits, and entertaining impure thoughts about unconscious women was one of them.

"To the house," he barked to the driver, who still stood by the horses' heads, looking as if he expected to be the next person to be struck senseless.

"I didn't see the beast till too late, yer lordship," he stammered, tugging at his cap. "I tried to beat it off with my whip, but it wouldn't go."

"It wasn't your fault," Stuart said impatiently. "You can't be held responsible for mad dogs or mad English-women, for that matter, so stop your yammering and get going. The girl's going to need a doctor."

"And the dog, yer lordship?" the driver inquired earnestly, his concern softening Stuart's heart. "Is the poor dog going to recover?"

"Never mind the dog—I'll take care of it. Get going before another catastrophe befalls me! God, *why* did I ever agree to come to this cursed place?" He wondered what Sir Harry would say when he heard that his house guest had been responsible for not only injuring one of his hunting dogs but one of his serving girls as well.

Three minutes later the carriage pulled up in front of Bigslow Hall, and Stuart barely registered the fine Elizabethan stonework he normally would have admired. He gingerly climbed out of the carriage, the girl still in his arms, her head lolling against his shoulder. The door flew open before he had a chance to knock and a stout, nearly bald-headed man appeared—the butler, Stuart assumed from his sober attire.

But there was nothing sober about his expression as he took in Stuart and his burden. "Oh, glory be!" he gasped, his face turning as pale as the girl's. "Dear Lord in heaven, what have you done to her, you filthy animal? And where's Maddie?" he demanded, rubbing his hand over the one small patch of hair that graced the front of his pate, causing it to stand up straight as a porcupine's quills. "She's never without the dog!"

Stuart drew himself up and assumed his most imperious expression. "She met with an accident, chasing after her dog. And as the dog met with an accident chasing after my carriage, I suggest you cease blaming me for their stupidities and call for a doctor. The girl gave herself one mighty crack on the head, and the dog's broken a leg."

The butler drew in a sharp breath of renewed alarm, but at least he stepped back from the doorway and let Stuart through. By the time the butler had guided Stuart to the upper landing, Stuart had an entourage of babbling servants in his wake, all creating a great commotion. Stuart was not fond of commotions and he turned and gave the lot of them a quelling stare, which had the satisfying effect of making them back away for all of five seconds. He could see that Sir Harry had not exerted much time or energy on training his staff.

"In here," the butler said shortly, opening a door to a large bedroom and Stuart just managed to enter the room when one of the most extraordinary creatures he'd ever laid eyes upon pushed past him, caterwauling in his ear.

"Oh, I knew it was shaping up to be a disastrous day indeed today, and wasn't I right," she sobbed, throwing back the bedcovers and practically yanking the unconscious girl out of Stuart's arms, settling her prize down onto the mattress and patting her all over as if she were a child of two. "My pet, my poor, poor pet, what has the wicked man done to you? And Sir Harry not even at home to shoot him as he properly deserves."

She raised her head and glared at Stuart. "It's not enough that you went and upended my darling, you had to break her dear little doggie too?"

Stuart looked the woman up and down. She was shaped exactly like a large sausage. A very large, overstuffed Cumberland sausage. Her complexion was about the same color as a sausage too, all spotty brown and red. She had the largest pair of feet Stuart had ever seen on a woman, stuffed into her shoes so that her ankles overflowed at the top like twin Yorkshire puddings. Her overlarge head was topped by an enormous white mobcap, and the hair that tumbled out of it in owlish tufts was such an unnatural shade of ebony that Stuart suspected she'd been at the boot boy's shoe black.

He opened his mouth and shut it again, took a deep breath to control his temper, and finally, when he felt slightly less explosive, said, "Who in sweet *hell* are you, who is this cursed woman, and has anyone in this lunatic asylum bothered to call for a doctor?"

The Sausage straightened and peered at him with puffy red-rimmed piggy eyes. "And I suppose you think you know all about it, do you? Well let me tell you, my fine lad, that I know all about *your* kind, indeed I do, and I shouldn't go throwing insults around if I were you. My darling is the sweetest young woman to ever walk this earth and the purest too, and if you've laid one filthy finger on her I swear I'll take the meat cleaver to that black, handsome head of yours if his lordship doesn't do it first." She snorted. "Cursed, indeed. She's perfection is what she is. And maybe she's been blessed by the Good Lord on top of it, for she'll never have her head turned by philanderers like you."

Stuart had had more than enough. He leaned slightly toward the Sausage in a menacing fashion, his hands planted on his hips. "Your name," he commanded, his nose only inches away from hers.

"Ella," she said, leaning backward, her hands grasping behind her for the edge of the bed.

"Better," he said, bending another inch forward. "And the girl's name?"

"J-Jane," Ella stammered, her capacious bosom pointing skyward. "Miss Jane Bigslow. S-Sir Harry's beloved niece."

Stuart straightened abruptly in alarm. Sir Harry's niece? He didn't even know Sir Harry *had* a niece. Oh, that was just wonderful. He'd inadvertently managed to knock out his host's beloved niece and he hadn't been on the premises above two minutes when he'd done it. The thought that Sir Harry ought to dress his beloved niece in a more seemly fashion to her station and give her a more suitable chaperone than a dog fleetingly crossed his mind, but he didn't stop to dwell on it.

"And the doctor?" he asked, hoping the damage wasn't more severe than it looked, for it didn't do to go about doing grievous injury to baronets' relations, especially female relations. Young, unmarried female relations.

"He's been summoned," Ella said, straightening the giant mobcap that had slipped to one side.

"Good," Stuart said. "Then why don't you look after your mistress until he gets here, and I'll go see to her dog. Maddie is her name?"

Ella nodded, and he was surprised to see tears well up in her piggy eyes. "Is—is she going to recover?" she asked tremulously. "Maddie's a good girl, she is, and Miss Jane would be beyond crushed if she didn't. That dog is her whole life."

"Miss Jane should keep her on a tighter leash then, if she dotes on her so much," he snapped. "But I don't think a broken leg will be Maddie's undoing. Where will she have been taken?"

"The kitchen," Ella said, wringing her hands. "That man of yours was just bringing the poor thing in when I heard about my darling girl. Oh, it's a black day indeed, and didn't Miss Jane predict this very morning that you'd bring disaster in your wake." Her face crumpled up and she pulled a large square of cotton from one apron pocket and splashed it around her platter-shaped face.

Stuart shook his head, took one last look at the pure and perfect blessing called Miss Jane Bigslow, lying still and pale under the covers like one of the nauseating illustrations from *Sleeping Beauty,* and thought he really might be sick at the cloying sweetness of it all.

"Have you a good strong piece of wood I can use as a splint?" Stuart asked the woman who hovered over him as if he planned on murdering the dog he was attempting to mend.

"Aye, and I should hit you over the head with it," Cook replied tartly, pointing one bony finger at him. "Running down innocent animals and people is no way for a body to behave if you ask me."

"I didn't ask you," Stuart replied, ready to tear his hair out in frustration. "I asked you only for a piece of wood, and I'd appreciate your fetching one as quickly as possible. It needs to be about six inches by two inches. This poor dog is in pain, and I'd like to help her." He ran his hands gently over the dog's trembling body, attempting to reassure her.

"A pretty sentiment from the one who put her in pain to begin with, never mind nearly murdering her mistress. But it's not Maddie's fault that you're a reckless fool, so I suppose I can oblige you. You'll be needing some strips of linen too, I reckon."

"Yes, please," Stuart said from between gritted teeth, glowering up from his place by the kitchen fire where Maddie had been placed on a pallet.

He couldn't believe the general insolence of the household staff, not to mention their extraordinary appearances. Gargoyles, that's what they were. The cook resembled nothing more than a witch, unnaturally tall and skinny with a long, sharp nose, most disconcerting in a woman who spent her life around food and not reassuring him as to the quality she produced if she couldn't manage to keep decent flesh on her bones. The butler, on the other hand, might have been one of the Seven Dwarfs, short and squat with little bowed legs and a belly that threatened to burst the buttons of his waistcoat. And then there was the Sausage, not to mention the rest of the odd-looking servants. They looked as if they'd all been put into a giant bowl, thoroughly mixed around and pulled out again, emerging with each other's bits and pieces.

He silently accepted the stick the cook returned with and concentrated on the task at hand, speaking soothingly to Maddie as he gently set the bone and secured the splint with the linen strips. She watched him steadily with trusting eyes, hardly moving throughout the process.

She was a beautiful animal, her glossy fur the color of spun gold, and although she was small for a retriever bitch, she was a fine example of the breed and clearly intelligent, for she responded well to his voice commands. Which made him wonder why she had been silly enough to bolt after a carriage.

He glanced down at the harness he'd removed, an interesting contraption and entirely unnecessary to his way of thinking. It made him wonder if Maddie hadn't been properly trained, that the perfectly perfect Miss Jane Bigslow foolishly believed restraining a dog took the place of commanding its obedience. And Maddie herself had proved the foolhardiness of her addle-pated mistress's theory this very day.

When he finished he sat down next to Maddie's pallet and put her head on his lap, stroking it as he whispered reassurances to her. "You'll be fine, girl, just fine if you stay off that leg as much as possible for a few weeks. I'm sorry that my horse injured you, but you have to admit you were asking for trouble. A little training is what you need to keep you on the straight and narrow and out of trouble, and I'd be happy to do the job myself if I didn't anticipate being tossed out of here as soon as Sir Harry learns what's happened."

He sighed heavily, idly scratching behind one of Maddie's soft ears. "Of course, that means I'll be forced to spend bloody Christmas with Penelope and Noddy after all, and believe me, it's a fate worse than death."

Maddie gazed up at him, her clear brown eyes only half-open, which he hoped meant she'd soon be asleep. He hated to admit it even to himself, but at heart he was a terrible sentimentalist, especially when it came to animals. It had been hard enough growing up with an artistic nature, especially at Eton where the boys had bullied him interminably for drawing in his spare time. He quickly learned to disguise anything that gave away his sensitive side, excelling at sports, playing down his intelligence to the point that his father despaired he would ever receive a decent grade. It was no wonder he loved animals so much—they were far superior to the kind of ignorant people he'd been forced all his life to be around.

But by the time he'd reached adulthood he'd gone so far as to give up owning dogs, mostly because he cared far more about them than he did his friends and it showed. Still, he missed having dogs around. For one, they were largely silent, not disturbing his concentration with a lot of foolish chatter. And they were loyal. You wouldn't find a dog running off into the arms of another man. Running after a carriage, perhaps, but that wasn't the same thing as outright desertion.

His mouth drew into a tight line as the unwelcome image of beautiful Penelope drew itself in perfect, minute detail on the canvas of his mind. Penelope with her glossy hair the color of ripe walnuts and almond-shaped eyes only a shade lighter, eyes that had gazed at him with what he thought reflected love, but turned out to reflect nothing more than a heart filled with treachery. And greed.

An earl's title was apparently worth far more than that of a mere viscount's in her estimation, and since Noddy's fortune was nearly as large as his, she had nothing to lose. She used her beauty and her charm to secure that higher title when Noddy returned from the Peninsular War and tossed Stuart aside like an old shoe, caring nothing for his honor, never mind his heart.

Stuart shook his head hard, banishing the memory. He ran a gentle hand over Maddie's golden head.

No, dogs were vastly preferable to women, no question about it. And he'd never be fool enough again to forget it.

"I think you had better explain yourself, Blakeney," Sir Harry said without preamble when Stuart was eventually conducted into the library to meet his host.

"Actually, Sir Harry, my name is Middleton. I only use the family name of Blakeney on my paintings."

"Oh, is that it? Yes, I suppose it would have been a deuced inconvenience to change it when you inherited. But never mind that, what is all this about your mowing down my niece's dog and then my niece?"

Stuart was relieved to find that Sir Harry's appearance was relatively normal, for as Stuart quickly scanned his face, he decided that he looked rather like St. Nicholas without a beard. His cheeks were full and fat and ruddy, his head thick with white hair, and his belly comfortably round. And he had exactly the right spectacles with bright blue eyes that twinkled behind them, eyes that were now fixed on him in expectation.

"Perhaps you'll first tell me what the doctor said about your niece's condition," Stuart said, for despite his annoyance with the prostrate princess, he had been concerned about her injury. Not as concerned as about her dog, but concerned nonetheless.

"According to the old sawbones my niece has sustained a concussion," Sir Harry said, pouring them both a large measure of whiskey. "Nothing she won't recover from, but it still don't do to run people down in the middle of the road, especially when they don't see you coming. But I suppose you had your mind on more important matters? Art and all that, what?" He raised two bushy white eyebrows at Stuart in what Stuart could only interpret as a hopeful fashion, and he realized to his surprise that Sir Harry was trying to give him a reprieve, although for the life of him he couldn't understand why. He wasn't sure he even wanted a reprieve from the madhouse of Bigslow, although he had to admit he did want to see how Maddie's leg mended. Actually, he wanted that very much.

So instead of giving himself an easy way out of a situation he'd been dreading, Stuart launched into a truthful explanation of events. "I'm very sorry, sir," he said as he finished his account. "I had no desire to bring harm to any member of your family and certainly not a valuable dog. Should you wish me to take myself away at once, naturally I will oblige you."

"Nonsense, my boy," Sir Harry said with an expansive wave of his hand. "Jenny shouldn't have been running in the first place. A nice steady pace I always say, but does she listen? Certainly not, although I can't fault her temperament. Sweet as the day is long, and biddable too. A true comfort to me in my old age." He nodded to himself. "Yes, indeed, as good a girl as they come, and I'm grateful she wasn't injured any more severely. She's had enough bad luck, poor poppet. On top of everything else, she suffers from the headache, you know, although she never complains, even when it keeps her confined."

Stuart felt another rush of nausea creeping up on him. Penelope had wielded the supposed fragility of her health like a weapon, claiming the headache any time she wished to avoid an obligation, never mind an argument. It seemed Miss Jane Bigslow was prone to the same feminine deception.

"I'm sorry to hear it, sir," he lied, disliking Sleeping Beauty more by the minute. He might almost believe she'd pretended her swoon to gain some manipulative end if he hadn't seen the bruise on her head for himself. "If there is anything I might do to lessen her present distress, seeing as I was the cause of it . . ."

Sir Harry's expression suddenly darkened. "Distress, you say? Ha! Jenny's distress is nothing in the face of my own, for as I said, she'll recover with no trouble. But will I? That is the question." He waved his clenched fist in the air, his face growing alarmingly red. "My wife stabbed me viciously through the heart this very morning in a fit of pique. It's a miracle I'm not dead from the shock. How am I to recover from her act of treachery, I ask you?"

Stuart stared at him, wondering if Sir Harry was entirely in his right mind. "I—I beg your pardon?" he said, only vaguely registering the crystal tumbler Sir Harry thrust into his hand.

"You heard me. A black-hearted harpy, that's what Lucinda is, and I'm being charitable." He pulled out a handkerchief and blew his nose soundly. "Ah well, never mind. It's not your fault, for you weren't to know. You're here now and here you'll stay, and I don't want to hear a word to the contrary—not from any quarter, so don't you even think of making a protest, good manners or no. I won't have you run off." He rubbed his nose vigorously with his handkerchief and stuffed it back in his pocket. "So that's settled. You'll be my guest for as long as you wish, and I have every reason to believe that you can create a masterpiece during your stay here. That you try is all I ask in return." He shot Stuart a speculative look from behind his little round spectacles. "I've heard all about it, you know. They say you're capable of great things, but you're lacking in heart. Perhaps you'll find it here at Bigslow."

Stuart stared down at his glass, badly shaken. He wasn't accustomed to people speaking so bluntly to him, certainly not about his work—or lack of it. Well, what did he care? He had a sanctuary for the time being, as odd a place as that sanctuary seemed to be. He could keep to himself, see to Maddie's recovery, maybe even train her when she'd mended.

The perfectly perfect Miss Jane Bigslow could use

some training as well from what he'd observed, the first lesson being to watch where she was going.

As soon as she regained her senses, he intended that the first face she saw would be his, and it was *not* going to be a pleasant sight.

Chapter 3

Jenny groaned as she struggled to sit up the following morning. She still wasn't exactly clear as to what had happened. She had a vague memory of running after Maddie, and nothing after that until she had woken last night with a pounding headache, not helped by Ella's fussing.

The headache was still there, but it wasn't like her usual, which left her feeling sick and her head spinning dizzily. This was centered in the middle of her forehead, directly beneath the thick bandage wrapped around her skull. Her hand crept up and gingerly touched the linen. She winced at the contact, and then at her own stupidity. She knew better than to go careening off across the lawn without Maddie at the other end of her harness to guide her.

Maddie! What had happened to Maddie? She remembered now, Maddie's howl of pain, a man's voice. And then she'd fallen. She carefully reached her hand over the edge of the bed, feeling for Maddie in her usual place, but there was nothing there. No soft fur, no cold nose nuzzling into the palm of her hand. No snuffles of pleasure. No sound at all.

"Ella! Ella, come quickly!" Jenny cried, her heart racing in alarm. Dear God, where was Maddie? Horrible possibilities crossed her mind and her mouth went dry with fear, her fingers clutching on the bedcovers as she prayed for Ella to appear. "Ella!" she howled again.

Her prayer was answered as the door opened abruptly. "Oh, Ella, thank heaven," she began, then abruptly stopped. The footsteps that approached her bed were wrong—not Ella's heavy plodding, but softer, surer somehow. And completely unfamiliar.

"Who—who are you?" she asked nervously, pulling the covers up higher over her chest.

"Middleton," a man's voice answered immediately. "At your service, Miss Bigslow."

A ridiculous image of a man sweeping off a hat and bowing low flashed into Jenny's mind. For a moment she couldn't think who this Middleton could be, for she knew no one by that name, and then realization dawned. She'd heard that voice before, swearing loudly. "You're the person who hit my dog!" she choked. "Where is she? What have you done to her?"

"She is in the kitchen, by the fire," he replied, and she heard the scrape of a chair as he pulled it close to the bed and had the nerve to sit down uninvited. "Her leg is broken, I'm sorry to say, but the fracture was clean and she'll mend in good time. In the meantime, she's resting comfortably."

Jenny let out a long shaking breath, torn between relief that Maddie was alive and not *too* terribly injured, and outrage that this—this monster could sit there and blithely inform her of her dog's injury as if he were discussing the weather. As if he had no responsibility for Maddie's distress. Or for hers, for that matter.

"You wretch!" she cried, outrage taking over. "How dare you invade my bedchamber, sit yourself down as if you belong here, and offer no apology for running my dog over? Or for causing me grievous bodily injury on top of it?" She pointed an accusing finger toward where she imagined the chair was. "You're just like all the others, immoral and selfish, thinking of no one but yourself, taking what you can get with no care to anyone's welfare but your own. My poor aunt has lost her home because of you, but I'm sure *that* causes you no stirring of conscience. You play at being an artist when you haven't the slightest idea what that means, the discipline and hard work that have to be earned in order to call yourself by that name."

"My dear girl—"

"I'm not your dear anything!" Jenny said, all of her anger and frustration flooding out as if a dam inside of her had been unstopped. She'd kept her peace for all these years as the artists had come and gone, taking whatever they could, using Bigslow like some giant playground, and this horrible man was the last straw. "And don't you try to mollify me. It's your fault that Maddie is crippled! I heard the speed at which you were driving. It's a miracle that nothing worse happened to her, that she's not in pieces all over the road, no thanks to you."

Stuart stared at her, wondering if everyone in Sir Harry's eccentric household, Sir Harry included, had lost what little wits they had. Sweetness and light? Pure perfection? Sleeping Beauty had woken, and she was the most ghastly harridan he'd ever had the misfortune to meet. Her hair, the exact shade of corn silk, fell in wild disarray over her shoulders and arms as if it had never known a brush. Her sky blue eyes snapped like a madwoman's, and her rosebud mouth spat nothing but thorns. A charming creature indeed. He doubted she'd seen herself in a mirror this morning, for if she had, she'd be buried under the bedclothes in mortification.

But then, she appeared to be too shortsighted to see much at all, for even in the midst of her temper tantrum she didn't focus on him, but at a spot somewhere over his right shoulder. Stuart sighed and rubbed one cheek. It was just his luck to be cooped up in the same house with a woman who was not only of unfortunate temperament, but who was too vain even to wear eyeglasses. Which explained why she'd taken such a tumble the day before. Stupid girl.

"Have you nothing to say for yourself?" she demanded, thumping a small fist on the bed.

"Indeed I have, most of which I am certain you'd rather not hear," he retorted. "I am sorry about your dog, but if you'd trained her better, she wouldn't be in the predicament she's in now. I'm sorry about your aunt, although I have no idea of what you mean. I assure you I had nothing to do with her or her home— or her absence from it, and I rather resent your implication that I had." He fixed her with a level gaze. "And

I'm sorry that you fell down and bumped your head, but it's your own fault that you weren't looking where you were going, and I don't see how you can possibly hold me to blame."

Miss Jane Bigslow's rosebud mouth slowly opened and then closed again. Her face crumpled up as if she were about to sneeze and he waited for the inevitable torrent of weeping as her hands crept to her face and covered it. But instead, and to his considerable astonishment, instead of tears came a peal of laughter, and then another until she was laughing so hard that he feared she might actually be insane.

Finally she calmed and looked up, wiping the tears from her porcelain cheeks. "You really are a jackass, aren't you?" she said, addressing that point over his right shoulder. "I must say, for a supposed artist you're singularly unobservant. My dear Lord Middleton, I'm unable to look where I'm going. I'm blind."

"B—blind?" Stuart stammered, shaken out of his usual self-control. "I'm so sorry, I had no idea! No one said a word, only that you'd concussed yourself . . ." He trailed off, feeling awkward and off-balance. And guilty as sin, as an appalling thought occurred to him. "Oh, dear Lord—not from your fall?"

"Not from my fall," she retorted, looking annoyingly self-satisfied. "I was blinded in an accident when I was six. But that's beside the point. The point is that thanks to you I've lost the only eyes I have."

Stuart frowned, trying to puzzle this peculiar statement out, wondering if her wits hadn't been scrambled in the same accident. "I beg your pardon. I don't understand."

"Naturally you don't. I don't believe you understand very much at all, but that comes as no surprise. I'll try to explain it to you as simply as possible," she said as if she were speaking to a dimwitted child. "My eyes are lying downstairs by the kitchen fire."

"Your—your eyes?" he said, feeling a stirring of genuine pity for the poor, addled creature.

"Yes. With a broken leg. It's unlikely that they'll be any use to me for a good six weeks, which leaves me at a great disadvantage."

The light finally dawned. The strange harness—of course! He'd heard of dogs being used for such a purpose, to guide people who lacked sight. Naturally it hadn't occurred to him that Maddie might be a guide dog—why should it have? No one had thought to mention that her mistress was blind, a rather salient point to his way of thinking. "I see . . ." he said slowly. "I mean—I mean I understand," he added, cursing himself for his lack of tact.

To his irritation, she grinned. "You needn't tiptoe around me, my lord. I may be blind, but I'm not particularly thin-skinned. You don't have to use euphemisms."

"No, no of course not," he said, feeling like a fool. "I'm sorry. I'm not—that is I'm not accustomed to being in the company of blind people. Oh, damnation," he said, thoroughly frustrated. "Look here, Miss Bigslow; if you think to put me at a disadvantage, you already have. There's no need to take any further vengeance. I feel an idiot as it is."

"Good," she said. "It's a beginning as far as apologies go. You weren't to know I couldn't see when you came barreling up the drive, but you might have been looking a little harder in the direction of my dog."

"She practically ran under my horses' hooves!" he replied, stung.

"Lord Middleton?" she said, her tone gently reproving.

"Oh, very well." She was right, of course. He ought to have instructed his coachman to go at a slower pace once they left the main road. "But you must admit, you should have trained Maddie better. She was lucky she didn't have her neck broken with the way she was yapping and leaping about."

"It is her drive, is it not? She has every right to protect it from intruders."

There wasn't much of an answer to that rejoinder. "I suppose that is true to a certain extent. But the dog does seem to be lacking in common sense if she tries to suicide herself every time a strange carriage comes down her drive."

"It seems to me that you are attempting to shift all the blame onto Maddie and away from yourself. You emerged unscathed from the encounter. She did not. As a result, neither Maddie nor I can go anywhere at all for some weeks."

Stuart released a deep sigh, seeing he wasn't going to win this battle. Miss Jane Bigslow's eyes might be sightless, but her wits were apparently in fine condition.

"You are correct. In which case, what might I do to make up for the inconvenience I have caused you? I can't mend your dog's leg any more than I have, but . . ." He stopped as an absurd idea occurred to him.

"Yes, Lord Middleton?" she said, resting her chin on her fist, her face filled with curiosity.

"Well, I—that is . . ." He forced himself to continue. "I suppose *I* could act as your eyes. If you will permit, of course." He hoped against hope that she wouldn't permit, that she'd offer all sorts of protestations that such an arrangement would be unseemly. Which indeed it would be.

Much to his surprise, her face lit up. "You will? I mean you would? You would only have to take me walking every day, for that is my greatest pleasure." She pulled her bottom lip between her teeth and chewed on it for a moment. "Replacing Maddie in her duties does seem an apt penance, but you would have to promise to behave with complete propriety," she continued, blushing slightly. "I am not unaware of the unfortunate proclivities to which you artists are inclined, and I must insist that you do not entertain any such thoughts while in my company."

"Believe me, such a thought would never cross my mind," Stuart snapped, instantly regretting his impulsive suggestion. He couldn't think what had come over him to suggest it in the first place. The idea of being forced into this overbearing shrew's company for an hour or two every day was singularly unappealing.

But then he supposed that was what penances were for.

So it was that three days later Stuart found himself escorting Miss Jane Bigslow out of the house, her small hand firmly tucked in the crook of his elbow. The day was bright but chilly, the wind from the north, and he hoped that she might find it too cold to walk for long. He had no intention of spending more than the minimal necessary time in her company.

"There are four steps in front of you," he said, ignoring Partridge's heavy scowl as the butler shut the door behind them.

"Yes, I know," his charge said. "I've lived here since I was six. You need only warn me about things I might not be aware of, things I might walk into or trip over."

"I beg your pardon," Stuart said tightly, feeling as if he'd just been told off by a snip of a miss. "I've never been anyone's guide dog before."

Jane turned her face up toward his. "Are you always so ill-tempered?" she asked.

"I would hardly describe myself as ill-tempered," he retorted, absently noting that the sapphire blue of her cloak complimented her eyes nicely, although the wool was two or three shades darker. "How is your headache?" he said, strongly desiring to change the subject, for she had a point. He had been in a bad mood for two years now, not that she needed to know that. Or why.

"Completely vanished, but thank you for asking. Ella tells me the only remaining sign of my fall is a fading bruise on my forehead. I can hardly complain about that."

He was happy to hear it, for Penelope would have complained endlessly about her spoiled looks. But he supposed what Miss Jane Bigslow couldn't see would hardly give her cause for hysterics. And it was just a small bruise, more of a faint purple smudge directly below her hairline.

"Maddie is in good spirits, don't you think?" he said conversationally. He'd actually been rather touched to see the bond between the dog and her mistress when he'd taken Jane into the kitchen before their walk. Maddie's tail had thumped furiously when Jane had kneeled down and enveloped her in a warm embrace. And he'd been fascinated to see how sensitively but thoroughly she had explored every inch of the dog's body, her fingers feeling carefully over the bandaged splint as if they could pull a complete visual image from touch alone.

"She seems content enough, but I imagine she knows that there's nothing she can do but be patient while she heals. You do believe she will make a full recovery? That is to say, she won't be left with a limp?"

He looked down at Jane's anxious face and felt an unwelcome twinge of guilt. "I believe she will heal soundly, yes. I've had some experience in these matters, and Maddie was fortunate that the break was so clean and low in the foreleg. She's still young, and that will help."

"Yes," Jane said, her brow furrowing. "Yes, I suppose so. I can't help but wish that it was my leg that

was broken. It's so hard on a dog to be confined—
maybe by Christmas she'll be able to get around a bit."

Stuart shot her a quick glance. He had to appreciate
Jane's concern for her pet, an admirable quality, even if
it was the only one she had. "Please don't worry yourself overmuch," he said, leading her around a bench
that sat under a mulberry tree. "Maddie will be back at
your side before you know it." And that couldn't be
soon enough for him.

They walked in silence for a time, Stuart's thoughts
glumly wandering back to the studio Sir Harry had
ensconced him in. It was an airy room, the light southern but still strong. Not that the light made any difference. He'd set up his easel and laid out his paints, but
the surface of the canvas was as white and pristine as
when he'd taken it out of the trunk.

He had no clue what to paint. And he was no further along in making a decision than he had been when
he'd arrived.

"How do you like our Yorkshire countryside, Lord
Middleton?" Jane said, interrupting his black thoughts.

"It's very attractive," he replied politely. "Tell me,
what is the name of the river that runs through the
property?"

"The river Swale," she said. "Our rivers are re-
nowned for their fishing, but perhaps you know that."

"Yes, I'd heard," he said, casting his gaze over a
flock of sheep that grazed on a hillside. Boring. It was
all so boring. Yorkshire, Hampshire, Hartfordshire,
what difference? Hill and dale, river, trees, hedgerows,

all the same. Maybe he should take himself off to the Mediterranean for a change of scenery.

"Lord Middleton?" Jane asked hesitantly. "I was wondering if you might tell me . . ." She trailed off.

"Yes, Miss Bigslow? You were wondering if I might tell you what?" He waited for the pestering questions to begin. They always did. Where was his country seat, how large was his estate, how many horses did he keep, how many months of the year did he live there. Boring.

"I was wondering if perhaps you might describe it to me. The countryside I mean."

Stuart's gaze snapped to her face. "You want me to describe the countryside to you?" he repeated blankly. "Why?"

"Because—because I can smell it, and I can feel it around me and under my feet, but I can't see it," she said, raising her face to the wind. "And you can, and you're an artist, so I thought it might be easy for you to describe."

Stuart thought this over. It really wasn't much of a request and it would give him something to say, he supposed. "Very well. Before you is a sweep of meadow and below it the river. Most of the trees have lost their leaves, so there's not much to be seen in the way of color." He looked around, then up. "The sky is clear today with a few clouds drifting across it. And there are sheep grazing on the hill to your left."

Jane was silent for a moment. And then she nodded. "You might call yourself an artist, but I wonder if I don't see more with my imagination than you see with your eyes."

Stuart stared at her. The gall of the girl! He couldn't believe that a blind woman was telling him—Stuart Blakeney, Viscount of Middleton, an artist who had been called brimming with talent—that he couldn't bloody well see. "Are you criticizing my descriptive abilities, or are you merely going out of your way to annoy me?"

She laughed and he glared at her. He had half a mind to leave her where she was standing. If Miss Jane Bigslow was so scornful of his company, she could make her own way back to the house.

"Neither," she said, still looking amused. "I'm sure if you put your mind to the task you could describe the scenery perfectly well. But the way you're going about it, you could be reciting any landscape, anywhere." She pointed at the sky. "What about birds, my lord? They come in varied colors and shapes, as do clouds. And grass has many different hues of green as trees have many different shades of bark, even when they don't bear leaves. How do the branches look against the sky? Are they black, or brown, or perhaps even a mossy green?"

"What difference would it make to you?" he retorted. "How can I possibly describe colors to one who has no idea what I mean?"

"Oh, but you're mistaken. I do remember colors, all of them, I think, or nearly all. I dream about colors every night and in the day I try to take the memories with me." She smiled wistfully. "It's not unlike music, you know. Can't you remember the melody of a piece of music in your head, hear the notes perfectly clearly? But remembering the melody isn't the same as hearing it played, and it's the same with sight.''

Stuart swallowed hard. Her words had shaken him, for he'd never before considered what blindness really meant. He opened his eyes in the morning and there was light—very often too much of it. And from that moment until he closed them at night, his eyes fed him information about his environment. He didn't think about his sight any more than he thought about his hearing. Both performed the tasks they were designed for without any trouble.

He tried to imagine what it would be like to live in a dark world, to be able to see the vibrancy of color and shape, light and shadow only in memory, never to be able to appreciate the simple beauty of nature unless someone verbally described it . . .

He slowly looked around him, seeing the country-side as if for the first time, looking, really *looking* at all the things he'd always taken for granted. Yes, there were birds. All sorts of birds. A flock of sparrows on the wing, and there a hawk, circling overhead. And in the distance the red flash of a grouse taking low flight over the moor.

And the clouds. They weren't just clouds, but fat white pillows of softness slowly skimming across the cerulean blue of sky, with a fine streaking of cloud cover higher above, these steadier, not pushed so speedily along by the wind.

She was right about the trees, too. Their stark

branches shaped themselves in various forms, some heavy and uniform, black as ebony, some delicately fanning out weblike, green as sea algae, each splendid, unique. What had he been looking at these last two years, or the last twenty-six for that matter? He wasn't sure he knew. Or had ever known.

Stuart cleared his throat and began to speak, the words coming out at first hesitantly, and then pouring faster and more surely as he translated sight into pictures full of life and color, as if he were drawing a brush across a canvas and painting everything he saw in glorious, minute detail.

For the first time in his life, Stuart began to realize what vision really meant.

Chapter 4

J enny listened with only scant attention to her uncle and Lord Middleton's conversation that night at dinner, even though it was her first meal in their company. Her ears still rang with the word-pictures that her companion had painted that afternoon, pictures that shone with utter clarity in her mind's eye.

For the very first time since arriving at Bigslow all those years ago she had a true idea of the magnificence of her environment, which before she'd only been able to imagine. Oh, people had described the rolling hills and dales of Yorkshire to her before, but never with such exquisite detail so that she could picture every blade of grass, see the backlit sun shining on a hawk's delicate but powerfully outstretched wing, practically feel the soft ivory wool of a sheep's coat beneath her fingertips.

There had been something sharp and alive in his voice, an excitement, as if he too was discovering the splendor that surrounded him. His words had poured forth like poetry as he spun images in thin air, and she'd wanted to cry with their simple beauty.

She still didn't know what had possessed her to accept his offer to take Maddie's place on her walks, other than sheer pique and a desire to inconvenience him.

She didn't even like him, not one little bit—he was cold and curt and unfeeling. And yet . . . and yet he had surprised her by describing the landscape to her with great sensitivity. And he had been sensitive to Maddie too, she did have to admit that, speaking to the dog with obvious tenderness and caring.

Jenny frowned, trying to fit the odd pieces of the puzzle that was Lord Middleton together. He had been quiet as they'd walked home, but it had been a different quiet than the stony silence to which he'd treated her on their way out to the viewpoint. This had been more of a stillness, as if he'd gone to a private place only he could enter, a place where nothing but his art existed.

She understood that place well, retreating there often enough herself when she went to her music room, lost to everything but the sweet sounds of the pianoforte, mingled with her own voice, sounds that filled her head as uncounted hours drifted by.

Could it be that he really was an artist in the true sense of the word? All the others that her uncle had brought to Bigslow had been nothing more than dilettantes in her opinion, playing at their painting as they played at life, full of silly, boring conversation and grandiose airs.

She couldn't accuse Lord Middleton of boring conversation, for he was now discussing Rubens' works with a keen intelligence.

"For example, look at his use of glowing light and form in *Ganymede*," he was saying as she turned her attention back to the conversation. "The eagle is a masterpiece, so vital and alive that one can almost feel oneself carried up upon its wing. There is such a warmth of nature expressed, such pagan energy. I can only deeply admire his mastery in his handling of the oils."

No, no grandiose airs there, no pompous criticism that implied he could do it better.

Jenny had to admire him for that, if for nothing else.

"Jenny, my dear, you are unusually silent tonight," her uncle said, interrupting her thoughts. "You are not feeling unwell again?" he asked anxiously.

"No, Uncle, I am in very good health," she replied truthfully. "I was merely enjoying my meal and your conversation. My walk with Lord Middleton gave me a prodigious appetite."

"Ah, that is good to hear, and it is kind of Lord Middleton to offer to escort you. I feel you are entirely safe in his company, a great relief to my mind as you no longer have the companionship of your aunt. A terrible

shame that, but what can I do in the face of her attitude?" He cleared his throat loudly. "Well, what's
done is done, and nothing I can say will change matters. Just take note, Jenny, for it don't do to go flying in
the face of a husband's wishes."

"Yes, Uncle," Jenny said dutifully, although she
didn't anticipate ever having a husband's wishes to fly
in the face of. As her aunt had often said, what man in
his right mind would want to marry a blind woman? In
any case, she never met eligible bachelors, for her aunt
didn't think her fit to go out in society.

Her aunt was probably right. Jenny knew she completely lacked social graces and couldn't do the simplest
things required of a woman out in society, like dancing, for instance. She could just imagine trying to perform the complicated steps of a quadrille and knocking
everyone flat. Oh, she'd be a wild success, she thought
with a wry smile.

In any case, she'd long ago resigned herself to living
out a solitary life at Bigslow. It really wasn't so bad, she
told herself firmly, stifling the longing for adventure
that ate at her: she had her walks to enjoy, and her
music, and her uncle would often read aloud to her in
the evening. And she had her dreams.

They would have to be enough.

Stuart tried to keep his attention on Sir Harry's endless questions, but he couldn't keep his gaze from drifting over to Jane. Jenny, her uncle called her fondly, and
it was a name much more suited to her, he decided,
wondering why she wore such a wistful expression.

He hadn't realized until that afternoon how paintable she was. There had been something about the entranced way she looked as he tried to draw a picture for her, her face turned toward the horizon, her clear blue eyes focused on something beyond.

She hadn't interrupted him once, and he knew that she was truly listening as few people ever listened, that she drank in every word as if it were nectar poured down a parched throat. That alone had spurred him on. And as he talked he'd been struck by a brilliant inspiration—why not paint exactly what he was describing? And why not paint *her* with her pale, ethereal beauty, just as she looked in that moment? A woman gazing rapturously out on all that winter splendor. A woman who couldn't see a damned thing except in her mind.

It was a brilliant idea, a complete twist, and he knew just where he wanted to begin. He hadn't been so excited in years. There was only one small obstacle, and that was the ornery Miss Jane Bigslow herself. How was he ever going to convince her to model for him? He hadn't exactly made a good impression on her, but that hadn't mattered in the least until he'd decided that he needed her for his landscape. His nice, bleak mid-winter landscape.

Stuart gazed down at his pudding of blancmange, its snowy surface perfectly smooth, just like a snowdrift. Yes. Snow would be good. He'd pray for a decent snowfall before Christmas, unlikely as it was, but in the meantime he'd lay down his base. Anyway, he had as good an imagination as anyone. He could already see the sunlight shimmering on the snow, icicles hanging like crystals from the bare branches of the trees.

And Jenny with her cloak pulled fast around her, one hand peeking from beneath the sapphire folds, her corn-silk hair tumbling down her back, her face in semiprofile as she stared sightlessly out from the canvas. He'd have her other hand resting on Maddie's golden head. Yes, that was a good idea, to include the dog.

He could hardly wait to start sketching her. All he had to do was employ a little friendly persuasion. It was a pity that it was impossible to sway her with his good looks, but that couldn't be helped. He'd just have to drag some charm out from somewhere.

He sighed, thinking that at least he wouldn't have to argue with the dog.

"You want to do *what*?" Jenny said, her mouth falling open in shock as Lord Middleton finished his startling proposition.

"I said I want to paint you," he replied levelly. "Right here as you look on this bluff, but adding your dog at your side. A winter scene."

Jenny couldn't believe her ears. Who would want to paint her? And why Lord Middleton of all people in the world, who clearly disliked her as much as she did him? He'd be forced to spend hours and hours in her company. And she in his.

"But—but why?" she stammered, desperately trying to gather her wits. "I don't understand . . ."

"Because you'd be the perfect subject," he answered in his deep, velvety voice. "And you're here, which is always useful. It's also another way I can make up Maddie's accident to you. You'll be so busy that you won't have time to miss her."

Jenny bristled. "I'll miss her regardless," she said, glaring toward him. He really did have an extraordinary nerve, thinking he could replace Maddie's company with his own.

"Well then, why don't I carry her upstairs to the studio and she can sit with you while you sit for me," he said smoothly. "I'm sure she'd enjoy that and you would too."

"Oh," Jenny said, unable to deny the truth of that argument. "But why would I be the perfect subject? I'm not exactly a beauty."

There was a long silence. And then very quietly he said, "You think not? Do you have any idea of what you look like?"

"Yes, of course I have!" she replied, thinking that he really must believe her to be stupid as well as blind. "My aunt's told me any number of times. My complexion is pale and bland, and my eyes are the color of the sky on a cold English day. My nose is too long and my hair is too straight and the color of a hayseed. In short, I am ordinary, my lord, and not about to set the world on fire with my looks."

Lord Middleton burst into laughter. "Is that what your aunt told you? She sounds a most disagreeable woman and sorely lacking in observation."

"She is not disagreeable in the least," Jenny said, lying through her teeth out of loyalty to her aunt. "She may be of strong opinion and temper, and she does

have firm ideas about what is socially acceptable and
what is not, but she is certainly not unobservant and it
is most rude of you to say she is when you have never
made her acquaintance."

"I'm beginning to be grateful," he said with a
chuckle. "Tell me, Miss Bigslow, why did your aunt
leave her home? I gather it was in a fit of pique over
something, and from what you and your uncle have
implied, I can only guess that the something that sent
her packing was my imminent arrival."

"I—yes, that's true," Jenny said reluctantly, for the
truth was bound to offend him. "She has lived with a
constant stream of artists coming and going for years,
and her nerves couldn't take any more. When my uncle refused to withdraw his invitation to you, she said
he'd made his choice between you and her and removed herself to the Dower House."

"I see," he said, not sounding at all offended. "I'll
add unreasonable to my assessment."

"You wouldn't say that if you knew what she's had
to put up with," Jenny said darkly. "I don't blame her
for not wanting to see her house burned down around
her ears or the wine cellar drunk dry yet again. Uncle
Harry would rather spend his money supporting untalented artists than on buying his wife a new wardrobe or
sending her to London for the season. It's no wonder
she feels unappreciated."

"I see," he said again. "And you include me in that
list of untalented artists, do you?"

Jenny shrugged uncomfortably. "I would hardly
know. Do you consider yourself talented?"

"Yes, as a matter of fact I do. But why don't you let me prove it to you? Allow me to paint you, to show the world what real beauty is."

Jenny shook her head with a wry smile. "And now you try to flatter me to have your way, is that it?"

"I do not," he said, sounding injured. "I speak the truth. I have been looking for inspiration for a long time, and now that I've found it I don't want to have it snatched from my grasp just because you decide to stand on your pride, or stubbornness, or whatever."

"I am neither proud nor stubborn, my lord. It is true that I have a mind of my own and I can make it up for myself. You needn't resort to false praise to make my mind up for me."

He touched her shoulder lightly. "I swear to you, I have not praised you falsely, Jenny; you are in truth a most becoming woman and it's a pity you can't see that for yourself. But I can be your eyes in this as well. I can describe you as well as I can describe a landscape and paint both even better, if you'll but let me. Will you?"

"Oh, very well," she said, thoroughly tired of the whole conversation. And then she heard what she had said and almost took it back. But the idea intrigued her. Maybe he really would describe to her everything he was painting, and that would be interesting, more interesting than spending her time alone. It might even be an adventure. "But don't call me Jenny," she added for good measure.

"I most certainly will," he said baldly, dropping his hand from her shoulder as if now that he had her capitulation he didn't need to be pleasant or sensitive for another minute. "I only address models by their Christian names, for anything else would create an intolerable formality between subject and artist. For the same reason you will call me Stuart, and I don't want to hear another word on the subject. From now until the time we are finished you will do exactly as I say, within reason, naturally."

Jenny smiled. "We'll see about that," she said, beginning to relish the challenge of bringing the overbearing, oversighted Lord Middleton to his pompous knees.

For two weeks they fought like cats and dogs. Stuart, as Jenny had learned to call him after being corrected every time she addressed him by his title, insisted on impossibly long hours.

She sat. And she sat. And she sat some more. Outside of arguing with her, Stuart wasn't interested in conversation, working in silence at a fever-pitch. At least she was able to sit inside in the warmth of the studio, although given his complete lack of regard for her comfort she was surprised that he hadn't insisted on forcing her to sit on the bluff in the freezing cold and blowing wind.

For entertainment she listened to the sound of his brush moving swiftly across the canvas, the rattle of what she assumed were his paint tins as he dipped into them, the soft swearing that hissed from between his teeth when he didn't like the way his work was going.

As he'd promised, he carried Maddie upstairs every day, and she slept peacefully by Jenny's side, oblivious to the sparring matches that occurred when Jenny objected to being forced to sit in one position for hours on end.

"Would you rather stand?" he curtly asked on one occasion when she complained about her stiffness. "I'd be happy if you would, for that's the position in which I'll be painting you. *I* thought I was being particularly kind, allowing you to sit comfortably. And stop twitching, if you please. Anyone would think you had fleas . . ."

And so on and so forth every single day, until Jenny wanted to throw something heavy at him that would knock some reason into his hard head.

Until one day at the beginning of the third week, when everything changed.

Jenny by now had memorized every step of the way to Stuart's studio and could get herself there without Ella's help, a distinct advantage since she no longer had to listen to Ella's daily litany about the Imminent Danger of Ruin Jenny was placing herself in.

Fifty paces down the hallway from her bedroom to the door that led to the west wing. A left turn and another thirty-five paces, then down the stairs, sharp right, and ten steps to the studio door, being careful to avoid the table and chair along the right side of the wall. Her nose guided her as well as her hands and feet, for she could smell the oil paints as soon as she reached the top of the stairs, a pleasantly rich scent.

The grandfather clock chimed the hour of ten, telling her she was exactly on time, and she knocked, then opened the door.

"Good morning," she said, her hand firmly on the doorknob. There was no answer, which meant Stuart was late. She sighed, for if she was ever late there was the devil to pay, but not the other way around. Stuart behaved as if he were the King of England and she his lowliest subject.

It was only ten steps in a straight line from the door to her chair, so she started on her way, one hand stretched out in front of her for good measure. But it was her shins that unexpectedly met with an obstacle and she tripped and fell over it, bringing what felt like a low table on top of her.

"Oh!" she cried, more out of surprise than pain, although her shins smarted and her palms felt bruised from taking the brunt of her weight. "Oh, damnation!" she added furiously, a particularly satisfying epithet she'd learned from Stuart. She pushed the table away, then sat up and rubbed her shins vigorously.

"Jenny? Good God, what happened? Did you hurt yourself?" Stuart arrived at her side almost immediately, and he gently helped her to her feet, brushing off her dress with quick, efficient strokes.

"You moved a table, didn't you?" she said accusingly, pushing his hands away, rattled by the feel of them on her body. She hadn't realized how large and strong his hands were, how different they felt from Ella's.

"So I did. I thought you might like to have it by your side so that you could put things on it. It never occurred to me that you'd trip over it—you're not usually clumsy."

"It has nothing to do with clumsiness," she said, beginning to be extremely annoyed, now that she was over her shock. "You seem to forget that I have no way of knowing when you've moved something unless you tell me!"

"Yes, of course," he said, leading her to her chair. "I—I'm terribly sorry. I didn't think about that. *Are* you hurt?"

He did sound genuinely contrite, she decided, which took the edge off her irritation. "No, I only barked my shins. But please, in future will you keep things just as they are? I have to live in an extremely orderly world if I'm to stay in one piece."

"Of course you do. My mistake. Will you forgive me?" he asked, lightly squeezing her fingers.

She quickly pulled her hand out of his, flustered by the warmth of his touch, but she couldn't help smiling. She rather liked the humble side of Stuart. "I forgive you, but only on one condition," she said, not above exploiting her momentary advantage.

"What is that?" he said, walking over to the easel, and she heard the familiar whoosh of cloth as he uncovered the canvas.

"Will you talk to me?" she replied, waiting for the inevitable explosion. But it didn't come.

"Talk to you? Do you want me to talk to you about anything in particular?" he said, sounding amused.

"You might start by telling me about the painting, how it's coming. Are you pleased?" To her surprise she felt anxious about his reply, but then she did have a vested interest in his progress.

"In truth I am," he said after a moment. "I'm a long way from being finished, but what I have is not bad. I don't know, though. There's something missing, and I can't put my finger on it."

"Why don't you tell me about what is there? Maybe I can help you decide what it needs."

Stuart wanted to laugh. He didn't know how she thought she could help when she couldn't see the damned thing, but he didn't imagine that it would hurt to talk it through. In any case, he owed her something after causing her to fall, and if she wanted a little conversation, he supposed he could provide it.

"Well, first there's the background, which I've already told you about—the river winding through the valley, the sheep on the hill, all the rest. A hard frost covers the ground and the trees are laced in ice. And a mist hangs over the left side of the valley in the distance." He paused, tapping his brush against the corner of his mouth. "If it ever snows, I'll probably paint some in, but I need to see the reflections first. In any case, I haven't come that far yet. I've been concentrating on you. You're standing in the foreground in your sapphire cloak, Maddie next to you—by the way, I didn't bring her up since it's the first warm day in a fortnight, so I put her outside on her pallet in a patch of sun. I didn't think you'd mind."

"That was kind of you—she'll enjoy a sunbath," Jenny said softly. "Tell me more about the painting."

He turned his attention back to the canvas, frowning. He'd done a beautiful rendering of Maddie, her fine golden coat fading to a near white on her chest and legs, and her brown eyes shone with bright intelligence. He could practically feel the texture of her fur beneath his fingers as he looked. Indeed, he was pleased with Maddie. Jenny was another question.

She looked exactly like her beautiful self, but there was something lacking in her face and he couldn't for the life of him work out what it was. "I don't think I've captured you yet," he said, scratching the back of his neck.

"I'm not surprised when you hardly know me," she replied, a smile hovering on the corners of her rosebud mouth. "It must be hard to paint someone properly when you haven't the first idea of how they think or feel."

Stuart's head snapped up. The idea had never occurred to him that one had to actually *know* a person to paint her. His art was driven by technique, not by establishing a personal relationship with his model, for God's sake. Anyway, he had no interest in developing a relationship, having finished with those for all time. "Don't be ridiculous," he said curtly.

"I don't see why I'm being ridiculous. They say the eyes are the windows of the soul. Oughtn't you know something about a person's soul if you're going to reflect it in the eyes?" She paused suddenly, biting her lip, a little frown drawn on her brow. "Unless, of course, my eyes don't reflect anything at all . . ." She trailed off uncertainly.

Stuart stared at her. Of course! That was it—the

eyes. The eyes were wrong, lifeless. And Jenny wasn't the least bit lifeless. Her eyes sparked when she was angry, they shone merrily when she was amused. And when she was lost in thought they became distant, unfocused. But he had captured none of those things. He'd been concentrating on making her *look* blind, idiot that he was, instead of giving her an inner vision . . .

A surge of excitement started in his belly and flashed up to his brain. *The soul . . . the eyes are the windows of the soul. You have to paint the soul . . . you have to paint the soul.* The words hammered in his brain over and over again until they almost jumped out of his mouth.

But how was he going to paint her soul when he didn't have the first clue what her soul was about? Maybe if he started at the beginning he might be able to work it out.

What was it like to be blind? What was it like to live in a world where one had to rely on all of one's other senses? He'd watched her over the course of three weeks, the way she walked so deliberately when she was on her own, hand outstretched. He'd seen how she felt for her utensils at dinner, her glass always in the same location, the footman telling her what was on her plate and in what position. And yet he'd never thought beyond the darkness of her world, had never considered the other aspects of her life.

She had a maid to dress and undress her, naturally, but what about the rest of her needs? How heavily did she have to rely on others for the simplest things? How terrible to be so thoroughly dependent, he thought with an inward shudder, wondering how he'd cope with blindness, knowing he'd chafe not only at the loss of precious vision, but also at being so helpless.

She couldn't pick up a book and read to entertain herself, or work at a piece of embroidery, or paint watercolors, or do any of the things that other women her age did without thinking. He knew she didn't go out except to attend church on Sundays, not exactly a thriving social life. And to his knowledge, no one came to visit.

And then there was her aunt: from everything Stuart had managed to divine, she was a selfish old biddy who for some reason had made Jenny feel as if she were no more than ordinary. Such beauty, such silent strength in her adversity, and Jenny thought herself ordinary.

He shook his head with disgust. He'd like to get his hands on her aunt and set her straight. Maybe she was jealous of Jenny's youth and exceptional looks, he decided. Or maybe she was just a silly old cow who couldn't see what was under her nose—more likely, considering the way she'd left a husband who adored her, half-breaking his heart in the process.

Stuart had come to enjoy Sir Harry, finding him most agreeable and undemanding company, and sensible to boot. Look at how he hadn't stood on any absurd old-fashioned notions of propriety when Stuart had asked his permission to paint his niece, instead beaming happily at the prospect. At least Jenny had her uncle who loved her, if no one else—with the exception of the motley crew of household staff, he amended, but they didn't really count.

"Stuart . . . you've lapsed into silence. Have I lost you to your work already?" Jenny said, breaking into his racing thoughts. "Or are you just begging the question?"

"What question?" he replied with distraction.

"About my eyes. Are they cloudy?" she asked tentatively, and for the first time he noticed that her hands were clenched in her lap.

"Cloudy? You mean as if you had cataracts? Good God, no, they're anything but!" he said, astonished that she'd think such a thing. "They're azure blue, as clear as the sky. But why wouldn't they be?" He stopped abruptly as another question occurred to him and he realized how very little he did know about her. "How did you lose your sight, Jenny? You said it was in an accident when you were six, but what exactly happened?"

"I—that is, my parents and I were in a carriage going to Bath for a holiday," she said, her brow puckering in what he could only interpret as misery. "One of the wheels became dislodged and the carriage went over an embankment. I don't remember much, but when I regained consciousness I learned that my parents had been killed. I was lucky—I only struck my head and broke an arm. My arm healed, but I never saw again." She passed a hand over her temple as if that was where the blow had been struck. "The doctors said my optic nerve had been damaged beyond repair and there was nothing to be done."

"How awful for you," he said quietly, trying to imagine what a nightmare she'd woken to. If it had been him, he probably would have torn the hospital to pieces. "And so you were sent here to Bigslow?"

She nodded. "Yes. Uncle Harry is my only close relative. He and Aunt Lucinda were kind enough to take me in, although it must have been especially difficult for them, given my blindness. I owe them a great deal that I'll never be able to repay."

"I know for a fact that your uncle considers you a blessing. He loves you very much, Jenny, and certainly has no regrets about adopting you."

"Yes, I know," she said, and he swore he caught the glimmer of tears in her eyes before she quickly lowered them.

"If you know that, then why do you feel guilty about living here?" he persisted, wanting to get at the whole truth. "You obviously do."

"Because I've been a terrible trial to my aunt," she said, swallowing hard. "I think she would have liked a daughter to present to society, a daughter who at least would have married well and left home. Instead she had me dropped into her lap, a girl with no prospects for whom she'd be responsible forever. I think . . . I think maybe that was one reason why she finally left. I was too much of a burden."

Jenny turned her head to one side, her chin lowered, and he knew she was struggling not to cry. Something in Stuart's chest, something hard and almost unbearably painful, twisted so tight he could hardly breathe. Brave, brave Jenny, never thinking of herself or her own tragedy, but only of the people she believed she had inconvenienced.

Without reflecting on the consequences, he crossed the room and dropped to his knee in front of her, encompassing one small fragile hand in his own.

"My dear girl," he said softly, wishing harder than he'd ever wished for anything that he could take her pain away, that he could wave a hand and give her everything she'd lost back again—wishing that he could somehow make her feel whole and loved and appreciated as she so deserved to be. "I don't believe you have the right of it, not this time." He looked down at her fingertips, trying to find the right words. "There is something to be said for bringing joy into people's lives, after all, and you have surely done that."

She raised her sweet face, now tearstained, to his. "I have? But how?" she said, her voice full of question. "I am nothing but a trial, and I know everyone tries to be nice to me because they feel sorry that I can't see, but I make so much extra work, and the servants always have to go out of their way, and . . ."

"And you can't see their faces, can you?" he interrupted abruptly, refusing to let her believe she was a burden for a minute longer. "But I can, and therefore I can tell you that they all worship the ground you walk on." He dug a handkerchief out of a pocket and dabbed her cheeks with it. "When I first arrived I thought that you must surely be the most revoltingly saccharine creature that ever walked the earth, for I was not only hailed as a monster for having inadvertently hurt you, but I was also assured by every last person who crossed my path that you were kind and good and disgustingly perfect. I am delighted to say that I have been happily disabused of the latter sentiment, since you are nothing even close to approaching perfection."

She hiccuped, her smile lopsided. "And you, my lord, are so far from perfect that the idea is laughable. Perhaps we are better suited to be friends than either of us thought. I am not sure we are so well suited to being enemies, since it has been taking far too much energy."

He gazed at her, thinking that maybe she was right. Maybe they were alike in ways neither of them had previously fathomed. They were both stubborn, both argumentative, both independent of spirit, which had probably rescued them from the true depths of despair. Her world was limited by a lack of sight, caused by a scarring of her nerves. His world was limited by an inability to feel, caused by a scarring of the heart, with both conditions incurable.

It sounded like a fine friendship to him.

Chapter 5

Five days later the snow came. Jenny woke knowing that something was different, and she slipped out of bed and made her way to the window, pressing the palms of her hands against it.

The glass was cold, nothing unusual, but she could *smell* the snow in the air, and the way it changed the sound of the outside world. She felt for the latch and pushed the window open, her fingers meeting lovely soft powder that had gathered on the sill.

She scooped some up in her hand and dipped her head to it, inhaling the fresh, clean scent with a thrill of excitement. They hadn't had snow in December for at least three years, and she knew Stuart would be pleased. He'd really had his heart set on a snowfall, she thought with a grin. He'd probably gone so far as to insist that heaven send him one.

Stuart was utterly impossible when it came to insisting on having his way, which he generally got. But she didn't mind anymore. They were getting along so much better, and where she once had found him acutely aggravating, he had ceased to irritate her. Actually, beneath his gruff exterior she was beginning to think he might have a heart after all. She had been touched by his generous words when she'd been upset, touched that he cared enough to try to make a difference. And in his own way he had.

She looked forward to sitting for him now, for instead of silence he amused her with silly stories as he painted. He'd described the household staff to her in hilarious detail—she could just see Partridge with his squat form and round face and the one last persistent lock of hair that sprouted from his bald head, the picture endearing him even more to her. She'd laughed herself silly when he'd described dear Cook's chicken-bone legs and arms, an image that fit exactly with the image Jenny had always had of her. And Ella with her sausage-shaped body and overflowing ankles, blackened hair and mottled skin, which made Jenny wonder if Ella's alarming stories about all the awful artists' lascivious pursuits were nothing more than wishful thinking.

She didn't mind Stuart's devilish humor, for he offered it with no malice, his descriptions helping to flesh out the people she loved. He always offered himself as the butt of the joke, telling her just how blackly he was regarded by everyone and recounting outrageous and probably highly embellished stories about that too. One of the more amusing things she had learned was that her uncle filled his house with the most eccentric-looking people he could find, simply for that reason. He thought they gave creative motivation to those who beheld them. It was just like dear Uncle Harry to do such a thing.

But best of all were Stuart's stories about his life. She'd learned a great deal about Stuart himself as he talked away, more than he probably realized.

She knew, for example, that he loved animals—not because he'd said so, but because the stories he told her of his boyhood were littered with dogs and cats and horses—even a pet pig he'd once trained to come running to him, much to the chagrin of his mother. She'd laughed herself silly at that one.

And she knew that although he'd wanted to be an artist from the time he could remember and had worked hard at realizing his dream, he'd run into some sort of trouble two years before and had been unable to paint until he'd come to Bigslow. No matter how hard she pressed him, she hadn't been able to learn anything more than that, but she didn't mind. She was happy that being at Bigslow had inspired him to work again, and happy too that she was a small part of helping him.

Humming a little melody she started to dress.

Christmas was only a few days away and there were a
hundred things to do. She had to finish the red scarf
she was knitting for Stuart from soft lambswool, and
the hall had yet to be decorated with boughs of holly
and garlands of fir.

She wasn't much help as far as decorating was concerned, but she loved to sit and smell the tang that
filled the air and listen to the general bustle as Partridge
directed the proceedings.

They might even have a white Christmas if the snow
held. She hadn't looked forward to Christmas so much
in years. Her persistent headaches had mysteriously
vanished, and she no longer dreaded the long hours of
ceaseless pain and misery. Maybe that was why she felt
happier than she had since the day her accident had
taken away both her parents and her vision: her life was
interesting and full and not marred by the threat of
migraines.

The only unhappy note left was the absence of her
aunt. Jenny missed her, and she knew that her uncle,
despite his proud silence on the subject, missed her
even more. But there was nothing else she could think
to do that would bring her aunt home. The letters she
had dictated to Partridge had been returned unopened
and she had to wonder if Aunt Lucinda was even there.
As difficult as her aunt could be, Christmas wouldn't
be the same without her.

Jenny pushed the thought from her mind, determined not to let her aunt's stony silence cast a pall over
what promised to be a wonderful day.

*   *   *

"No, no, Jenny," Stuart said impatiently. "Turn your head just slightly to the left. That's it. Perfect— don't move." He hadn't bothered to bring a sketch pad out on their walk, knowing that he could memorize everything he wanted to add to the painting. He only wanted to see Jenny in the right pose, standing on the bluff in the snow, her rosy cheeks glowing, a merry smile turning up the corners of her sweet mouth just as he had imagined it in his mind's eye.

She looked enchantingly lovely, the loveliest thing he'd ever seen. She had a glow about her, a vibrancy that he could feel singing in his own veins as if she were life's blood itself. He didn't know what had brought about the change, but over the last few days she seemed to have come fully awake, as if before she had only been dreaming about life. And he felt as if he'd come awake with her, as if he'd been away somewhere dark and cold and solitary and suddenly the sun had come out and life had meaning and beauty again, more meaning and beauty than it had ever had before.

He supposed it was because he was finally pleased with his work for the first time in a long while. He couldn't paint fast enough, working into the early hours of morning as his brushes flew over the canvas. Nearly everything was done now—everything but Jenny's eyes. He wanted to work around them, leaving them for last, until he felt he *really* knew the inner recesses of her soul. He wanted her eyes to be the final touch, the spark that would bring the painting to life.

He wanted—oh hell, he didn't know what he wanted, but something burned in the very center of his being, a longing, a hunger that neither food nor drink nor even his art could satisfy and he didn't have any idea what it was or how to quench it.

It was damned frustrating to feel so alive and so empty at the same time.

He walked over to her and ran a fingertip down her cheek. "You're cold," he said, relishing the feel of her soft silky skin, not wanting in the least to take his hand away, but dropping it anyway, not about to start behaving like a rogue now.

"I'm not at all cold," she said with a light laugh, and he was delighted that she didn't move away. "I'm—I'm exhilarated. Tell me, Stuart! Tell me how the snow looks on the ground, how the trees look, how everything looks!"

"It's glorious," he said, catching her lighthearted mood. "The sun is shining brightly and the river is banked with snow. The dark bark of the trees is streaked with white and billows of snow have gathered on top of their branches like icing. The sheep look like little moving puffs of cotton on top of a huge alabaster sheet, but the sky—oh, Jenny, the sky! It's a turquoise blue with not a cloud to be seen, and the river sparkles beneath it, catching sunbeams on the water as if it is trying to capture the sun itself."

He paused only to draw breath, desperate to make her see what he saw. "The surface of the snow dazzles like a field of crystal daisies and the grizzly old farmer who is trying to dig his wagon out of a drift looks as if he's not enjoying one minute of all this splendor and wants nothing more than the heat of his hearth, a hot bowl of soup, and even the acerbic conversation of his wife."

Jenny burst into laughter. "Really? Oh, the poor man. He really must be miserable."

"Miserable? I'd say cursing his rheumatism, bad luck, and God in that order."

He caught her hand up in his and pulled her over to a huge plane tree that rose a good seventy feet in the air. "Here, put your hands on this," he said, pulling off her gloves. "Do you feel the bark? If you pull at it, it will peel off in your hands. It's a dappled gray in color with creamy patches beneath the flaking, and the snow is caught in the rough edges—feel it? It's the tallest tree in sight, far higher than the roofs of Bigslow."

Jenny nodded. "It feels so—so solid and strong. I know the sap is sleeping, but I can still sense the life force inside, just waiting for spring so it can surge through the trunk and burst into life."

"Just so," Stuart said, feeling unexpectedly discomfited. It seemed that his sap had started surging in the dead middle of winter, and he thought it might be a good idea to back off a pace or two from the human sunshine that had suddenly and unexpectedly brought him to life.

"Stuart . . ." Jenny said, turning toward him, her face full of expectancy. "Have you—have you ever made a snow angel?"

"A snow angel? Not since I was about eight, but I think I remember the mechanics. Why? Do you want to make one?"

She beamed up at him. "Oh, I do! I know it's childish, but I can't help myself. Would you just make sure I don't drop down somewhere dangerous?"

He took her hand and kissed the tips of her fingers with a laugh, his lips lingering for just a moment. "What sort of guide dog would I be if I led you into danger? Your wish is my command. But you'd better come over here where there's a clear spot, and you should put your gloves back on first."

He tucked each of her hands into the soft leather of her gloves and led her over to a perfect place, a smooth stretch of meadow on an incline covered by a good six inches of new-fallen snow. "You're on your own," he said, standing back with his hands on his hips, watching her with an amused shake of his head.

Jenny grinned, then flung herself backward, arms stretched over her head. She fell, embraced by the gentle cushion of snowflakes and with a shout of laughter she brought her arms down to her sides and up again and repeated the motion several times until she'd made the wings of an angel.

Stuart couldn't help himself. He felt all the wild abandon of the eight-year-old he'd once been as he threw himself down at her side and did the same thing, flapping his arms and legs until he'd duplicated a larger, more masculine-looking angel.

And then he looked over at her and said, "Shall we move on to the next piece of idiocy?" Without waiting for an answer he tucked both arms around her waist and with a lean of his body he sent them rolling over and over down the incline of gentle hillside.

They tumbled, laughing wildly as snow collected

everywhere, turning them into one giant snowball. And finally they came to a halt as the ground leveled off.

Jenny lay underneath Stuart, still gasping with laughter. "I don't think I've had so much fun since I can remember," she said gleefully, pushing the hair out of her face.

"Nor I," he replied softly, gazing down at her, his heart pounding furiously. Jenny. Jenny, who looked like a Snow Queen, flakes clinging to her fair hair and eyebrows and lashes like spun sugar.

Fire pounded through his veins, eradicating any sense of cold. He could think of nothing but the feel of her pliant body in his arms, her smell that reminded him of roses—winter roses, soft and sweet and utterly enticing, and strong enough to bloom in the midst of December. He wanted to take her lips under his, taste their nectar, show her what she couldn't see in his face. That he wanted her.

Stuart sat up in alarm, appalled with himself. He *wanted* her? *Oh God. Oh God, oh God, oh God.* What was he thinking? What could possibly have come over him?

His love for Penelope had had nothing to do with this kind of burning desire—indeed it had very little to do with carnal need and very much to do with blind devotion.

But this very real woman he'd just been holding in his arms sent his thoughts, his very senses, soaring in a completely different direction. He ran his hand through his wet hair, sending sprays of snow flying as he tried to regroup himself.

Jenny pushed herself upright, a smile lingering on her lips, with no idea that he looked more like a wild wolf than a man. "Oh, that was wonderful! Thank you!"

"My pleasure," he said, thinking it was nothing near as wonderful as some other things he could show her.

"Stuart?" she said, her expression sobering. "I'd like to ask something of you."

Oh God. What more could she want from him? What more could he give her that wouldn't require his bringing her to the ground and taking what *he* wanted? He cleared his throat with an inhuman effort. "Yes? What would you like to ask?" he said hoarsely.

"I know this is probably a most improper request, but I—you see, I don't know what you look like. Ella says you're devilishly handsome, and she always says it so darkly that I think you must be, but that means nothing to me. Do you think . . . do you think I could feel your face with my fingers?" She glanced down shyly.

Stuart looked away, his teeth gritted painfully. Oh, now she wanted to feel his face. He'd have to endure the torment of her fingers tracing delicate paths over his flesh with no way to respond in kind. God really must hate him.

"If you wish," he said, not believing his lack of will to refuse her. Yes, God really did hate him.

She nodded solemnly. "Thank you. I know it must be an imposition, but I do appreciate your tolerance."

She removed her gloves, then stretched her hands out, first cupping his face in her palms, feeling the shape of his bone structure, moving them slowly but surely over his jaw, his cheeks, up over his forehead and down again.

Stuart thought he might die. But she wasn't finished with him yet. When she took the tips of her fingers and the pads of her thumbs and traced the line of his eyebrows, his eyelids, his nose and mouth he knew he had truly gone to hell.

Never had he been touched in this way. Her fingers felt like a butterfly's wings brushing against his skin, so light, so sensitive, and he knew that she was drawing in an enormous amount of information. He looked into her face as her hands traveled over his features; she wore that incredibly focused but distant expression she assumed whenever she was absorbing important information, whether it was a simple description or a story or the flavor of a particularly good meal.

"What color are your eyes?" she asked, her fingers pausing.

"Brown," he said, choking the word out.

"What shade of brown?" she persisted.

"I don't know, I suppose the shade of Amontillado sherry." He really didn't know if he could hold on to his self-control much longer.

Jenny smiled merrily. "As I lost my sight before I was of an age to be a connoisseur of fine sherries, perhaps you might find another comparison."

"Er, well," he said, running his tongue over his lips,

"then I suppose you could say my eyes are the color of umm . . . walnuts."

"Walnuts. Yes, I can imagine that. And your hair? Ella says it is very dark, but how dark?" She smoothed a lock between her fingers. "It is certainly soft and silky."

He closed his eyes, sweat beading on his forehead even on this cold day. "Not as dark as a raven's wing, but not so light as a hawk's," he said. "Somewhere in between. Jenny . . ."

"What?" she said, her fingers making one last sweet excursion down his cheeks. "I think Ella is right. You're very handsome."

"That's most generous of you," he said, taking her hands away.

"Not at all. I think I have a very good idea of your appearance now. Maybe—maybe if you touched my face in the same way with your eyes closed you would have a better idea of how you can tell how a person looks from touch alone."

Stuart wanted to cry. "But I *know* how you look, little goose," he said, quite sure he wouldn't be able to withstand temptation if he laid even one finger on her.

"But you still don't know what I mean," she said, pulling his gloves off and lifting his hands to cup her cheeks.

Stuart's pulse threatened to jump out of his throat as he felt the warmth of her skin burning into his palms. But he couldn't help himself. He closed his eyes and gently caressed her face, tracing her delicate bones, running his thumbs down her straight little nose and over her full mouth. A mouth that he very, very badly wanted to kiss. His head inclined toward hers as if of its own volition.

And then somehow, drawing on a hidden reservoir of strength, he managed to stop himself at the very last second.

"I think I see," he said, abruptly pulling away from her and jerking his gloves on, knowing that he was in imminent danger of making a terrible mistake. One stolen kiss and his life would be in irretrievable shreds.

"I don't know how you can have gotten a very good picture with such a cursory examination," she said, but her voice was shaky and her cheeks had flushed scarlet.

So, Stuart thought ruefully, she wasn't immune to his touch either. Well, he was some kind of saint, because now he knew he could have that kiss, but he was going to save them both from disaster. "It's cold," he said, standing. "We should head back."

Jenny nodded and let him help her to her feet. "I'm sorry," she said in a low voice.

"Sorry? Sorry for what?" Stuart couldn't think what *she* had to be sorry for, but he could think of all sorts of things he was sorry for, and his damned nobility topped the list.

"Sorry that you found the exercise so repugnant," she said tightly, turning her face away.

Stuart had a strong desire to howl with frustration. "I didn't find it repugnant in the least." *Anything but.* "It is only that your cheeks are frozen," he lied. "And as I am soaked through, I thought you must be too. We can't have you catching cold right before Christmas."

He tucked her hand through the crook of his arm. "Why don't we hurry back to the house and sit in front of the fire with something warm to drink?"

Jenny glanced back at him, her face full of question. But she said only, "Yes, that's a good idea. Maybe Cook has made up her excellent Wassail."

"Good, it sounds just the thing. We'll go at a fast trot and stir our blood up." Wrong thing to say, he realized belatedly, and started off at a pace closer to a canter.

Jenny couldn't sleep, and she had a good idea why not. She'd been feeling out of sorts ever since Stuart had abruptly terminated their walk, and every sense told her that she had done or said something that had annoyed him. He'd gone to the studio almost immediately after returning to the house, insisting that he didn't need her to pose that afternoon. He hadn't been particularly cold or curt, just distant.

She had a terrible feeling that she knew what had caused his withdrawal, and she had no one to blame but herself. She didn't know what had come over her to behave so foolishly, to *touch* him like that. She felt as if she'd been touching fire as her hands had traveled over his face, drinking in every detail of his strong features. Never in her wildest dreams had she imagined they would be so beautifully put together, so devastatingly masculine.

And never had she imagined that she would so enjoy being held close by him. She hadn't wanted their tumble down the hillside ever to stop, loving the feel of his arms wrapped close and strong around her, his breath warm on her cheek, his face pressed hard against hers. That had been what gave her the idea to ask him if she could feel it, for she suddenly longed to know the face of the man she had come to care for.

To care for. To love was more like it, she thought miserably, sitting up and huddling her knees to her chest. Idiot that she was, she still wasn't so stupid as to deny that her feelings for him had been slowly changing, but she hadn't realized just how much until that afternoon when they had played and laughed and held each other, *touched* each other, causing a yearning in her that reached into the deepest well of her heart. Kindled a desire that reached into her very bones.

Yes, she loved him. And loving Stuart was futile. Hopeless. Not only was she blind, which made the situation impossible, but he certainly didn't love her or desire her in return. He had jerked his hands from her face as if he found touching her acutely uncomfortable. And why shouldn't he? She was nothing more than a model to him, someone whose form and face he wanted to paint.

She knew perfectly well that his lightheartedness and enthusiasm that day had been caused by the snow, not by her, and it was her fault that her own lightheartedness had led her to behave in such a reckless fashion.

She could only pray that he had no inkling of how she felt, that nothing in her behavior or facial expressions gave her away.

She wanted to cry, but that would get her nowhere. She'd learned long ago that self-pity was futile, would not change her situation. There was only one thing that might help her to forget, give her a few precious hours of peace.

She slipped into her night robe, put on her slippers, and made her way to the upper floor of the west wing. This path she knew well, although she hadn't taken it in some weeks, too tired after a day with Stuart to want to do anything but sleep.

In a matter of minutes she'd managed to get a small fire started in the grate without burning herself. She settled herself at the pianoforte, taking a minute to think about what she needed most to express.

And then she raised her hands and when she was ready she lowered them, striking the keys and letting the music come pouring forth, her fingers her medium, her aching heart her vehicle, her voice her messenger.

Stuart couldn't sleep. He was hardly surprised, but he was excessively annoyed with himself. He'd been sixteen the last time that he'd allowed lust to cloud his brain to this extent. He had his work to think of, but he couldn't even bring that into focus, for every time he brought his painting to his mind, Jenny was there, the image of her dear face leaping out at him, her ripe body calling every last lustful feeling back with complete clarity.

He could hardly help that she was beautiful and desirable. He certainly couldn't help that she was everywhere he looked, physically as well as mentally. She had burned herself into his mind, damn her anyway, and his mind was his sanctuary. But there she was and she wouldn't go away.

He'd been about to jump out of his skin at dinner as Jenny sat there so silently, so innocently, with no idea of what was raging through his brain and body. It was everything he could do to keep his gaze averted, but even as he managed that, he felt her in every nerve, every cell of his body. He hoped to God that Sir Harry hadn't noticed anything, but he seemed not to have, for he carried on conversation in his usual haphazard fashion.

It wouldn't do to have his benefactor realize that Stuart cared a great deal more about seducing his niece at this point than about completing his painting.

Stuart cursed fiercely, then shrugged himself into his trousers and shirt and pulled on his boots. Pacing. That was the only solution, and the hallway was the only place that would accommodate the amount of pacing he had in mind.

He started down the corridor, taking long, fast steps, and when he reached the end he spun around and started back again. And then something stopped him mid-stride, an unfamiliar sound that came from directly above. The sound of music, a sweet, plaintive melody that flowed like a river, rushing and falling and rising again, moving endlessly on and on.

He couldn't think who played it, but he knew he had to hear more. He walked swiftly to the staircase and climbed to the next story, following the resonating notes down the corridor until he reached a door.

He placed his hand on the cool brass knob and softly turned it, cracking the door and then pushing it wider.

His heart stopped as he took in Jenny's back, her hair cascading down it like a shower of starlight. Her head was slightly bowed, her body swaying as she started to pour out notes of liquid gold into the dark, her voice soaring over the music her fingers coaxed from the instrument.

The sound of her singing was the purest thing he'd ever heard, running like quicksilver up and down the scale in an Elizabethan melody. She might have been a nightingale, but this nightingale sang words, words that tore at his heart and spirit and brought tears to his eyes. They were nothing he'd ever heard before, but surely the most beautiful ever to touch his ears, and he knew in his heart that they were hers as much as the melody from which they sprang was hers.

She was gifted, truly gifted, and he was humbled by her talent. But that was the least of what struck him. Her ability to compose so purely and beautifully, to execute her music so skillfully, awed and surprised him, but Jenny herself awed and surprised him far more.

This was the core of her soul, her music.

In the deep night shadows, I sing my song alone
Snow has lightly fallen, and I am in my home
But winter's depth has taken me, and none can melt the
   cold.
I cannot melt the cold, my love, that seeps into my soul.
I see your face so clearly, though no light shines my way

*And love you just as clear and strong, that night might
    still be day.*
*If night were day and I could love, and love were mine
    to take*
*What secrets would my heart reveal, what pledges might
    I make?*
*But mine is not to choose or take, your love belongs
    elsewhere*
*And if I gave my heart to you, 'twould only fill with
    tears.*

She paused for a moment, then touched the keys
again, replaying the last stanza of the haunting melody,
but with different words.

*I am as the snow to you, a moment here, then gone
And I am left in darkness, a darkness without dawn.*

The last notes faded away and Stuart stood stunned
as they rang in his ears, just as her words rang in his
ears, over and over again. There was no mistaking their
meaning.

She had opened her heart in her song, and she was
far braver than he. She had faced her feelings, and he
had hidden behind a mask of indifference when he felt
anything but. Anything but.

He had been so stupid not to realize that he loved
her. That he honored her and cherished her for everything she was. She had given him more understanding
in their brief month together than he'd received in a

lifetime, more vision than his own eyes had ever offered him.

He stood there, a man who had for so long been alone, alone far before Penelope, he finally realized. But now he had been lucky enough to find a woman strong enough and wise enough and tolerant enough to love him. Really love *him*. Not his title or his money, his lands, or even his looks, just him, as he was. Jenny loved his soul, as surely as he loved hers.

And he, fool that he was, had caused her to believe that she meant nothing to him when she meant everything.

With a blinding flash of insight Stuart realized that he wanted to spend the rest of his life with this woman.

And he always got his way.

Chapter 6

Jenny's back stiffened as she sensed a presence in the room. She quickly wiped away the hot tears that streamed down her cheeks and turned.

"Who is there?" she whispered, praying with all her heart that it wasn't Stuart, that he hadn't heard her singing her pathetic ballad.

"It is only me, Jenny," he said from the doorway, and her heart fell further than she thought possible. "I couldn't help but hear the music from downstairs and I came up to see who was playing so beautifully."

"I'm sorry if I disturbed you," she said, bowing her head, hoping he hadn't seen her tears.

"Disturb me?" Stuart softly closed the door and she heard his footsteps approach, but to her relief he only crossed over to the fire and added more coal. "Not at all. I've never heard anything so enchantingly lovely. I had no idea you played. Or sang."

"You never asked," she said defensively.

"I suppose there are a good many things I've never asked you," he said quietly. "But then I've only recently started to realize how very much I want to know. You must have played all your life to achieve such a level of expertise."

"Music gives me solace," she said uncomfortably, wondering what he could be thinking. Did he have any idea that he'd listened to a song she'd written to him? And yet he made no mention of it, only that he'd thought the music beautiful. She began to relax slightly, for Stuart never missed making a point when an opportunity presented itself.

"It gives me solace too," he said. "May I sit next to you? You obviously couldn't sleep any more than I could. Perhaps we can both find comfort in music tonight." He slid onto the bench next to her.

"What would you like to hear?" she asked, thinking that there was nothing of comfort to be had with Stuart sitting only inches away from her. She could feel the heat emanating from his body, sense the mass of his physique. His body so close to hers . . . his heart so very, very far away.

"Christmas is only two days away," he said. "Maybe you could play a carol or two to put us in the mood?"

"A carol? There are so many . . . which are your favorites?"

"Nothing sad. I think we've had enough of sadness. I've always liked 'Lo How a Rose Tree Bloometh,' if you know it."

Jenny nodded. That was one of her favorites too, and she'd sing anything to take her mind off her misery. Her fingers rippled over the keys and she started the first stanza:

Lo how a rose tree bloometh, from tender stem hath
  sprung
From Jesse's lineage cometh, as men of old have sung.

To her surprise Stuart joined in with the harmony, his voice a pleasant baritone that blended nicely with hers.

It came a flower bright
Amidst the depth of winter, when so cold was the
  night . . .

Stuart abruptly stopped with a laugh. "I never can remember the second verse. Never mind, do you know 'The First Noel'? I've always liked the image of all those shepherds standing watch over their sheep on a bitter winter night, eyeing that alarming star shining huge in the sky and wondering what was happening to the world. And then suddenly an angel appears and tells them in no uncertain terms, scaring the daylight out of them in the process."

"How typical of you to put it like that," she said with an attempt at a smile. But she played it for him and this time Stuart remembered three full verses. By the time they'd finished, Jenny began to feel better. They sang "God Rest Ye Merry Gentlemen," and *"Venite Adoremus,"* and a handful of others at full volume, and when Jenny finally lowered the lid of the pianoforte she was laughing with pleasure.

"I hope it's not my singing that amuses you so much," he said dryly. "I am happy to say that I paint a great deal better than I bellow. I sound like a wounded bull next to your clear soprano."

"You don't bellow in the least. You have a fine voice," she said. "And I can't paint at all," she added to be fair.

"Oh yes you can," he said, shifting on the bench to face her. "You paint in your mind, dear heart, beautiful breathtaking pictures that I can only catch glimpses of. I am far more earthbound than you, limited by my tedious eyesight."

Jenny closed her eyes for a moment, a stab of pain grabbing at her heart. She wished he wouldn't say such tender things, for they only made her love him more.

"What is it?" he asked gently, covering her hand with his own. "You look so sad again, just as you did when I first came in."

"I—I can't . . ." She pulled her hand away and turned her head, willing away the tears that pricked at the back of her eyes, a hard knot forming in her throat.

"Jenny. Sweetheart. Do you think me so stupid that I don't know you were singing about yourself? About me?"

She froze. *No, oh no, oh no. This couldn't be happening.* He had known how she felt about him all along, all the time they were singing and laughing? She shook her head furiously as if she could shake away the humiliation that burned at her. He must think her the silliest fool who ever walked the earth.

"Listen to me," he started to say.

"Please don't," she choked. "Please, Stuart, if you care anything about me, don't pursue this."

"Why shouldn't I? Who else is going to set you straight?"

"I don't need to be set straight," she said, clenching her fists in her lap. "I understand the situation perfectly well. There's no need to point out the error of my ways." Jenny wanted to die.

"I think there's every need to point out the error of your ways," he retorted. "You seem to think you are the only one who feels what is between us, that you are the only one capable of love in this relationship. You're sadly mistaken, for I love you with all my heart."

Jenny slowly turned her head and stared toward him blankly, shock numbing her body. Her sense of hearing was so heightened by the loss of her sight that in place of reading meaning from a person's facial expressions she had learned to listen to every nuance of every word.

There was nothing but sincerity in Stuart's voice, but she still couldn't believe she had heard him correctly. "You—you can't mean it," she stammered, her head reeling. "How could you?"

"How could I love you?" he said, toying with her fingertips. "I'm not sure myself. I thought I would never love again, not after having my heart ripped to shreds two years ago by a woman I was to marry within days. But I recently discovered that I never loved her at all, not really, or at least not for any of the right reasons." He paused, releasing a long breath. "And then I came here, still filled with anger and bitterness and a bleak cold that reached into my very soul. And I met you, Jenny. I met you and my soul began to thaw as if winter had finally loosened its grim hold."

"But why?" she said, thoroughly bewildered. "Why because of me? I did nothing!"

"Nothing? You showed me how to look at the sun shining in the sky and birds on the wing, and yes, even the bark on the trees." He chuckled softly. "And you harangued me day and night to talk to you, to describe things to you until I realized I was describing them to myself in a way I never had before. I was the one who was blind, Jenny, not you. Never you. *You* taught *me* how to see. You set me free."

She couldn't help the tears that overflowed and poured down her cheeks. "No," she said, her heart breaking for them both because of what she had to do now for his sake. "You set me free. You taught me how to laugh and be silly and carefree. You taught me about courage as you struggled to find your art again. And you did, Stuart, you did, and you found yourself in the process. You don't need me anymore."

"Are you out of your mind?" he said incredulously. "What, do you think I consider you some sort of mascot or good luck talisman? I *love* you, Jenny. I don't say that easily or lightly. God knows I never thought I'd say it again, and certainly not to you." He cupped her face between his large, capable hands and stroked her cheeks with his thumbs. "There are a hundred other reasons—your sweetness, your sense of humor, your innate wisdom. I love the myriad of expressions that cross your face and tell me what you're thinking, the way you drink in life with such intensity. I love the way you make my heart pound and my blood boil and every last one of my senses rage."

Jenny's breath caught in her throat, for he did the same thing to her. He was doing it now: her body shook with longing for him and she had to fight to keep her wits about her.

"Can you deny that I make you feel the same way?" he asked softly.

She shook her head between the cup of his hands. "I cannot lie to you. You do—you know you do, but that is beside the point."

"Then what is the point, for God's sake?" he roared with frustration.

"You don't love *me,* you love what you have found here through me," she said desperately, determined to have nothing but the truth between them, as much as it pained her. "If you were honest with yourself you'd see that when you leave here you'll take all of what you found away with you."

"Yes, I will," he said fiercely. "And part of that includes you."

Before she could register what he was doing, Stuart slipped his strong arms around her and brought his mouth hard down over hers, kissing her with such passion and intensity that she couldn't help but surrender to him. She had never felt anything so breathtakingly wonderful as the feel of his lips moving over hers, his mouth opening and his tongue tangling with hers.

Her heart pounded with excitement and fire burned in her veins until she thought she really might die. He drank her in, drowned her, took her beyond herself and beyond him to a place that made them one, and in that moment they both flew free.

She knew it was the one and only kiss they would ever exchange, for she loved him so fully that she had to relinquish him to his destiny—a destiny that she knew could not include her.

As he finally pulled his mouth from hers, Jenny released him even as her heart broke.

"Marry me," he said, burying his face in her hair, his breathing ragged against her chest.

"No," she said, wanting nothing more, but wanting even more for him to fly unfettered. She would only clip his wings and in the end, he would resent her, chafe at the chains that would inevitably bind him.

He lifted his head. *"No?"* He took her by the shoulders, his fingers biting into her skin. "Have you even bothered to think about it, you little fool? I can offer you everything—freedom, independence, a life of luxury, but most important, a heart that belongs wholly to you."

"No," she said again. "I can't."

"Why not, for the love of God? I know you love me, and it's no good trying to tell me you don't, because no woman kisses a man like that if she doesn't love him."

"I *do* love you," she said, steeling her resolve. "I will always love you, but I love you too much to shackle you with me for the rest of your life. You have no idea, Stuart, none at all how much of a burden I would become to you. I won't do it." She shuddered against the searing pain that gripped at her very core. "I would rather lose you now than know that eventually you would regret your decision, realize that I was right all along. I am happy to have been an inspiration to you, but you will move on to other inspirations. I was never meant for marriage."

His silence beat impossibly still in the night. "And where have you come up with this idiotic idea?" he finally said, his voice as hard and cold as steel. "Or can I guess? Your dear aunt Lucinda told you that you were never meant for marriage, just as she told you that you were ordinary. And a burden."

"Please leave my aunt Lucinda out of this," Jenny said sharply. "I know what I say is true. If nothing else, you are a viscount, Stuart. You have social obligations and when you take a wife she must be able to fulfill them also."

"Poppycock. I rarely fulfill my social obligations as it is." He expelled an impatient breath.

"But I cannot do any of the things expected of a wife. I cannot run a household, I cannot go out in society, I can't even dance, Stuart," she said desperately. "I'm not the woman for you, I'm not! I won't accept your offer, as flattering and tempting as it is, and then be a disappointment to you, which inevitably I would be. In any case, I couldn't possibly leave my uncle—he depends on me completely now that my aunt has left him. I would be the most ungrateful person in the world to desert him after all he has done for me."

Stuart briefly stroked his hand over her hair. "I think I see," he said after a moment. "Very well, I won't bore you anymore with my intentions, as you obviously think you have the right of it. You're stubborn as the day is long and probably always will be."

"Probably," she agreed, vastly relieved he'd accepted her refusal so gracefully, even though a very large part of her wished he hadn't.

"I'll take you down to your room," he said, rising. "But, Jenny, be warned. I'm not going to play the disappointed suitor and leave tomorrow in a fit of pique. I'm here for the duration."

"Of course," she said, wondering how she was going to bear to continue to be in his company. "But I think we had better agree to stay within the boundaries of friendship for both our sakes," she added cautiously.

"Boundaries are a matter of interpretation, my dear, as is friendship," Stuart replied cryptically, but he took her to her room without any further ado and bid her a polite good night as if nothing out of the ordinary had passed between them.

Jenny spent the rest of the night crying her heart out.

Stuart woke in a righteous fury after having passed a nearly sleepless night. He had divined perfectly Jenny's reasons for refusing him and discounted every last one.

The conveniently absent Lucinda Bigslow was at the bottom of the entire mess, and he intended to set the situation straight as soon as possible so that he could get on with the rest of his life.

He only just managed to tolerate Newton's fussy administrations, but he needed to look his finest. He had serious business ahead and he knew exactly what sort of impression he wanted to make. And how he wanted to make it.

He ordered his carriage brought around and he spent the twenty-minute drive putting himself in the right frame of mind—this was an encounter that was going to require every last bit of arrogance he had ever learned, as well as a good dose of carefully planned manipulation.

When the carriage arrived in due course, Stuart alighted and presented his card to the startled house-maid.

"Tell Lady Bigslow that Lord Middleton is here to see her on a matter of urgent business," he commanded, giving the poor girl his most imperious stare. It was a stare that had brought many far above her station to their knees, and although he had not had occasion to practice it in some weeks, he knew its effect had not diminished, for the housemaid bobbed a curtsy and vanished instantly.

A few minutes later he strolled into Lady Bigslow's drawing room in the housemaid's wake.

"My dear Lord Middleton, this is indeed an honor!" A woman of uncertain years but distinctly diminished looks greeted him with a simpering smile and curtsy. "How very kind of you to call on me. I believe I once made the acquaintance of your mother, a most admirable woman. Are you in the neighborhood for the Christmas holiday?"

"I am, although I have been in the vicinity for some four weeks now," he replied, declining her offer of sherry. "To come directly to the point, I have been staying at Bigslow Hall at the invitation of your husband."

Lucinda Bigslow paled. She paled most satisfactorily to Stuart's way of thinking. He used his advantage and gestured to a chair. "Forgive me for being so blunt, but I believe I am the reason that you left Bigslow, and for that I am most sorry."

Lucinda Bigslow developed two very pink spots on her cheeks and began to fan herself furiously, sputtering incoherently. "But—but my husband said the name was Blakeney, I'm sure of it!" she finally managed to blurt out.

"My family name," Stuart said. "I sign my work with it. Your husband forgot that I use my title in all other areas of my life. Does it make a difference?"

"But I . . . had I only known! Oh, dear, how very

distressing! I'd never heard of a Lord Blakeney, so naturally I assumed you would be another of my husband's bounders. And now to discover that it was you, my lord, all along . . ."

She blinked rapidly, apparently trying to absorb the implications of her mistake. Stuart was well aware that the wealth that went with the Middleton title was legendary, even though the title itself was nothing grand. Lucinda Bigslow was surely kicking herself for a lost opportunity.

Stuart took the moment to assess her more closely. She had probably once had some decent looks but they had failed her, for her bones had not held and her cheeks now sagged unfortunately into jowls. She'd developed bags under her eyes, and her waistline had expanded until it matched the girth of her hips, topped by an equally sagging bosom which she had decorated with a vast quantity of blue ruffles better suited to a woman in her twenties.

To top it all off, her white hair was curled unattractively into girlish ringlets about her face.

She was a woman who refused to grow old gracefully, he decided. No wonder she had downplayed Jenny's glowing beauty to such an extent, the selfish old bag.

"I am sorry for the misunderstanding," he said, crossing one leg over the other. "I can certainly sympathize with the distress you must have felt assuming that an irresponsible dandy was about to arrive on your doorstep and turn your household upside down—not an unreasonable assumption, given what your niece has told me about your previous guests with an artistic bent."

"Well, yes," she said, pulling fretfully at the frivolous bodice of her dress with one hand, still fanning herself with the other. "We have suffered many of those already, but there was one in particular, a man of most unfortunate temperament . . ."

"Indeed. It happens in the best of families," Stuart said blithely.

The last thing he wanted was Lucinda Bigslow launching into the subject of Jasper Ogilvy. Jenny had told him all about Jasper's disastrous visit and he hadn't been the least amused, knowing Jasper a little too well. And given that, he could understand why Lucinda had balked at the idea of a repeat performance, although he thought her decision to run away from home rather extreme behavior.

Now that he had met her, he couldn't entirely dislike Lucinda Bigslow, although he felt deeply sorry that Jenny had been subjected to her for so many years. There was no doubt that she was a silly, selfish woman and a snob to boot. But since he intended to take Jenny away from Bigslow Hall, there was everything to be gained by returning Lucinda to her home, for Jenny would no longer be able to use her aunt's absence as an excuse. And he did owe Sir Harry a debt, which he wanted to repay. For whatever odd reason, Sir Harry truly did love his ridiculous wife.

"To come to the reason for my visit," he said, "I must tell you that I am deeply concerned by your husband's melancholy over your absence. He is a proud man, and although I have sensed that he finds himself at a deep loss, he will not speak of his great sorrow. It is perhaps an admirable quality, but not a productive one in this instance, for here we are with Christmas nearly upon us, and I fear for his health."

"His health?" Lady Bigslow said, forgetting to fan as she sat up at attention. "He is not unwell?"

"Not as yet, but he seems to slide into a deeper state of depression every day," Stuart said not entirely untruthfully. "I believe that he finds facing this season of celebration nearly unbearable without you. As attentive as his niece is, she cannot be everything to him that you once were."

"Oh," Lucinda said, her hand moving to her heavy jowl. "Oh, dear! I had no idea . . . my poor, darling Harry. I did think he would come for me long before this, I do admit. I have missed him terribly."

Stuart considered this real progress and he was well pleased with himself. He pressed his advantage. "The household is in terrible upheaval as well, hardly surprising when it lacks you at its helm."

"Oh, my goodness. Yes, I can see how it would be with only Harry and poor Jane to manage."

Stuart pounced. First he bowed his head and sighed heavily. Then he raised his head again and gave her a long, and what he hoped was a heart-wrenching gaze. "Yes," he said. "And then there is Jenny. It is very forward of me to say, I know, but I love her, Lady Bigslow. I wish to make her my wife."

Lucinda stared at him. "*You* want to marry Jane?" she gasped. "But she is blind!"

"I can hardly help but be aware of that," he said, trying to keep an edge on his temper, for it was obvious that Lucinda had never been able to get beyond Jenny's blindness to love and appreciate Jenny herself. Yet Jenny remained steadfastly loyal to her, despite the poor treatment she had received at her aunt's hand.

He wanted nothing more than to throw the silly, thoughtless woman through the window and plant her on her head in a snowdrift, arms and legs akimbo, but he managed to restrain the desire. He had a goal to pursue and he would not let his temper get in the way.

"But you could marry anyone," Lucinda said, still staring at him. "You are titled and rich beyond measure. Why would you want to marry my niece?"

"Why wouldn't I?" he retorted, nearly nauseated by her attitude. "Your niece is not only a beautiful woman, she is also a woman of unusual heart. I regret that you have been unable to point out either quality to her, but I suppose that beauty is in the eye of the beholder, just as blindness is."

"I do not understand you," Lucinda said uncertainly.

Little wonder, Stuart thought dryly. "It is really not so complicated," he said as patiently as he could manage. "You see, Lady Bigslow, I don't think of Jenny as a blind woman. She is a woman who is blind, yes, but she is a great many other things as well, all of which I cherish."

"Yes. Yes, I see. Well, I can hardly argue with the match. It is a brilliant one, far beyond my wildest hopes for dear Jane. I never thought she had a prayer for marriage."

"An absurd sentiment that you've unfortunately transferred to Jenny," he said bitterly. "And there won't be a match, brilliant or otherwise, unless you return home."

Lucinda sat up straight, her eyes popping wide open in alarm. "Do you mean to say that Jane has *refused* you?"

"She has. She does not believe you are ever coming back and she refuses to leave her uncle alone." He paused for effect. "It would behoove you not only to come home but also to further my cause with Jenny, for I shall naturally settle a large sum of money on her, yours and your husband's on the day we are married, to do with as you please."

Lucinda's small eyes gleamed with sudden excitement and Stuart could see her already counting his money and the luxuries it would provide her. "But of *course* I will return home, for my dear ones need me," she said quickly, as if the large carrot he had dangled in front of her nose had nothing to do with her decision. "I was only trying to make a point."

Stuart exhaled with profound relief. "As long as you relinquish the point, I will not quibble with you. I only ask that you bring yourself home this night. It is Christmas Eve, after all, and your family will be glad for your return."

"Then I will make my entrance this very evening before dinner," she said, nodding happily, now that all the benefits to herself had sunk in. "I will be my dear Harry's Christmas miracle."

And mine as well, Stuart thought, praying that with her help he could bring Jenny around. *And with the grace of God, mine as well.*

Chapter 7

Jenny sat bleakly in her chair in the studio, wondering why Stuart was in such a disgracefully good mood when she'd never been more miserable in her life. He'd returned from wherever he'd gone that morning in the best of spirits, saying only that he was seized with inspiration and wanted her to sit for him.

He said not a word about their conversation the night before, talking instead about how much he was looking forward to their Christmas celebrations. She wanted to murder him. Did he think that because she'd refused him her feelings had disappeared, that they could go on as if nothing had happened?

"After dinner we'll go to Christmas Eve services," he was saying. "And then there's the lighting of the Yule log to look forward to, but first I have a wonderful surprise for you. Jenny? Are you listening?"

"I'm listening," she said tonelessly. "You have a surprise for me."

"I have indeed. I think you'll be getting two surprises tonight, but I can say no more without giving one of them away."

"If one of them is finishing your painting, you had better stop chattering and get on with it."

"Wrong guess," he said, "although I am very nearly done."

Jenny's heart sank. He'd said he intended to stay for the duration of his invitation, but what reason would he have once he had finished his work? "Are you thinking of starting another landscape?" she asked, not sure she wanted to hear the answer either way.

"I'm not sure if I'll do another landscape," he said, clattering around for something. "I haven't really thought beyond this piece, to tell you the truth."

Jenny reached down for Maddie's head and scratched her ears, trying to comfort herself.

"Sit up, dear heart. I can hardly see your face when you're bent over double and it's your eyes I need."

She straightened obediently, wishing he wouldn't call her by an endearment. It was hard enough keeping tears at bay as it was.

Only an hour later Stuart gave a gleeful whoop that nearly made her jump out of her skin. "What happened?" she asked nervously.

"That's it!" he shouted. "Done. Finished! Not another brush stroke to be made. God in heaven, Jenny, I wish you could see this. You're more beautiful than Aphrodite herself, and that's saying something."

Jenny colored. "If I am it's because you made me that way."

"Not I. God," he said, crossing the room and dropping a kiss on her hair. He smelled of paint and turpentine and his own special male scent. Oh, how she was going to miss him, she thought with a terrible pang.

"Come along, sweetheart, it's time to change for dinner. Let the celebrations begin."

Jenny didn't feel the least bit like celebrating, but she washed and let Ella help her into her best evening dress and fiddle endlessly with her hair. Jenny didn't really care how she looked, but she didn't want to diminish Ella's bubbling Christmas spirit.

"There you are, my darling, and don't you look just like one of God's angels tonight," Ella said, steering her toward the door. "Now down you go and enjoy yourself."

Little likelihood of that, Jenny thought as she descended the staircase. One more burst of goodwill from Stuart or anyone else and she'd scream. Or cry. Or throw a temper tantrum worthy of her aunt. And just as that tempting thought crossed her mind, her aunt's voice drifted up from the hall.

Jenny stopped dead in her tracks, her hand clutching at the banister. "Aunt Lucinda?" she whispered in disbelief.

"Jane, my darling girl!" came the answering reply. "Yes, it is I, your devoted aunt, returned to the bosom of her family. Come and give Auntie a big kiss."

Jenny moved as quickly as she could manage and found herself swept up in her aunt's capacious arms, being hugged and kissed and petted as she never had been before.

"But how—what made you change your mind?"

Jenny said, utterly confused by this sudden reversal of affairs, but unbelievably relieved.

"That darling Middleton," her aunt cooed. "He came to visit me this very morning and explained how unhappy you and dearest Harry have been without me. And of course when I saw for myself that he was nothing like the others, well, I could hardly stand on my pride a minute longer."

"Stuart visited you?" she said, taking a startled step backward.

"He did," her uncle said, touching her shoulder to let her know he was behind her. "And I have nothing but thanks to give him. It is a miracle, Jenny, a true miracle. I feel like a new man! I cannot wait for him to appear so that I might shake his hand in gratitude."

Tears pricked at the back of Jenny's eyes. So this was Stuart's surprise. He knew how much Uncle Harry had missed his wife, how much she had missed her aunt, and so he had set out to give them both the best Christmas present he could think of. And being Stuart, he had managed it.

Oh, she did love him. She loved him so much that her heart fair wanted to burst. She didn't know how she'd ever repay him, for in truth, she had been worried sick about her uncle.

"He is very kind," she said. "Very, very kind."

"Well," her aunt said, patting her hand, "I must say that since Middleton went to all the trouble of bringing me home, the least you could do is marry him, isn't that right, Harry?"

"It's the first I've heard of it," her uncle said cheerfully, "but it's a dashed good idea, now that I think of it. But does Middleton want to marry Jenny, that's the question."

Jenny closed her eyes and covered her face with her hands. She didn't know whether to laugh or cry. Of course. Stuart had worked it all out. Bring her aunt home and that excuse would be out of the way. He really was incorrigible.

"Well, girl?" her uncle persisted. "Does he, or is this just another one of your aunt's harebrained schemes?"

"But I do. I want to marry Jenny more than anything in life. The question is actually whether she wants to marry me."

Jenny dropped her hands and spun around at the sound of Stuart's voice. "Stuart . . ." she said, half-tempted to strangle him.

Chaos ensued for a moment while her uncle Harry poured profuse thanks upon Stuart for bringing his wife home to him, and Lucinda carried on in her usual silly fashion. Jenny was glad for the distraction, for it gave her time to gather her badly scattered thoughts.

And then Stuart took her hand and drew her off to one side, resting his hands on her shoulders. "Well, my sweet love?" he said softly. "Have I managed to make any inroads on that hard head of yours? Will you marry me?"

She laughed, but it came out more as a hiccup. "You think *my* head is hard? I don't think there's a harder, more determined head in all of Christendom than yours," she said, shivering at his warm touch.

"Maybe not, but I cannot help loving you, and since

you know I can match you in stubbornness and probably best you at that, you might as well save yourself a great deal of trouble and accept me. I won't stop loving you, you know, and I won't stop asking. I'll plague you until the day I die, or you die, whichever comes first." He pressed a kiss against her temple. "I don't want to be miserable any more than I want you to be miserable. Be my wife, Jenny. Let me make you happy. Let me give you children to love, let me keep you warm through the long winter nights, let me paint the whole world for you."

Jenny leaned her head against his chest with a sigh. She couldn't fight him for the rest of her life any more than she could fight her love for him. She was starting to wonder if she wasn't being an idiot, turning her back on happiness, for Stuart truly did love her, she knew that now. She could hear it in his voice, feel it in his touch. And she knew it from his sheer determination to have her, despite her lack of sight.

It was she who had made her blindness an issue, not he, she who had insisted that she would make his life a hardship, not he. Stuart didn't care in the least that she couldn't see. So why should she?

A great weight lifted from Jenny's heart as she made her decision, the last shackles that had held her back unbound.

"Jenny?" he whispered. "Please marry me?"

She raised her head, tears streaming down her cheeks. "Yes. Oh yes, I'll marry you, Stuart," she said, crying and laughing all at the same time. "I'll marry you and have your children and I'll do everything in my power to make you happy." She wiped her eyes with the back of her hand, smiling up at him. "If you really want my hand in marriage, it's yours, but I warn you. You won't be able to let go of it for long."

"I'll never let go of it at all if I have anything to say about it," he said, his voice suddenly rough. "God, how I love you, Miss Jenny Impossible Bigslow. And I thank you with all my heart."

He bent his head and kissed her thoroughly, without a care that he was standing in a hall filled with people. Jenny kissed him back just as thoroughly, with even less of a care.

Shortly before midnight they all returned from church, where Jenny had given every kind of thanks she could think of to the Good Lord for guiding her way to happiness. And she was so filled with that happiness that she hardly knew what to do with herself.

To her surprise Stuart stayed Partridge's hand when he started to remove her cloak. "We're going out again," he said. "Not to worry, we'll be back in time for the midnight Yule lighting." He whispered in her ear. "Did you forget that surprise I had for you?"

"I think I've had enough surprises recently to last me a lifetime," she said with a smile.

"Oh, I don't know about that. But stay here. Don't move, I'll be right back."

He was as good as his word. Jenny's ears pricked as she heard him come across the hallway, but it wasn't the sound of his boots that made her catch her breath. It was another familiar sound, a sound she hadn't heard in over a month. The sound of Maddie's four feet rushing toward her.

She dropped to her knees with a cry of delight, her arms outstretched as a warm bundle of fur flew into them, depositing wet licks all over her face.

"Maddie! Oh, sweet, sweet dog, you can walk! You're all better . . . oh, *Stuart*!" She rose and threw her arms around him, laughing with joy. "Thank you. You couldn't have given me a finer present."

"She's thoroughly sound," he said, laughing with her. "I thought we'd take her for her first proper walk. Not a long one, just enough for her to stretch her legs and enjoy her freedom."

"It's a wonderful idea," Jenny said, tucking her hand into the crook of Stuart's elbow. "Oh, it has been a wonderful night."

"It's not over yet," he said, leading her down the steps, Maddie running in front of them, her footfalls suddenly silenced as she reached the soft snow and bounded off. "I wanted to take you out under the Christmas stars. It's a clear night and only a quarter moon, and the sky is lit up with thousands of tiny, shimmering lights."

"Oh, how lovely it sounds," she breathed, imagining it all as he described. "Where does the moon hang?"

"Just above the trees to your right, a large golden crescent that curves from left to right. Good God," he said suddenly. "There goes a shooting star, right over our heads! Make a wish, my darling, make the biggest wish you could think of."

But Jenny didn't have time to make a wish. A dreadful pain shot through her head as if she'd been stabbed through the temple with a sharp knife and she cried out, dropping to her knees in agony.

"Jenny? Jenny, my love?" Stuart said, dropping down beside her and gathering her up in his arms. "What is it, sweetheart? What's happened?" His voice was filled with alarm.

"My head," she moaned. "Oh, my head . . . it hurts so . . ." She heard Stuart talking to her, but his voice receded and she could no longer make out the words. She squeezed her hands against her temples, trying to still the terrible throbbing that consumed every part of her until there was nothing else.

And then as suddenly as it had come the pain was gone. Gone as if it had never been. Jenny released a deep breath, testing. No, there was nothing left of it.

She opened her eyes and tilted her head back, breathing deeply, infinitely relieved to be released from such vicious torment.

Brilliant pinpricks of light punctuated the blackness.

She had no idea where they came from, only that they were so bright that she had to close her eyes against their cold fire.

When she cautiously opened her eyes again, they were still there. Along with a large golden crescent that hung sideways in the sky.

Jenny cried out in wonder. The moon . . . It was the moon, rising in the night sky. A sky that was filled with stars, thousands and thousands of stars. Brilliant, brilliant starlight that shone down from the heavens.

"Jenny? Oh, God, sweetheart, what's happened to you?" Stuart's desperate words penetrated through her amazement.

"Stars," she choked. "I see stars . . ."

"Stars in your eyes, dear heart? As when you knocked yourself out?"

"No! In the sky. Stuart, I see stars in the sky . . ."

She blinked and turned her head, gazing up at him. And she saw him, his face gazing down at her, even more beautiful than she had pictured it, his dark eyes filled with concern. And love. She saw the deep love in his eyes, and knew that she'd been a fool ever to question it.

"Stuart—oh, Stuart, I can see! I can see you, the moon, the stars, everything. How is it possible?"

"Are you sure?" he whispered, his voice filled with awe. "Are you really sure?"

"I can even see Maddie," she cried as her beloved dog ran toward her, her coat gleaming silver under the starlight, and for the first time Jenny saw how truly lovely she was. "She's beautiful . . . oh, Stuart, everything is so beautiful."

She turned her gaze back to him, only to find that his cheeks were wet. "Don't cry, my love, don't cry," she said, wiping his tears away with her fingers—fingers she would never again have to rely on to describe the world to her. "It's magic."

"It's a miracle," he said, stroking her hair. "Jenny, we've been given a true Christmas miracle this night, praise be to God."

"We've been given two," she said. "We've been given each other as well."

He bent his head and kissed her in answer.

"It is a true mystery," the doctor said, when he'd finished examining Jenny. "I don't know how it happened, although there have been rare documented cases of sight restored after years of blindness. The only thing I can think is that a blood clot might have put pressure on the optic nerve and Miss Bigslow's recent mishap might have dislodged it . . ."

"We don't need explanations," Stuart said, gripping her hand tightly. "We only need to know if the change is permanent."

"I believe it must be, my lord. If my theory is correct, then your fiancée's sight will remain as it is now. It appears to be perfect, and I have tested it every conceivable way I could think of."

"Thank you for your time," Stuart said, smiling broadly. "If that is all, we'll let you get back to your Christmas dinner. . . ."

He pulled Jenny into an embrace as soon as the doctor had left. "In that case," he said, dropping a kiss on her nose, "there is something I want you to see."

He took her downstairs and called her aunt and uncle and every member of the staff he could find, and he led them into the studio. "My good friends," he said, "I have something to show you, but most especially to show my bride-to-be." And so saying, he went to the canvas and pulled the cover off.

Jenny gasped with disbelief. She stood in the midst

of a snowy landscape, one hand resting on Maddie's back. Stuart had painted the landscape with a sure touch, bringing all of its sensual beauty singing to life. She knew that now, for he had taken her out to see it. But *how* he'd painted her took her breath away. She gazed out from the painting, her eyes all-knowing, shining with an inner light she had never seen depicted before by any artist.

The eyes are the windows of the soul, she'd once told him. And he had taken her words to heart, for she knew herself in his portrait of her. Stuart had found his true talent at last and could only rise higher.

She turned to him, able to do nothing but take his hand and kiss its back. Able to say nothing but, "I love you."

Her uncle did much better.

"Genius," he cried, waving his hands in the air. "I've finally found genius!"

And Jenny knew that at last he had. She could see the truth with her very own eyes.

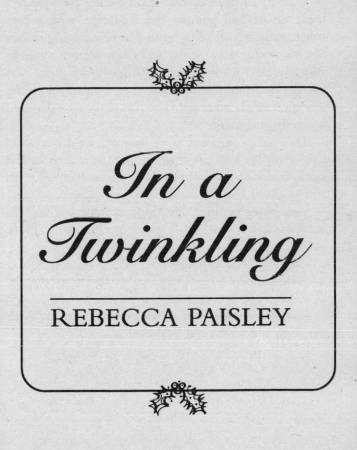

In a Twinkling

REBECCA PAISLEY

Chapter 1

Tymbrook, England

"Would you please cure my hurt reindeer, Sir Doctor?"

Savin barely had the door open when he heard the question, and when he opened it a bit wider, he didn't know which was more astonishing—the girl on the doorstep of his office or the reindeer that stood patiently behind her.

The girl's striking beauty demanded his full attention.

But since reindeer did not live in England, the oddness of the animal's presence also vied for his undivided focus.

"Sir, you *are* a doctor who cures animals, are you

not?" the girl queried. "The lady who lives down the road that leads into town told me you were. I stopped at her house because she has the loveliest Christmas wreath on her door. Fresh greenery bent and braided into a perfect circle and a wonderful red velvet bow that she said she uses every year. She did not tell me a falsehood, did she? You *are* a doctor who cures animals."

Again Savin failed to answer. The girl's voice sang through his mind, unlike any sound he'd ever heard before.

It was the sound of a harp, he thought. No, a flute. Bells and a violin. Or maybe a combination of all.

Music. That's what her voice was. When she spoke, it was as if she were singing a song.

"My reindeer and I," the girl continued, lifting her hand toward her throat, "we have traveled a great distance, Sir Doctor. And to return home, we must travel the same distance again."

She had such tiny hands, Savin mused. Almost childlike, with dainty fingers and perfect little nails. And she possessed a curious accent, one he couldn't place, and her perfume . . . He couldn't think of what she smelled like, either, but it seemed quite familiar to him for some reason.

"But my reindeer cannot possibly make the journey in his condition," the girl went on. "He has torn his back leg on a tree and is bleeding and limping."

Instantly Savin recovered his full sense of awareness, the thought of an animal in pain overcoming every other notion in his mind. The cold November wind ruffling his hair and chilling his neck and arms, he stepped outside, brushed past the girl, and stooped to look at the reindeer's leg.

The beast suffered a jagged laceration down the entire length of his thigh. Although some blood had dried around the edges of the wound, fresh blood continued to soak the reindeer's thick fur.

"You say he tore his leg on a tree? Do you mean a bush?"

"No, I mean a tree. A tree limb."

"But how was it possible for him to tear his leg on a tree limb? Was the tree on the ground? It had been cut down?"

"No, the tree was alive and rooted in the ground, standing up and reaching toward the sky."

Savin straightened, turned toward the girl, and saw tears slipping from her impossibly blue eyes. The droplets shone on her pale face like ice crystals on snow, and as he watched, one tear slid over her mouth and settled on her full bottom lip.

Preferring to deal with animals rather than people, Savin shuffled his feet on the ground and pointed to a stone barn across the yard. "Lead him into the stable. I'll tend to his injury there."

Without a word, and with tears still trickling from her eyes, the girl turned and led her reindeer toward the barn. Savin followed along behind, unable to miss the way the late-afternoon winter sunshine shimmered through her long hair.

Her hair. A peculiar hue it was. Silver, but not exactly. Rather like the color of white lightning, but a tad golden as well, and she wore a long sprig of holly in it as a hair decoration, complete with red berries.

Silver, white, and gold hair? How could that be?

And what of her garments? Green leggings hugged her slender legs, and her feet disappeared into red leather boots that laced up around her slim ankles with what looked to be ribbons of green satin. A green velvet tunic encased her tiny upper torso, its long sleeves edged at the cuff with red lace that fell over half her hands. He'd never seen a woman dress the way she did.

The chilled breeze brought her perfume to him again, and he finally recognized what it was. The scent of peppermint assaulted his senses. She smelled of candy.

Her hair, voice, clothing, scent, and her pet . . . all quite odd.

As he followed her, still pondering all the curious things about her, Savin watched the gentle sway of her hips as she walked toward the barn. It wasn't until he felt a long-forgotten warmth seep through him that he realized the effect her beauty had had on him.

A feeling he hadn't experienced since—

Instantly he snatched the memory from his mind, angry at himself for allowing it to resurface, irritated at the girl whose loveliness had weakened his will to forget.

"Will he be ready to return home by tonight?" he heard her ask.

"Tonight?" he bit out. Frowning, he chose not to answer her absurd question. Her character was as fantastic as her hair, voice, scent, and pet.

"Why do you growl so, Sir Doctor? It was a simple query—"

"We're going to have to restrain him while I clean and stitch the wound." He interrupted her while he collected the medical supplies he would need to dress the reindeer's injury.

"That will not be necessary."

"You don't seem to understand, miss." Fighting to keep his temper, Savin turned up the lamps in the dim barn. "When I begin to sew up the wound, it's going to hurt—"

"He will stand as still as he must while you tend to him, Sir Doctor. I told him to."

Savin turned from the lamp and stared at the girl again. "Look," he flared, "*I* am the doctor here, and *I*—"

"Of course you are the doctor. I would not have brought him to you if I did not believe in your skills. You will cure him in a twinkling. Of that I am most sure."

"My skills won't be of any use at all if he bucks and rears and runs out of this barn, as he most certainly will do if he's not restrained while I sew up his—"

"You do not believe in magic."

He saw that she was looking at him with a mixture of disbelief and sadness. He squelched the urge to address her ridiculous statement. Magic, indeed.

Ignoring the girl, he reached for the four ropes suspended from the ceiling, all of which were fashioned into loops at the bottoms. He would use them to suspend the animal off the floor of the stable and then tie the beast's hooves together so he would be unable to thrash overly much.

"I said you did not need to restrain him, Sir Doctor," the girl said, then took a moment to coo to her animal. "Why do you doubt what I say? I have never told a falsehood in my entire life. I said he would not move, and he will not."

Damn the girl! Fine, Savin thought. Fine. He'd show her how wrong she was. He would dab some water on the reindeer's leg. The animal would react as all hurt animals did when their injuries were handled.

Bending at the waist and prepared to step away quickly, he ran a wet cloth down the edges of the reindeer's injury.

The beast released a long, shuddering breath but made no other movement.

"You see, Sir Doctor? I told—"

" 'You so.' " Savin finished for her. "Well, dabbing a bit of water is one thing, miss. We still have to clean the wound and stitch it."

Still wary that the reindeer might bolt, Savin began to clean the injury thoroughly and then poured a thick liquid made of water, a bit of rum, and an assortment of herbs. He had concocted the medicine himself and believed it helped speed recovery.

Through it all, the reindeer remained absolutely still. Astounded, Savin looked up at the girl and saw a tender smile on her face as she continued to whisper to her pet. She then turned and looked down at him, her lips mouthing a word.

Magic.

Ha! Savin mused. The thread and needle part had yet to come.

As gently as possible he held the edges of the wound together with one hand and inserted the needle into the reindeer's skin. When the beast continued to stand absolutely still, Savin then began the slow and tedious procedure of sewing the wound together, all the while astonished by the uncharacteristic behavior of the animal.

Apparently the reindeer was as atypical as its owner.

When he finished stitching, he applied a soothing salve and then wrapped the animal's thigh with clean white bandages.

"We may leave now, Sir Doctor?" the girl asked.

"You can, but your reindeer can't." Savin took the animal's halter from her hands and led him into a nearby stall filled with fresh hay. "I need him here so I can watch for signs of infection or fever. Surely you can understand that. Can you not?"

"What? But—"

"You want him to get well, don't you?"

She nodded. "Yes. But how long will it—"

"Could be as long as a month, maybe a bit less, depending on whether the wound becomes infected. You saw the cut, miss. It was far more than a mere scratch. It was a jagged—"

"But will he be well by Christmas?"

Christmas. The mere word summoned memories Savin tried to forget every year but never could because of the village's annual holiday festivities. Green wreaths decorated every door in Tymbrook, red bows fluttered from fence posts and windowsills, and the children ran around the streets as if crazed by some mental illness. People held parties and dances everywhere and sang songs that grated in his ears year after year.

As many times as he'd been invited to share the merriment, Savin would have no part of the season.

To do so only reopened years-old wounds, wounds never fully healed.

"Sir Doctor?"

"What? Oh. Uh, that's about three weeks away, isn't it?" he asked the girl.

Her eyes widened with incredulity. "You do not know when Christmas is?"

Savin gathered up his medical supplies and put them away. "No."

"Christmas Eve will arrive in twenty-two days!"

"How wonderful for Christmas."

"You are a very sad man."

When she reached out and touched his arm, he felt warmth trickle through his body. The feeling was not at all unpleasant, but he stepped away from her anyway.

The longer he was with her, the stranger she became. How was it possible for one simple touch of her hand to fill him with heat?

"It is my guess that you do not even celebrate your birthday. Do I guess right, Sir Doctor?"

Deciding it was none of her bloody business what he celebrated, Savin ignored her comment.

"I am not going to leave my reindeer, Sir Doctor. I shall stay here with him."

Savin shook his head. "You cannot stay in the barn.

It's cold in here, and it will be colder still when the sun goes down. There's an inn not far from here. Straight down the road you came into town on. On the right. You will see it as soon as you come upon it. You may stay there and come visit your animal tomorrow."

"Sir Doctor—"

"Now about my fee, miss . . . it depends on how long I keep your pet boarded and fed here, of course, but—"

"I shall stay here with him. I do not wish to go to the inn. And I think you should know that he will not eat the hay in the stall."

Momentarily taken aback by the girl's stubbornness, Savin could only watch as she entered the stall and circled her arms around the reindeer's neck.

But in the next moment irritation swayed through him. "Now, see here, miss. You cannot—"

"He will eat naught but rose petals and sugar cubes and onions, and sometimes he'll nibble at raisins, although they do not set very well with him. Raisins make him sneeze. And a very strange thing about him—"

"Sneeze. Onions? He eats—"

"No, onions do not make him sneeze. Raisins do. That is what I said."

"I know that's what you said, but that's not what I'm questioning. It's the onions—"

"He likes them with the sugar cubes. But of course I have to peel them for him. He does not like the peel. I think it must become stuck in his teeth, for he throws his head and stomps the ground whenever he happens to eat a bit."

"Uh, yes. Of course."

"Would you be so kind as to answer a question for me?"

"What? I—"

"The rose petals he likes . . . well, I find it entirely odd that he will not eat yellow rose petals. He will eat red, pink, coral, white . . . any color but yellow. Why is that?"

Savin could not form a reply. Never in his life had he been confronted with such bizarreness.

"Obviously you do not know either," the girl said. "So it will always be a mystery to me. Would you be so kind as to bring him some onions and sugar cubes? And any color rose petals but yellow? As for myself I think I would enjoy some bread and honey and a cup of hot spiced tea. I have not eaten since this morning, and even then all I had was a tiny cake my grandmother made for me. It was a vanilla cake dusted with cinnamon, and I had it with a drink she makes with oranges and all sorts of berries."

Again Savin felt stunned by her audacity. "I do not run a restaurant here, miss, and I am afraid I cannot allow you to stay in that stall with your reindeer. You may buy your meal at the inn I just mentioned and find lodging there as well."

"I will not leave him, Sir Doctor. He would be horribly upset if he knew I was far away."

The adamant tone he heard in her voice irritated Savin anew. "You will not stay here in this barn tonight, that is the end of it, and my name is not Sir Doctor. It's Dr. Savin Galloway."

"Oh, that is a very nice name. Savin Galloway. My name is Lyrical, and it is with great pleasure that I accept your kind offer to stay in your house with you. Your home is near enough to your barn so that I will not feel far from my reindeer, whereas the inn you spoke of would be much too far away to suit me or him."

Having made her intentions clear, she kissed her reindeer's snout. "You will be comfortable and fine here, my precious. I shall not be far."

She'd know if the animal needed her? In spite of his irritation, Savin almost smiled. Many people thought that talking to animals and expecting them to understand was ridiculous. But he'd worked with beasts long enough to know that while animals might not understand the exact words spoken to them, they certainly understood tone of voice and emotions.

The fact that the girl obviously loved and comprehended animals did much to soothe his annoyance with her.

He watched her exit the stall, noticed the look of relief on her face, and he wondered if the reason why she didn't want to stay in the inn was that she had no money. Her attire was certainly not that of a woman of means.

Actually her attire was not that of anyone he could think of, rich or poor. "Listen to me——" he began, but stopped speaking when he saw the pocket on her tunic move. Something looked as if it were rolling around inside.

"Settle down, Emo," she said, and patted the pocket.

Savin guessed she had a pet mouse or some other tiny creature named Emo in her pocket. "I understand your hesitation to leave your pet. I really do. But you cannot stay—"

"So you have said, Sir Savin, and I have already accepted your invitation to stay in your home. Did you not hear my acceptance?"

"My invitation?"

"It is really so good of you, Sir Savin, to worry about my sleeping in the barn and offering me the warmth and comfort of your home."

"But I didn't—"

"I am very fortunate to have met such a kind man. You may be quite sure that I will do everything within my power to see that your kindness is rewarded."

Before he could argue further, she sashayed out of the barn and headed toward the house.

Chapter 2

Savin started after her but stopped abruptly when he remembered her reindeer had not been watered or covered. Muttering curses under his breath, he dipped a bucket into a large trough of clean, fresh water, then lifted the full bucket over the stall door and set it on the floor. He retrieved a thick, heavy horse blanket from a hook in the wall and tossed it over the reindeer's back.

"I'm really very sorry, but you won't be getting your favorite meal of onions, sugar cubes, and rose petals," he told the animal. "You'll eat that hay if and when you get hungry enough. Now, if you'll excuse me, I've a bit of business to take care of with your very misguided owner."

Satisfied that the reindeer would fare the night well, Savin turned down the lamps and stalked out of the barn toward the house. When he didn't spot Lyrical, he realized she had already let herself inside his home.

The brazen wench! How dare she enter his home! With each step Savin took, his irritation mounted, until by the time he reached the front door of his house he felt true anger narrow his eyes.

He burst inside, uncaring that the door banged into the wall as he pushed it open. He didn't see Lyrical anywhere, but he spied his young niece, Harriet, sitting on a stool in front of the fireplace. Her hands were cupped as if she cradled something within them, and she held them in front of her face.

Wondering if Harriet held the little creature named Emo that had been stirring inside Lyrical's pocket, Savin approached the little girl and looked down into her hands.

He saw nothing there, yet Harriet continued to stare into her hands. Reaching down, he started to take her arm and pull her from the stool, but a musical voice stopped him in mid-action.

"Why do you interrupt her play?" Lyrical asked, standing near the stove with a few potatoes in her hands.

"What do you think you're doing?" Instantly Savin released Harriet's arm and approached Lyrical.

"I thought I would endeavor to prepare a meal with these potatoes I found in that basket over there," Lyrical said, using one of the potatoes as a pointing stick when she indicated the basket that sat on the floor near the wall. "I am not at all accustomed to cooking and really have no notion what to do with these potatoes, but making supper for you and your little girl is the least I can—"

"I don't *want* you to make supper!" Savin took her hand, barely noticing the potatoes drop and roll across the floor. "I *want* you out of my house!"

Intent on making her leave, he pulled her toward the open door. The woman had *no* right to make herself at home in his house, and he'd had enough of her boldness!

But a small body, a little body called Harriet, came between him and the door.

Savin stopped immediately, alarmed by the distraught expression on his niece's face.

Harriet pulled her cupped hands apart but continued to cup her left palm. With her right hand she tried to push Savin back, shaking her head all the while.

"Little girl," Lyrical asked, pulling her hand from Savin's grasp, "what is the matter?"

"Her name is Harriet, and she can't hear you," Savin said, struggling to overcome his impatience.

"She's deaf, and she is not my little girl. She's my niece."

"She can't hear?"

"Well, that's usually what happens when people are deaf." Savin reached down and tried to move Harriet away from the open doorway.

Harriet moved straight into Lyrical's open arms.

"She does not want me to go, Sir Savin," Lyrical announced. "She wants me to stay here with her."

"She's known you for all of five minutes! Why—"

"That is true. But she sees with a child's heart. To a child, five minutes are sufficient. I learned all about children from my grandfather. No one knows them as he does. Harriet likes me and wants me to stay."

Savin could have continued arguing, but the look of hope in Harriet's huge brown eyes told him Lyrical was right. Good God, he thought. Harriet was acting as if she'd known Lyrical her whole life.

He felt a sigh fill his chest. He wasn't certain how to handle the little girl. Never had been, not since his sister had died and left Harriet to him three years ago. So what he did was just give her what he thought she wanted and allow her to do whatever she pleased. She never wanted much, and she didn't do much, so everything usually went very smoothly.

Of course she did have those weeping fits of hers when nothing he thought of to do could console her. He didn't know why she cried like that, wished she wouldn't, but saw no help for it.

He didn't want her crying now either. "Very well,"

he said, finally releasing his sigh. "You may stay, Miss— What is your surname?"

"Lyrical is fine. That is my name."

He was in no mood to press her further. If she chose to dispense with proprieties, he would allow her her wish. He owed the impertinent chit no courtesy in any case. "All right, Lyrical. You may stay here tonight. But tomorrow you move to the inn, and that is my final word on the subject. Do you understand?"

In answer Lyrical only smiled. "Come along now, Harriet. You can watch me peel the potatoes, and we can laugh together too." Taking Harriet's arm, Lyrical led the little girl to the kitchen table and sat her down.

"I told you she's deaf," Savin said wearily. Damn the woman! Was there no getting through to her?

"I know that is what you told me, Sir Savin," Lyrical replied, gathering more potatoes from the basket. "I am not the deaf one. Harriet is."

"And she doesn't laugh."

Lyrical stopped and turned to face Savin. "What do you mean, she does not laugh?"

"Precisely what I said. She doesn't laugh. She's been with me for three years now, and I have never heard her laugh."

"But all children should laugh!"

"Maybe, but she doesn't. Now, if you'll excuse me, I'm going to change clothes."

Lyrical waited until Savin disappeared into the back part of the house before she sat down across from Harriet. For a long while she simply watched the young girl, wishing there were something she could do to make Harriet laugh.

After a while an idea came to her. Gently she laid Harriet's cupped hand on the table. "Emo, dance for Harriet."

"I don't feel like dancing," came a crabby little voice. "I want to go home. I told you you were getting too far away from—"

"We will return soon, and I was just getting ready to turn around and go back home when that tree got in the way. An unfortunate occurrence, yes, but there is naught we can do now but wait. Now, if you do not dance for Harriet, I shall tell Grandfather on you."

His tiny chest rising and falling as he huffed and puffed with irritation, the tiny elf named Emo started to dance on the table.

Lyrical watched as Harriet's eyes began to glow with surprise and delight. In the next moment the little girl smiled, her plump cheeks turning pink with pleasure.

When Savin returned to the great room, he heard a sound he'd never heard before: Harriet's bright laughter.

Chapter 3

Lyrical looked up and saw Savin across the room. She hadn't really studied him before. At first she'd been too worried about her reindeer and then much too preoccupied with Harriet to pay much attention to him.

She paid close attention now.

Firelight glimmered through his wavy black hair, gleamed within the depths of his dark brown eyes, and cast a glow over his sharply defined features. He had a long, straight nose, high cheekbones, and a dimple in his chin. His parted lips were full, and they shone, as if he'd just licked them.

He was very tall, Lyrical thought, broad-shouldered and quite muscled, probably from all the heavy work he did with livestock.

As she continued to watch him, Lyrical felt an unfamiliar happiness that made her smile without knowing why. The way Savin looked just made her feel happy. Plain and simple.

She liked the feeling very much and hoped it would last as long as her stay with him, which would be at least three weeks, for she fully intended to stay with Savin and little Harriet until her reindeer was well enough for the journey home.

And yet . . .

She felt another feeling too. The feeling was quite apart from the feeling of happiness she felt when she looked at him.

It was a sense of worry mingled with sadness, and she realized the feeling came from her suspicions that Savin Galloway was not a contented man.

A bit of magic would remedy whatever sorrows or bitterness that dwelled within him. A pity he did not believe in it.

"Sir Savin?" she called softly, finally noting the dumbfounded expression on his handsome face. "Is something the matter?"

Vaguely he heard her say his name. "She's—she's laughing. Harriet is."

His low voice touched Lyrical's ears like the caress of a sunbeam. "Yes. She is. Does that not make you feel like laughing with her? She might not hear your laughter, but if you laughed in front of her, she would see it and know that you are happy. And I am thinking that you need to laugh as much as she does."

Savin crossed to the table and stopped beside Harriet's chair. With a gentle hand he touched her shoulder, and when she looked up at him, he saw that her big brown eyes were filled with a deep joy he'd never once seen in them before. "What—what did you do to make her like this, Lyrical?"

Lyrical began to peel one of the potatoes she'd found earlier. "I did not do anything," she replied, casting a sweet glance down at Emo, who had stopped dancing and was now standing on the table with his hands on his tiny hips and glaring up at Savin in a most vicious way.

"Then what is she laughing about?" Savin pressed.

He most assuredly did not believe in magic, Lyrical thought. If he did, he would be able to see Emo frowning up at him.

Of course no one had ever been able to explain to *Harriet* about magic, but she knew that what she saw was not ordinary. And she accepted it. So she believed in magic.

"Lyrical?"

"Yes, Sir Savin?" Lyrical replied without looking up from the potatoes.

"I asked you—"

"I know what you asked me."

"Well, answer—"

"I do not choose to answer you."

"What?"

"I do not choose—"

"Why?" Savin yelled.

His shout startled Lyrical so badly that the knife slipped in her hand and cut into her palm. Bright red blood oozed over her wrist, staining the potato she'd just finished peeling. "I'm fine," Lyrical blurted when she saw Emo's expression of horror. She gave the elf a look of warning and attempted to calm his concern. "It is a scratch, nothing more."

"Let me see it." Dragging his fingers through his hair, Savin walked around the table, then reached down and took Lyrical's hand.

"I am truly very sorry," Lyrical squeaked.

"Sorry? For what?"

With her free hand Lyrical picked up the blood-stained potato. "For tainting dinner."

"What? For tainting—"

"Dinner." Lyrical finished for him. "I did not mean to—"

"There's a whole larder full of the blasted things. Almost everyone in Tymbrook pays for my services with vegetables out of his garden, bread out of his oven, or cider from his press. If anyone pays at all, that is."

"Onions too?"

Her question, which he knew she'd asked because of her reindeer, convinced him she wasn't seriously hurt. Indeed, as he examined the injury, he found it to be just as she described: a minor cut.

But he felt obligated to dress her wound anyway. His own shouting, after all, had been the indirect cause of the wound.

He found the supplies he needed in a large leather bag he kept by the door. In little time at all he'd cleaned the small wound and applied a bit of balm to it.

"I would not have cut myself had you not seen fit to yell at me the way you did, Sir Savin. You are indeed a most peevish man at times, aren't you?"

Savin tossed the bloodstained potato into a pail, then washed the knife Lyrical had been using. "I am not peevish, and I am not Sir Savin. I am Dr. Galloway. I told you that—"

"But I am fond of the way *Savin* feels on my tongue when I say it. The feeling is not unlike the way something sugary and soft tastes. You know how soft, sweet things feel and taste upon your tongue."

Savin was about to tell her in no uncertain terms that he didn't give a damn about what she was or wasn't fond of but refrained when he saw Harriet scoop up a handful of nothing from the table and return to the stool in front of the fire. "What in God's name does she think she's holding?"

He followed his niece to the hearth and took her cupped hand.

Harriet tried to yank her hand away, to no avail. Her action only turned her hand over.

"I'm spilled!" Emo shouted as he tumbled down to the braided rug before the fire.

"Savin, no!" Lyrical shouted when she saw him begin to step back. "Do not move! You will smash him!"

Savin turned his head sharply toward her. "Smash him? Smash who? What—"

He broke off when Harriet finally freed her hand from his hold and threw herself to the floor. On her hands and knees she began to crawl around near the fire, looking under a chair, a small table, and then behind the broom that leaned against the wall.

The little girl made deep, hoarse sounds at the back of her throat as she burst into tears.

"Oh, Harriet, do not weep!" Lyrical hurried to the fireplace, knelt on the floor, and gathered the sobbing child in her arms, rocking the small body gently and tenderly. "I promise you on all the miracles in the world that all is well."

Some promise, Savin thought bitterly. Miracles never happened. They were only fantasy, as were magic and whatever other outlandish beliefs Lyrical entertained in her fanciful head. "She isn't going to stop crying for a long while," he said, dreading the coming hours of Harriet's sobbing. "When she's like this, her tears last for—"

"She will cease her weeping in a twinkling." Lyrical

reached out her arm and placed her hand near the
floor, smiling when Emo scampered out from behind
the pile of firewood and hopped into her palm.

"The big brute might have killed me," the elf muttered. "His bootheel came within a fraction of an inch
from—"

"But you are alive and well," Lyrical reminded him.

"I'm alive and well?" Savin repeated. "What—"

"Yes, you are alive and well too, Savin. And now
you will see that Harriet will cease her weeping when I
show her that what she feared was lost or hurt is not
lost or hurt at all."

Savin watched as Lyrical emptied her empty hand
into Harriet's lap. His bafflement deepened when his
niece's forlorn expression died away like a spark in the
wind and a brilliant smile appeared on her little pink
mouth.

Once more he watched as Harriet scooped nothing-
ness into her hands. She then leaned forward to kiss the
air she held. "Lyrical," he said, knowing full well that
Lyrical was in some way behind his niece's strange behavior, "what is she doing?"

"She is kissing her playmate," Lyrical explained, and
sighed. Savin would not understand, she knew, would
not believe.

But Lyrical was not one to lie. Savin had asked a
direct question, and she'd answered it truthfully.
"Harriet wept because she thought that Emo had been
hurt or lost. Now she knows that he is fine, and so
she—"

"Emo?"

Lyrical helped Harriet off her lap, then rose to her feet. "Yes. That is his name, and he is a rascal. It is good that you did not hear what he yelled when you knocked him out of Harriet's hand, for he has the tendency to . . . Well, shall we say he is prone to colorful language when he is angered?"

"Emo," Savin repeated, his gaze traveling from Lyrical's face, down to Harriet, and back up to Lyrical again.

"A crotchety little fellow, to be sure, but his heart is as big as the sky itself. Now that I ponder that, the two of you might be very much alike. But of course only time will tell me if your heart is as big as the sky, is that not true? I must become better acquainted with you before I will know with any certainty."

Before Savin could answer, he saw Harriet kiss the nothing in her hand again. With much effort he managed to keep tight control of his features so Harriet wouldn't notice his anger. Stuffing his hands in his pockets, he walked casually to the table near the stove, motioning with a nod of his head for Lyrical to follow him.

She did.

After making sure Harriet wasn't watching him, Savin asked the foremost question in his mind at the moment. *"What* have you been teaching her? I have *never* seen her act as strangely as she has since you arrived. *Never* seen her—"

"Do not thank me," Lyrical said merrily, waving

away his words with her hand. "I would do no less for any child in the world."

"She is playing with nothing," Savin growled from between clenched teeth. "For that you believe I am thanking you?"

"She frolics with Emo, and he is not a nothing. He is a someone. But hearing such information perturbs you dreadfully because you don't believe in—"

"Because it's nonsense, Lyrical. And I don't appreciate your doing whatever it was you did that made Harriet—"

"Laugh? Cease to weep?"

Her questions silenced him. He snatched his right hand out of his pants pocket and drove his fingers through his hair, unable to think of a single argument that would overcome or even lessen the points she'd made.

She *had* made Harriet laugh. She *had* succeeded in stopping Harriet's tears.

She'd done in a little more than an hour what he'd failed to do in three years.

"Savin?"

His reply was simply to glance into her startling blue eyes. But the longer he looked, the deeper his gaze into them became.

And he found he could not look away. It was as if her eyes possessed some bizarre power over him. First he felt his inclination to look away from them weaken and disappear, and then he knew a potent desire to stare into them for as long as she allowed him to do so.

At that moment Savin realized that Lyrical, whoever

she was and from wherever she came, was unlike any woman he'd ever known.

Or ever would know again.

Chapter 4

After forcing down the worst meal he'd ever eaten in his life, Savin sat down in his big chair by the fire, stretched out his legs, and watched as Lyrical and Harriet washed the dishes together. Their task was quickly accomplished, for Lyrical had used only one skillet in which to prepare the entire supper.

Indeed, Savin had never sampled a fare that consisted of potatoes, carrots, turnips, cabbage, walnuts, and dried fish all mashed together into one heaping pile of thick, sticky mush. While he'd tended to the sick and injured animals he kept in pens in the room he used as a clinic at the back of the house, the daft woman had simply thrown various foodstuffs she'd found in the kitchen into the pan, added water and lard, and pressed it all together with the back of a spoon.

Baked atop the vegetable-fish mixture had been a layer of what Lyrical said was a *delicate* crust. She'd given the chore of making the *delicate* crust to Harriet, who had simply mixed together all the ingredients Lyrical furnished: flour, water, eggs, sugar, and salt.

Savin was no baker himself, but he didn't think there was much wrong with what the *delicate* crust had been made of. The problem, he reasoned, was that Harriet had used a dozen eggs, a cup of flour, several heaping spoonfuls of sugar and salt, and only a sprinkling of water. She'd plopped the gooey mess right on top of the thick, sticky mush Lyrical had been responsible for making, and then the two untutored females had baked the pan of culinary chaos in a hot oven for more than an hour.

The *delicate* crust had come out so hard that Savin had no doubt that if thrown with enough strength, it could have knocked down an oak tree. And the mixture inside the pan had burned on the bottom but remained glutinous in the middle.

Savin hadn't known whether to eat his meal with a spoon or a mallet.

"We are all finished washing the dishes and cleaning the kitchen, Savin," Lyrical announced, drying her and Harriet's hands within the folds of a blue towel. "It would not make you shout at me if I made Harriet ready for bed, would it?"

Savin glanced at his niece, who appeared as though she'd just emerged from a barrel of flour. The little girl clung to Lyrical's legs, hugging her with all her might. She'd been hugging Lyrical all evening, all through the preparation of supper and the chore of washing the dishes and tidying up the kitchen.

Savin couldn't understand why or how Harriet had become so quickly attached to a woman she'd never met.

"Savin?"

"What? Oh. She needs a bath."

"I have already filled the tub I found in her room," Lyrical informed him, picking out a bit of dried egg from one of Harriet's pretty brown curls. "The water was very hot when I poured it in, but it should be perfect for bathing by now. And I added a few drops of vanilla bean oil that I found in one of the kitchen cupboards."

Oh, wonderful, Savin thought. His houseguest smelled like candy, and his niece would smell like a cake.

He was too tired to argue. "Fine. I'll be in to bid her good night in a bit."

"And I shall have her in bed waiting for your night love in a twinkling."

Savin shifted in his chair. He'd never been demonstrative with his affection for Harriet. She hardly responded to the little pats or hair rufflings he gave her. "Uh, yes. My night love."

"That is right. Night love." Lyrical led Harriet toward the threshold that opened into the hall. "Your hugs, your kisses . . . and your prayers that tomorrow and all her days will be filled with every joy," she called over her shoulder as she disappeared into the short corridor.

"I don't like him," Emo declared from within the hollow of Harriet's palm as the little girl walked alongside Lyrical. "He hasn't said a single nice thing to you since we got here. Hard is what his heart is. Hard as rocks and metal and—well, hard like hard things."

Lyrical escorted Harriet into the child's room and began to unfasten the little girl's frock. "He is a sad and angry man, and he does not believe in magic, Emo. You should not dislike someone because he has not the capacity to trust in miracles. If Grandfather had heard you say that, he—"

"Well, he didn't hear me say it, and he won't know I said it unless you tell him," came Emo's gruff reply.

After finishing undressing Harriet and settling the elf on her own shoulder, Lyrical assisted the child into the tub of warm vanilla-scented water. "One day will come when I make good my threat, Emo," she warned.

Emo knew better. Moving into the warm, minty hollow between Lyrical's shoulder and neck, and holding on to a lock of her silken hair so he wouldn't accidentally fall into the tub, he contemplated the young woman he'd known since her birth twenty years past.

Kindness incarnate she was. Sweet as sugar sprinkled from the hand of God Himself.

Leaning to the side, he smoothed his hand across her pinkened cheek. Her skin was soft, but he knew her heart was softer.

The only problem with Lyrical, he mused, was her lack of any talents whatsoever. Her grandparents and all their workers had tried their hardest to teach her whatever abilities they possessed—and of those there were many—but Lyrical had proved inept at them all.

She and the kitchen were not compatible, as that brute of a man in the other room had come to learn tonight. Her grandmother had tried to teach her to sew, and Lyrical's accomplishment had been a haphaz-

ardly stitched–together wad of fabric that was supposed
to have been a new pair of curtains for her grandfather's workroom. The ball of material was now used to
clean the windows rather than hang from them.

Her grandfather's workroom.

Many a wonderful thing happened within the walls
of that large and extremely busy room. It was a place
where wishes and dreams and hopes took shape and
came to life, that main part of the grand old house.

Much to her grandfather's dismay and that of his
multitude of workers, Lyrical had demonstrated no
proficiency there either.

So she spent her days doing whatever it pleased her
to do, whether it was listening to her grandfather's
tales, singing for her grandmother, reading letters, or
playing with the animals with which she kept company, one of which was the reindeer in the stable outside.

But Emo wanted Lyrical to feel needed, as did her
grandparents and all the other workers who lived on
the estate. He gave a small sigh, doing his best to remember the words of her wise old grandfather: *Somewhere in this big and wonderful world there are people who
need and will find Lyrical's hidden gifts. You will see, Emo,
you will see.*

So intently did Emo deliberate upon his thoughts he
failed to keep in mind the fact that he needed to continue holding on to Lyrical's hair. When she leaned
over the tub as she finished rinsing Harriet's hair, he
slipped off her shoulder.

"I'm drowned!" he screamed right before he splashed into the water.

Lyrical let out a shriek of surprise, Harriet laughed with delight, and both reached for the tiny being at the same time.

Hanging on to Harriet's pinkie, Emo came up sputtering water and a few choice words that Lyrical was glad Harriet couldn't hear.

"You know I didn't bring any extra clothes," Emo griped after he'd finished cursing. "What do you want me to do? Go around here naked?"

"I did not bring other clothes either," Lyrical replied.

"But yours aren't soaking wet."

"And yours will dry." Grinning, Lyrical assisted clean little Harriet from the tub, toweled her dry, and dressed her in a soft white nightgown. After settling the sweetly scented child in bed, she placed Emo upon the pillow.

That accomplished, she began to look for a pencil and a sheet of paper on a small desk that sat by the window. She could not find a blank piece. Every sheet of paper she found had one of Harriet's drawings on it. The illustrations of flowers, sunny skies, trees, and all kinds of animals were done in what looked to be charcoal. The rainbows were the only designs she'd painted. Done in bold swashes of watercolors, they were bright and cheerful.

There were dozens of drawings of a woman. Although Harriet had depicted the woman in various positions and clothes, Lyrical knew it was the same woman. There was something about the lady's face. Harriet had managed to make the face the same in each illustration.

Lyrical picked up one of the pretty pictures of the rainbows, then glanced over at Harriet, who was laughing softly while Emo tickled her ear. "Do you know what we are going to do, Harriet?" she asked, uncaring that the child could not hear her. "We are going to give you a new name. From now on Emo and I will call you Rainbow."

"Rainbow," Emo repeated, nodding his little head in approval.

"Yes, Rainbow." Lyrical found a pencil, gathered up all of Harriet's drawings, and returned to the bed to sit down beside the child. There she showed all the sketches to Emo, who, after viewing them all, kissed Harriet on the cheek.

"Very well, Rainbow," Lyrical said, "we are going to write your letter to Father Christmas. I am quite sure he has never received one from you, and I think getting one from you this year will make him very happy indeed. And we'll write it on the back of one of your drawings. He'll like getting your picture too."

"How do you know what she wants for Christmas?" Emo asked, hopping off the pillow and sitting atop Harriet's chest.

"Well, to begin with, I will just write down some of the things all little girls want. Let's see . . ."

She began to write on the back of one of the drawings of the woman Harriet was obviously so fond of. "A doll, a soft doll she can sleep with. A picture book, maybe of castles or seashores or gardens or some such. Some pretty hair ribbons, and a dainty necklace with a heart on it. There. That is a nice list, do you not think so, Emo?"

"What kind of list?" Savin's voice filled the room.

Lyrical turned and saw him standing beside the tub. "I have made Rainbow's Christmas wish list for her. There are many who believe that such a letter must be posted, but that is not true. Once the list is complete, it is instantly received."

Savin wondered if confusion was to be his perpetual state of mind during the time Lyrical was in his home. "Who, if I may ask, is Rainbow?"

"Oh, that is Harriet's new name. Harriet is a much too grown-up-sounding name for one as little as she. She needs to grow into it before it fits her. Besides, she likes rainbows. Have you seen these, Savin?" She held up Harriet's drawings.

Savin didn't bother to look at them. Instead he frowned into Lyrical's eyes. "You are talking to that imaginary friend of Harriet's too? That Emo thing?"

"I—"

"And you're making a wish list for Harriet? To send—"

"To Father Christmas. Yes. So he will know what to bring her on—"

"That is ludicrous," Savin flared. "Not only can't she understand what you're doing, but there is no such thing as Father Christmas!"

Lyrical gasped so deeply and quickly that she fairly

choked. "You are wrong! The wrongest kind of wrong!"

Savin crossed to the bed. "I'm glad Harriet can't hear you, Lyrical. If she could, you'd fill her mind with all manner of nonsense. She's already invented some invisible Emo character, and although I don't know how you got through to her, given her deafness, you *did* have something to do with that. After all, Emo did not exist before you got here."

"He—"

"Do not, I repeat, *do not* attempt to make her believe in Father Christmas, do you hear me? Some imaginary creature called Emo is one thing, but I will not have her waiting for some gift-bearing old man—"

"But—"

"You may sleep in my room, Lyrical," Savin declared, intent on ending the discussion and the evening. "It's down the hall to your left."

It took some time for Lyrical to manage her flustered emotions. Finally, after reminding herself that Savin could not help the way he was, she gave a small nod. "Where will you sleep?"

Savin could tell by the faint hint of sadness in her voice that he'd upset her. But he refused to apologize for making sense. "There's a cot in the room where the animals are. I'll sleep there."

"May I see your sick animals tomorrow?"

Savin shrugged. "If you like. Now, good night. Oh, and for the last time—just so you truly understand— stop teaching Harriet balderdash. I mean what I say, Lyrical. She is *my* niece and under *my* care, not yours."

Lyrical stood and handed Harriet's drawings to Savin, keeping only the one upon which she'd written the wish list. "I find you very lacking, Savin."

Savin could only glare at her for a moment. "And I find *you* very ——"

"You do not lack whatever something special it is that makes me feel happy when I look at you," Lyrical explained. "You possess an abundance of that special something."

"When you look at me?"

Lyrical nodded. "When I look at you, I feel an odd happiness that I have not felt before. It is a very pleasant feeling. The way you look is what brings me the feeling."

The only conclusion Savin could come to was that she meant she thought he was handsome. He appreciated the compliment but wanted no part of what it might lead to.

Women had not been a part of his life for years, and he meant it to stay that way. So far he'd been successful at fending off female attentions with relative ease.

If indeed Lyrical were attempting to attract his interest, she would soon understand the endeavor was futile.

"Lyrical——" he began.

"But," she continued, "you are lacking in happiness and the sweet acceptance of magic. You do not have to remain in such a sad state for the rest of your life, however. You can be cured of your tragic malady. I will do my very best to find a way."

"If I am possessed of any sort of malady, it has nothing to do with my beliefs about magic. It has to do with insanity, a state of mind that you seem intent on pushing me toward."

"That is quite the silliest thing I believe I have ever heard." Harriet's wish list still in her hand, Lyrical bent down and kissed the pretty child. "Sleep well, Rainbow. Dream of happy and nice things. Dream of Father Christmas and all the wishes he can make come true for you. I will see you in the morning. You too, Emo."

"Good night, Lyrical," the elf said. Yawning and stretching, Emo crawled up to Harriet's pillow again and lay down.

Lyrical winked at Emo, then turned to face Savin again. "Good night." Quickly and quietly she left the room.

When she was gone, Savin performed his usual good night action and patted Harriet's cheek. He then moved to turn down the lamp. But before he did so, he thumbed through the collection of Harriet's illustrations that Lyrical had handed to him, finding the trees, the sunny skies, the flowers, the rainbows, and the many drawings of the lady.

Harriet was fond of drawing women. Savin had seen her drawing ladies many times in the past. She really did possess a talent for drawing them, he mused as he examined the lady pictures more closely.

And more closely still . . .

Savin frowned, consumed by bewilderment and disbelief.

That the woman in the pictures was the same woman was clearly evident. Something else was obvious as well: The woman in the sketches was Lyrical.

And Harriet had drawn the portraits before ever having met her.

Chapter 5

Before Savin opened his eyes the next morning, he knew she was there. Lyrical.

The scent of peppermint filled the room.

Slowly he opened his eyes and saw that dawn had barely pinkened the sky. Sure enough, there stood Lyrical, by the window, holding a pitifully thin black cat. She'd removed the animal from its pen and was stroking its bony back.

He took a moment to watch her before letting her know he was awake. The tender light of the early morning shimmered through her hair, making those oddly colored locks look as though they were made of pure silver and gold.

She was really a tiny woman, he mused. Almost fragile-looking, as if a strong wind could shatter her to bits.

His final thought before falling asleep the night before had been of Lyrical. Then he'd dreamed about her. Now she was his first sight this morning.

Harriet's drawings had put Lyrical in his mind to stay, at least until he could make some sort of sense out of how his niece had known Lyrical before meeting her. He wanted to think the whole matter was coincidental, but nagging doubts kept him mystified.

"She won't eat," he said, rising from the bed and stretching out his arms. "I've offered her everything I could think of. I have even tried force-feeding her with a dropper, but everything I managed to get into her stomach comes right back up. I can't find anything wrong with her, though. If I had a sickness to work with, I could try to cure her. But try as I have, I cannot make a clear diagnosis. If she loses any more weight, she's going to die."

Lyrical turned from the window, cradling the cat in her arms as if it were a baby. "Die?"

Savin walked toward her. When he reached her, he took the cat from her arms and held it in his own. Bright green eyes gazed up at him, and he felt his heart being squeezed by the fist of regret. "I found her about a week or so ago. She was obviously homeless. Starving even then. She can't last much longer."

Lyrical watched closely as Savin continued to hold and pet the cat. A deep sadness filled his eyes. A look of helplessness passed over his face.

A wave of tenderness enveloped Lyrical even as the same sorrow he felt touched her own heart.

He loved animals the way she did. He understood their natures, their needs. He might not get along well with people, but he certainly had a way with animals.

"Animals make you happy," she said.

He put the cat back in its pen. "I doubt I would do what I do if they didn't."

"But . . . it must be terribly difficult to lose one," Lyrical whispered.

Savin nodded, opened another pen, and stepped back as a white puppy with black spots shot out.

"Oh, what a dear little thing!" Lyrical exclaimed when the animal went scampering toward her.

"That's William. He belongs to Mrs. Pembers."

Lyrical scooped William off the floor and laughed when he licked her face. "He does not seem to be sick or injured."

"He's not. Not anymore. In fact he's going home today. Mrs. Pembers will be here to collect him in a few hours, and I've no doubt she will pay my fee with something she's baked. Whatever she brings, we'll have for breakfast, so don't bother preparing anything. In fact I'd prefer it if you left the cooking to me from now on."

"But I want to be of some use to you while I stay here, Savin. Cooking is a woman's task—"

"Not if she possesses no cooking skills, it isn't."

Hard pressed to keep hold of the squirming puppy, Lyrical set him back down on the floor. "You did not care for the meal I made last night?"

"I didn't see you clean your plate either."

His answer made her laugh. "My grandmother has done her best to teach me how to cook, but—"

"She failed."

"Well, yes. But it was not her fault. It was mine. I have no talents. Without talents one cannot do very much, do you disagree?"

Savin took a moment to ponder her question. "What do you mean you have no talents?"

"Not in the kitchen, or with sewing, or in my

grandfather's workshop . . . I cannot do anything. Or if I can, I have not learned what it is yet. What was the matter with this little dog called William?"

So intently was Savin concentrating on her comment of possessing no talents, he almost didn't catch her question. "William? Oh. He was hit by a fast-moving carriage on the road outside the village and broke his leg. I just took the splint off last night. There was really no need for him to stay with me while his leg healed, but Mrs. Pembers said she couldn't bear to see him suffering, so she asked me to keep him until he was well."

Lyrical walked over to the row of pens. "And what is wrong with all the rest of these animals?" she asked, looking at two more dogs, another cat, and a fat brown rabbit.

"One dog has an infection in his eye, the other dog needed stitches in his neck after indulging in a fight with a dog three times as big as he is, and the cat is going to give birth. She had a difficult time with her last litter, lost three of the kittens. So her owner asked me if I would assist her this time."

"She—she lost three of her babies?"

Savin watched as the slight smile on Lyrical's soft mouth disappeared and realized she felt the mother cat's loss as if it were her own. "Yes."

Lyrical slipped her hand into the cat's cage and laid her palm upon the animal's swollen belly. The unborn kittens moved against her hand, and she sent a silent prayer to heaven that all the babies would live.

"I'm sure they're all going to be fine this time,"

Savin said softly, knowing exactly what she was thinking. "I will make sure of it." He sincerely hoped he
sounded more convinced than he felt. The truth was
that the cat was going to have another extremely difficult time.

Many moments passed before Lyrical spoke again.
"And when she gives birth, may I watch?"

"Of course."

Satisfied, Lyrical moved to the next cage. "And this
rabbit?"

Savin didn't miss the squeak in her voice. Obviously
the news about the three dead kittens had made her
afraid to hear what he might say about the rabbit. "Par-
asites. But he's on the mend, really. He should be going home to his owner in a few days' time. A lad by the
name of Christopher who has already paid for my services with a cart of firewood."

"You would rather have money than firewood and
the other things with which people pay you?"

Savin crossed back to the window and looked
through the glass. From where he stood, he could see a
few houses down the road.

He sighed. The people who lived in those houses
had little. Many needs but little money. "Of course I
would rather be paid with money. There are many
things I can't buy without it. I'm in dire need of a
horse and wagon, for one. I had both some six or seven
months ago, but they were stolen one night. It's not
that I can't walk to most of the houses or farms where
I'm needed. Nothing around Tymbrook is very far

away. But it's often difficult for me to carry the various supplies I need."

"There is no one at all who pays you with money?"

"A few people manage to see to my fees with coin, but the only person around here of any means is Lord Bleser."

"Lord Bleser?"

Savin finally turned away from the window. When he did, he saw that Lyrical had removed the dying cat from the pen again and was holding the frail animal up on her shoulder and stroking its side. "Lord Bleser is the Earl of Wyldon. His estate is but a short ride from Tymbrook. Lady Bleser owns a trio of greyhounds. One of them needs medical attention every now and again, but none has recently."

Lyrical returned to the window and laid her hand on Savin's upper arm. "You must believe that all will be well, Savin. You are a good man, and such goodness never goes unrewarded. Beneath your blustering exterior there beats a gentle heart. I know this to be true because I have seen how you fret over these animals. And you have Rainbow as well. She is not your child, but you took her into your home, and you have cared for her."

Ill at ease with such tender praise, Savin felt the urge to shrug and walk away.

But the sensuous warmth of her hand and the genuine expression of honesty and interest in her oh-so-blue eyes compelled him to stay right where he was.

Like before, he found looking away from her an impossible thing. But it wasn't only her astonishing beauty that kept his gaze locked with hers. It was that same bewildering yet potent hold she possessed over him. This time he felt it even stronger.

Only barely cognizant of his own actions but led to perform them by a power he found impossible to resist, he leaned down to her, his gaze centered on her mouth.

Then his lips were a breath away from hers.

"Dr. Galloway!" a woman shouted from outside.

A loud knock at the door followed the woman's call. Abruptly Savin straightened, ran his fingers through his mussed hair, and tucked his shirttail into his trousers. "Uh, I—That will be Mrs. Pembers. With breakfast, I'm sure. Where did William go?"

"You were going to kiss me."

Glad for an excuse to avoid answering her statement, Savin began looking around the room. What the bloody hell had gotten into him? He *had* been about to kiss her.

Damn the woman and the infuriating control she somehow had over his senses.

"I will find him, Savin," Lyrical said. "You mustn't keep Mrs. Pembers waiting outside." Quickly she returned the sickly cat to its pen and began seeking and calling the rambunctious dog, which she soon found in Harriet's room. The little animal was sound asleep beside the child.

"This mongrel woke us both up," Emo complained from his spot on the pillow beside Harriet's ear. "Came flying in here and leaping onto the bed like some deranged thing."

"Oh, but he is not a deranged thing, Emo," Lyrical replied, and smiled. "He is only a puppy that Savin has cured and whose owner is at the door with breakfast."

"Breakfast?" At that Emo raced into Harriet's cupped hand and pointed toward the door.

Harriet got out of bed and followed Lyrical into the great room.

"There's the pretty little poppet!" Mrs. Pembers exclaimed when she saw the child. "You know, all of Tymbrook is waiting to see when you will provide Harriet with a mother, Dr. Galloway. True, the woman you take to wife will be Harriet's aunt, but she would be like a mother as well."

Savin resisted the urge to roll his eyes. Nearly every person in the village took it upon himself or herself to remind him that he needed to wed.

For all the good it did them, he mused, somewhat satisfied by the knowledge that their nagging would get them nowhere. He would not marry, and that was that.

Never mind the fact that he'd almost kissed Lyrical a short while ago. That was—well, it was naught but physical attraction. Lust, plain and simple, and regardless of Lyrical's confounded ways of getting around his better judgment, he would not allow himself to fall prey to her mysterious wiles again.

"I appreciate your concern, Mrs. Pembers," he said, tugging at his shirt cuffs, "but—"

"And just who might you be, holding my dear little William, miss?" Mrs. Pembers queried, looking at the woman who'd come into the room with Harriet.

"My name is Lyrical, and I—"

"I'm seeing to her injured reindeer," Savin interjected. "He's out in the barn."

"Reindeer? In England?" Mrs. Pembers thrust a bundle wrapped in paper and string into Savin's hands, then bustled into the house without invitation and approached Lyrical. Upon reaching her, she took careful note of Lyrical's odd attire.

A circus person, she decided. Yes, Lyrical was a member of a circus or some other kind of traveling fair. That explained her strange clothing and the fact that she had a reindeer.

Harriet certainly seemed to like the pretty stranger in town. The little girl clung to Lyrical's leg like a vine. "How long until your reindeer will be well, my dear?"

"About three weeks." Savin, impatient for the woman to leave, answered for Lyrical.

"Three weeks," Mrs. Pembers murmured. Lyrical would be with Dr. Galloway for three weeks. Smiling, she tousled Harriet's hair, then took William out of Lyrical's arms. "Well, thank you very much, Dr. Galloway," she said, turning and walking toward the door again. "William seems to be in fine form."

"Do have a very merry Christmas, Mrs. Pembers," Lyrical called. "And if you have any children, I am sure that Father Christmas will be good to them."

Mrs. Pembers turned once more and stared at Lyrical. The girl was young and beautiful. She'd won Harriet's affection and believed in and enjoyed Christmas as well.

A fine match for Dr. Galloway, who shunned Christmas for reasons no one understood.

And three weeks were plenty of time to fall in love!

"Yes," she said. "I'm sure Father Christmas will be good to us all, Lyrical. Thank you."

"Oh, Mrs. Pembers?" Lyrical called as the woman stepped outside into the winter sunshine. "Would you be so kind as to tell me where I may gather rose petals? Yellow ones will do me no good at all, but any other color would be fine."

"Roses?" Mrs. Pembers said. "It's winter, lass. Look about you. There is nothing in bloom now. Well, cheery-bye!"

"Good day, Mrs. Pembers," Savin said as he shut the door.

"Savin?"

He turned and immediately saw her distress. The word might as well have been etched on her forehead. "Lyrical?"

The memory of his almost kiss still wafted along the edges of her memory, but a more important thought took precedence in her mind. "The rose petals," she squeaked.

"Yes? What about them?"

"He—he must have them, Savin. They are the most important part of his diet."

Dismissing her statement as nonsense, Savin walked to the table and unwrapped the package that Mrs. Pembers had given him. Instantly the tantalizing smells of fresh bread, creamy cheese, and fried sausages permeated his senses.

It was true that he'd rather receive money for his services, but when one was as hungry as he was, one did appreciate such food as that which Mrs. Pembers had brought.

After setting the table, he motioned for Harriet, sat his niece down, and squelched his irritation when she emptied her invisible playmate beside her plate of food. "Lyrical, come eat while breakfast is hot."

"I cannot eat, Savin," Lyrical replied, still standing in the middle of the room. "It would be terribly selfish of me to fill my belly when my reindeer is in the barn starving for—"

"I assure you that when we check on him after breakfast, we will see that he has eaten the hay I gave him yesterday. Granted, as you say, he might not care for it, but hunger will have induced him to—"

"No, Savin. You are wrong. You do not understand. The rose petals are—"

"Very well," Savin snapped, weary of arguing and still less than pleased with himself for surrendering to the temptation to kiss her. "You may feed him some onions and sugar. Surely that will tide him over until you are successful in your search for nonexistent rose petals."

"The big brute is right for once," Emo called from the table, perched on the rim of Harriet's plate with a piece of cheese in his hand. "Onions and sugar will have to do for now, Lyrical. And there is no sense in your going hungry until you find the rose petals. Indeed, if you do not eat, you will be too weak to look for them. Your grandfather wouldn't want anything to happen to you."

Nibbling at her bottom lip, Lyrical acquiesced with

a nod of her head, crossed to the table, and sat down in front of the plate Savin had filled for her. As she picked up her fork, she noticed that Harriet was looking at her with a worried look in her huge brown eyes.

Realizing that her fretful demeanor was causing the child to worry about something she neither understood nor could help, Lyrical forced herself to smile. "Eat your breakfast, Rainbow, and then we shall go to the barn and feed my reindeer some onions and sugar."

"Her name is not Rainbow." Savin stabbed at another piece of sausage and stuffed it into his mouth. "That name—it's not even a person name. It sounds like a name for a calico cat to me."

"It is a better name than Harriet for a child so small," Lyrical said. "I explained that to you last night, Savin. Besides, she cannot hear me call her Rainbow, so what matter does it make?"

Because she'd managed to make a tad of sense, Savin chose to disregard her question. Instead he changed the subject altogether. "Lyrical," he said, "had you ever been in Tymbrook before yesterday?"

She pushed her food around on her plate with her fork. "No. I have never been here."

"Where are you from?"

"From?"

"Where do you live?"

"North of here. Far north of here."

Finishing the last of his breakfast, Savin wiped his mouth with his napkin and sat back in his chair. "Did you happen to notice anything peculiar about Harriet's drawings of the woman?"

"They were nicely done, but I do not see how that would be peculiar."

"They all bear a striking resemblance to you. Indeed striking might not be the word. The woman she's drawn looks exactly like you."

Lyrical ate a piece of bread. "How nice."

"How nice? That's all you can say?" Savin pushed his plate to the side and leaned over the table. "You don't find it at all odd that she drew pictures of a woman she had never met?"

"If I told you what I think, you would only scoff."

"Indulge me. Tell me anyway."

"Magic."

"Magic." Savin curled his fist around his napkin. "And what, might I ask, is the reason for your magical arrival?"

Lyrical smiled broadly. "Oh, Savin, one does not question magic. One simply accepts and is grateful for it."

Savin stood and threw his napkin down to the table. "I wonder," he said, "if I will ever have an intelligent conversation with you."

"And I wonder if you will ever be rid of the sadness and anger inside you that lie in the way of your believing in magic."

Savin stared at her. How had she sensed the bitter emotions he carried inside him? "Only a short while ago you spoke of—You—Never mind. It isn't important."

"A short while ago I spoke of your gentle heart," she said, reading his thoughts. "That is true. But while your heart beats with a wonderful gentleness, your soul is tormented with bitterness and anger. Is what I say not true, Savin?"

"I've a horse to see outside Tymbrook, and then I'll tend to a few sheep nearby. When Harriet is finished with her breakfast, would you be so kind as to help her dress? I need to feed the animals in the pens first, but I shall be ready to leave within the hour."

"You are taking her with you?"

Savin carried his empty plate and his fork to the pan of water that sat on the table in front of the window. "I take her everywhere I go, Lyrical. She's too young to be left—"

"Oh, but I am here, Savin. Can she not spend the morning with me? I will let her feed the onions and sugar to my reindeer, a task I am sure she will find delightful because of the velvety softness of his lips. When he nibbles out of your hand, it is a most wonderful feeling."

Savin's first impulse was to deny her request and take Harriet with him on his rounds the way he always did. But he remembered how bored and restless his niece became at times. He often spent hours tending to sick or injured animals, and there was little for the child to do while he worked. And the long walks to and from the farms made her very weary.

"Very well," he finally said, wondering if Lyrical would soon give him cause to regret his decision. "If all goes well, I should be home by early afternoon. I'll arrive with food, no doubt, so you needn't worry about supper."

When he disappeared into the hall, Lyrical hurried Harriet along with the rest of her breakfast and then washed the dishes. That done, she found and peeled several large onions and filled a bowl with sugar cubes she found in a clay pot in the larder.

After dressing Harriet in a warm woolen dress, she led the little girl out to the barn. "Rainbow, this is my reindeer. You may feed him if you like." She opened the stall door and allowed Harriet and Emo to enter first.

Harriet gasped in wonder when she saw the strange-looking deer, an animal she'd never seen before. Tentatively she stretched out her hand and caressed his ear.

"Oh, Lyrical, he's in a bad way," Emo said upon seeing the animal. He sat on Harriet's shoulder, holding on to her hair. "Look how he's hanging his head. I've never seen him do that before."

The reindeer was indeed hanging his head. "He— he is hungry," Lyrical replied. Fighting back continued apprehension, she reached into the bag that Harriet held and withdrew one of the onions.

The reindeer gobbled it up as if it were the last food on earth. Lyrical then placed another onion into Harriet's hand and watched as the reindeer consumed that one and then another as well.

"Now you may feed him his dessert, Rainbow." Lyrical pointed to the bowl of sugar.

Her eyes still wide with amazement, Harriet fed the reindeer the sugar handful by handful, laughing when the beast's soft lips caressed her palm.

"Onions and sugar are all well and good, Lyrical, but we have to find the rose petals," Emo said.

Lyrical felt her eyes sting. "I know."

"If we don't—"

"I know, Emo." Tears spilled down Lyrical's cheeks. "If we do not, he will die."

Chapter 6

When Savin walked into the house after a long, trying day of working with horses and sheep, the sight that met his eyes created a tempest of emotions inside him.

Confusion.

Disbelief.

And finally anger.

Harriet, wearing a spray of holly leaves in her hair, held her cupped hands in front of her face and was dancing around as if to some grand and glorious waltz.

And she was dancing around a small tree.

An evergreen tree.

A *Christmas* tree.

The tree was decorated with lacy snowflakes cut out of white paper. Strings of red berries snaked through its branches, and at the top was a yellow star that Harriet had obviously painted with her watercolors.

A few other Christmas decorations adorned the room as well. Red candles and bows garnished the fireplace mantel, above which hung a wreath of fresh evergreen boughs. And an array of angels with paper cone bodies, walnut faces, and yellow yarn hair was scattered upon various pieces of furniture.

Christmas had come to the Galloway home.

Savin closed his eyes, damning each memory that flooded his mind. He shook his head and tried to think of other things, to no avail.

Two sets of memories. One from his childhood and one from only nine years past.

Jerome.

Madeline.

Though he'd known and loved them years apart from each other, he'd lost both on Christmas Day.

Now he hated the season with everything that made him what he was, and nothing or no one could ever make his loathing disappear.

Tense with years-old anger, he opened his eyes and threw down into a chair beside the fireplace the packages of food with which he'd been paid for his veterinarian services of the day. "Where is she?" he demanded. "Harriet, where is that insane, meddling woman who—"

He broke off. Bloody hell, he thought. Harriet couldn't hear a word he said. Lyrical had so confounded and angered him that he was beginning to lose his own sanity.

"Lyrical!" He stalked into the back of the house and checked each of the rooms. When he didn't find her anywhere, he realized she was probably out in the barn with her rose petal–eating reindeer.

Refusing to look at Harriet, who he knew was upset

by his irate behavior, he stormed out of the house, headed into the barn, and finally stopped before the reindeer's stall. Sure enough, there sat Lyrical on a pile of hay.

She held the dying cat in her arms, and although Savin couldn't quite understand what she was saying, he heard her murmuring to the pitiful animal.

The sight tempered his fury somewhat, but he still wasn't going to let her get away with what she'd done. "Lyrical, I'd like to talk to you, please." He tried to speak softly, but he still heard a hard edge in his voice.

"Both of them," she whispered. "They both are going to die, Savin."

"You decorated the house without my permission. I know you do not and will not understand, but I don't like Christmas, Lyrical. Moreover—"

"They'll both be gone soon for lack of food. My reindeer because he must have rose petals to survive, and this cat . . . I have been holding her nearly all day. Even when Harriet and I went out and found a nice man to cut the Christmas tree for us, I took this poor little cat along with me. I thought if she received undivided attention, if she were kissed by the magic of love for the very first time, she would want to live and enjoy her life. She's been in her little cage for a while, after all. I understand that you cannot give her constant devotion because you are so very busy with the other animals, but I can, for I've little else to do."

Savin thrust his fingers through his hair. "Are you listening to a word I say?"

Lyrical shifted the cat in her arms so that she could

see into the animal's green eyes. "I even gave her a name so she would feel important. I call her Linda Lime because her eyes are the color of limes."

Savin stared at her. "Linda," he repeated. "Linda Lime." It was the stupidest name for a cat he'd ever heard.

"It is a beautiful name for this dear little cat."

"Linda . . . Never mind that! I asked you a question. *Haven't you been listening to a word I've said*?"

"Yes." Lyrical looked up and met his gaze. "Are you listening to a word *I* say? I do not think so. Because if you were, you would understand that what *I* am saying is infinitely more important than what *you* are—"

"Your reinder is not going to die, and there's nothing more than can be done for Linda Lime. Now—"

"My reindeer *is* going to die. Look at him, Savin. Come in and look at him."

"I already looked at him this morning. I changed the dressing on his leg, and I'm quite sure he's going to be fine."

"Please look at him again."

Savin did as she asked. Not so much out of obedience as to ease her fears so he could talk to her about what she'd done.

Once inside the stall, he grabbed the lantern Lyrical had lit and neared the reindeer. He felt the animal's nose and ears and was satisfied that the beast suffered little, if any, fever.

Still, the reindeer did appear to be in some sort of distress. He was hanging his head low, lower than he had in the morning, and his eyes held a glazed look.

"He did not eat the hay you gave him," Lyrical said, still stroking the dying cat she held in her arms.

"Did you give him the onions and sugar?"

"Yes, but they are not enough. He needs—"

"Rose petals, but not yellow ones." Once again Savin pushed his fingers through his hair. "Listen, Lyrical. I know you believe he really needs those flowers, but there are other foods that we can try—"

"Not for him, there aren't. He is no ordinary animal, Savin. He's—"

"Well, of course he's not ordinary to you. You own him. Owners always think their pets are special. But—"

"I do not say that because he is mine. He is not really mine anyway. He belongs to my grandfather. And what I tell you is true, Savin. He is different in that he is—"

"I do not wish to talk about the reindeer any longer, Lyrical. I came out here to discuss the blasted Christmas decorations you—"

"I did that for Rainbow. She—"

"And her name is not *Rainbow,* dammit!"

Lyrical bowed her head. "She has never had a Christmas. Or if she ever had Christmas with her mother, she does not remember. Evidence of that was that she did not know how to decorate the tree, make the star, or—"

"None of that is any of your concern!"

"Yes, it is. It is very much my concern."

"No—"

"She did not even know who Father Christmas was."

Savin's only consolation upon hearing Lyrical's last statement was that because Harriet was deaf, she couldn't hear and therefore could not believe any explanation about some fantasy grandsir whose only responsibility in life was to fly around the skies on Christmas Eve and deliver gifts to good little boys and girls around the world.

Good God, what a ridiculous tale *that* was.

"I want those decorations out of the house, Lyrical. Tonight. Do you understand?"

"Yes."

"Good." Savin turned to leave the stall.

"I understand, Savin, but I am not going to take them down."

Suddenly it didn't matter anymore that she was holding or loving the dying cat. Savin's rage returned full force. Spinning on his heel, he turned toward Lyrical again. "What did you say?"

Lyrical got off the mound of hay and stood to face him. "I am not going to break her heart and take down the decorations that have made her so happy, Savin. Has it never occurred to you that she has noticed that other houses are decorated while hers never has been? She is deaf, yes, but she is not blind. And Christmas, whether you like the holiday or not, is a time mostly for children, a time when their innocent hopes and fantastic wishes can come true. It is a season for magic."

"Magic." Savin growled the word. "Tell me something, Lyrical. Were you raised in some sort of fairy-tale land? You're a grown woman, for God's sake, yet you—"

"Magic can happen to anyone. Children and adults alike. But only to those who believe in it or at least wish to."

"You—"

"And if you are truly adamant that the decorations be removed from your home, then *you* take them away."

Damn the woman! Savin raged inwardly. He'd tended to her injured reindeer and knew without doubt that she had no means with which to pay him. He was allowing her to stay in his home, and he was feeding her as well.

Not only that, but he'd been putting up with her nonsensical beliefs and outlandish behavior.

Thus far he'd done what he'd done for Harriet's sake. But now, Harriet or no Harriet, he'd had enough.

"Very well," he muttered. "I'll take them out of the house myself, and *you*, Miss Lyrical No Surname from fairy-tale land in the far North, are leaving with them!"

When he left the barn and started toward the house, Lyrical hurried along behind him, apprehension caus-ing her to stumble several times. It wasn't so much what he'd said about making her leave that worried her as it was that Harriet's first taste of Christmas joy was about to be killed. "Savin, how *can* you do this?" she demanded as she entered the house.

"How can I do it? Watch and see!"

He wouldn't do it, Lyrical told herself. He wouldn't. Something would happen to keep him from taking the decorations away.

Something would happen.

She watched as Savin approached the Christmas tree, then saw Harriet's bottom lip begin to tremble. The sweet child might not understand exactly what was happening, but she sensed it was going to be unpleasant.

Quickly but gently Lyrical placed Linda Lime on the pile of packages that lay upon the chair by the fireplace. She then crossed the room to where Harriet stood and took the child into her arms.

"That brute is going to take Christmas away, isn't he?" Emo yelled from within the cup of Harriet's hand.

"No," Lyrical replied firmly. "He isn't. We must believe that something wonderful will happen to keep him from committing such an outrage as taking Christmas away."

As Savin lifted the small tree and its base off the floor, intricately cut paper snowflakes floated down upon his black boots. He shook them off and walked toward the door.

But he stopped before reaching the portal, stopped beside the chair by the fireplace.

In the chair stood the cat, Linda Lime. Frantically, using her claws and teeth, she was tearing open one of the packages of food that Savin had tossed into the chair earlier.

In only a few moments more she began to devour the roasted chicken that had been wrapped up in the package.

For many long minutes Savin simply watched the starving cat eat. And then, softly spoken words began to drift through his memory: *I thought if she received undivided attention, if she were kissed by the magic of love for the very first time, she would want to live and enjoy her life.*

Savin turned and met her beautiful blue gaze.

Lyrical.

The daft woman had made Harriet laugh, had somehow found the way to make the dying cat eat, had almost impelled him to kiss her.

Whatever special something Lyrical possessed, Savin could deny it no longer.

The Christmas tree still in his hands, he walked back to the spot in the room where the evergreen had stood.

And the magic that Lyrical had hoped for happened then.

Savin set the tree back down on the floor. Questions clouded his mind like a swarm of biting mosquitoes. So many that he could not untangle them sufficiently to ask even one.

Time, he thought. He needed time to deliberate upon the inexplicable.

Time to contemplate Lyrical.

"Savin?"

He looked at her again, but a long while passed before he spoke. "You win," was all he said before leaving the house and shutting the door quietly behind him.

Chapter 7

"Who are you?"

Standing beside a fence post in the front yard of the house and staring up at the bright December moon, Lyrical did not answer Savin's question. Instead she moved her gaze from the pretty moon to the glorious array of stars.

"Lyrical." Savin moved closer behind her, so close that he could smell her scent of peppermint. The spicy fragrance mingled with the essence of the wintry night air, and in spite of his less than tranquil state, he admitted to himself that the scent was not unpleasant.

The hour was late, well after midnight. But sleep would not come to him. His mind was too full of questions, uncertainties, and bewilderment to rest.

It had been this way for almost two weeks now, ever since the night he'd left the house after returning the Christmas tree to its spot in the great room. He walked at night now, trying to understand things. All through Tymbrook and even along the edge of the oak forest that surrounded the village. He usually ended up in front of a small stream, and there he'd stay for a while longer.

Watching the moonlit water splash along its course and thinking. Trying desperately to find some logical explanation for the outrageous happenings that had occurred since Lyrical's arrival.

No justification he'd come up with had accounted for the unbelievable events.

So he'd decided that the only thing he could do was ask Lyrical herself.

Tonight.

"Lyrical—"

"He is dwindling, Savin," she whispered. "My reindeer. I just came from being with him. The onions and sugar are keeping him alive, but he—"

"I know." Savin rubbed the back of his neck. He too had become concerned over the reindeer. The animal's leg was healing nicely, but the beast was definitely not well. "Lyrical—"

"I know. You asked me a question." She walked alongside the fence, stopped beside a wooden cart, and turned toward him. "Might I ask you one first?"

Her request entered his mind, but he could not concentrate on an answer. Moonlight and the spill of star glow washed over her. Her extraordinary-colored hair shone even more vibrantly beneath the bright night sky. Her eyes glittered like polished sapphires, and her lips shone as well, as though she'd just moistened them.

Her beauty might as well have been unreal, for Savin had never seen the like in all his life.

He watched her glide her hand along the surface of the fence. The wood was rough and dark; her hand looked so soft and white. Such a contrast was that, a simple one, yes, but one he found oddly pleasing.

She moved like sunlight. Soundlessly, as though guided by the unseen hand of grace itself. It mattered not that she wore the most unfeminine clothing he'd ever seen on a woman. At that moment she seemed the very epitome of femininity.

"Savin? What do you ponder?"

"You."

Lyrical bowed her head for a moment and stared at the shiny pebbles that lay near her feet. "And I you." She lifted her face up toward his. "You have not spoken much during this past fortnight. You stay away working almost all day, and when you come home, you work more and then leave to walk. You are angry with me still? For filling your home with Christmas—"

"I'd be lying if I said no. But I'm more mystified at the moment."

"Oh." Lyrical bowed her head again and moved a few of the pebbles with the toe of her shoe. "I do not know whether to apologize or not. The decorations made Rainbow so very happy, yet they tore at and opened wounds inside you."

"You—" He broke off. "Why do you think they opened wounds—"

"I am not a bad person, Savin," Lyrical murmured, still playing with the little stones on the ground. "I only sought to give Rainbow a bit of joy. A tad of—"

"How is it you know so much?"

"I do not know the reasons behind the pain and sadness inside you, if that is what you are thinking. Why do you not enlighten me?"

Savin stuffed his hands into his pockets. "That is not why I came out here to talk to you."

"But there is no reason I can think of as to why we cannot discuss more than one thing. Unless, of course, you are afraid to."

He frowned. "Afraid?"

"Yes, that is the word I used. It is the proper one, I believe."

"Oh? Well, you believe wrong."

"No, I do not think so."

"You don't even know me, Lyrical." Savin flared. "Therefore, you cannot stand there and make accusations—"

"I already have, but they were not accusations. I only spoke the truth, and you know that full well. You are afraid to talk about what makes you sad and angry. If you were not, you would have already told—"

"I haven't told you because I do not see how anything that has to do with me and my life has anything to do with you."

Playing with the ends of her hair, Lyrical strolled away from the fence, crossed the yard, and paused in front of the trunk of an ancient oak. Leaning her back against the tree, she looked up at the twinkling sky again. "And yet," she said when Savin reached her side, "the first thing you said when you joined me out here tonight was 'Who are you?' "

He saw she was watching him out of the corner of her eye. "What bearing does the question I put to you have on the fact that my past doesn't concern you?"

Lyrical smiled, then laid her hand on the tree trunk and began to pick at a bit of the bark. "You asked who I was. If I answer that question, I must dwell a bit on my own past, must I not? Unless of course you want to know who I am only at this precise second, which is the present but even now is already in the past."

Savin wondered if her daftness was somehow rubbing off on him, for her explanation actually made sense to him. "I'm really quite unaccustomed to speaking of my past. It's—"

"I think you are unaccustomed to speaking at all. Rainbow cannot hear you, so you do not talk to her. It is true that you must discuss certain subjects with the owners of the animals to which you tend, but such discussions usually center upon the pets themselves."

He'd gone outside to talk about *her*, Savin mused, and in only moments she'd changed the subject to him. Well, he didn't care to discuss himself. So he wouldn't, and that was that.

Perhaps the best thing to do would be to forget his quest for answers to the enigma she presented. She would after all be gone as soon as her reindeer decided to get over whatever strange depression he was in. Savin could live with his confusion, curiosity, and astonishment for that long, and once she'd departed, the three states of mind would begin to wane and soon disappear altogether.

"You obviously came out here to enjoy the night air," he said. "Forgive my intrusion upon your privacy and solitude. It's late. I've many things to do tomorrow, so I will bid you good night."

As soon as he turned toward the house and took his first step forward, he felt her small hand curl around the side of his waist. He knew it was coming, that peculiar yet inviting warmth of hers. But this time he was prepared for it. This time he swore it would not weaken his resolve.

His oath melted away in the next second.

Even as he damned her command over his will, he turned back around to face her.

"Savin, tell me why you so dislike Christmas."

He thought her voice as soft as the night breeze.

But the softness of her voice was not going to make him talk about Christmas.

"I imagine your feelings about Christmas and the sadnesses you bear are somehow related, are they not?" Lyrical moved her hand from his waist up to his face and smoothed her thumb over his chin.

He decided that God had never made a pair of eyes such as hers. Surely they'd been created from bits of the azure sky itself.

Of course, just because she had gorgeous eyes, there was no reason to divulge information he did not wish to share.

"Savin, I would not ask these questions of you if I did not care. I do not know for certain if there is any way that I can help you, but perhaps just speaking of them will somehow ease you."

He felt her concern touch him as if it had fingers and hands.

But the caress of her caring was insufficient reason to—

"Jerome," he heard himself murmur.

"Jerome?"

It was far too late to stop now, he told himself. He'd given her a name, and she'd annoy him endlessly if he did not explain. Yes, there was naught else he could do now but continue.

Her hand remained on his cheek, and he felt her thumb still gliding upon his chin. "He was my dog."

"Was." Suddenly Lyrical realized that Jerome was lost to Savin. "I am sorry."

Savin took her hand from his face and held it in his own. "He was only a puppy when I found him, and I was but a child of seven."

"Puppies and little boys: They are like bread and butter, thunder and lightning. They go together."

Savin managed a small smile. "Yes." Her hand still enclosed within his, he began to walk Lyrical around the yard, from one side to the other. He'd have liked to walk around the village but dared not stray too far from Harriet, fast asleep inside the house. "When I found him and brought him home, my parents allowed me to keep him."

Lyrical struggled to keep her emotions balanced, a difficult task since she realized the story she was about to hear was going to be sad. "What did he look like?" she asked.

Savin stopped for a moment and looked down at her. Her features registered a combination of curiosity and dread. He hadn't known her long, but he realized exactly why she felt the way she did.

And her soft-hearted reaction pulled at his own tender emotions, feelings he had not felt toward another person in many years.

"Jerome," he said quietly, "was of such a mixture that even now, as a veterinarian, I could not begin to tell you how many breeds might have created him. He was squat, with a long, bushy tail that dragged on the ground. His ears were small and erect, his snout was long and pointed, and his neck was so short it almost looked as though he didn't have one. Most of him was a tan color, but he had white on his belly and some black on his ears and left hind leg."

Lyrical squeezed his hand. "He sounds beautiful."

"He was. To me he was." Savin paused for a moment, gathering his thoughts and all the feelings that went with them. "He—he was my best friend. For six years we ate together, played together, and slept together. And each day of those years our affection and loyalty toward each other grew deeper."

A cold December breeze whipped past him, but he didn't feel the least bit chilled. He wasn't wearing much in the way of outer wear and could only believe that it was the warmth of Lyrical's sweetness that kept the cold from affecting him.

The thought made it easier for him to keep talking to her. "One morning I took Jerome for a walk through the woods near our house. I was thirteen. The forest was cold and quiet, but then I heard something moving within a nearby thicket. The hair on Jerome's back stood straight up, and he began to growl and snarl. In the next moment a wild boar came running out of the brush. I—I couldn't move. But Jerome could . . . and did. He met the beast head-on."

Savin swallowed then. Even now, years later, the tragedy of that day was horrible to remember. "The sounds that followed: a hideous scream and then the explosion of gunfire. The scream was Jerome's; the gunfire was my father's. The boar was dead, but Jerome was still alive. He lay there on the forest floor, bleeding from where the boar had gored him."

"Oh, Savin," Lyrical whispered.

"I snatched him off the ground and ran . . . ran as fast as I could to where the doctor lived. There was no veterinarian in the town where I grew up, but I just knew in my heart that Dr. Hoffman would know what to do."

When Savin began to walk around the yard again, Lyrical stayed right by his side, still squeezing his hand, still feeling his sorrow and pain. "What happened?"

"There was an evergreen wreath on the doctor's front door. With a red bow and a note attached to it. The note said, 'Gone to London for the holidays. Will return December thirtieth.' "

He began to walk faster, as if speed would somehow outdistance the sadness and he could leave it behind. "I took Jerome home, and my parents and sister and I did the best that we knew how to stop the bleeding. But— but he   Jerome died that night. In my arms, looking up into my eyes, and I knew he was saying good-bye. I knew he was, but I told him over and over again that I would see him again. I promised him. It was the last thing he heard . . . my promise."

Lyrical could barely see where she was going, so blurred with tears was her vision. "You—you said the doctor's door was decorated with an evergreen wreath. Christmas—"

"Years later came Madeline," Savin continued quickly.

"Madeline?" Lyrical asked, confused by his sudden change of subject. "She was another dog you had?"

"No. Madeline—Madeline . . . She was a woman with ebony hair, dancing green eyes, and a sparkling smile. I met her at a parish dance, and after it was over, I knew I was in love with her."

"Madeline," Lyrical repeated. A woman, she thought. Savin had loved a woman once upon a time.

"Yes. Madeline Chatham." Savin finally stopped beneath the towering oak tree. He breathed heavily, but not from exertion. He hadn't spoken of Madeline in many years. Doing so now seemed impossible.

But somehow, from somewhere, came the courage and strength to put words to the memories. "I courted her for three months before asking for her hand. She accepted, and her parents gave us their blessing."

"You were married? I did not know you ever had a wife."

"I didn't. I never have."

Lyrical tensed, prepared for yet another tragic story. "She—she died before the wedding?"

Savin spied a rusty bucket beside the porch steps. He stared at the bucket for a very long while. "She might as well have. She—"

He resumed his walk around the yard, holding Lyrical's hand more tightly than he had before. "We were to have been married in February. In December she— Well, she met someone else and ran away with him. I don't even remember his name. They married on Christmas Day. In London. On Christmas Day."

Before Lyrical could form a reply, she saw a change

come over Savin's features. While his expression had been sorrowful before, it was now tightening with the beginnings of anger. "Savin—"

"*Now* do you know why I hate Christmas?" he barked down at her, stopping suddenly beside the oak tree again. "*Now* do you know why the season—"

"Yes, I understand—"

"Do you really, Lyrical?"

Was he defying her out of anger? she wondered. "I—"

"Two loves," Savin snapped. "The love of my boyhood and the love of my manhood. *Both* lost to me on Christmas Day! And you expect me to embrace the season?"

Her left eyebrow raised high, Lyrical looked straight into the storm in his dark brown eyes. "Yes. I do."

Not having expected the answer she gave him, Savin scowled and stepped away from her. "Oh, really? You think it is that easy, do you? You think—"

"What I think is that you should try to remember the Christmases you had before Jerome was killed. Even the Christmas season during which he died. Before the accident. If you can stand there and tell me in all honesty that you did not love Christmas as a small boy, then I will cease my arguments and leave you be with your bitterness and sorrow."

Savin squared his shoulders. "That was a long time—"

"Yes, a very long time ago. But I know you still have happy memories of Christmas tucked away somewhere within the folds of your heart, Savin."

He looked away from her, refusing to be softened by the gentle, imploring look in her vivid blue eyes. "If indeed I have such memories, I have no wish to resurrect them. I can see no reason why I should."

"No?" Lyrical reached up and locked her hands around the back of his neck. "I can think of one very good incentive. Her name is Harriet, but Rainbow suits her better. Granted, you have your reasons for feeling uncomfortable during this holiday season, but your painful memories are not Rainbow's. Moreover, if you give her her first Christmas, it is possible that the merry season will take on a fresh meaning for you as well. Now, given that, would you deprive Rainbow of—"

"I allowed her the Christmas decorations, did I not? What more—"

"I shall leave the 'more' up to you, Savin. As you said, this is none of my concern."

Her last statement quickly erased his frown. "None of your concern?" For someone who believed the situation none of her concern, Lyrical had certainly worked hard to learn information previously denied to her.

And she'd succeeded. She had pressed for and received every secret he'd been determined to keep.

Three, he thought. The count was up to three now. She'd managed to bring about three things he never thought would happen. Harriet had laughed. The dying cat had eaten. And *he'd* talked of sorrows he'd sworn never to speak of to anyone.

The word *magic* filtered through Savin's mind. Instantly he attempted to kill the thought.

But the notion remained, quiet and unassuming.

Very well, he mused. So he'd thought of magic. It was only a word after all. Just because he'd thought of it didn't mean he believed in it. He could think of dragons and witches and fairies and elves and all manner of other fantastic things. It didn't mean he considered any of them as true.

"Savin?"

Finally he looked back down at her. The mischievous slant of her lips and the bright twinkle in her eyes made him smile back at her.

"You are smiling," Lyrical whispered.

He saw that her gaze settled on his mouth. His own gaze watched her smile as well.

That smile of hers, he thought. Enchanting.

He wanted to sample it. To taste it. To know the flavor of enchantment.

Her peppermint scent floating through his senses, he slipped his arm around her waist and brought her closer. Next to his chest, and he felt her breasts and her legs touch his body.

He felt her warmth steal around him like an embrace from soft and gentle unseen arms.

And then he kissed her.

Her entire body seemed to sigh in his arms. Realizing she had no objections to his advances, he took his fill of her, moving his mouth slightly across hers at first, but then slipping his tongue between her lips and finding yet more sweetness within.

Her sigh became his own, and at that moment he felt his every defense come down, felled by the odd power Lyrical had over him.

He stood before her then a vulnerable man, a naked one, stripped of all emotions and thought save those her nearness had given him.

A delicious contentment ribboned through him, drifting past all memories of Madeline, of holding Madeline, of kissing Madeline.

He could no longer envision ebony hair and dancing green eyes.

Now he could only remember silvery white hair kissed with hues of gold. Now blue eyes blinked in his memory, blue pools that shimmered with joy and caring and gentleness.

He'd sought a taste of enchantment.

He found it in Lyrical's kiss.

And its taste was . . .

"No word," he whispered, his lips moving upon hers. "There is no word to describe it."

She had no idea what he meant, but it didn't matter. The feel of his lips on hers was surely the most glorious sensation she'd ever known. "Oh, Savin, do it again. Kiss me—"

He did, and her fiery response revived yet more of the feelings he'd buried so long ago. Desire caught him unaware, a need so fierce, so long denied, that it was only with the greatest effort that he managed to end the kiss and break the force of the power she held over him.

He said nothing but only took her hand and led her

inside the house and into the hall. There, in the dimly lit corridor, he slid his fingers through her hair and smiled at her. "Sleep now, Lyrical."

Without waiting for her answer, he turned and walked to the room where he kept the animals, where he'd taken to sleeping since Lyrical's arrival.

It wasn't until he lay stretched out in his bed that the realization came to him.

He'd met her in the yard tonight to find out more about her. Indeed, the first thing he'd said after stepping out of the house and finding her standing beside the fence had been "Who are you?"

Instead he'd ended up telling her everything she'd longed to know about him.

The woman called Lyrical remained a mystery.

Chapter 8

When Lyrical walked into Harriet's room the next morning to awaken the little girl, she found only Emo there. The elf was jumping and turning flips on the pillow. "Emo? Where is Rainbow?"

Not having heard Lyrical enter the room, Emo shrieked with surprise, promptly fell off the pillow, and rolled down to the mattress. "You scared me!"

"For that I am truly sorry." Lyrical reached for her tiny companion and slipped him into the pocket of her tunic. "Now, where is Rainbow?"

"He came in and woke her up some time ago. Got

her dressed, and away they went. I do not know where they went or why because he didn't say a word the whole time he was in here. You know, Lyrical, we have been here for almost a fortnight already, and I have yet to see that man show Rainbow any affection. He does not talk to her, rarely touches her, and—"

"*He* has a name, and it is not *he* or *that big brute,*" Lyrical replied as she left the room and walked down the hall. "It is Savin Galloway."

His head poking out of her pocket, Emo did not miss the way Lyrical's voice softened when she said Savin's name. Wondering what her face looked like, he wiggled his upper torso out of her pocket and stretched out his body so that he could see her eyes.

She accommodated him by looking down at him. "Emo, what are you doing? You are about to fall on the floor." With one finger, she pushed the elf back into her pocket.

But he'd already seen her face, her eyes. "Have you lost your mind, Lyrical?" he blasted. "You know we cannot stay here! We have to—"

"What—"

"—go home as soon as—"

"—are you talking about?"

"Him!"

Lyrical entered the great room and quickly collected onions and sugar to feed to her reindeer. "Emo, I've no idea what you are talking—"

"You've fallen in love with him, haven't you? That Savin. That Dr. Savin Galloway!"

"Love?"

Lyrical left the house and started toward the barn. As she walked, Emo clambered out of her pocket, scaled up her chest, and climbed onto her shoulder. Next to her ear and holding onto her hair, he began to rant. "You've fallen in love with him. Don't deny it. I've been around a lot longer than you have, young lady, and I've seen my fair share of the beginnings of love! I've seen the look you have on your face before. I've seen the glow you have in your eyes before, and I've heard that soft tone you have in your voice before. Lyrical, how *could* you let this happen? You know we have to return in only days, yet you have gone and fallen in—"

"Oh, Emo, *look!*"

He turned his head away from her ear and peered into the stall.

The reindeer was lying on the hay-strewn floor, his chest rising and falling so slightly that it almost appeared as though he were not breathing at all.

"Savin," Lyrical whispered shakily. "Rose petals. We must find Savin!"

Emo hanging on to her hair, she raced out of the barn, through the yard, and back into the house. "A note," she panted. "Maybe he left us a note."

Frantically she searched every part of the house she could think of where Savin might have left a note that explained his and Harriet's whereabouts. She found nothing. No note.

But she did come upon something else. In the room where Savin kept the sick or injured animals penned.

The cat. She was about to deliver her kittens.

One look at her told Lyrical something was very wrong.

Harriet's soft, little hand firmly clasped within his large, calloused one, Savin led his niece out of the Fogel barn. Outside, he turned to face Mr. Fogel. "Angel Eyes should be right as rain within a few days, Mr. Fogel. There's really nothing for you to worry about."

Mr. Fogel looked back into the stable, watching as his beloved cow stuck her head out of the stall and chewed the hay he'd just given her. "I do hope so, Dr. Galloway. I know she's only a cow, but . . . I've had her since she was naught but a calf, and she—well, it might sound a bit odd to say, but I do love her."

"Not odd at all," Savin replied. "All animals are lovable. Just keep the infected udders clean, and don't forget to apply the salve twice a day."

Mr. Fogel nodded, then reached down to pat Harriet's shoulder. "She's grown since the last time I saw her, Dr. Galloway. Taking her out for a bit of Christmas shopping now, are you?"

"What? Uh—"

"Have a grand afternoon," Mr. Fogel said. He smoothed his hand over Harriet's cheek. Feeling quite sorry for the deaf little girl whose uncle hated Christmas, he hunkered down beside her and pointed to his cottage. "Listen to me, pretty girl. I believe if you go and knock on my door, Mrs. Fogel will give you a slice of gingerbread. She made some this morning, you know."

"Mr. Fogel, you know she can't hear you." Savin frowned, wondering why so many people, including Lyrical, talked to Harriet as though she could hear them. "She's—"

"Deaf. I know." Mr. Fogel stood. "But she can still see lips moving. So she must know when someone talks to her. Why don't you take her to see Mrs. Fogel, Dr. Galloway? It's long past breakfast, and she might be hungry."

Savin decided that the piece of gingerbread for Harriet was to be payment for his services. Sighing slightly, he nodded and walked Harriet to the cottage. There Mrs. Fogel did indeed give Harriet a slice of warm gingerbread. And to Savin she gave another.

When he'd left the Fogel cottage and was walking down the street in the direction of his own home, Savin wondered when and if he would ever receive coin for payment. It seemed as though he would never have enough money to buy the horse and wagon he needed so desperately.

The thought had barely entered his mind when a shiny black lacquered coach drawn by four prancing black horses came to a halt beside him. The door was embellished with a gold coat of arms, and when it opened, Savin saw Lady Bleser, the Countess of Wyldon, sitting inside.

"Dr. Galloway!" she cried, clutching at her substantial bosom with a bejeweled hand. "I was just on my way to your home to ask you come straightaway!"

"The greyhounds?"

Lady Bleser nodded. "Charles Alexander, George

Randolph, and Mary Frances are all limping, and I am quite beside myself because of it! You know they are my children, Dr. Galloway, and when something is amiss with any of them . . . well, I am just quite beside myself!"

Savin could see that the lady was indeed quite beside herself. Her eyes glittered with unshed tears, and her body trembled. "I'm sure the greys will be fine, Lady—"

"Will you come with me now, Dr. Galloway? In the carriage? Of course your niece may come as well, and I will have you both taken back home when you are finished seeing to Charles Alexander, George Randolph, and Mary Frances."

Savin would never have refused treatment to any sick or injured animal, but he was especially happy to treat the greyhounds. He assisted Harriet into the luxurious coach, sat down beside her, and closed the door. As the carriage rumbled down the street, he thought of the money with which Lord and Lady Bleser would pay him.

"I do hope you will be able to cure my darlings of whatever horrible malady has attacked them, Dr. Galloway," Lady Bleser exclaimed, dabbing at her eyes with a delicate lace-edged handkerchief.

"I feel certain that that will be the case, milady," Savin answered. He sent the distraught woman a reassuring smile, for he already suspected what he would find when he examined her dogs. All three dogs were limping. That alone indicated they'd found and gotten into a thorn patch somewhere upon the vast estate.

A short while later the coach pulled onto the winding pathway that led to the mansion. In front of the
house one of the footmen assisted Lady Bleser and
Harriet out of the carriage, and Savin alighted behind
them. Once inside the elegant home, he heard Harriet's small gasp.

Looking down at his niece, he saw that her face
fairly glowed with amazement. Her bright gaze
touched everything that existed in the grand entryway
from the shining spiral staircase and polished marble
floors to the glittering chandelier that hung on the ceiling above.

She'd never seen such wealth, such expensive things,
he mused. She had no idea that the items she saw were
expensive, of course. But for all their pretty radiance
she certainly had to see them as beautiful.

Harriet had never owned anything in the way of
shiny or pretty, he recalled. She had no way of asking
for such things, and he'd never thought to buy her any.

Perhaps he would. With a bit of the money he made
from seeing to the greyhounds. A little necklace,
maybe, or a few satin hair ribbons.

"Dr. Galloway?"

Leading Harriet along, Savin followed the countess
up the winding staircase and down a long, spacious
corridor. When Lady Bleser turned into a hot and very
humid room, he noticed it was filled with luscious
green plants and a wild and colorful array of various
hothouse flowers.

"This is the conservatory," Lady Bleser explained.
"Charles Alexander, George Randolph, and Mary

Frances enjoy being in here. The plants and flowers remind them of springtime, I think, when all the world is blooming."

"I see. Of course." Biting back a smile, Savin let go of Harriet's hand and approached the greyhounds, all lying on the marble floor in the bright sunlight that streamed through the clear, glass ceiling.

Hurt though they were, the gentle dogs wagged their long, skinny tails when he got down on the floor with them. "There, now," Savin cooed to them. "Let's see what terrible affliction it is that has you feeling so poorly, shall we?"

A quick examination confirmed his suspicions. The dogs' paws were quite wounded with thorns. Some of the spines were large and thick, and others were so small that Savin was forced to use a pair of tweezers to remove them. The procedure on the three dogs lasted for a few hours but was relatively easy to perform.

"Very well, Lady Bleser," Savin said when he had finished removing the thorns and was applying a soothing ointment to the dogs' paw pads. "They'll be fine; really they will. It would seem they trampled through a mass of thorns, but their injuries are really quite mild. Why, they should be up and around in only a bit, actually."

Tears of gratitude and relief in her eyes, Lady Bleser nodded. "I do not know how to thank you, Dr. Galloway."

As he followed her back downstairs, Harriet walking beside him, Savin thought of how the countess could thank him. And when she left him in the grand entryway for a moment and returned with a sealed ivory envelope, he hoped she'd thanked him generously.

But it wasn't greed that compelled him to hope for a nice tidy sum of money. It was need. Of course he realized his payment would not be sufficient to purchase the horse and wagon, but however much it was, was more than he'd had before Lady Bleser had come for him.

Savin smiled all the way home.

Lyrical heard the door open as Savin and Harriet returned. Sweat dripped from her brow, and her eyes stung with fatigue.

She'd moved the mother cat from the pen to the bed where Savin slept, and now she watched as the animal strained to deliver another kitten. The exhausted feline had already given birth to two others, each a terrible struggle to bring into the world and one not faring well at all.

Emo stood beside the ailing kitten, stroking its tiny ears and neck. "He's barely breathing, Lyrical. I think the poor little thing is going to—"

"Don't say that!" Lyrical frowned and wiped her brow with the back of her hand.

"Don't say what?" Savin asked as he entered the room and set down his medical bag. "Who are you talking—"

He broke off when he saw the mother cat on the bed. "Dear God, it's too soon," he muttered as he crossed to the bed. "She's got at least another week and a half before—"

"She did not wait, Savin. She's delivered two. Both times were all but impossible for her—"

"How long has it been since her labor began?"

"Several hours."

"You helped her with both the kittens?" Savin took off his coat and rolled up his shirtsleeves.

"Well, yes. I did not know exactly what to do, but it seemed to me that if I—"

"Whatever you did worked just fine." Savin knelt on the floor beside her and felt the mother cat's belly as she strained with her next contraction. "This one is trying to come out sideways."

Lyrical watched as Savin carefully inserted a finger into the mother cat in an effort to turn the kitten around. "Oh, Savin, doesn't that hurt her?"

"No. The kitten she's delivering is much bigger than my finger." Slowly, and with much caution, he pushed the kitten more deeply into the birth canal, then hooked his finger around the baby's front leg and gave a gentle pull.

He smiled when he felt the kitten's head move up into the right position. "There. Now let's see if the mother can finish the delivery herself."

"Lyrical," Emo said, standing beside the mother cat and watching, "you cannot see what I see. She needs more help."

"What kind of help?" Lyrical asked as she stroked the cat's head.

"I beg your pardon?" Savin said.

"She needs more help," Lyrical answered. "What can you do?" she asked Emo.

Emo watched the mother cat for a moment longer. "She's still having trouble pushing the baby out."

Lyrical saw the cat strain as another contraction ripped through her. "Do something!"

"What?" Savin asked.

"She's still having trouble, Savin," Lyrical explained. "She—"

"You're right." Savin wondered how Lyrical knew about the kitten's struggle but had not the time to dwell on it. The mother cat appeared to be in extreme distress now, and Savin realized that if the kitten were not soon born, its mother would die. "I'm going to have to pull—"

"I'm going to pull the kitten out," Emo announced. He rolled up his sleeves and, as gently as he could, slipped his tiny arms into the birth canal and wrapped them around the kitten's head.

"Yes, pull the poor little thing out," Lyrical said.

"I am," Savin said.

"No, Savin." Lyrical stayed his hand. "It is all right now. The kitten will soon be born."

"Lyrical, what are you talking about?" Savin queried. "You just told me to pull—"

"I know, but it is not necessary anymore." Lyrical watched as Emo carefully began to pull the tiny head. "You will trust me with this, please?"

Savin remembered when she'd told him her reindeer wouldn't move as his injury was being stitched and recalled how she'd somehow coerced the dying cat to eat.

You will trust me with this, please?

He gave a slight nod, questioning himself about whether he'd lost his mind. He was, after all, the animal doctor, the one with all the experience.

Yet for some reason he couldn't fathom, he trusted Lyrical's strange faith.

His trust did not go unrewarded. In the next moment the kitten slipped into the world and began to wiggle upon the mattress.

"I did it!" Emo squealed, his little chest heaving. "I did it, Lyrical."

"Yes, you did," Lyrical said, "and he looks fine. But the other kitten—"

"Did what?" Savin asked.

"Savin, you must tend to the sick one." Lyrical touched the ailing kitten, the second one born. "He hasn't been breathing well."

"I know. I've been watching him." Savin picked up the unwell kitten, held it in the palm of his hand, and began to massage the tiny body. "Sometimes rubbing these little lazy ones gets them to wake up."

Lyrical watched as the kitten began to wiggle and squirm upon Savin's hand. "He doesn't appear to like it."

"He's not supposed to. Being irritated is what's making him come to life."

Lyrical put her arm around Savin's shoulders. "You are a wonderful man, Savin Galloway."

Savin detected a hint of sorrow in her voice and looked into her eyes. Tears shone within them. "Lyrical?"

She wiped at her eyes with the back of her hand.

"It's my reindeer, Savin. He's—he's dying. Like that kitten, he's barely breathing. And—and although you do not believe me, he will not live without the rose petals."

Savin thought of all the things she'd said and done that he hadn't believed.

He thought of many things.

About Lyrical.

Her extraordinary sweetness and gentleness. Her way with little Harriet and the animals. The song of her laughter, the sparkle of her smile and eyes, the warmth that she brought with a single touch of her hand.

He even thought of her outlandish way of thinking. Her whimsical character.

And he thought of what she'd done this afternoon, delivering the kittens when her own beloved pet lay dying in the barn.

From a place so deep inside him that he knew not where it was, a realization came to life.

Lyrical was without doubt the sweetest, most caring person he had ever known.

He placed the kitten next to its mother, who had already begun to clean and nurse her offspring. "There's something I need to do, Lyrical. I'll be back shortly."

After one last glance at the tears in her eyes, Savin grabbed his coat and left the house.

It was a long, long walk back to Lord and Lady Bleser's estate. The whole way there he thought about the horse and wagon he needed so badly.

It would be a very long time before he'd be able to acquire those things.

But rose petals were far more important.

Chapter 9

Emo and Harriet in the stall with her, Lyrical lay down beside her reindeer. She slipped her arm around his neck and did not attempt to stop her tears. The animal's breaths were so shallow and irregular now that she knew in her heart that within only moments he would take his last one.

She had no idea where Savin had gone. He'd left several hours ago. But even if he'd been there, he could not save the reindeer, she knew. Unlike the kitten, the reindeer would not respond to a vigorous massage.

The animal would not live without—

"Rose petals."

Savin's words finished the thought in her mind. Lyrical looked up and saw him standing on the other side of the stall door. "What—"

"I just hope he's not already too weak to eat them," Savin said as he opened the door and walked into the stall.

Lyrical saw that he carried a large burlap sack in his hand. "Savin—"

"Move over a bit, Lyrical," Savin instructed.

She did as bidden and sat up. "What have you in the bag?"

He didn't tell her. He showed her by pouring the sack's contents in front of the reindeer's face.

Lyrical gasped with surprise and joy when she saw hundreds and hundreds of fragrant rose petals flutter to the floor. Pink, red, white, coral, ivory . . . every color except yellow.

"Savin, where—how—"

"That doesn't matter." Savin knelt in front of the reindeer. "Let's get him to eat, shall we?"

Working side by side, Lyrical and Savin pushed the velvety petals into the reindeer's mouth. Harriet decided to help as well and crawled closer. She and Emo both tucked more petals upon the animal's tongue.

"He's not chewing them," Emo said.

"No, he's not," Lyrical answered.

"He's not what?" Savin asked.

Lyrical shook her head. "He is not chewing the petals. He—I— Do you think he is past—"

"Saving?" Savin finished for her. "Not if I can help it. Stay here with him. Keep talking to him. I'll be right back."

Savin stuffed several handfuls of rose petals into his coat pockets and left the barn. A half hour later he returned with a bottle full of liquid and a glass dropper with a bulb at the end.

"I crushed the petals and then simmered them for a bit," he explained. "Whatever properties are in the petals that your reindeer needs are still there but in a form easier for him to swallow."

Quickly Savin removed the whole petals from the reindeer's mouth and then, cradling the animal's head in the crook of his arm, began to feed him the rose water with the dropper.

The reindeer choked and sputtered at first but gradually began to swallow the liquid that trickled down his throat.

Night fell; Lyrical lit several lanterns.

Patiently and carefully Savin continued to feed the reindeer, drop by drop. Two hours passed before the bottle of rose water was empty.

"Now we wait," he said, "wait to see if the rose water gives him enough strength to eat the petals by himself."

Lyrical stroked the reindeer's fur. "And," she whispered, "if he eats, he will grow stronger and stronger. Then—then he can travel? I can take him home to my grandfather? I mean, his leg—"

"His leg is already sufficiently healed."

Overcome with gratitude, Lyrical fairly threw herself into his arms.

So did Harriet.

Harriet's show of affection took Savin aback. The child had never been cold or distant toward him, but she'd never demonstrated her feelings the way she was doing now.

Lyrical. Lyrical had done this.

For the rest of the night Savin held woman and child. Both fell asleep within his embrace.

And when dawn seeped through the cracks in the ceiling and walls of the stable, two momentous things happened.

The reindeer lifted his head and began to eat the rose petals.

And Savin realized he didn't want Lyrical to go. Didn't want her to return to her home, wherever it was. He wasn't at all certain why he felt the way he did.

But he wanted her to stay.

Then he can travel? I can take him home to my grandfather?

Her words swept through his mind. She wanted to go home, to her grandfather.

He had no right to ask her to stay. She had a life somewhere. Family.

Another Christmas.

Another loss.

For the next four days a fresh supply of roses arrived daily from the conservatory in Lord and Lady Bleser's estate. Confused though Lady Bleser had been when Dr. Galloway had returned the money to her and asked for a regular supply of rose petals instead, the kind woman had agreed and made sure that the blossoms were delivered each and every morning.

The reindeer made steady progress toward a full recovery. Not only had the injury to his leg healed properly, but he was eating bag after bag of rose petals.

Lyrical soon realized that she had to return to her home. She'd never known such sorrow could be felt.

"You don't want to leave him, do you, Lyrical?" Emo asked. Perched on her shoulder, he watched as she brushed Harriet's hair in front of the fireplace.

"It doesn't matter what I want," Lyrical answered. "You know as well as I do that I have to—"

"What you *have* to do is far different from what you *want* to do, though, isn't it?"

Lyrical did not answer. Could not. To speak of leaving Savin only deepened the pain.

And there was Harriet too.

Would Savin become closer to his niece? Begin to show her more affection?

Lyrical didn't know. But there was naught else she could do. She had to leave.

When she was gone, it would be up to Savin to see to the sweet child's happiness.

But who would see to Savin's?

"Lyrical," Emo said softly, caressing her cheek, "I've changed my opinion of him, you know. He— well, he's not a brute. You wouldn't have fallen in love with him if he were."

With slow and steady strokes Lyrical continued to brush Harriet's hair. She said nothing until the door opened and Savin stepped into the house. "Savin."

He drank in the sight of her. She looked so pretty there by the fire, with the mellow light dancing through her hair and eyes.

The entire sight he beheld was beautiful, he decided. Lyrical and Harriet sitting in front of the fire together. He could become quite accustomed to seeing what he was seeing now, for it seemed right in some way.

Very right.

"You were gone a long time, Savin," Lyrical said. "Is everything all right?"

"What? Oh. Fine, really. A lot of livestock and pets to see today." He took off his coat and laid it on the back of the chair by the fire. "Seems that half of Tymbrook's animal population decided to become ill or injured."

"Well, you arrived in time to say good night to Rainbow. I was just putting her to bed."

Savin walked to the table and laid down the packages of food he'd received as payment during the day. "Go ahead and get her ready for bed. I'll be right back. I want to check on your reindeer one more time today."

He left the house, and when he returned, he saw Lyrical sitting by the fire again, staring into the flames as if they were the most interesting objects on earth.

"Lyrical?"

Not having heard him come into the house, Lyrical started. "Oh. Savin. Rainbow. She —she fell asleep almost as soon as she crawled under the blankets. She and I had a busy day today. We walked all around Tymbrook, collected pretty rocks from everywhere we could find them, and went fishing. But we did not catch anything."

"I see." He sat down in the chair by the fire. When would she leave? he wondered. How much time did he have left with her? "You've been good for Harriet."

Lyrical smiled. "She's become very special to me."

He wondered if *he'd* become special to her as well. Obviously not, since she was still planning on leaving.

"Savin? Umm, there is something else we did today. Something I could hide from you but choose not to."

"Oh? What is that?"

Lyrical rose from her chair and collected a stack of drawings from within a drawer in the kitchen. "You might be angry at me for doing this, but—well, I told Rainbow the story of Father Christmas."

"You told her? How—" .

"Well, she could not hear me, of course, so I told her through a series of drawings."

Instantly alerted and feeling a tad of irritation prick at him, Savin frowned and leaned forward in the chair. "Let me see them."

She handed him all the drawings except one, which she would show him last. "They're in order. You must look at them in the right succession."

As Savin looked through the drawings, his irritation grew to anger. Deaf though Harriet was, he knew without doubt that she now knew not only who Father Christmas was but also what he did on Christmas Eve.

Some sketches showed him flying in the sky in his sleigh. Stealing into houses. Spreading gifts beneath Christmas trees.

Others showed children waking up in their beds. Running into the room where the Christmas trees stood. Finding the gifts that Father Christmas had left.

Every tender emotion Savin had felt toward Lyrical earlier vanished like a drop of water thrown into flames. Slowly he raised his head and glared at her. "You *know* how I feel about this. *Why* did you—"

"Because Rainbow—"

"Her name is not Rainbow!" Savin stood and threw the drawings to the floor. "The Christmas tree and other decorations are one thing, Lyrical. I indulged you and Harriet and allowed them to stay. But making her believe in some fantasy—"

"But Father Christmas is not a fantasy, Savin!"

"How do you think she's going to feel when she wakes up on Christmas morning and doesn't find her gifts beneath the tree?"

"But she *will*—"

"What did she ask for? From this Father Christmas?"

Lyrical took a few steps backward. She'd seen Savin angry before, several times. But he was in a true rage now.

She handed him the last drawing. On the paper Savin saw sketches of a doll. A picture book. Some hair ribbons and a dainty necklace with a heart on it.

He rammed his fingers through his hair. "I cannot afford these things, Lyrical! You know my clients don't pay me with coin! My only consolation is that she does not know when Christmas Day is. Or did you find a way to make her understand that as well?"

Lyrical chewed her bottom lip and nodded. "I put three beans in a cup, then took them out one by one. When all the beans were out of the cup, I showed her the paper with all the gifts drawn on it. I did that over and over again until I began to see the light of comprehension in her eyes. So, yes, I believe I found a way to help her understand that Christmas is but three days away and that that is when Father Christmas will—"

"Enough! Do you hear me? Enough!" Paper in hand, Savin began to storm around the room. "You've done many good things since you got here, Lyrical, but *this*"—he held out the paper—"*this* negates them all! To build such ludicrous hopes in a little girl's mind, knowing full well that those hopes will be dashed—"

"But, Savin—"

He left the room before she could finish and disappeared into the hall. She realized he'd gone to bed.

Her eyes filled with tears, Lyrical walked into Harriet's room. Staring down at the sweet sleeping child, she felt her tears slip over her cheeks.

"Good-bye, Rainbow," she whispered, bending down to kiss the little girl's forehead.

"Good-bye, Rainbow," Emo echoed. He too kissed the child before hopping into Lyrical's hand.

After one final glance at Harriet, Lyrical quit the room. In the corridor she stared at the closed door at the end of the hall, where Savin slept.

"Good-bye, Savin," she whispered. "Thank you for everything you did for my reindeer."

Emo on her shoulder, she left the house then and crossed the yard to the barn.

In a twinkling, woman, elf, and reindeer were gone.

Chapter 10

Nothing Savin did made Harriet stop crying. When the child awakened and found Lyrical, Emo, and the reindeer gone, she fell to pieces like a shattered crystal.

Nor would she eat. For two days Savin coaxed her with all her favorite foods—meals he'd asked Mrs. Pembers to prepare—to no avail.

Only when she was asleep did her tears cease.

It was during those quiet times at night that Savin thought about Lyrical. Outside in the yard, standing beneath the starry sky, sitting in the chair beside the hearth, staring into the flames, or lying in his own bed where Lyrical had slept, he remembered everything he knew about her.

And pondered the things he didn't.

He berated himself continuously for shouting at her the way he had, deeply regretting the fact that his fury was the last thing she'd seen of him before she'd left.

The house was empty now. Void of all smiles, laughter, song, and joy.

Savin felt empty as well. He missed Lyrical's warmth, the sweet way she had about her. He missed her touch and even the silly things she used to say.

He dealt with another adversity as well. Along with his regret and sense of loss, he struggled with his worry over Harriet. It was not only that the child would not stop crying for Lyrical.

It was that Harriet firmly believed that Father Christmas would come.

The little girl carried around with her everywhere the sketches Lyrical had drawn. She even slept with them.

When Christmas Eve arrived, Savin was at a loss as to what to do. Without money he could not purchase the items Harriet expected to receive the next morning.

In an effort to find the least bit of coin, he went through every pocket of every garment he owned. He searched inside containers in the kitchen, through all the drawers in the house, and even under the beds.

He found naught but a few tuppence and the pocketknife he'd misplaced long ago.

Frustrated and anxious, Savin found the bottle of wine a client had given him months ago and sat down at the small writing desk in his bedroom. There he began going over his accounts, attempting to find at least one person who had yet to pay for his veterinarian services.

There was only Mr. Bish, a ninety-year-old man who owned and loved a very old dog. Savin stared at the man's name for a long while while he drank the wine.

He could not collect from Mr. Bish. The man lived in abject poverty, and what little money he managed to acquire from the parish he needed to survive.

Savin soon finished the bottle of wine. Still sitting at his desk, he picked up a pencil and began to draw nothings on a sheet of blank paper. He drew and he wrote, hardly paying attention to what he was doing, so lost in thought he was.

Finally he laid the pencil down and looked at what he'd drawn and written.

Besides various drawings he'd jotted down a letter. A short note:

Dear Father Christmas,
Lyrical.
Signed,
Dr. Savin Galloway

Savin sighed and pushed his fingers through his hair. Dammit to hell, he was drunk, he decided. The wine had gone straight to his head, and now he was writing letters to some chimerical grandsir.

Still not knowing how he would deal with Harriet's disappointment in the morning, he took off his clothes and went to bed.

God, how he hated Christmas.

Sunlight and a pounding headache woke Savin up the next morning. He wanted nothing more than to roll over and go back to sleep, but he knew he could not.

It was Christmas morning.

Harriet would soon be crushed by the biggest disappointment of her young life.

Savin dragged himself out of bed, got dressed, and walked into the great room. When he did not see Harriet anywhere, he decided she was still asleep.

He was in the process of making a pot of tea when she entered the room. When he saw her head for the Christmas tree, he abandoned the tea and joined her. There, by the tree, he tried to pick her up.

But she squirmed out of his arms and knelt on the floor.

Savin knew she was searching for the gifts she believed Father Christmas had left for her. A sigh gathering in his chest, he reached down to pick her up again.

But he stopped in mid-action.

And couldn't believe what he was seeing.

Beneath the tree lay a pretty doll. A picture book of flower gardens. A substantial supply of multicolored satin hair ribbons. And a dainty necklace with a heart pendant.

Totally astonished, he watched as Harriet examined each of her Christmas presents. "Presents," he murmured. "What, how, where, who—"

A knock at the door interrupted him. He thought about not answering it, but the banging became louder and more insistent.

His mind reeling with bewilderment and incredulity, he staggered to the door and opened it.

There, on the doorstep, stood Lyrical.

"Savin."

Her soft, musical voice drifted through his senses. "Lyrical. She—Harriet—you—gifts—how—"

"Merry Christmas, Savin!" Lyrical threw herself into his arms, nearly knocking him over. "Grandfather got your letter last night, but not until he was well away from home! When your note reached him, he finished his tasks and then came home to get me. I was his last delivery!"

"Delivery?" So confused that he could not keep a single thought in his head, Savin looked down at Lyrical. "My letter? Lyrical, those gifts. Under the tree Harriet found—"

"Well, of course she did, Savin! My grandfather

would not have let her down! Rainbow!" Smiling broadly, Lyrical left Savin standing by the door and hurried to join the little girl by the Christmas tree.

Harriet burst into laughter when she saw the woman she loved and crawled right into Lyrical's lap.

"Lyrical, what—"

"Savin, shut the door. You are letting the cold air in, and Harriet is still in her nightgown."

He did as she bade, then joined her and Harriet by the Christmas tree. "Lyrical—"

"Savin, I could not believe it when Grandfather came home at dawn and showed me your letter. I have never known such happiness."

"What letter?"

Shaking her head, Lyrical pulled out a folded piece of paper from the pocket on her tunic and handed it to Savin.

He unfolded it.

Yet another wave of disbelief crashed over him when he read the note.

> Dear Father Christmas,
> Lyrical.
> Signed,
> Dr. Savin Galloway

"Savin, does this mean you love me as much as I love you?" Lyrical asked softly.

Savin didn't answer. Instead he turned, walked to the chair by the fire, and sat down.

Harriet's gifts beneath the tree.

The note.

How had they come about? What possible explanation was there?

A loud scratch at the door nearly stopped his heartbeat, so intently had he been contemplating. Still dazed
with disbelief, he got up and opened the door, wondering if yet another inexplicable thing would meet his
eyes.

A dog stood outside. He was squat, with a long,
bushy tail that dragged on the ground. His ears were
small and erect, his snout was long and pointed, and his
neck was so short it almost looked as though he didn't
have one. Most of him was a tan color, but he had
white on his belly and some black on his ears and left
hind leg.

Savin's eyes widened. His mouth fell open. "J-j-j-j,"
he stammered.

"Savin?" After taking Harriet's hand, Lyrical led the
child to the door and looked at the dog outside. "A
stray?"

"Jerome," Savin managed to whisper. "The dog.
Jerome."

"Jerome?" Lyrical looked at the dog again. "But,
Savin, you said Jerome was killed when you were a
child. Surely this is a dog that only looks like Jerome."

The dog was Jerome. Of that, Savin had no doubt.
His markings and coloring were all the same, and the
wonderful look in his eyes was the same look Savin had
never forgotten.

A remembered promise came to him then. An oath

he'd made many, many years ago, the night that Jerome had died.

He'd sworn he would see the dog again, had uttered the oath to Jerome right before the dog had died.

He reached down and picked the dog up, whereupon the loving little animal began to lick his face.

The Christmas gifts left beneath the tree, Savin thought.

The note.

Now Jerome.

And Harriet's drawings of the woman, he recalled. The sketches of Lyrical. The child had been waiting for her, he realized. Somehow, silent little Harriet had known Lyrical would come.

Magic.

There was no other explanation in all of God's universe that could explain the things that had happened this morning.

"Lyrical," he said, hearing the shake in his own voice, "your grandfather . . . he is Father Christmas."

She smiled so broadly she felt her ears move. "Yes! He is!"

Before Savin could speak again, he saw something move inside the pocket on Lyrical's tunic. In the next moment he saw a tiny man crawl out.

Harriet reached for the elf immediately, cupping him in her hands and laughing in utter delight.

"Emo," Savin whispered, "that is Emo."

"Hello, Savin Galloway," Emo called out, and waved. "So you love our Lyrical, do you?"

The elf's question prompted Savin to look back up at Lyrical. In her eyes twinkled joy, and on her mouth there shone a smile so beautiful that he was completely mesmerized by it.

She was wrong, he mused, wrong about her lack of skills.

Her natural talents were her abilities to love and bring joy to those around her. She did them well.

He'd never known anyone who'd done them better than she.

"You believe now, Savin," Lyrical pressed, "in magic. You believe in it now."

His gaze still centered on her lovely face, Savin nodded. "I believe something else too." He closed the space between them and felt her special warmth and fragrance drift around him, cloak him like a peppermint-scented sunbeam. "I believe you are the best thing that has ever happened to me. I believe that I love you. That I have loved you since the day you first knocked on my door and asked me to cure your hurt reindeer."

He took her hand. "And I believe, Lyrical, that if you agree to be my wife, I will do everything within my power to make you happy."

Too astounded to speak, Lyrical could only nod. Tears of joy hazed her vision, making it all but impossible to see the man who would soon be her husband.

But it didn't matter. She carried his image in her heart.

And it would be there forever.

"Savin," she finally whispered. "Rainbow . . ."

"Rainbow," Savin repeated. Leaning down, he placed a loving kiss right on his niece's soft little mouth. And then, Jerome still tucked beneath his arm, he put his other arm around Lyrical and pulled her and Harriet closer. "I woke up this morning angry, sad, worried, and not a little frustrated," he explained softly, almost achingly. "Minutes later my entire life changed."

He bowed his head and touched his lips to Lyrical's.

"And it all happened," he whispered, "in a twinkling."

Angels in the Snow

STEPHANIE MITTMAN

Chapter 1

With a fortifying glass of thirty-year-old scotch in his hand, Graham Taylor Trent looked out the window of his lower study. He took a shaky breath as Francine Morrow was helped into the piano tuner's rickety black wagon by her latest suitor, Mr. Milton Beaufort. The pane, festively garlanded for the season, fogged over too quickly for him to be sure, but he could have sworn she was searching the house for a sign of him. Of course, it could have been just his wishful thinking.

"A napkin for your drool?" his brother, Perry, asked, holding out one of the fine damask linen squares Rogers had left next to the cold supper they had requested earlier.

"Am I so obvious, then?" He wondered just what

having Miss Francine Morrow in his house, with her pretty little smile and her happy little voice, had reduced him to, and dragged himself away from the sight of the tradesman's wagon as it sped down Fifth Avenue and was lost in the confusion of New York City traffic.

"I don't know what in the world you see in her," Perry said, shaking his head as he let loose the tiebacks and closed the heavy Friesland velvet draperies against the cold night air. "She's the worst governess you've hired for Gregory thus far, and I can't say her conversational skills at the dinner table have exactly been a boon to my appetite. While I can understand the tuner, not to mention the floor waxer last week and the butcher the week before . . ."

"The worst governess?" Graham asked, unwilling to hear the litany of Miss Morrow's escorts repeated to him yet another time by yet another member of the household or staff. "In what way?" Actually, he rather liked Miss Morrow's handling of Gregory. He wasn't blind to his son's shortcomings, and neither, it seemed, was the boy's new tutor. Whereas Gregory had found it easy enough to push around teachers twice the young woman's age—and three times her weight— Miss Morrow seemed to hold her own with his son.

"Oh, Graham, really!" Perry said, and sighed a heavy, theatrical sigh before perching on the arm of the leather wing chair. "The girl doesn't know an egg spoon from a sugar shell. And worse, she doesn't care. You realize, don't you, that it isn't fair to her or to Gregory to put her in the position of preparing him to assume his rightful place in society when the time comes for him to—"

"He's six," Graham reminded his brother. "I'm grateful he's using any spoon at all, never mind the right one. As I recall, the tutor you hired couldn't even accomplish that." The picture of the previous teacher's face covered with soft-boiled egg was not a pretty one.

"She's peasant stock, Graham. Face it, old boy. She may have managed to get off the farm, but she's still got manure on the bottom of those fine kid boots."

"Peasant stock! An odd thing to say for someone raised by a man who had more ambition than ability and more aspirations than . . ." He shook his head, at a loss for words. "You, dear brother, are a pompous ass, and you know it."

"And you, brother equally dear," Perry said, rising and bowing slightly at the waist, "are smitten!"

"With Miss Morrow? Don't be ridiculous. I'm nearly old enough to be her father." He meant for the idea to sound ludicrous, but supposed his intentions did little to mask the longing he felt—a longing for what he'd never had and doubted he ever would.

"And wealthy enough to build a considerable moat between your heart and her little form, inviting though it might be to you."

The large clock in the hall began to chime. It had belonged to Katherine's grandfather. Graham was sure because, like most things in the house, Katherine had mentioned daily that it signified a heritage to which he could never even aspire. It was one of the many things he did not miss about Katherine.

Often he had wondered if it wasn't some terrible flaw in his nature that he felt no guilt about how easily he had adjusted to his wife's passing. Finally he had reconciled himself with the knowledge that without question, Katherine would have coped quite well had he been the one to have been killed in the derailment. In fact, he doubted she would even have noticed, provided his railroad stock was left intact.

"Aren't you going to be late for Amelia's little soiree?" Perry asked when the clock had finished all its noise.

Amelia's party. He had forgotten it entirely. Well, perhaps not entirely, but not for lack of trying. Compared to the men and women who would be at Delmonico's for Amelia Becquith's get-together, Perry was only an amateur ass. After all, Graham and his brother had been mere imitators. Their father had barely been able to scrape enough together to keep them both at Deerfield Academy, where they had been expected to make the right connections and to find their way into the upper classes. And they'd done it, too.

Done it all. Graham had made their fortune and Perry had managed it. Graham had married well and Perry, well Perry had formed several important, albeit discreet, liaisons.

"I think I'll pass tonight," Graham said, stretching and affecting a yawn. "Turn in early."

"Amelia won't like it, and neither will her father," Perry warned. "These are perilous times, financially. And appearances are everything. I don't think—"

Graham held up his hand. All his life he had done what was expected of him. With his business success, he'd been able to take his father from the jaws of poverty and deliver him to the steps of one of the finest mansions on Fifth Avenue. But a Hunt-designed house within a stone's throw of the Vanderbilts and Sloans and Shepherds hadn't been enough. So he'd married Katherine Proctor and linked his name with one of the finest families in all of New York. Still it hadn't been enough.

Even on his deathbed, his father had continued to give instructions and make demands. Graham had met them all; if he couldn't give the man love, at least he could give him obedience.

Two months after his father's death, he and Katherine welcomed into the world the requisite son.

He'd thought his father's death would end it, but Katherine had taken over where Richard Trent had left off. There were all the trips, always without Gregory. There were the parties, the associations, the endless obligations. He'd met them all; truly, if he couldn't give his wife love, the least he could give her was obedience.

And now of course, there was Perry. Perry who managed his finances and his life.

"I'm tired," Graham said, tucking the bottle of scotch under his arm as he headed for the door. "Much too tired for roistering, or for Amelia and her father. Or . . ."

He waved over his head without turning around, then switched the bottle to his right hand. With his left he fumbled amid the ridiculous evergreen boughs with which Mrs. Rogers had decorated the marble staircase that led to the second floor until he finally located the banister and then more or less hauled himself upward.

First he'd check on Gregory. Then perhaps there would be a moment for his dreams.

She'd gotten home too late. First Mr. Beaufort had insisted on taking her dancing, something that a man of his considerable weight and lack of skill should endeavor to avoid in the future, as certainly she would, and then his carriage had gone and thrown a wheel in a nearly deserted section of Central Park.

While losing a wheel did not appear to be a particularly unusual occurrence for Mr. Beaufort, as he had three spare wheels stored in the back of his truck, he did seem to find it very surprising when she demanded that he find help to fix it immediately so that he could return her to the Trent home.

And now here she was, barely able to keep her head up, trying to set a good example for a rebellious, fractious, arrogant six-year-old who had egg running down his chin.

"You might make good use of that napkin so handily set beside your plate," she suggested, slipping her feet out of the carpet slippers she had hastily put on and resting them on the fine Axminster rug beneath them. Heavens, but she had worn her feet to the bone last night, wearing out the bottoms herself and leaving the tops for Mr. Beaufort and his inimitable dancing skills.

"It's already soiled," Gregory said sullenly, removing the cloth from beside his plate and dropping it to the floor. "I need a clean one."

"Oh, perhaps Miss Morrow can help," Perry Trent suggested, while the boy's father bent down to retrieve the napkin, a grimace on his face. Really, she could hardly be held accountable for the boy's poor manners. She'd only been at this position for the better part of a month. And frankly, if this was what private tutoring was like, it wasn't any more to her liking than the public school at which she'd started the year.

Maybe the truth was she didn't like children. Wouldn't that be just dreadful? A teacher who didn't like children? She'd grown up the baby in a family of six, and rather preferred to be the one being spoiled than the one who had to do the spoiling. Especially when it came to Gregory, who quite obviously was spoiled enough.

Or maybe the truth was that she just missed home. Missed her brothers and sisters and a bed that was truly her own. Missed stringing cranberries and popping corn and assembling baskets of bounty for the less fortunate of her neighbors. The Trent house might have all the trappings of Christmas, but there was some indefinable something missing, some feeling that all the fancy glass ornaments from Woolworth's couldn't replace.

A breeze eased the pain in her feet just as Graham Trent returned to an upright position with a very surprised look painting those aristocratic features of his. His Adam's apple bobbed furiously as he stared at her while absentmindedly handing the napkin back to his son.

"Problem?" Perry Trent asked his brother. Graham Trent shook his head and gulped his orange juice in one swig.

He wasn't particularly handsome, not that it mattered. Looking like a Greek god would only serve to make the impossible all that much more unbearable. No, Graham Trent had the kind of face that revealed everything the beholder was required to know. His grooming indicated his wealth, two wrinkles in his brow spoke to his seriousness, and his direct gaze underscored his honesty.

After her first interview with him at the Columbia School for Teachers, she'd gone as far as to allow herself a small fantasy—imagining him a possible husband and herself as lady of the house. After all, he would certainly be considered a good catch by those who were fishing.

Oh, the trolley ride uptown had been a good time for imagining. But then she'd seen the house. A true mansion, and he quite rightly the lord of it. Not that he'd done or said anything at all to make her feel uncomfortable, but Sissy, who had raised Francie from birth after their mother had died, had always told her that the truest sign of a person's good breeding was his ability to make everyone feel welcome in his presence.

"I'll get it," Perry Trent offered rather quickly when Gregory once again threw down his napkin.

For the second time she felt the cool air waft under the table and wiggled her toes wishing there was a pond nearby in which to dunk her aching feet as she'd done after so many dances back home in Van Wert, Ohio.

Perry Trent came up red-faced and rang for a maid. When Daisy came running hurriedly in, he requested a fresh cloth for the tyrant and then turned to Francie.

"Too much dancing?" he asked, his glance darting to his brother.

Now why would he . . . her feet! The fork she was holding—she hoped to God it was the right one—clattered noisily against her plate.

"Nothing like—" Perry Trent began, but was interrupted by Gregory yelling, "Don't touch me!" and swatting at Daisy as she tried to wipe at the egg on his face.

"—a nice quiet—"

Mr. Graham Trent, having followed his orange juice with a healthy gulp of water that obviously went down the wrong way, began to cough hard enough to make the crystal glasses on the table sway and clink against one another.

"—breakfast."

"Only my father can touch me," Gregory told Daisy. "And only when I say so."

"Perhaps Miss Morrow can help? Maybe you could aim some of that charm that seems to so enchant grown men toward my nephew there," Perry Trent said. "Or maybe we Trents are just immune to that sort of thing."

She thought that Graham Trent's eyes were going to pop out of his head. Truly she did, as he choked on his water and glared at his brother and wiped the egg off his son's face all at the same time. He really was much too nice a man to have to tolerate such unsociable behavior from everyone around him.

"Bite your tongue," Graham Trent mumbled in his brother's general direction.

"But it's so much more fun when someone else does it," Perry Trent answered. "Don't you think?"

He was looking at her, waiting for an answer, when Graham Trent stood up and pulled his son's chair from the table. "You will finish your meal in your room, young man, since you are not fit company for those around you." He turned to his brother. "I could say the same to you, but I don't think it would do any good."

Gregory refused to get up from his chair, crossing his hands over his chest until his father tried to lift him, then grabbing onto the edges of his seat and kicking his feet out in his father's direction.

Francie had three brothers, but one would have been enough to know that Gregory hit his mark when Graham Trent grunted and turned away from the table, his back hunched, his breath short.

"Position is everything, I always say. Perhaps Miss Morrow can help," Perry Trent suggested one last time, his eyebrows raised, his smile wide.

Heavens, but they all gave him a difficult time!

"Of course I can," she answered as sweetly as she could, knowing full well Perry Trent's meaning and choosing to ignore his implication. "I'll take Gregory up to his room."

"Thank . . ." Graham Trent's voice came out in a squeak and he cleared his throat, then spoke over his shoulder. "Thank you, Miss Morrow. That would be helpful, indeed."

He really was quite the gentleman, Francie had to admit as she pulled his son up the stairs, prying the boy's clawing little fingers from one baluster and gaining a step before starting the process all over again.

And he *was* trying to do something about Gregory, who, at that very moment, was attempting to get his teeth around her hand.

"I've been fighting little boys since long before you were born," she warned the child. "I haven't been bested since I was three."

She put her hand on Gregory's head in an effort to keep him at arm's length. It would have worked, too, if he hadn't stomped down on her instep, grabbed at the lovely greenery Mrs. Rogers had festooned the staircase with, and begun to run.

It was instinct that made her reach out and trip him. Instinct that got the better of her in what was a dirty fight, but still she should have known better. Not only was she older, wiser, and employed by the boy's father, but she certainly should have guessed that he'd cry the minute his father could see him and she'd be out on her ear.

Which was, of course, just what he did. He screamed bloody murder, taking breaths to yell "Ow!" and groan "Oh!" between howls.

"Stop it this instant!"

Graham Trent was on the steps before he finished his

edict, and she expected he'd give her about as long to pack. "Anyone who can make so much noise can't be all that injured," he said impatiently to his son. "But I can—and I will—remedy that if you aren't in your room and silent by the time I count to ten."

She supposed she looked as surprised as Gregory.

"His uncle used to do the same thing," Mr. Trent explained once Gregory had sullenly made his way to the top of the stairs. He extended a hand to help her stand. "Don't know how many whippings I had to endure because he was the loudest crybaby in Boston."

For a six-year-old boy who couldn't weigh more than ten pounds for every year, he had surely done a good job on her foot. It felt like when Henry the cow had decided her milking days were over and wanted to be sure Francie knew it.

"Are you all right?" Graham Trent had one hand under her elbow and the other was smoothing the hair out of her face. She was close enough to see for the first time the flecks of brown in his green eyes. She was close enough to smell the eau de Pinaud that her own father used to wear. He was taller than she thought. And freshly shaved. And his front tooth was chipped a tiny bit.

Somewhere a doorbell rang.

"Someone's at the door," Perry Trent sang out.

Graham Trent's hold on her didn't waver.

"Your son's crying his capacious lungs out," Perry said in the same sing-songy voice, crossing the front hall on the butler's heels.

Up so close, she realized that Graham Trent's hair

was really auburn, not brown as she'd thought, and there was just a touch of silver in it.

"Oh look, Rogers! Flowers! But whoever are they for?"

Neither one of them looked away.

"Miss Morrow! And they're from Milton Beaufort! Isn't timing just everything in life? Shall I read the card?"

Francie knew just what it would say. *Thank you for a lovely evening. Looking forward to seeing you again.* The men she stepped out with were nothing if not predictable. She could count on them to always say and do the right thing. Never a surprise to make her blood rush or her heart pound.

"Shall I?" Perry Trent asked again.

Graham Trent's eyes rose to the ceiling, where he studied the mistletoe that hung several feet above their heads, while Francie felt the color rush to her cheeks.

"I'm going out," Graham Trent said rather suddenly, and let her go so abruptly that she had to grab the banister to keep her balance. Little spikes of evergreen needles pierced her palm and brought tears to her eyes so that his retreating figure was just a blur.

"But—" she began to say as he hurried down the steps and grabbed his hat from the hall tree beside the door.

"Graham, boy—" Perry Trent started, then jumped when the door slammed behind his brother.

"Wasn't he . . ." she said slowly, coming up beside Perry to peer out the window.

"Yes, he was," Perry answered as they both stared at

the man sliding down the icy steps without a coat and wearing his bedroom slippers.

Chapter 2

Two nights later Graham sat in the darkened study, awaiting Francie's return. It was foolish of him, worrying about her as he was, but he couldn't seem to help it. He didn't like the idea of her out with tinkers and tradesmen. With a sigh he admitted to himself he would be no happier to see her leave on the arm of one of his business associates either. She was a young woman from the country, alone in a big city full of snake-oil salesmen with fancy names like Rockefeller and Morgan and . . .

"Mr. Trent? Are you in there?" The light from the hall lit a path across the room to find him in the leather chair by the window.

"Yes, Rogers, I'm here."

"Are you quite all right, sir?" asked the silhouette in the doorway.

"Yes, Rogers, I'm fine. You can go on to bed now. Thank you. And tell Mrs. Rogers I enjoyed tonight's rack of lamb immensely."

"Yes, sir," Rogers said, hesitating. "And it was mutton, sir. But I'll tell her." Again there was a pause, then Rogers cleared his throat and asked, "Is there anything I can do, sir? You don't seem quite yourself."

Rogers had hit the nail on the head. He wasn't himself. Not at all himself. Not since that moment on the stairs when he had tucked Francine Morrow's silky blond hair behind her tiny shell ear and felt the blood in his veins warm to boiling. Even the icy December wind on his front steps hadn't cooled his excitement. Nor had two days of polite conversation at the table complete with Gregory's howls and Perry's jibes.

For the first time since he was six years old and wanted a store-bought Snow King sled like every other kid on the block, Graham Trent wanted something. Something purely and selfishly for himself. Not wealth for his father, not prestige for Katherine, not acceptance for Perry, nor security for Gregory, all of which he had willingly provided.

No, he wanted Francine Morrow, in his home, in his arms, in his life, and—God help him—in his bed.

And while he had managed to get all those other things for everyone else, Francine Morrow wasn't something he could buy. At least, he didn't think so, although he just might be willing to pay whatever the cost.

"Sir?"

"Rogers! I forgot you were there. Go on, now. Go to bed. Truly I'm all right."

"Mr. Perry is still out, sir. As is Miss Morrow. I'll just . . ." Rogers's voice trailed off as he backed away from the door.

"Mr. Perry has a key, and I believe that's Miss Morrow's carriage, now," Graham said, feeling his heart race as outside a horse and wagon slowed at his front door. "I'll get the door."

"As you wish," Rogers said, bowing slightly. "I'll just say good night then."

"Good night," Graham answered absentmindedly, taking up a position against the wall that allowed him to view the goings on outside without being seen. He craned his neck and after a while began thrumming his fingertips against his thigh. Did that Beaufort fellow have the back of one of those highly skilled hands on Francie's porcelain cheek? Was he touching her exquisite softness? Had his hand strayed to her collarbone? Beyond? What strings was he working on now? What tune was he hoping to play?

Graham wet his lips with his tongue, feeling thirsty for the taste of Francie on his mouth. Parched, like a man who had been too long on the desert, he burned with the need to know her sweetness. The thrumming fingers balled into fists and pounded against his thighs. What the devil was taking them so long to say good night?

He was kissing her. Graham knew he was. What else could they be doing in that wagon all this time?

She would have to leave his employ. A loose woman was certainly not an appropriate tutor for his son. Could he look at those lips across the table every day and know they had touched another man's?

The door to the carriage swung open with such force that the vehicle shook and he could hear the smack of wood on wood as it hit the body of the coach. Francie half tripped, half fell, out of the wagon, missing a step and pulling at her cloak as she hurried away.

"Ever!" she yelled loudly enough to rattle the windowpane in front of him.

She was pounding at the front door before he was halfway across the foyer.

"Rogers! For the love of God, let me in!"

He threw open the door and she raced past him, turned after a moment as if she had just realized it was he and not Rogers who had answered the door, and stood staring at him, tears glistening on her cheeks.

"Oh! It's you. I . . ." Flustered, she covered her mouth and cheeks with two gloved hands.

"I'll kill him," Graham said, surprising himself as much as he apparently shocked her.

"Don't you move!" he shouted out the open door. He tried to think, but those moss green eyes of hers were overflowing and it muddled him. "A sword! I . . . no, I don't have a sword. How absurd. A pistol! I need a pistol."

He dashed to the hall tree and opened the small drawer, flinging mittens and gloves in every direction.

"I don't have a pistol, do I?" he asked, turning to find a small smile tipping the corners of her slightly swollen mouth.

She shook her head and shrugged questioningly. "I don't know, but it doesn't seem likely that you would. Besides, I don't think it's really necessary. I think you've scared Mr. Beaufort halfway home."

She pointed toward the doorway and Graham could see that the curb in front of his house was quite empty and deserted.

"I suppose I shouldn't ask what's wrong," he said,

closing the door as silently as he could and coming to take her wrap. "Nor should I mention that you are very lovely looking with a little color in your cheeks."

"Oh, I'm sure. And with a red nose, to boot. Serves me right for listening to the wrong sister. Della always said let a man nibble your pinkie and soon you'll have him eating out of your hand. But Sissy always asked what fellow it was that could eat just one pig's knuckle and not want to devour the whole ham hock."

He had no idea who Sissy was, but knew she was probably right. Especially when it came to Miss Francine Morrow's hocks . . . knuckles . . . pinkies . . . oh, Lord!

He took a deep breath and tried to compose himself. Miss Morrow was shaken enough and didn't need his lack of composure further rattling her poor nerves. He studied the delicate features warmed to pink by her embarrassment and felt his anger simmering yet again. Anger, and something more.

"You are all right, aren't you?" he asked, bending his knees slightly to get a good look at the moss green eyes which were studying the blocks of marble that made up his foyer floor. "I mean, he didn't hurt you, or . . . I could have used my fists. I used to be quite the fighter. Had to be. I should have just dragged him out of that wagon and . . ."

She put one of those tiny, precious hands on his chest and he was sure that his heart stopped. "I'm fine. My pride's a little tarnished, but the Reverend Winestock always warned me about pride going before a fall."

He wasn't sure he was still breathing.

"Is something wrong with Rogers?" she asked, removing her hand and restoring his lung power.

"Rogers?"

"Yes. He's usually the one to get the door." She looked at him intently and then bit her bottom lip. He felt his head cock slightly to the side and his mouth open ever so slightly. "You weren't waiting up for me, were you?"

The moss green eyes got even bigger. He had to shake himself to respond. "Me? You? No . . . no. Oh no."

She grimaced slightly and he realized that even frowning she had the most beautiful mouth he had ever seen. He tried to concentrate on her words, but her tongue distracted him.

"What? I beg your pardon?"

"I said that I'm a big girl now and that you needn't wait up for me like I'm some errant child, Mr. Trent. You'll no doubt have enough years of that which Gregory reaches adolescence. Between my father and five older siblings, I think I've had enough looking after. I hardly need another guardian."

"Mm," he agreed, stung by the fact that she saw him as some father figure. He wasn't *that* old, after all. Sarcastically, he said, "Tonight obviously proved you can take care of yourself."

"Well," she conceded with a shrug. "At least I'm not much the worse for wear. Sissy always says you learn more from your mistakes than your successes."

"Who is this Sissy?" he asked, leading her toward

the stairway and sitting down on the third step. "She sounds like a very levelheaded woman. You don't suppose she'd mind if I never availed myself of Mr. Beauford's services again, do you?" The third step put her breasts at his eye level. He wished she'd sit beside him, but her standing there wasn't exactly torture. Or was it?

"Oh no, I don't think so! And Sissy's my oldest sister, hence the name. My mamma died when I was born, and Sissy raised me. Me, and all my brothers, and my sister Della, and most of my nieces and nephews, and Noah's girls, and now she's got a couple of her own."

There was just him and Perry, and of course, Gregory, left to the Trent family. His mother had walked out on his father when he and Perry were little more than babies and had moved in with some stockbroker who owned a four-bedroom townhouse on Thirty-fifth Street. One of the first things Perry had done when the brothers' investments had begun to turn a profit had been to help the man lose everything he owned. Graham hadn't lifted a finger to stop him. Family meant nothing to his mother, and that feeling was her lasting legacy to her sons.

"Big family," he said, hoping to prolong the conversation.

"Yes," she said, examining fingernails that reminded him of little opals. "Well, there are a lot of us, but somehow it still seems small. I mean they're all practically within shouting distance of each other, and for good times or bad they all manage to fit into our parlor." She got a faraway look on her face and added, "Guess it's Bart's parlor now."

"Miss them? Bart and Sissy and the rest?" Christ, what was happening to him? Now he didn't just want her. He wanted the whole damn family.

She chewed at her lip and sat down on the step next to him. "Well, this time of year is always hard. Sissy makes such a thing out of Christmas, making us all gifts, and oh, the baking! Nobody makes plum pudding like Sissy. And hot milk with honey, and Santas in the Snow for all the children—"

"Santas in the Snow? Is that like those angels where you fall down and wave your arms?" He'd done that! Maybe it was a hundred years ago, but he'd done that. Cold snow on the back of his neck, creeping up his pants leg, between his mittens and his coat. He shivered at the memory.

"No, they're cookies. Cookies all decorated like Santa and walking across fields of pudding, and every now and then there'd be a present that fell from his sack, and Samuel and James, those are Della's boys . . ." She fell silent and wrapped her arms about herself as though she felt a sudden chill.

"What about Samuel and James? What do they do?"

She swallowed and stood up, smoothing her skirts and blinking rapidly. "They used to fight over Santa and . . ." She shook her head sadly. "Samuel died three years ago. Choked to death in front of all of them. A holy terror one minute, and . . ."

She shrugged and put one hand gingerly on the banister, then lifted her skirts slightly with the other.

From where he sat he could see the top of her boot and a small bit of stockinged leg. He'd have given his house, his fortune, anything he owned, to be able to reach out and touch what wasn't even an arm's length away.

"I think I'll just go check on Gregory," she said, unaware of what she was doing to him, of how she twisted his insides with new feelings so foreign to him he couldn't even give them a name. "It's been a long time since I kissed a little boy good night."

His head was sweaty, as she expected it would be, with little dark curls clinging to his forehead. At her touch he opened his eyes and blinked up at her.

"It's dark," he said.

"I didn't mean to wake you," she said softly. In his nightshirt, its ruffly collar framing his small face, Gregory had a vulnerability that his little combination suits hid in the light of day. "I just wanted to say good night."

"I don't like the dark," he said, peering around the dim room, whose only light came from the open doorway.

She knew better than to ask him if he was afraid. Boys never admitted fear beyond the age of three or four. "Would you like me to stay a little while?" she asked. "Until you fall back to sleep?"

"You don't need to," he said, pulling the covers up tighter against his chin.

"Would you mind if I did?"

"I guess not."

She decided to press her luck, her thoughts still on Samuel, who would have been just about Gregory's age had he lived. There was still James, Samuel's twin, but none of them, most especially James, had ever been quite the same. "I surely am tired," she said, stretching. "Would you mind if I sat down on your bed?"

She hadn't been home since Samuel's death. Hadn't taken a child in her arms, hadn't shared a bed with a sibling or a niece or a nephew.

Gregory looked at her suspiciously. Finally he shrugged, albeit reluctantly, and moved over slightly to make room.

"Thank you. I surely would like to tell someone a story," she said. "Okay?"

At his nod, she puffed the pillow up behind her head and got comfortable. "Once upon a time there was a family with no mama and a very sad papa."

"Like mine?" Gregory had turned on his side, and was resting his hand on her arm.

In truth, she had intended to tell him one of the Morrow family stories that Sissy used to tell her—a tale in which one or the other of the Morrow children triumphed over adversity and found happiness. But looking down at the boy next to her, his head drooping against her arm, a lump formed in her throat.

Somehow amid all the luxury of the Trent mansion, she had lost sight of the fact that Gregory had a great deal less than other little boys. He had no mama, and no brothers or sisters to fill the aching void that Francie knew so well. She reached out and gently ruffled his hair.

"And there was a little boy with dark curly hair and big brown eyes and a smile that could light up a room as dark as this one."

"But the boy wasn't happy, was he?" Gregory asked sleepily.

"No," Francie agreed. "He wasn't."

"Because nobody liked him."

"No, nobody did. At least not very much." She put her arm around the boy and pulled him closer against her. "But that was because he didn't know the secret."

He pulled back from her embrace a little so that he could look up at her. In the darkness they couldn't see very much, and she wondered if he could even see her reassuring smile.

"The secret?"

"Yes. The secret to being liked. And if I tell you, you must promise to keep it to yourself until Christmas, or the spell will be broken. Do you think you can do that?"

"When is Christmas? Is it very far away?" His head lay innocently against her breast and she wondered about his mother. Had she held him like this? Did he miss her terribly? He seemed like the kind of boy who had always been alone.

"A little more than two weeks," she answered. "Not very long, really. Unless you're waiting for something wonderful. Are you?" she asked, stalling for time.

"For Christmas? I want the same thing I always want. Someone to play with. What about the secret? Can you tell?"

"Well, I think that you just might get your Christmas wish if you keep this secret close to your heart. Ready?"

He nodded. Her mind raced ahead. What would Sissy tell him? What had she no doubt told Samuel and James and probably Francie herself?

"Well," she drew out slowly. "The secret is . . . to be liked you must be likable. That's it." She smiled at her cleverness in the dark, quite pleased. Much more satisfied apparently than Gregory was.

"But that's not a secret," he whined.

"Well, the special power comes from not telling anyone," she added, groping for a miracle recipe that she hoped would satisfy him. "You just do things that people will like you for and magically, by Christmas, they will."

"Like what? What could I do?"

Heavens, but Sissy would be proud of her!

"Well, you could say nice things, like telling your father he looks handsome, or your uncle that he's very clever. You could tell Mrs. Rogers that you like her applesauce . . ."

"That's all?"

"Oh!" she said, getting caught up in the spirit herself. "We could make presents, like we did back home—special things that no one else in the world could give the people we love!"

"And that would make them like me?" Gregory asked, catching her enthusiasm.

"Better," she said, kissing him on the top of his head. "It'll make *you* like you! Now quick to sleep. We've got a big day tomorrow."

The boy snuggled up against her. After she'd hummed every carol she could remember, she felt his full weight against her side and realized that he'd fallen back to sleep. As gently as she could, she extricated herself from his embrace and stole quietly from the room, glancing over her shoulder once more at the little boy in the bed who looked liked none of her nephews and every one of them at once.

"You were very good with him," a deep voice whispered once she was in the hall and the door was closed behind her.

Startled, it took a moment for her eyes to adjust to the bright light only to find Graham Trent studying her. With his top two buttons open she could see the same dark curls which capped Gregory's head dusted his father's chest. He looked older than the men she'd met in New York—older and wiser.

"And what do you want for Christmas?" he asked, leaning his shoulder against the wall and pushing a stray lock of her hair out of her eyes.

"Me?" she asked. *I want to be with my family—people I can trust, people I can love.* "Oh, I suppose a piece of Sissy's plum pudding would make me happier than just about anything."

"And a Santa in the Snow?"

He was standing so close to her that she could hear his breathing, smell the faint odor of pipe tobacco that clung to him, see each and every whisker that painted his chin so black. Why had she never liked the dark coarse hair on a man's face or chest before? Why had she never noticed how very manly a dark curl by the collarbone could be?

"Oh, at least one," she agreed. "And what about you? What do you want for Christmas?"

He placed his finger against her lower lip as if to silence her. Very quietly he whispered, "It's too soon to ask, Francine Morrow. But you'll be the first to know."

"But perhaps Gregory and I could make it," she suggested, anxious to have some ideas to give the boy in the morning.

"I think perhaps you could," he said cryptically without telling her what.

Down below somewhere the door opened and closed. Perry Trent's voice spiraled up the staircase. "I'll just go up and find him. I'm sure he hasn't retired yet."

He took the steps two at a time, judging from the leap he made when he reached the top.

"Oh. There you are." He took in the two of them and despite the fact that they had jumped apart at the sound of his voice, Francie knew they must look guilty of something. Thrusting out her chin, she reminded herself that, regrettably, there really was nothing to feel guilty about.

"I've brought Amelia and her father home with me," Perry said to his brother. He looked at her and then waved his hand as though he were casting, or breaking, a magic spell. "So consider this party over. You must come down right away, Graham. They've arrested President Keeney of the Commercial Bank and stocks are falling faster than snowflakes!"

"Oh, is it snowing?" she asked inanely, as if that mattered when a bank was on the verge of collapse.

"What?" Perry asked her, treating her like the fool she most certainly was.

"Snow," Graham Trent repeated as though there was nothing else in the world that concerned him. "Is it snowing, she asked."

"Yes, it's snowing," Perry said impatiently. "It's snowing drifts of debt out there, now come on downstairs. I promised Amelia . . ."

Francie didn't hear the rest of Perry's words. Her eyes were locked on Graham's as he descended the staircase with his head twisted back toward her.

She could swear that his eyes said *snow angels in the morning*. But she must have been mistaken.

Chapter 3

It had snowed on and off all the next day, and the one after that. Graham had been too embarrassed to ask Miss Morrow to somehow enjoy with him the white blanket that was falling one tiny flake at a time. And so he had just watched it pile up and cover the city with its magic.

Now, as dusk began to fall, through his bedroom window he could just make out the figures of his son and Francine Morrow making their way up to the corner on Fifth Avenue. Cloaked in a navy coat and bonnet, she had several packages in her left hand and Gregory's hand in her right. Big clouds punctuated the air above them as they spoke to each other, making them look like the Sunday funnies awaiting the dialogue within the speech balloons.

When the carriages had passed and it was safe for them to cross the street, Gregory climbed atop the mound of collected snow at the corner until he was nearly as tall as the woman who still held his hand, her arm raised above her head now in order to keep him steady. Graham watched in awe, or was it envy, as Gregory plucked the hat from her head and then took off on the top of the snowbank with Miss Morrow chasing him.

When she finally caught him, only a few steps away from the staircase that led to his front door, Graham waited for her to deliver to Gregory the scolding that he deserved. Instead he saw her tweak the boy's nose and draw an imaginary line vertically over his head as if he had scored a point over her.

Not a second later she scooped up a handful of snow and squeezed it into a ball, hurling it out of Graham's line of vision.

"Hey!" His son's voice carried up through the cold clear air and straight into Graham's room.

Miss Morrow's laughter followed it, finding the way to his heart. *Francie,* he thought, and tasted the word with silent lips.

Nearly falling down the marble stairway in his haste, he hurried to the front door, grabbing a scarf along the

way. He could show those two something about snowball tossing. He'd been the first boy chosen for the
army in more snow battles than he could count.
Funny, he hadn't thought about that in years. When he
remembered Deerfield he invariably recalled feeling
separate and apart from his wealthier classmates, but on
a snowy field of battle he had always been welcome.
He had forgotten that.

"Oh, my!" Francie said, nearly tumbling through
the doorway as he yanked the big door open in hopes
of joining them. "Thank you!"

Both her cheeks were aglow with the cold, and one
temple bore a bright red circle where apparently she
had been hit by a good hard snowball, the remains of
which were still clinging to the pale blond curls that
framed her face. If she weren't smiling so broadly and
laughing that musical little laugh of hers, he would
have been alarmed by her injury.

"He got you, did he?" he asked, pointing toward
her forehead only to find that he was still holding his
muffler, which now dangled without purpose over his
arm.

"Oh, but I gave as good as I got, didn't I?" she asked
over her shoulder, looking rather smug for a tiny little
thing with bits of ice melting in her locks and running
down her pretty face.

Gregory tromped in noisily, his heavy boots smack-
ing the black-and-white marble floor, all the while
complaining that Miss Morrow wasn't supposed to get
him back because she was a grown-up and worked for
his father, no less. Then he reached back and dug a

mound of snow out from inside the collar of his cashmere coat.

Miss Morrow, as if the reminder of her place in the household had just hit home, looked contrite.

"Hm," Perry said, gliding in from the dining room and surveying the puddle that was rapidly growing beneath the two as the melting snow ran down their coats, fell in clumps from their boots, and turned the foyer into a treacherous pond of icy water. "Now all we need is a cat."

"Pardon?" Graham wasn't following anything but the movement of Francie's hands as she unbuttoned her coat, sliding the black horn button through the slit that rested between her breasts.

"It appears we already have what one would have dragged in."

She slipped off her coat, and Graham took it from her, along with her packages so that she could assist Gregory with his outer things.

"I don't need your help," his son said sullenly. So far, Graham had seen no indication that the little talk Francie had had with the boy had done any good. Of course, he had been foolish to expect that it would. She wasn't, after all, some kind of angel. With her skin glowing and the last of the snowflakes melting in her hair, she only looked like one.

"I never thought you did," Francie said evenly, still crouched in front of Gregory and obviously awaiting his permission to assist him. "I was just trying to be nice. You might give it a try."

There was something about the tone in her voice—

not quite a dare, but more than a suggestion—that seemed to leave everyone waiting for something wonderful to happen. But since it was up to Gregory, and Graham's son was anything but cooperative, nothing wonderful did.

"All right, then," Francie said, getting to her feet. "Have it your way, but don't expect miracles if you aren't ready to meet them halfway."

"Don't expect them at all," Perry said as he took her place in front of Gregory and unbuttoned the boy's coat with enough flair to announce that he could easily accomplish what Francie could not. "Unless they are on sale at Hilton, Hughes, and Company. In which case, expect two."

Francie rubbed her hands together and blew into them daintily. Graham hefted the coat he still held in his hands, weighing its ability to fight the cold of a New York winter and shook his head. No wonder she was shivering.

"There's hot tea in the study," he offered. "Perhaps you'd like—"

"Thank you," she said, then spoke loudly enough to make her point to Gregory. "How very nice of you."

"We need to buy you a new coat, Miss Morrow," he replied, pleased to see Gregory's jaw drop slightly as he watched the adults play out their little scene. "Fur is much better at keeping out the chill."

He put his hand at the small of Francie's back and propelled her toward the study, noting that her jaw, too, had dropped—and quite a bit farther than his son's.

Sable, he thought as he steered her toward the small table upon which the tea service had been set. *Yes. Sable was ever so much more elegant than mink.*

They weren't brown flecks that dotted his thickly lashed green eyes, Francie noted in the electric light of the study. They were golden. He was smiling to himself as he poured their tea, as if he had a secret that was hard for him to keep.

"A letter came for you today," he said, fishing in first one pocket and then another. "From Van Wert, Ohio."

"Oh!" she said, clapping her hands together as if she were still a small girl. Just thinking about home brought back all the feelings of her youth, of being safe and cosseted in the bosom of her family. She looked at the return address as he handed her the familiar blue envelope. "It's from Sissy!" she said, then composed herself, realizing that, of course, Graham Trent had no interest in her correspondence.

"Mrs. Noah Eastman is Sissy, then?" he asked, at least feigning an interest in her life. "The oldest one, right? The one that raised you?"

She nodded.

"The one with the Santas in the Snow?" he asked eagerly, as if he really cared.

Again she nodded, and put the letter in her lap. It was terribly rude to read at the table, even if she could feel the warmth of her sister's love burning through her woolen skirt.

"Go ahead," he encouraged, pointing at her lap.

"I'm sure you want to make sure everything's all right."

She could feel his eyes watching her as she carefully opened Sissy's envelope and unfolded the letter which would later join all the others she had received since coming to New York.

Everything was fine at home. Willa, Bart's wife, was expecting again. Ethan, the youngest of her brothers, was still hoping to go West, but in the meantime was turning out to be quite the ladies' man. Della was still mourning the loss of Samuel, and Peter, her husband, was burying his sorrow in work at the bank, where he was now senior vice president.

"Is she fine?" Graham asked her anxiously. "Everyone all right back home?"

"Yes," she said, folding the letter and slipping it into her pocket. "Seems I'm going to be an aunt once again."

"Sissy?" he asked, as though it really mattered to him.

"Willa, actually," she answered, trying to end the subject and move on. "We purchased a few things down at Best and Company today. I put them on your bill, as you said. I hope that's all right. Gregory needed some new mittens, and—"

He dismissed her worry with a wave of his hand. "And Bart? He happy about the baby?"

Sissy hadn't said, but she was sure he would be. The way he doted on his wife and son was still a surprise to the rest of his family. "I'm sure," she said. "And beside the mittens he needed a few—"

"What about the others? The boy who lost his brother? What was his name?" He replaced the Royal Crown Derby teacup in the saucer and moved his chair closer to hers so that now their knees were nearly touching. "John?"

"James," she corrected, finding it harder to breathe with him so very close. She tried not to stare at those eyes of his, admitting to herself that she found them fascinating, that she could study them for hours, watching the brown flecks turn to gold, watching the green deepen until it was the color of the evergreen that stood just beside the porch at home. Instead she focused on his upper lip where the shadow was darkening daily and realized that he was growing a mustache.

"Ah, yes," he said. She watched as he pouted slightly as if it annoyed him that he'd forgotten her nephew's name. "James," he agreed, appearing to commit it to memory.

One last cold trickle, at least she hoped it was the last, inched down the back of her neck and she felt herself shiver despite how warm the room was growing with Graham Trent's body only inches from her own, and his intent attention blanketing her soul.

"Cold?" he asked, long fingers reaching out toward her and stroking her cheek, touching the tip of her nose as if taking her temperature. "Maybe some brandy would do you more good than this tea."

His breath warmed her forehead as he spoke, and she risked another look in his eyes, so very close to her own. She'd been kissed before—heavens, she was nearly twenty—but a kiss had never seemed so long in coming, had never been her own heart's desire, but always that of her beaux. Now, with the fire in the grate flaring to light the concern in his eyes, with the heady smell of the evergreen boughs that decorated the room, with the first few icy pelts of sleet against the windowpane, there was nothing she wanted more than to feel the very soft lips of Graham Trent against her own, to test the prickliness of his new mustache, to taste the forbidden fruit of his tongue within the warmth of her own mouth.

"Oh!" she said, jumping back from him and nearly toppling the chair in which she sat. What in the world was she thinking? She hated that kind of kissing! In fact, she much preferred a kiss on her hand to anything more intimate, although she had actually submitted to more than one chaste kiss when the situation de-manded—which she had to admit it did more and more often since she was of an age when men expected . . . well, when a kiss on the hand would no longer do.

"I'm sorry," Graham said, backing away himself un-til there was a respectable distance between them.

There was such hurt on his face, such disappoint-ment in his eyes, that it was all she could do to stop herself from reaching out and laying a finger against his lips to silence him, from running into his arms and letting them close around her, from brushing the soft curl of auburn hair that teased the eyelashes of his left eye.

She settled for picking at a piece of imaginary lint on his lapel. "I see you're growing a mustache," she said, using the excuse to stare at his lip and trace with her gaze its upper edge as though she had any right at all to look so brazenly at him.

It wasn't until she saw him struggle to swallow that she realized he was having the same difficulty with his emotions as she was. That, standing so close, he too might be wishing there was more between them than there could ever be.

"I noticed that Milton Beaufort had quite a soup strainer settling in there," he said, self-consciously stroking the new growth above his lip and glancing toward the doorway at the sound of approaching steps.

"I like mustaches," she said. Then quickly she backed up several feet toward the enormous fireplace and set to warming hands that already stung with the heat of Graham Trent's nearness.

"It itches," he admitted softly, then turned his attention to the couple in the doorway.

"And we'll put a small trio in here, perhaps a flute and a violin and . . ." Perry Trent's voice trailed off as he and Amelia Becquith swept into the room. "Oh," he said, not even trying to hide his displeasure at finding Francie there with his brother. "I suppose a duet might do . . . but it would have to be the right pairing. Done incorrectly there is simply nothing more gauche. Isn't that right, Amelia?"

Chapter 4

"I expect that Amelia would like a little more co-operation on your part, Graham, with regard to this Christmas bash we're throwing," Perry said pointedly at breakfast three days later. The entire idea had been Perry's, and Graham saw no reason to be dragged into the planning of a gala he had no wish to host and even less wish to attend. Christmas Eve was meant for church and prayer and tradition. It was meant for hanging stockings, decorating trees, and gathering the family.

"Graham, boy, I'm only saying, for perhaps the thousandth time, that Amelia is trying desperately hard to please you and you are making it damn difficult for her by making her guess at what it is you really want." Perry put the water goblet down on the table with such conviction that a good portion of the water in it managed to overflow the glass and cause a small puddle on the white linen cloth.

"Uncle Perry spilled," Gregory announced. "And he said a bad word!"

"Well, maybe Miss Morrow will take me over her knee and spank me," Perry said, crossing his hands over his chest as if he was daring her to.

"Apologize," Graham said with as much control as he had ever exercised over his emotions, for surely he was about ready to take both his brother and his son and lock them each in their rooms until they could learn their manners. "Now, Perry. Or your ridiculous party is off."

He wasn't sure he'd ever seen Perry quite that shade of red. It certainly wasn't attractive on a man with such fair skin and hair to have splotches of rage paint his cheeks and his ears, though it did lend a Christmas air when contrasted with the green moiré-covered walls behind him.

"That party is every bit as important to you as it is to me," Perry said. "If you ever expect to consummate "

"I expect you to apologize," Graham said as evenly as he could, avoiding Francie's gaze as surely as she was avoiding his. "In fact, that is not only what I expect, it is what I demand."

"I don't even remember what for," Perry answered, daring him to repeat what had obviously been so offensive to himself and to Francie and which had luckily sailed right over Gregory's small head. "What was it that upset you so? The water?" He pointed at the spill on the table.

"Rogers," Graham called, his patience with his family well and truly exhausted. "I need a pen and note card, and then I'll require a messenger."

"Now, Graham," Perry said, a nervous laugh trapped in his throat. "You are overreacting, which is so very unlike you. One idle comment . . . You know how I am . . ."

"Eat your applesauce," Francie said very quietly to Gregory. "We've a big day and you won't want to be hungry."

"A big day?" Perry asked, as if it mattered to him in

the slightest what his nephew and the boy's governess had planned.

Rogers came forward with a silver tray on which were a few sheets of Graham's notepaper, the ivory bond with his monogram at the top, one of those new Waterman fountain pens, and a fresh bottle of ink. "Thank you, Rogers," he said, handing the butler his breakfast plate in order to clear a space in which to compose his note. Amelia would be furious at first, but some ear bobs from Tiffany's would go a long way toward calming her anger. Lord knew what she'd do for a necklace.

"I apologize," Perry said quickly. "Miss Morrow, I was quite out of line. Hired help you may be, but you are still a lady. I meant no harm, but my sense of humor sometimes overshadows my good taste. Please forgive me."

"Certainly," Francie said quickly, staring at her plate and finally lifting a spoonful of applesauce to her lips. The spoon disappeared and then slipped gracefully out from her flawless mouth making the pureed fruit seem like nectar from the gods. "Isn't this delicious?" she asked Gregory encouragingly.

The boy shrugged.

"Perhaps you'd like Rogers to let Mrs. Rogers know just how much you're enjoying it," she suggested, while Graham pondered whether or not to make an issue of Perry's referring to her as *hired help*.

Gregory looked at her suspiciously, but didn't open his mouth.

"Rogers," she said so pleasantly that the room

seemed brighter and warmer as she spoke. "I wonder if you'd be so kind as to tell Mrs. Rogers how very much Gregory enjoyed her applesauce this morning, and every morning, in fact. I don't know how many times he's mentioned it to me, and I keep forgetting to tell her myself. And he forgets, and then no one ever—"

It was clear to Graham that she was babbling, making excuses for his son just as he had always had to make excuses for his brother. But Rogers was lapping it up, his face beaming with pride over his wife's cooking skills, such as they were.

"I'll tell her right away, miss," he said. "If that's all, sir?" He gestured toward the letter Graham had started.

Amelia's father owned two banks and interests in several more. Graham's finances had been tied to his for years, just as his name had been linked with Amelia's. And Graham had Perry to thank for both. In fact, it was Perry's goal for Graham to wed Amelia and marry the Becquith and Trent fortunes at the same time.

But Graham had wanted this Christmas Eve to be different. He had wanted to sit alone with Francie in front of a fire, light the candles that adorned the tree, and listen to stories of the Morrow family while he dreamed about what still might be. He had wanted to remember the Christmas when he was four and his mother was still living with them and they had all hung up their stockings and wished on the shining star atop their feeble tree. His wish hadn't changed in over three decades. He still wanted only to wake up happy in the morning.

On Christmas morning 1865 his mother was gone.

Perry cleared his throat. "The *Times* financial section says the New York and Northern Railway just went into foreclosure. Public auction on the twenty-eighth. Damn it all! I believe Andrew Becquith had more than a million wrapped up in the Northern. I told him it was all but over, but he simply wouldn't listen."

Andrew Becquith had been one of the men who had opened his doors and his brains to Graham for the picking. He'd taken him to his club before Graham had a prayer of ever joining it, taken him to the places he needed to be seen, and sat him next to the people he needed to be seen with to make the success of himself that he was. No one ever made it on his own. No matter that it felt like it. One only fell on his own, never rose that way.

"Sir?" Rogers asked, reminding him that he was still waiting for the note to Amelia.

"That'll be all, Rogers. Thank you." He ripped the letter he had begun into two even pieces. "Was his apology satisfactory?" he asked Francie, knowing that there was really no way she could say it wasn't, but wanting her to know it mattered to him that she was satisfied. Mattered a great deal. Perhaps too much.

"Of course," she said with a forced smile that was still brighter than the midday sun glinting off the snow. She touched her lips with the linen napkin and pushed her seat back slightly. "If it's all right, I think Gregory and I will leave you gentlemen to your business and begin our day, sir."

Sir. He could throttle Perry right there, lay him out flat cold between the crystal and the silver.

"Let me apologize once again for my brother," he said, the words catching in his throat as he added, "I do not regard you as the *hired help.* There is no need for you to address me as *sir.*"

"But I am the hired help," she said as if he needed reminding, then rose and made sure her starched white shirtwaist was well tucked into her blue serge skirt, which had a tendency to rustle slightly as she walked and made him think of breezes in the palms of Florida.

"Gregory? Are you ready to begin your lessons?"

"I think perhaps he's already started," Perry said dryly, his eyes jumping back and forth between Graham and Francie as though he were at some lawn tennis match.

"Excuse me, sir," Rogers said from the doorway, coming in with a tray of some of the most elaborate desserts Graham had ever seen, and certainly never at breakfast.

"What's all this?" he asked, Gregory's wow of approval ringing from the chandelier.

Rogers walked right passed him and held the tray just to Gregory's left. There was a small Battenburg cake covered with almond paste and decorated with what looked to Graham like actual violets, a Jenny Lind cake, individual trifles, some fancy cream pastries, and a meringue that looked suspiciously like Santa Claus, smack in the middle of the silver tray. "Mrs. Rogers has been practicing," he said. "She says it's been a long time since we had any festivities in this house and she wanted to be sure she still had all her skills about her."

"I would suppose there will be a great many more galas in the future, Rogers," Perry said, eyeing the tray of treats and settling on a cream puff in the shape of a swan. "What with Miss Amelia and Mr. Trent about ready to declare, now."

"Yes, sir," Rogers said. "Well, seeing how Master Gregory enjoyed the bit of sweet applesauce so, Mrs. Rogers thought he might like to try one or two of these, seeing as how he won't be attending the party."

Gregory's eyes were as wide as two shiny Christmas balls as he looked first at the Battenburg cake with its swirls of icing, and then at the Santa meringue, and finally at a cream puff with chocolate dripped over its top.

"How very nice of Mrs. Rogers to think of Gregory like that," Francie said, still standing by the table, now with no place to go and apparently even less inclination to stay.

Gregory's gaze slowly lifted from the temptations within his reach up and across the table until he found his governess. In a whisper that was nearly a gasp, he said, "It *is* magic, Miss Morrow."

Francie stood straight and tall and as proud as Graham had ever seen her. She gave his son half a smile and a very quick wink meant for no one but him. Then she put one finger to her lips to remind him about the secret nature of the magic she had told him about that night in his bed.

"Won't you have something, Miss Morrow?" Graham asked, wishing she would return to her seat, wishing she would bestow that smile on him, wishing that life didn't demand of him that he remember her place and his own. "They aren't Santas in the Snow, but traditions have to start somewhere. Why not here?"

"I'm sure the Becquiths are just crawling with tradition, Graham, if that's what you're after," Perry said, reaching over and helping himself to the pastry swan.

Amelia was certainly big on tradition, as Perry suggested. She had everything mapped out for Graham, and Gregory as well. Just yesterday she'd written a letter to the Deerfield Academy making sure that Gregory's place was being reserved. And she'd told Graham that she expected next year's Christmas Eve gala to be even finer than this year's. She would, she assured him, wear red velvet once again, and on and on she went until he was numb to her words.

"Amelia's traditions are not what I'm after," he said.

Perry choked on his cream puff.

Francie's eyebrows lifted until they nearly reached her hairline, and her mouth formed the dearest little "o" as she eased down into her seat.

"Now who needs to apologize?" Perry said after he caught his breath, delighted to make an innuendo when none was meant. He put his hand to his ear as the front door bell rang. "Are those wedding bells I hear?"

It wasn't hard to imagine Francie Morrow as a bride as she sat there at his table, her pale face lit by the morning sun, her high-collared white blouse with its tiny edging of lace imitating a wedding gown. It wasn't hard to imagine sitting down across the table from her like this every day for the rest of their lives and watching each emotion play across her face, leaving, as it did now, a telltale trace of pink on her cheeks.

"Perhaps they are," he answered his brother, just as Andrew Becquith and his daughter entered his dining room and Amelia bent down and presented her cheek for a kiss.

"Now a dab of glue," Francie told Gregory as the two sat huddled over the wooden scraps scattered about the newspaper-covered mahogany desk in the boy's room.

"Do you really think he'll like it?" Gregory asked dubiously as he assessed the picture frame he was decorating for his father.

They had decided on the picture frame with a photograph of Gregory in it after Francie had searched the house and found that except for the portrait of Katherine Trent, which hung in the hall next to the room she used to occupy—which, Francie noted, was not the same one in which Graham Trent slept—the house was devoid of a single framed photograph.

When she'd asked Perry Trent if Graham—she'd begun to think of him simply as *Graham,* despite the dangers of familiarity she knew existed in even thinking of him that way—had some aversion to photographs, Perry Trent had assured her it was the people, and not the photographs, to which his brother was averse. That seemed to include their mother, their father, and,

Francie noted with some satisfaction, even Amelia Becquith.

The Morrow farmhouse had photographs everywhere. Noah, Sissy's husband, had bought a Hawkeye camera from the Sears, Roebuck and Company catalog and each niece and nephew had been captured on film and caged in a homemade frame on the mantel. Their parents' wedding picture, a daguerreotype, was on the dresser in the bedroom where it had sat since Zena and Jack had gotten it back from the traveling photographer two months after their marriage.

"Miss Morrow? Do you really think he'll like it?" Gregory asked again.

"I do," she said honestly, thinking about the family portrait that she kept next to her bed so that she could see the people she loved first thing each morning.

"I wouldn't practice that phrase too much if I were you," Perry Trent said as he leaned against the frame of the doorway.

"What?"

"You're a pretty young thing, Miss Morrow. Sweet and appealing in your way. Perhaps I'm mistaken. Has the piano tuner popped the question, then?"

"Mr. Beaufort?" She still didn't catch the drift of his conversation, but she had the uncomfortable feeling that he was warning her to stay away from his brother. A warning that, in light of the fact that Amelia Becquith was downstairs in Graham's library going over menus and flowers and she was upstairs being paid to watch a little boy barely anyone could tolerate, seemed hardly necessary.

"Mr. Trent asked me to let you know he'd like you to be ready to go out with him after lunch to run some errands for the Christmas season.

"I offered to deliver the message," he continued, still lounging against the door frame and running his tongue along his teeth as though there was something distasteful in his mouth he'd like to be rid of, "because I wanted you to clearly understand how things stand."

He pushed off from the door and entered the room so that he couldn't be overheard. "Finances are precarious right now, and I wanted to be sure you understood before you and he went off on this little spree . . . You do know about the railroads?"

She nodded. Of course she knew. There was more talk of money than of the menu at every meal.

"And the banks?"

She nodded again. Did he think she didn't read the newspapers? "Yes?" she prodded. If only he'd get to the point and leave. Gregory was gluing his fingers together and there was more glue than wood on his gift for his father. "Go and wash up, now," she told the boy gently, taking the bottle of paste and setting it out of his reach. "It's almost time for lunch."

Perry Trent took the seat his nephew had vacated, looking disdainfully at the mess just inches from his bespoke suit. "That was good—getting rid of the little one," he said conspiratorially, leaning toward her. "I'm trying to tell you that despite appearances, the money is not what it seems, so don't let my brother be recklessly extravagant, Miss Morrow. Do you understand?"

"Mr. Trent wants me to go shopping with him?" Francie asked, surprised. "Is it for Gregory?"

"Don't tell him I told you," Perry insisted. "He's a proud man, but a fur coat is simply not in the budget in times like these."

"A fur coat? For Miss Becquith?" Perry Trent hardly had to convince her that a fur coat was certainly an unnecessary extravagance when it came to Miss Becquith. With the winter hardly begun, Amelia had already come over draped in half a dozen different skins.

Perry Trent grimaced and stood up, holding his hands away from his body as if he had no idea what he ought to do with any glue that had the audacity to cling to him. "I believe," he said, looking her up and down with obvious disapproval, "that you are the intended recipient."

"Me?" she asked incredulously. Graham Trent wanted to buy her a fur coat?

Gregory was right—it *was* magic!

Chapter 5

"I am *not* trying to be difficult," the obstinate little blond said, her hands on her slim hips, her eyes wide with indignation.

"Then get your things and let's go," Graham insisted, reaching for his silk muffler as if that would put an end to the first argument he could remember having with a woman in his life.

"I'm sorry," Francie said without any conviction, obviously not as much a stranger to disagreement as he.

"You're not!" he said back, his voice rising enough for Rogers to poke his head through the sitting room doors, look surprised, and then discreetly close the heavy mahogany sliders behind him.

Graham lowered his tone and spoke through gritted teeth. "You're not sorry, but you will be when you come down with pneumonia from going about in that threadbare little cloth thing."

"My twill raglan is not threadbare. It's only two winters old and I'll not have you maligning it. It cost me over a month's salary and that was on sale at Bierman-Heidelberg."

Of course it had. Embarrassed, he retreated some. "It's a very nice cloak. Very attractive. And probably an excellent value. But it simply isn't warm enough for a New York winter."

"I didn't spend last year in Florida, Mr. Trent, nor the year before. And I'll have you know that unless they've moved Van Wert several hundred miles south since last I've been there, we get our fair share of Jack Frost in Ohio, too!"

"Well, maybe I don't want Jack Frost nipping at that nose," he said, reaching out only to have her back away. "Maybe I want to keep you warm . . ." Lord, he ached to keep her warm.

"Well, maybe that's no more your job than shopping with you is mine!"

"Damn your job, and damn mine!" he shouted, pulling her coat from the rack and snapping it toward

her much like a toreador would with an enraged bull.
He felt just a bit like a matador, and found, to his
amazement, that fighting was invigorating. In fact, he
could fight with Francie Morrow from now until the
cows came home, and on Fifth Avenue that would be a
good long time. Maybe the rest of their lives.

"You watch your tongue, Graham Trent," she said,
snatching her coat from his hands and returning it to
the hook from whence it came.

He liked the sound of his given name on her lips. It
melted his bones and made him feel limp. The thought
of her in sable, a high collar of dark fur up against her
peachy cheeks, those delicate hands lost in a soft muff,
pushed him to try another tack.

"A growing boy needs to spend a good deal of time
in the out-of-doors. And Gregory has a lot of energy
which would be better spent running around outside
throwing snowballs than thrashing about his room
throwing tantrums.

"And a coat like yours, while certainly adequate for
an errand here and there, is simply not meant for—"

The fight seemed to leave her, but was replaced with
a melancholy that tore at him.

"I," she said quietly, "am not meant for furs. And
surely not from you. I'm touched, I'm flattered, but it
wouldn't be right. Don't you see? I live here in your
house, take tea with you, and suddenly I have a—what,
a rabbit or a mouton cloak? What would people think?
What would they assume?"

He hadn't thought. Not about anything but what he

wanted. And what he wanted wasn't rabbit or mouton or anything else so ordinary as that.

"What would Amelia Becquith think?" she asked, raising an eyebrow slightly in question.

It would be a simple matter to say that he didn't care what Amelia or anyone else thought. But that would be a lie, and a selfish one, at that. Amelia would suppose Francie compromised.

That anyone could think of Francie in those terms made him cringe. Furs were the gifts of husbands or lovers.

Francie stood proudly in front of him, her eyes a little too bright for him to meet.

Husbands or lovers.

He grabbed for his outer things. Coat on, hat in place, and hands jammed into leather gloves, he reached out and lifted Francie's chin with one gloved finger.

There were a hundred things he wanted to say to her, from *Let the world say what it will* all the way to *I love you.*

He settled for, "I'll be back, Francie."

She seemed resigned when she replied. "And I'll be here."

Graham stood by the window of his study, rocking on his heels, quite pleased with himself. All in all it could turn out to be a better holiday than he had ever dreamed. *If* things worked out as he had planned. And no amount of money could ensure that.

"Excuse me, sir." Rogers's voice cut into Graham's

thoughts, startling him into spilling the sherry he was pouring. "Oh, I am sorry," Rogers said, rushing to help and taking over, quite proprietorially, the job of serving.

"Hmm?" Graham asked, trying to pull himself back from the daydream he had been weaving. "Oh, don't worry about it. Don't worry about anything, Rogers."

Rogers eyed him warily. Well, it was nothing compared to the looks Graham would be getting soon enough.

"Did the mail come?" he asked Rogers, not caring if his eagerness showed to the servant who had been with him from the day he'd moved to Fifth Avenue and who had witnessed much of the good and even more of the bad that had affected Graham's life.

"No, sir, not to my knowledge. Late again. But there's a Mr. Saugus to see you, sir," Rogers said, replacing the soiled cloth and giving Graham a fresh little aperitif glass of sherry. "There seems to be some confusion about your order and he wishes to get it clarified at your convenience."

"Saugus?"

"The florist, sir," Rogers prompted.

Ah, the florist. No doubt he was upset that Graham had canceled his weekly delivery to Amelia. Setting down his sherry, he gestured to Rogers that he would follow him into the hall.

There he saw not only Mr. Saugus, a handsome young man somewhere in his twenties with a handlebar mustache that exceeded the width of his face by a good two inches, but also Francie and Gregory, all deep in discussion about the intricacies of some flowers they seemed much too interested in.

He cleared his throat to announce his presence and Mr. Saugus jumped back as if he'd been standing too close to a fire.

"Problem, Mr. Saugus?" he asked, keeping a tight rein on his temper. Francie refused to meet his gaze, but took Gregory's hand and headed for the stairway.

"Please," Mr. Saugus called after the pair, holding out the delicate pink flowers toward them.

Francie turned on the stairwell, looked first at the roses and then directly at Graham. She gave Gregory an encouraging prod, sending him back to capture the gift she was so willing to accept from the mustachioed merchant.

"Thank you, Mr. Saugus," she said, pulling her gaze from Graham's and turning her sunshine on the florist. "Gregory and I will see they get some water right away, won't we?"

Gregory took the two flowers from Mr. Saugus and stayed long enough for the man to ruffle his hair.

"Nice boy you have there, sir," the florist said, his eyes fastened to Francie's skirts as she made her way up the stairs, Gregory dancing up the steps beside her. *Nice boy, indeed!* He wasn't fooling Graham one bit. It was the boy's nice governess that had him drooling on the marble foyer tiles.

"Was there something I can help you with?" Graham asked the merchant. "Or are you just fascinated with my . . . chandelier?"

Mr. Saugus pulled his gaze from the top of the steps

and blinked at Graham, who knew the feeling all too well—Francie took the sunshine with her when she left a room.

"Yes, sir," he said, pulling himself up to his full height, which was several inches taller than Graham, who would have liked to have been looking down his nose at the man rather than just sticking his nose in the air. "There seems to be a little confusion about your order down at the shop. Miss Springer said you stopped by this afternoon around 2 P.M. to cancel your customary deliveries to the Becquith address—"

"That sounds perfectly clear to me," Graham said impatiently, turning toward the drawing room for something stronger than the sherry he had been sipping when the florist arrived. "Now if you'll excuse me . . ."

"But Miss Levy said that Mr. Trent came in shortly before three to send a poinsettia plant *in addition to* the regular order."

Graham turned back to face the florist. "I did not return to your shop at three or any other time. I want no further flowers sent to Miss Becquith, today, tomorrow, or any other time. Clear enough now?"

"Yes, sir, but it was—" he began, but was interrupted when Perry swept in from the library to finish for him.

"I. It was I that sent the poinsettias and I who reinstated the order," he said.

"Have you intentions with regard to Amelia?" Graham asked dubiously, and was rewarded with a sneer. "Then to what end, dear brother, are you sending floral bouquets? Misleading the woman would hardly be considered a kindness by her or Andrew."

"Misleading? I would never mislead. I simply corrected your error in judgment before any real harm was done."

"How could flowers from you . . ." He hesitated. Perry wouldn't have signed his name to Amelia's flowers, would never presume to . . . a look passed between the florist and his brother that assured him Perry would.

"Thank you," Graham said dismissively to the florist, now even more anxious for him to leave than he had been before. "Sorry to have made you come over this way, but I think things are more than clear now, aren't they?"

"Yes, sir," the young man said, too cheerily for someone who had squandered half an hour just two days before Christmas and lost a large order to boot. "No need to apologize. I wouldn't call it a wasted trip at all." He looked up the stairs once again. "Not wasted in the least."

"Care to elaborate?" Perry drawled, and Graham felt the tightening of a knot in his stomach of which he hadn't even been aware.

"It's really none of our concern," Graham said, hoping to avoid hearing, and allowing Perry to hear, what he suspected had the merchant grinning almost as wide as his damn mustache.

"It's the governess," he said in that dreamy way young men had that so irritated their seniors. "Miss Morrow. She's agreed to take a spin on the lake at

Central Park with me. Said she used to go skating back home and missed it, so I—"

"Rogers!" Graham shouted, startling both Perry and Young Handlebars, to whom he returned his attention. "When were you planning on this little outing?"

"Sir?" he asked, clearly uncomfortable at the question. Of course the man thought it was none of Graham's business, but then the man didn't know that Graham would sooner drown in the lake at Central Park than think of Francie Morrow skating on it in someone else's company.

"The skating. When did you think you were going skating?"

"Graham, that's really none of your concern," Perry admonished, trying to pull him into the drawing room and release the merchant to his business. "Miss Morrow is free to do as she pleases on her own time," his brother reminded him.

Rogers warily approached the trio, apparently unsure what was expected of him.

"Ah, Rogers! Please show Mr. Suckus out and then locate, if you would, my ice skates. I'll be needing them—" He paused and looked at Francie's newest suitor. He certainly knew Francie's schedule, but still he wanted to be sure. "—tomorrow?"

The man shrugged and reluctantly nodded.

"Good day to you, then," Graham said, dismissing both the florist and his butler with a wave, and headed for the library, where he prayed he had some manual or other that would instruct him in the basics of ice skating before he made a total fool of himself in front of Francie and half of New York the following morning.

"What do you think you're up to?" Perry said, trailing into the library behind him and shutting the doors. "You can't go out with Miss Morrow. One need only look at your face in her presence to know just what's in your groin."

"Watch it, Perry." He ran his fingers over the spines of his manuals until he got to the *i*'s, noted silently that he'd never opened any of them, and realized that he hadn't a clue what *ichnology* was. "As you may have guessed, I've made a decision with which you are going to have to reconcile yourself . . . or you'll have to begin to look for some other place to live."

Perry shook his head sadly. "No ultimatums, Graham. Not between you and me, please. We've been through too much together to let . . ."

"A woman come between us?" Graham finished for him.

"For years I've been your good sense, your good judgment, when your own threatened to fail you. We'd have lost thousands in the wheat market if I hadn't convinced you to sell. And our money would have gone right down the track with Andrew Becquith's if I hadn't stepped in months ago, and you know it." Perry's face was red, his temples pulsing. He ran his fingers through his thinning hair and then jammed his hands into the pockets of his fine worsted trousers.

"This isn't about money, Perry. This is a matter of the heart—a subject about which I'm afraid you are not qualified to advise me."

He'd closed his eyes to Perry's preferences as soon as he'd discerned them back at Deerfield. For years he'd covered for him even as he was repelled by his brother's choices. So what right had Perry now to be telling him who he could love?

Perry audibly sniffed back his hurt and put his arm around Graham, leading him to the leather Chesterfield sofa that always looked so inviting and comfortable but was in reality perpetually stiff and cold. Graham allowed himself to be led and took a seat beside his brother. Better that they get things settled civilly rather than duking it out or shouting the rafters down and in the process risking Francie's hearing both his and Perry's deepest feelings about her.

"I can't advise you about love? Who knows better what is and isn't appropriate? What society will and won't allow? And who, Graham, I ask you, knows you better? Who has watched after you all these years, making sure that no one did you harm, no one took advantage of you, no one strung you along?"

"She isn't Nancy Wallace, Perry," Graham said, touched by his brother's open wounds and the bare soul they exposed.

"No," Perry agreed. "And she isn't Julia Rift and she isn't any number of other women who would have happily picked your pockets clean and blown the lint in your face on the way out the door."

"That was years ago, Perry. Lord knows I'm older and wiser. Even you can see that Francie is different—"

Perry put his hand over Graham's and squeezed lightly, lovingly, as though he knew how much what

he was about to say would pain him. "Yes, Francie is
different. When Miss Francine Morrow walks out the
door, and she will, Graham, make no mistake . . .
when she walks out the door, she'll trample your heart
on her way and leave you lying in a pool of your own
sorrow, in which I think you just might drown."

Just the words, spoken aloud, shook him. The
thought of Francie walking out of his door, out of his
life, left him cold despite the roaring fire that crackled
and blazed just feet from where he and Perry sat, quiet
now, thoughtful.

"I believe that she could come to love me," he said
quietly after a while. "Even if, as you contend, it is the
money that she covets now, I think that she could
come to—"

"Then you, too, have your doubts?"

"No," Graham said, shaking his head adamantly and
rising to his feet. "I have no doubts at all. Francie Morrow hasn't a deceitful bone in that tiny little body. If—
when—she says she'll marry me, she'll love me. Love
me as I have never been loved."

He glared at Perry, refusing to so much as flinch at
the hurt written on his brother's face.

"Marry you? Has it come so far, so soon? What of
Amelia, who wants nothing from you? What of your
obligation to her?" Perry asked, as he too came to his
feet and then headed for the side table where the
brandy was perpetually laid out.

"Her wealth is nearly as great as yours, and yet she
worships the ground upon which you walk. And she

isn't dallying with every tinker and tuner and florist who crosses her path . . ."

"Don't," Graham warned, his fingers tightening around the ornate brass door handle as he made ready to leave the room.

"Miss Morrow would take everything you have and ask for more," he warned. "Amelia wants nothing!"

"And nothing is what I could give her. And nothing would never be enough."

"And what if you lost everything tomorrow, Graham? What then? How would you keep your Miss Morrow with you if the bottom fell out?"

"Perhaps," he said softly, opening the doors, "we'd learn to live on love."

He could hear behind him Perry's snort of disbelief, but he refused to turn around. At the steps he could still hear Perry, coughing now, sputtering.

"Rogers," he shouted toward the back of the house. "I believe that Mr. Perry is in need of assistance."

He climbed the stairs with a heavy heart that lifted only at the sound of Francie's giggle as he approached his son's room.

"Well," he heard her admit to Gregory. "I didn't draw them very well, so you'll just have to believe me. When Sissy makes Santas in the Snow they look a lot better than this. And they taste better. Just like a little piece of heaven. Like home."

Graham turned on his heel and hurried back down the steps, nearly running over Rogers on his way into his study. "The mail," he asked him nearly frantically. "Has the mail come yet?"

"On your desk," Rogers answered with a knowing smile.

"And?"

Rogers nodded. "It's there."

Chapter 6

From the moment Francie Morrow had laid eyes on Graham Trent she had known that he was a man who would be at home anywhere. He was the master of his house, the king of the boardroom. To see him in a shop was to witness a kind of majesty as he dealt with sales girls who hurried to cater to any whim he might have, clerks who jumped at his beck and call, and stock boys who cheerfully carried his packages to his waiting carriage. And all of it he handled with a grace and aplomb that spoke of success tempered with humility.

So the fact that he couldn't manage to let go of the willow branches that hung over the pond, couldn't make that regal bearing straighten up over the two narrow blades that were fastened to his oxblood Russian calf hand-sewn shoes, and couldn't hide the obvious humiliation he felt at his inability to master skating in as long as it had taken him to fasten on the skates, came as a bit of a surprise. A very endearing surprise. A surprise that touched her in a place that had laid dormant since she'd left Van Wert three years before to take on a world that cared very little about whether or not Francine Morrow was happy, whether or not she was lonely, whether or not she missed her home and family.

And that, of all people, Graham Trent should be the one who cared, and cared enough to make a laughing-stock of himself on a Sunday afternoon in front of his neighbors, his son, and the entire city of New York, warmed her insides more surely than any ray of sun-shine in August had ever managed to do.

"We could just watch," she offered, skating back to where he had planted himself, tottering precariously as he clutched a handful of thin willow reeds.

"I promised you a skate," he said through gritted teeth, "and a skate you will have." He straightened an inch or two and smiled proudly at his newest accomplishment. "Look! I've left the gorillas! Evolution at its most elementary!"

She reached out her two mittened hands to him. "Hold on to me," she said. "I won't let you fall."

He looked dubious.

"Come on," she encouraged. "There are worse things than a little tumble on the ice. Look at Greg-ory—he's spent more time on his bottom than his feet and he's having a wonderful time." He was, at that. In the last week she'd seen him laugh more, try harder, and smile wider as he tested the magic over and over again. Sometimes it worked, and sometimes she had to reassure him that every now and then it took a little longer—the magic would happen when least he ex-pected it.

She waved at Gregory, skating with the women and

children at the north end of the pond, and he waved back, showing off with a little pirouette that landed him on his tail for all his troubles. Then she turned her attention to Gregory's father. One by one Graham relinquished the branches until his left hand was free. She took it in her own and felt his strong grip. *Give me your fear,* she thought. *I'll keep you safe.*

"Now the other," she said, her left hand waiting to take his right. "Yes. Good."

She backed out slowly onto the ice, pulling him with her, trying to concentrate on teaching him as she had taught neighbors and friends back home.

But teaching neighbors and friends had never set her heart racing the way holding hands with Graham Trent was doing. Watching someone else's eyes fill with admiration had never swelled her head quite so large. Feeling the warmth of someone else's hands right through her woolen mittens had never burned her chest before. And sensing someone's complete trust had never clutched so at her heart.

She turned abruptly and placed his hands at her waist. Maybe if she wasn't staring into those deep eyes with their flecks of gold. Maybe if her lips weren't so close to his . . .

His hands held her waist for dear life as she skated slowly, encouraging him to do just as she did. Push off with the left and glide. Push off with the right and glide.

She didn't know when it happened, but somewhere into the second turn his arms bent and he pulled her closer to him, so close that she could feel the rise and fall of his chest against her back.

"This is wonderful," he said, his breath warming her ear. "How have I lived without this my whole life?"

"You've never skated?" she asked. "Not even as a little boy?"

"There are a lot of things I've never done," he admitted with a nervous laugh. "But I have a feeling I'm going to do them all now that I've met you, Francie Morrow."

Oh, how nice her name sounded on his lips!

"Aren't you going to ask me what else I've never done?" He leaned into her so closely she could feel his lips move against her cheek.

She turned her head to look at him and bumped his nose with her cheek. Naturally, that caused him to pull his head back, which threw him off balance, which set him to falling, which made him grab out for her, which landed her in his lap in the center of the frozen pond in Central Park.

"Well, I'll bet you've never fallen down in front of so many people, for one!" She laughed as she looked up at him, stopping the moment their eyes met. There was no laughter mirrored in his green eyes. And what she did see there was nothing to laugh about.

"I've never told a woman I love her," he said, not making a move to get up, apparently not caring that people were beginning to stare.

She tried to right herself and get to her feet, but her skirts were caught around Graham's legs.

"Not even Katherine," he admitted, ignoring her attempts to free herself.

She twisted and turned and felt as trapped as a baby bird with a broken wing who's been eyed by the cat.

"Because I've never loved anyone, Francie," he continued.

Her heart was breaking through her chest. Her breaths were coming in short little gasps as she yanked at her skirts with all her might.

"Until now."

There were other skaters on the pond, dozens of them. Gregory was falling in ever closer circles and the temperature was dropping and the sun was slowly sinking behind the new and luxurious Dakota apartments.

And Francie Morrow couldn't see any of it through her tear-filled eyes.

Graham Trent loved her! Little Francie Morrow from Van Wert, Ohio, whose shoes were four years old and whose underthings had holes from all the washing and wearing and who had to live in other people's houses and teach other people's children. Graham Trent loved her, despite all that.

A more unlikely pair she couldn't imagine. She pictured the look on Perry Trent's face. And her own brothers! Ethan thought that rich and evil were one and the same.

Graham Trent was the epitome of everything she'd ever wanted. He was caring and kind and strong and sure of himself.

And she, what was she? *The hired help.*

She supposed she'd have to leave Trent House.

Leave Graham and Gregory and Mr. and Mrs. Rogers and Daisy and . . . She knew she ought to leave. Staying would lead her down a path from which she could never return.

Because if Graham Trent wanted her, he would have her, and willingly, too.

And then what?

He bundled the fur lap throw around her, then suggested to Gregory that he might enjoy riding up front with Marlowe. The boy looked at him suspiciously and then at Francie, who hadn't met anyone's eyes since Graham's confession on the ice. Lord knew what she thought of him, a silly old man lying in a puddle of slush and groping her in front of half of New York, spouting words of love.

And yet he wouldn't have taken the afternoon back for two railroads and a chain of banks.

"All set?" he asked her.

She nodded, still silent. Was she never going to speak to him again?

"All right, Marlowe," he shouted, "through the park first, then home before it gets too cold, if you will."

"Yes, sir," his driver said. "Beginning to snow again, sir. Good thing we put the runners on."

"Yes," he agreed, enjoying the feel of the sleigh's metal blades gliding over the slick surface beneath, the sound of the horse's bells announcing the imminent coming of Christmas.

Beside him Francie burrowed deeper into the blankets. The gas lamps set aglow the blond curls that escaped her bonnet and showed her eyes a bit too bright.

"Comfortable?" he asked. "Cold?"

"I'm fine," she said as if she were in need of convincing herself.

"I suppose I've done this all rather badly," he admitted aloud. "Rushing at you like that. Pouring out my heart like a schoolboy."

"You took me by surprise, is all," she said, her gaze glued to the glistening trees that surrounded the path.

"I took myself by surprise," he admitted. He'd had it all planned out. Slowly, steadily he'd build a relationship between the two of them, ease her into the idea, make her see he wasn't so old or so boring as he must seem.

And then she'd been in his arms, within his grasp. Or so it seemed.

"You'd like me to just forget what you said," Francie said, trying to help him out. The bow that sat at her neck and held her hat in place bobbed as she swallowed. "I understand."

"No," he said, realizing at once the impression he'd given her and hurrying to correct it. "I don't want you to forget it. I want . . ." He searched for the words, looking out beyond the sleigh to the darkened woods, to the back of his son's head, to the snowflakes that melted on the fur wrap that surrounded the woman who held his heart. The words weren't there.

As gently as he could he touched her chin and guided her face toward his, trying to read in those moss green eyes in the rapidly deepening dusk what it was he needed to say to reach her, to convince her, to woo and win her.

"I want to marry you, Miss Morrow. I realize I'm not the best you could do—I'm old . . . well, not so old . . . and I come with a son who can be difficult at best and a brother who—"

Her bottom lip was trembling.

What else could he do but capture it with his own?

"My mother?" Gregory said incredulously as Graham helped him down from the sleigh at the curb in front of their door. "Miss Morrow would be my mother?"

Graham nodded, committed to the idea no matter how his son felt about it. Francie was the best thing that had ever happened not only to him but to Gregory as well.

"Hurrah!" the boy said, turning in his father's arms and throwing himself into a bank of snow. He righted himself and stood atop the pile like king of the mountain. "And she'll stay with us forever?"

"Forever," Graham agreed, taking Francie's hand and tucking it through his arm.

"Again, I say hurrah!" He raised his arms like some clown atop a diving board at Coney Island and took off once again for the snow.

"Wait!" Graham shouted and climbed up the mountain, pulling Francie along behind him.

They lined up, Gregory in the middle, their backs to the small field of snow that separated Graham's home from the sidewalk. He and Francie exchanged looks and nods.

"One," he said, and they all stood still as statues.

"Two!" she cried out and they began to fall backward like boards in the wind.

"Three!" Gregory squealed as they went down with a whoosh into the soft carpet of white behind them and then waved their arms up and down against the snow while the sound of Francie's laughter rang clear in the cold air.

Carefully they all came to their feet and turned to look at their work.

Three perfect angels lay carved in the pristine snow.

It was a relief to find when they had returned to the house that Perry had managed to move the entire party to Amelia's. Francie and Graham had sat in front of the fire along with Gregory and she had told them all about her growing-up years. As they kept careful watch over the candles on the tree, she promised that someday they would take Gregory out to Ohio to meet his cousins and swim in the lake and play with the animals and enjoy a world he could hardly imagine.

And Graham! Well, Graham would have to meet Sissy and Noah and the rest of her family now that he knew so much about them. Every morsel she gave him he had savored, asking questions about this nephew and that brother until Gregory had fallen asleep at their feet and Graham had had to carry him up to bed.

"Do you think I'll get my wish?" he'd asked her as she tucked him under his comforter.

"I do," she'd said softly, kissing him on the forehead and reveling in motherly feelings she now had a right to. "I think we all might get our wishes."

"What's that?" Graham had asked, but she'd winked at Gregory and refused to answer. Graham had to learn, as Gregory was learning, that Christmas was full of secrets and surprises.

He'd kissed her then, outside her door, the kiss of a man staking his claim on a woman. And she'd let herself be kissed, luxuriating in the feel of his warm arms surrounding her, intoxicated by the taste of his brandy on her lips, secure in the knowledge that it was the first of many, many kisses.

And she'd begun to get ready for bed.

The knock on the door startled her. If it was Graham, she wasn't certain she'd be able to turn him away.

Pulling her robe tightly around her and making sure it was closed at the neck, she cracked the door. Perry stood, still in his dress coat, just outside her room in the darkened hallway, a large box in his hands.

"Might I come in?" he asked. "I understand congratulations are in order and I didn't want to miss the opportunity to be the first . . ."

"Couldn't this wait until morning?" she asked, wishing Graham were there with her.

"Not really," he said, pushing his way through the doorway and placing the enormous box on her bed. He gestured toward it. "Open it," he said. "Go ahead."

"What is it?" she asked.

"Only one way to find out." He perched himself on

the edge of her bed, his hands folded, clearly in no rush to leave.

"Is it a Christmas present?"

"It certainly is," he said. "Probably the nicest one you'll ever get."

"I've already gotten the nicest present I'll ever get," she said, hugging herself at the memory of Graham's kiss and the promises they had made to one another.

"Well, this one will come in handy when we're huddled in front of a stove in some tenement, then."

"I beg your pardon?" she asked, noticing for the first time that he was slurring his words just a bit. A deep breath told her he'd had more than a little to drink at Amelia's.

"I'll help you," he said, pulling at the ribbon and lifting the cover from the shiny white box.

"Is something wrong?" she asked, ignoring the gift and searching Perry's face. "You look awful."

"I'm afraid, Miss Morrow, that everything is wrong. The Hanover National Bank closed its doors this afternoon for the last time. The Becquiths are bankrupt. The Morrises are bankrupt. And, dear little Francie, the Trents are bankrupt."

He stood and pulled from the box a dark fur coat. Francie had seen Amelia Becquith drag a coat like that across the foyer only a week ago. Sable, she'd said, instructing Rogers to exercise special care.

"Here. Better wear it before they get a chance to ask for it back." He strolled toward the door, draping the coat out in front of her, letting the soft fur brush over her bare toes. "And it might not be a bad idea to start packing up tonight. I suspect we'll have lost the house by the first of the new year."

"Lost the house?" The fur was heavy on her feet, rooting her to the spot.

"Everything's gone, Miss Morrow. Except, I'm sure, your love. They can't take that away."

Francie lifted the coat from the floor. It was surprisingly light for all that fur. Light and soft and warm.

". . . or can they?"

Chapter 7

Graham woke up in the same damn sweat that had greeted him every Christmas morning for as long as he could remember. And probably before that, as well. Having a mother who just walked out could do that to a fellow, he supposed.

Well, he told himself, forcing his breaths out evenly, that part of his life was done. He reached over and ran his hand across the pillow where very soon, and then forever, Francie would rest her head. He patted gently the place she would occupy in his bed and felt the warmth of the place she already occupied within his heart. After they were married he would be able to open his eyes each morning and instead of being alone in his big bed, there'd be an angel next to him. An angel in the snow of his white sheets, and she'd raise her arms and he'd fly into them.

He rose from his bed and checked the weather outside. Snow blanketed everything, revealing a path away from his front door. A shiver ran down his back and he pushed his feet into his slippers telling himself that it was just the day and his memories that plagued him with doubts.

Oh, but he just couldn't wait to see Francie in the coat he'd bought her! Wouldn't she be the talk of St. Thomas's Episcopal Church when she came strolling down the aisle on his arm wrapped in that sable? And first thing in the morning they'd go see old Justice Steckler about marrying them. Alfred owed him a favor or two. Unless, of course, Francie wanted a more traditional wedding. Whatever she wanted was all right with him. *Only please Lord, let her . . .*

He tried to banish the thought from his mind as he tied the belt to his heavy silk dressing gown about his waist. The sense of dread was overwhelming, pressing on his chest, cutting off his air.

He told himself that there was nothing to fear outside his door, and the sooner he got out there and proved it, the better off he'd be. Still, he had to drag his feet to the door, had to force his hand to clutch the knob, had to steel his heart for whatever might be laying in wait for him.

He stood with his hand on Gregory's shoulder, the two of them peering in at the three crates that contained every scrap of Francie Morrow that either of them had ever seen, and from the looks of it, a few they hadn't. Paper chains of red and green encircled each window and flowers cut from greeting cards lined the edges of the mirror where she fashioned her pretty hair.

A photograph sat atop one of the cartons and Graham was sure he could identify each and every person in it, down to two small twin boys, one of whom would never grow any bigger.

"But where did she go?" Gregory asked him.

The lump in Graham's throat was too big to force words around, the tears that stung his eyes threatened to spill over and embarrass him. Men, *fathers*, didn't cry. Not over governesses who stole away in the dead of night.

Had he frightened her off? Had his kiss been too brash? Too timid?

A shuddering breath escaped his lips and he steadied himself against the wall, unsure that on his own two feet alone he wouldn't simply crumble under the weight of such sorrow.

"Miss Morrow?" Gregory called out, only to have a faint echo mimic him in the nearly empty room. "The bathroom!" he shouted as if he'd figured out where the woman they had both come to love, to trust, must be hiding.

She was gone.

He'd known it before he'd even opened his eyes. After all, wasn't it Christmas?

"She's not . . ." Gregory said as he returned from his futile trip down the hall and thrust himself against his father's legs.

There was nothing to say, as there had been nothing to say thirty-odd years before, and so he just hugged his son closer to him and ran his hand up and down the boy's back offering and deriving what little comfort there was.

"Not to worry," Perry said cheerfully, coming up behind them and showing very little surprise at the evidence of Francie's sudden departure. "Governesses come and go, dear boy. You've had enough of them to know that. Come on now, presents are awaiting."

"You go on ahead," Graham urged Gregory when he could find his voice. "There's something I need to discuss with your uncle."

"But it's Christmas," Perry reminded him unnecessarily. Of course it was. Christmas meant the world caved in on him—once again. "Can't this wait until later? I've arranged everything for the day. Amelia's coming over later this afternoon, and Andrew, and even Cyril Phillips, recluse that he's become, has agreed to join us. A little reveling in honor of the holiday, and then it's time for some high finance if we're to save the country, not to mention ourselves."

"Where is she?" Graham demanded, both hands balled into fists. His brother had embarrassed him, disappointed him, even deserted him once. But never had he deliberately hurt him. Until now.

"How should I know?" But Perry's feigned innocence didn't fool Graham for a moment. He grabbed the satin lapel of his brother's robe and twisted it in his fist. The control he had cultivated his entire life was slipping quickly through those coiled fingers. "And why should I care? She's gone. I'm sure we'll get a note that tells us where to send the pathetic remnants of a rather unexciting life."

He released Perry's dressing gown and wandered deeper into Francie's private world, fingering the items in the wooden crates which sat on her naked mattress, a hairbrush with long blond hairs still clinging to its bristles, a small jar of powder he was afraid to open for fear of what the scent of Francie would do to his insides, the picture of the Morrow clan. "What did you tell her? That I was a closet drunk? That I beat my wife? That insanity ran in the family?"

"Nothing as dramatic as that, old boy. I knew what she was after and I gave it to her. That's all." Perry picked up the photograph and looked at it. "Quaint bunch, wouldn't you say?"

Graham was surprisingly offended at the assessment. Bart should mean nothing to him now. Bart and Sissy and the new baby—they would all be nothing to him now.

"Gave her what?" Graham asked. "What was it she wanted?"

"So naive. I told you but you wouldn't listen. But then you never listen. We'd be in the poorhouse if it wasn't for me. You know that? We'd have no money at all."

"I don't want money," Graham said, pulling the photo away from Perry and running his fingers over the faces of the family that wasn't going to be his. Perry never understood. No one did, except . . . No. Apparently, no one did. "I never wanted the money. The money wasn't what was important."

Perry sighed. "Well, it was to her. I told her it was gone, and then, so was she."

"The money's gone?" There had been so much of it. Too much. It was a relief to hear that the burden of wealth had finally been lifted from his shoulders.

"Bite your tongue," Perry said, sitting down on the bed in which Francie had slept all those nights that Graham had lain awake with want for her. "I told her it was. Gave her the coat and told her that was all she'd ever get."

"Did she take the coat?" he asked.

"Of course she took the coat," Perry shouted in exasperation.

"Then at least she's warm," he said, unashamed that he was worried about her. He had promised to worry about her for the rest of their lives. Just because she couldn't keep her promises didn't mean that he wouldn't keep his.

"You aren't hearing a word I'm saying," Perry complained. "And where the hell is Rogers? The damn knocker is going to come right through the front door."

Gregory appeared in the doorway, his bare feet sticking out from beneath his nightshirt. "There's a man at the door with packages in his arms. Do you think he might be Santa Claus?"

"Has he a red suit and a white beard?" Perry asked his nephew.

The boy shook his head sadly. "He's not hardly old and he's wearing the kind of jacket that a man wears to go fishing or something."

"Tell him deliveries are made at the back door only," Perry said, then turned to Graham waiting for correction. "Unless you think perhaps it's yet another of Miss Morrow's suitors."

"Go ahead," Graham told Gregory. "And we'll be down in just a moment. Tell Mrs. Rogers she can leave breakfast on the sideboard if she's anxious to get to church."

Gregory stood in the doorway

"What is it, son?" Graham asked, his heart breaking for the boy just as his own heart had broken and never really healed. "Don't you feel well?"

"Where is she?" the boy asked again. "My present isn't there and I know she knows how to get it for me."

"We'll discuss the present later, son," he said, wishing that his boy could be spared the feelings of abandonment he had come to know so well. His mother's legacy was being visited on yet another generation and there was nothing he could do about it. And no one to blame but himself for building up the boy's hopes and dreams. Fitting that he should have to be the one to pick up the pieces. If only he knew the magic that seemed to come so easily to Francie Morrow and her family.

Gregory dragged himself from the room, one slow step at a time the way he used to walk around the house before Francie Morrow's magic had invaded it.

"Is the fortune gone or isn't it?" he demanded of Perry, having lost the thread of their conversation. He wasn't sure he cared all that much, after all.

"Of course it's not gone," Perry said, as if he could read Graham's mind and found his lack of interest most annoying. "Just the fortune hunter."

"I'd give the one," Graham admitted aloud, "to have kept the other."

Heavens, it was like coming into a funeral parlor when she finally returned to the house and burst inside together with a gust of wind. As cold as it was outside, it felt ten degrees colder in the foyer, and quiet as a tomb. Well, when a fortune died, she supposed that a little mourning wasn't out of order. It was just that it was Christmas.

Couldn't they be sad tomorrow?

"Hello?" she called out tentatively. "Isn't anybody home?"

"Francie?" Graham's voice was incredulous. It matched the stunned look on his face as he came out from the library to see for himself. "Francie? Are you back?"

He came toward her slowly, looking at her peculiarly, as if he didn't quite believe she was real.

"Am I late?" she asked, sensing that he had been waiting for her despite the early hour. She'd tried to get back sooner, but there was so much to be done and no one anxious to do it on Christmas morning. "I was as fast as I could be. You did wait Christmas for me, didn't you?"

"Wait for you?" he asked, the clouds that hung in his eyes making way for the sunshine of his smile.

"We'd wait for you forever, Francie. Forever," he said quietly, solemnly.

And then his whole face smiled at her, rays radiating from his eyes, joy filling his cheeks. "She's back," he cried over his shoulder, rushing to her and pulling her against him so snugly that she had to fight for a breath. "I don't know what changed your mind, but I thank God for it."

He kissed her eyebrow, the edge of her temple where a cold damp curl beckoned him. "My God! You're freezing." He put his warm hands against her cheeks and pressed his lips to her forehead.

"Oh, don't worry about *me*. I'm fine," she assured him, though the truth of the matter was that her feet felt like two blocks of ice, she couldn't move her toes, and the shivering inside her chest still hadn't subsided. "It's you that—"

It was as though he didn't hear a word she said. "That's ridiculous. You're frozen stiff. Come by the fire." He put an arm around her and guided her into the library. "What in the world are you doing in this coat? I thought Perry gave you the sable I bought."

"Oh," she said, wondering how in the world she was going to tell him what she'd done. She took a deep breath and steeled herself for his anger.

And then she saw Perry, who stood staring at her openmouthed as though she were a ghost, shaking his head and mumbling something she couldn't quite make out. Gregory stood off to the side of the room kicking the edge of the rug as if he wasn't the least bit interested in the goings-on around him.

Well, if losing money could make people behave so very oddly, she was grateful she hadn't ever had enough to lose.

"Excuse me, sir," Rogers said from the doorway. "There's a gentleman down in the servants' hall who says he's—"

"Ethan!" Her brother pushed his way past the butler and scooped her up in his arms, swinging her around the room.

"Well, look at you!" he exclaimed, stepping back to take her in from head to toe. "Pretty as ever, even if you are getting a little long in the tooth!"

"Oh, Ethan!" was all she could say. Then followed it by looking over her shoulder at Graham and explaining, quite unnecessarily, "Look! It's Ethan. My brother."

"Well, about time you got here! I was afraid you wouldn't make it in time. You can't imagine how pleased I am to meet you," Graham said and extended his hand.

"So pleased you had me sent around to the back door," Ethan grumbled, not letting go of Francie to shake Graham's hand.

"What?" Graham asked, obviously confused. "You were in the kitchen? Rogers? Was this man in the—"

"No matter," Ethan said to Francie, pointedly ignoring now both Graham's hands and his words. "That Mrs. Rogers is a mighty fine cook. It's just that Sissy thought, from his letter," he gestured with his head toward Graham, "that things were different."

"Things *are* different," Graham said, refusing to allow Ethan to distance himself by coming over and patting her brother on the back. "They've moved a long way since my letter."

"Far enough to get out of the kitchen?" Ethan asked, taking in his surroundings and obviously being just as awed by the grandeur of Trent House as Francie had been when she'd first crossed over the threshold. And now it would be someone else's palace. To Francie it would always be the place her dreams came true, but she'd take what was important with her— Graham, Gregory, even Perry. "Even that end of the place is impressive."

"I'm afraid that was my fault," Perry said self-consciously. "I assumed from Gregory's description that you were a delivery boy. I had no idea that you were related to our governess . . . There really isn't any excuse for my behavior."

"Well," Ethan started, and Francie cringed, knowing what would come next. She'd heard it often enough. "My father always said that he had no use for excuses. They've no value to the poor and they're unnecessary to the rich."

"I take it then your father was poor," Perry said drolly.

"A condition you'd be wise to get used to," Francie said, not the least bit sorry to take Perry Trent down a peg or two.

"Francie," Graham began, naturally wanting to soften the worst of it, as if she really cared whether they stayed in this big old mansion or set up housekeeping in the shantytown up above Ninety-third Street.

"Oh! I almost forgot," she said suddenly, amazed that it could have slipped her mind. "And it's so cold out there!"

She gave Ethan a little nudge, encouraging him to go along. She was sure he'd catch on, what with all the nieces and nephews they had.

"You know," she said, peeking in Gregory's direction, "there was a package out on the lawn. I saw it as I was coming in. Now isn't that the strangest thing?"

"A package?" Graham asked, heading for the door. Ethan quickly stood in his way. "Hmm. Wonder where it could have come from?" he said, winking broadly at Graham, though not with much enthusiasm.

"You don't suppose Santa could have dropped it out of his sack, do you?" Francie asked with what she hoped was just the right amount of thoughtfulness.

"You're probably right," Ethan agreed, nodding as though he'd considered the suggestion and thought it valid. "Why, I bet it fell right out of his sleigh."

"How will we know who it's for?" Gregory asked quietly, being drawn in despite himself.

"Maybe there's a tag, or a note," Ethan suggested.

"I'll get it!" Gregory shouted, running past Francie and getting collared by Ethan, who pointed out the fact that he was barefoot and there was a good eight inches of snow on the ground outside.

"Maybe you could . . ." Francie started and Ethan whipped the boy onto his shoulders and ducked under the doorway. "Watch yourself there, cowboy," he warned Gregory. "You're nearly ten feet tall now."

"Hurry," Gregory said, kicking at Ethan as if the poor man had flanks. "Before someone else gets it."

"I hope it'll be all right where we're going," Francie said quietly when the two boys had left the room.

"Where we're going?" Graham responded.

"Perry said we're losing the house, but I don't want you to worry about it," she told him, digging into her pocket for the neatly rolled and tied stack of bills, pulling it out and handing it to him. His eyes widened, but he said nothing. Perry began coughing spasmodically, but waved away Rogers when he offered help.

"I sold the coat," she admitted, only now realizing how disappointed Graham would be. "But I don't want you to worry. Mine is warm enough, and with this we can get you started again. And I can go back to teaching. I really am very good at it, and—"

Ethan and Gregory came back into the room, the carton in Ethan's hands.

"You did what?" Graham demanded, casting a glance at Perry that should have finished the poor man off.

"Is it for Gregory?" Francie asked Ethan loudly, skirting the issue and hoping that the moment wouldn't be ruined for Gregory. After all, money or no money, coat or no coat, it was still Christmas. She just needed to teach them all that it didn't take fancy gifts and financial security to make for a happy time. Just like home, all they would need was each other.

"It says it's from Santa," Gregory said, nodding adamantly. "Put it down where I can reach it, Uncle Ethan. Put it down."

"Uncle Ethan?" Ethan mouthed at her as he placed the box on the floor in front of Gregory.

"Uncle Ethan," Graham nodded, placing a proprietary arm around Francie's shoulder.

"A puppy!" Gregory yelled as a small light brown bit of fluff jumped up and banged against his chin. "It's a puppy."

"Somebody to play with," Francie reminded him.

"That Santa is one smart man," Graham said, pulling her closer to him and kissing the top of her head.

"A lot smarter than your uncle Perry," Perry said, sniffing back tears. "And you are some woman, Miss Francie Morrow. Some woman indeed. I'd be damn proud to call you sister."

"Excuse me," Rogers said, clearing his throat as he stood in the doorway. "Mrs. Rogers and I would like to be off to church if that's all right."

"Yes, of course, Rogers, and a Merry Christmas to you," Graham said, then put up one finger and cast a questioning glance at Ethan. "Isn't there . . ."

"Yes, sir," Rogers said with a wide grin. "Mrs. Rogers is coming with it now."

And so she was, toddling in, carrying, with the utmost care, a silver bowl the likes of which Francie had never seen. And in the bowl, walking jauntily across a field of vanilla cream, was one of Sissy's Santas in the Snow, three presents dropped from his sack trailing behind him.

She couldn't help crying. She tried, but she couldn't stem the tears as they coursed down her cheeks and Ethan laughed at her and the puppy tried to lick them, climbing up Gregory's shoulder to get at her, and Graham tightened his hold and Perry took out his handkerchief with a flourish and presented it to her.

"Oh yeah," Ethan said when she had just about finished her tears. "Sissy thought you might be needing this." He fished around in his pockets, torturing her as he always did, pretending he'd lost Sissy's gift, and then took out a small felt pouch. Without even taking it into her hands, she knew just what it was.

"Will you do the honors?" she asked Ethan, wishing that Sissy could be there at that moment.

Ethan did his best to hide his disapproval. Heavens, she hadn't *meant* to fall in love with a wealthy man. Maybe Ethan would forgive him now that all his money had been lost.

Ethan cleared his throat and addressed Graham. "You know, I guess, that our mama died just after Francie was born, and our pa passed on a bit later. We never did have much, especially by your standards, but Sissy—who I guess by now you're sick to death of hearing about—managed to bring us all up and send us off with a bit of a dowry for each one that came direct from our parents.

"This is from my pa, with instructions to make every minute count and not let an hour go by without thinking about the one you love. Which in this case," he said, fixing Graham with a warning stare, "better be my sister!"

He handed the old watch to Graham. It was nothing special. Not gold, not fancy. But it had been her father's and now it was to belong to her children's father.

"You want me to have this?" Graham asked, his voice cracking with emotion.

"Hey," Ethan said with a laugh. "We're giving you our sister. The watch doesn't seem very important compared to that."

"No, not in comparison to Francie," he agreed. "But something that belonged to your father. I . . . I don't really know what to say."

"It's nothing all that special," Francie admitted. "But—"

"It is the only heirloom I've ever owned," Graham admitted with a whisper, fingering the watch reverently.

Ethan snorted and pointed around the room, which was filled with clocks and vases and tea sets made of pure silver.

"My first wife's," Graham explained. "Left to me, but never given."

"Well, it ain't much, as I said," Ethan repeated. "But it's what we've got and getting Francie is the real treasure, I'd say."

Francie felt her bottom lip tremble for only a second before Graham leaned over and kissed her.

"When you do that thing with your lip," he said so quietly that only she could hear, "it flips my insides over. I love you so, Francie Morrow."

"So for better or for worse?" Ethan said, reaching into the fine silver bowl, plucking a present out of the cream snow and popping it into his mouth.

"Speaking of that," Graham began.

Perry cleared his throat. "Ah, yes. Good news!

Good, good news! Seems we didn't have any money in the Hanover after all. Don't know how it slipped my mind that I'd withdrawn all those funds . . ." He looked sheepishly at Francie and offered half a smile. "I suppose it might be time for me to be looking for an apartment of my own."

Francie shook her head, knowing now full well that Perry had only been trying to protect Graham, and she couldn't fault him for that. That, after all, was what siblings did, protect and love and cherish. "Live without brothers and sisters around?" she asked as the puppy tugged on the hem of her skirt. "I don't think I could stand that."

"Brothers and sisters?" Gregory piped up as he tried to wrestle her dress away from the new puppy. "Are we gonna have some of those?"

Francie felt herself blush and Perry didn't help any when he added, "Oh yes, are we? Let's have lots!"

"How's tomorrow?" Graham asked her, a hand on her shoulder, another running up and down her arm leaving gooseflesh everywhere it skimmed. "Around three?"

Francie felt her cheeks redden. "For a baby?" she asked, shocked and confused.

"For a wedding," Graham stammered, glancing at Ethan cautiously.

"Tomorrow?" Francie looked around at all the men in her life, all of whom were waiting for her answer.

"I'm anxious to get your father's watch," Graham teased, and behind her back, where no one could see, his hand skimmed down her dress until it cupped her behind. "Very anxious."

She should have been shocked, outraged. But she couldn't pretend that it didn't feel wonderfully right for his hands to hold her body just as his heart held her soul. She leaned back into him and smiled. "Tomorrow would be just perfect," she agreed, slipping a hand behind him and brazenly doing to him just what he had done to her.

"I don't suppose we could find a judge today," he said, his breath a little irregular.

"On Christmas?" Perry asked, lowering himself to the floor between Ethan and Gregory as they played with the dog. "Oh, I wouldn't think so."

"Oh, please!" Francie said, her voice coming out like a little girl's. "Could you try?"

"First thing you gotta teach a dog," Ethan said to Gregory, "is *no*." He lifted the dog's tail for a quick look. "Oops. Forget even trying. Dog's a she-dog. Can't tell a girl no. Can't tell her nothing." He smiled up at his sister and gave her a wink.

"Sure would be nice to have a member of my family here to give me away," Francie pleaded.

"It'd take a bit of magic," Perry said, playing peeka-boo with the dog and making Gregory laugh.

"Did you know, Papa, that there really is such a thing as magic?" Gregory said, clearly convinced that Santa had granted his wish.

Graham turned Francie in his arms and looked down at her, his eyes bright with love. "Yes, son, I believe there is. And I believe she lives in our house."

Chapter 8

Graham had been watching the clock on the mantel tick away minute after minute for over half an hour now. And still Francie had not emerged from his—*their*—bathroom.

"Are you all right in there?" he asked, beginning to wonder if his new wife had somehow managed to drown herself in the marble tub that was roomy enough for two. If the two didn't mind being very close. He'd thought that they wouldn't mind, but now . . . "Francie?"

The heavy brass door latch turned and his beautiful bride of three—no, four—hours stepped through the doorway and stood shyly in front of him.

"Hello." She twisted a piece of the well-worn robe she wore—something he intended to replace first thing in the morning—in one hand.

"Francie, honey," he said, taking pride in the great patience he was exhibiting by not pinning her to the wall, ripping off her clothing, and touching every inch of her with every inch of himself. "Sissy did have a nice little heart-to-heart with you before you left Ohio, didn't she?"

Francie's big green eyes lifted to meet his. A tentative smile played at the corners of her mouth. "Lots of them," she said, and relief flooded through him, mixing with desire and need to form a very combustible substance that coursed through his blood. "But not about what you're thinking."

"Oh." His blood cooled slightly. "But once you got to New York, surely someone . . ."

She was shaking her head, those innocent eyes wide with questions.

"In a letter, then," he figured aloud. "Surely in a letter Sissy told you about . . ."

"What to expect?" She shook her head again.

"Oh, God." He sat down on the edge of the bed, his head in his hands, his blood now quite cold.

With baby steps she came closer and closer to him until his forehead rested against her belly. She had no idea what that could do to a man, a man who had just been granted all the rights of a husband but who was more than a little nervous about exercising them. His sigh ruffled the thin cotton nightgown and he realized with a start that her robe was merely a puddle around her feet.

"I'm a very good learner," she said reassuringly. "Before I was a teacher, I was a star pupil."

"I'm sure you were," he agreed. Francie would be stellar at anything, he was certain. It wasn't *her* part he was worried about.

"It was so nice of your friend the judge to come over on such short notice," she said.

He swallowed hard. "I explained that it was sort of an emergency." Funny, just a few hours ago he was certain how the evening would wind up, and now that it was legal, now that he wouldn't be compromising her, they were heading toward a chat about the weather instead of heading for their bed.

"And Amelia and her father standing up for us like

that," Francie said, her body swaying against his face and the exquisite scent of her filling his nostrils. "Especially considering everything . . ."

"Mm," he agreed, wishing he could drag her to the floor, peel the gown from her, and kiss every inch of the body he had worshiped only from afar.

"I'm ready for my first lesson," she said, her fingers running through his hair. "That is, if you are."

Ready? He'd been ready for love his whole life, and yet there was something so frightening about reaching out to take it. Until now, nothing in his life had ever been so close to perfect . . .

"Graham? I'm getting a little chilly. Maybe we could just get under the comforter?"

He stood and held back the covers for her, amazed at what a little slip of a thing she was without her crinolines and puffy sleeves to fill her out. She scooted to the far side of the bed and left the coverlet turned back for him.

Beneath his robe he wore nothing but his love for Francie, which would be apparent to her the moment he slipped the garment off, if it wasn't already.

She patted the bed.

"I'll just get the light," he said, quickly pressing the switch by the bed and then removing his robe in that first moment of darkness when all the world was black.

"I'm not scared, Graham." He listened for the lie in her voice, but there was none.

"I wouldn't hurt you for anything, Francie," he said, trying to prepare her for the pain he feared would find her.

"Nor I you," she said softly in the dark, her hand resting on the comforter which covered his bare chest. Again, he could hear no lie in her whispered words.

"Just do as I do, all right?"

He felt her nod against his arm, and leaned over her, kissing her cheek softly. She returned the kiss just as softly. He kissed her eyelid, the bridge of her nose. She kissed *his* eyelid, the bridge of *his* nose.

He touched her lips with his own while she waited patiently for her part. He opened his lips slightly and she followed suit by parting hers. He ran his tongue along her bottom lip, the lip that always so intrigued him, and then pulled back. Tentatively, she ran her tongue against his mouth.

Oh, dear, dear Lord!

He played at her collarbone with just one finger. She examined the hair at the base of his throat with two. He kissed the hollow of her neck. She missed and got his Adam's apple. He cupped one sweet young breast in his hand. She froze.

At this rate he was going to die a slow and painful death. But at least it would be in the arms of the woman he loved.

"Francie, I—"

"You're on my sleeve, Graham. I can't move my—" She yanked her arm free and connected with his jaw. "Oh, I'm sorry! I just wanted to—"

"To what, Francie?" he asked, testing his jaw. He was ready to grant her any wish, to do anything to make her happy. And that included doing nothing at all. Even if it was his wedding night.

"To love you," she said simply, rolling atop his chest so that she could kiss him full on the mouth, kiss him as no one else ever had, because, miracle of miracles, she loved him as no one else ever had. "I just want to love you, is all, Graham Trent," she said breathlessly.

"That's all?" he asked. "That's all you want?" What about sable, and diamonds, and pearls? All the things he wanted her to have. "It's Christmas, Francie. Ask me for whatever you'd like. Lord knows you've already granted every wish I ever had."

She was quiet for a moment. "Well," she said, as if she had given the matter some serious thought. "Twins would be nice. Could you give me twins, Graham, do you think?"

"I don't know," he answered honestly. Twins weren't something he could buy for her, yet he was the only one in the world in a position to give them to her. "I don't honestly know, Francine Morrow Trent. But no man on this earth would try harder."

It was Francie's laughter he heard ringing in his ears as he eased her beneath him and set about granting her only wish. No, no one would try harder.

Or more often.

About the Authors

Virginia Henley is the author of eight romances published by Dell, including the *New York Times* bestsellers *Seduced* and *Desired*. Her newest romance, *Dream Lover*, will be out in hardcover from Delacorte in February 1997.

She divides her time between Ontario, Canada, and St. Petersburg, Florida.

Katherine Kingsley was born in New York City. She spent her childhood there and in England. She now lives in the Colorado mountains with her English-born husband and their son. Look for her previous Dell romance, *In the Wake of the Wind*, and for *Once upon a Dream*, coming to bookstores in spring 1997.

Rebecca Paisley grew up in Southern Pines, North Carolina, and confesses she's sometimes homesick for the longleaf pines and wonderfully warm folk who dwell there. Presently she lives near Dallas with her family.

———————

Stephanie Mittman lives on Long Island with her high-school-sweetheart husband, her bird, her cat, and two phone lines to keep in touch with her grown children. She readily admits to separation anxiety. Sometimes she just can't let go. She tried to say good-bye to her fictional Morrow family, but no sooner had she finished Francie's story, *Angels in the Snow*, than Ethan came knocking on the door demanding a story of his own. Look for *Sweeter than Wine* in bookstores spring 1997.

Stephanie loves to hear from readers and can be reached c/o MLGW, 190 Willis Avenue, Mineola, NY 11501, or on line at Smittman@aol.com.